## Praise for *Western Swing*

"Tim Sandlin writes about crazy people. Not scary crazies, but the kind of interesting, funny eccentrics with whom the reader would like to spend an evening drinking beer...*Western Swing* is funny, wise and a bubbling joy to read."

—*Kansas City Star*

"Tim Sandlin never forgets that he is a storyteller, and an exceptionally entertaining one. He writes with humor and a cheerful energy that keeps the narrative going at breakneck speed...*Western Swing* is a spirited novel of love and loss, and Loren and Lana Sue are genuine modern-day folk heroes."

—*The Toronto Globe & Mail*

"Droll and high-spirited...Two vividly sympathetic characters whose adventures have something of the grit and pathos of a funky country-and-western ballad."

—*Publishers Weekly*

# Praise for Tim Sandlin

"Pound for pound, Tim Sandlin's stuff is as tight and funny as anyone doing this comedy novel thing."

—Christopher Moore

"Sandlin can see that there is a kind of gruesome comedy in what happens to us, but the humor is never mean, and he loves his people too much not to understand that their grief and nostalgia and frustration is real."

—Nick Hornby

"Sandlin is Tom Robbins with a heart."

—*Atlanta Journal-Constitution*

"This man is writing himself into a richly deserved place of honor on all our shelves."

—John Nichols

"Sandlin just keeps getting better and better."

—W. P. Kinsella

"In a region heretofore dominated by Larry McMurtry, Tom McGuane, and Ed Abbey, Tim Sandlin, of Oklahoma and Wyoming, is emerging as a new and wickedly funny talent."

—*Publishers Weekly*

"Tim Sandlin is among the growing coterie of writers who are shaping the fictional territory of the New West."

—*Kansas City Star*

# Praise for *Skipped Parts*

"There is no more compelling subject than young human males and females coming together in the spring of their lives...A thoughtful, surprising and delightful entertainment."

—*St. Louis Post-Dispatch*

"A sparkling tale...*Skipped Parts* offers some big helpings of western wit, down-home adult humor and once-in-a-while sorrowful truths...It's a classic story of the well-read, old-before-his-time young teen and hip mom learning to cope...Excellent."

—*Indianapolis News*

"Wittily told...reminiscent of Larry McMurtry's *The Last Picture Show*."

—*Library Journal*

"Chock-full of wonderful characters and good writing."

—*Dallas Morning News*

"This witty, often touching portrayal of a dirt-streetwise youth's coming-of-age sparkles with intelligence."

—*Booklist*

# Praise for *Sorrow Floats*

"A raucous, surprisingly original tale."

—*New York Times*

"Unforgettable...*Sorrow Floats* has a multitude of gifts to offer—laughs, real people, high drama, and a crazy cross-country journey that makes it hard to put aside for long, if at all."

—*West Coast Review of Books*

"Sandlin understands that the best black comedy is only a tiny slip away from despair, and he handles this walk without a misstep."

—*Dallas Morning News*

"A zany road trip across America starring an engaging heroine and two AA devotees occupies talented novelist Tim Sandlin in *Sorrow Floats*."

—*Cosmopolitan*

"Able storytelling and an engaging cast of dysfunctional modern American pilgrims animate this winning tale of the road...Sandlin fashions a convincing tale of redemption."

—*Publishers Weekly* (starred review)

"A rousing piece of Americana...rowdy, raunchy...A total delight."

—*Library Journal*

"Funny and poignant...Sandlin's sustaining insight and faith in humanity give the book compassion and hope."

—*Winston-Salem Journal*

"A kinder, gentler Tom Robbins and/or Kurt Vonnegut... funny...compelling, sad, a weird brand of black comedy, and important modern fiction."

—*Nashville Life*

"Some writers make you laugh out loud. Tim Sandlin is one."

—*Winston-Salem Journal*

"Hilarious."

—*Copley News Service*

"The best moments in *Social Blunders* come from Sandlin's sense of the inevitable comedy in even the most tragic situation. But to describe them too fully is to betray their sense of art and delight."

—*Planet*

# WESTERN SWING

## TIM Sandlin

sourcebooks
landmark

Grateful acknowledgment is made for permission to reprint the following lyrics:

From "Wine Over Matter" by Pinto Bennett and Baxter Black. © 1983 by Motel Cowboys, Inc. All rights reserved. Used by permission.

From "Leavin' on Your Mind" by Webb Pierce and Wayne Walker. © 1962 by Cedarwood Publishing Company (A Division of Musiplex Group, Inc.). All rights reserved. Used by permission.

From "You Are My Sunshine" by Jimmy Davis and Charles Mitchell. © 1940 by Peer International Corporation. Copyright renewed assigned to Peer International Corporation. International copyright secured. All rights reserved. Used by permission.

From "It's My Party and I'll Cry If I Want To" by J. Gluck, W. Gold, and H. Weiner. © 1963 by Arch Music Co., Inc., and World Song Publ. Inc. All rights administered by Chappell & Co. Inc. International copyright secured. All rights reserved. Used by permission.

From "Echo of an Old Man's Last Ride" and "Hole in My Life" by Bruce Hauser. © 1980 by Up the Creek Music, Inc. All rights reserved. Used by permission.

Published by Sourcebooks Landmark, an imprint of Sourcebooks, Inc.
P.O. Box 4410, Naperville, Illinois 60567-4410
(630) 961-3900
Fax: (630) 961-2168
www.sourcebooks.com

Originally published in New York in 1988 by Henry Holt and Company.

Library of Congress Cataloging-in-Publication Data

Sandlin, Tim.
  Western swing : a novel / Tim Sandlin.
      p. cm.
  1. Authors—Fiction. 2. Women country musicians—Fiction. 3. Married people—Fiction. 4. Marital conflict—Fiction. 5. Self-actualization (Psychology)—Fiction. 6. Wyoming—Fiction.  I. Title.
  PS3569.A517W47 2011
  813'.54—dc22
                              2010051764

Printed and bound in the United States of America.
VP 10 9 8 7 6 5 4 3 2 1

For Emily and Rocky

# *Acknowledgments*

I HAD A LOT OF HELP WITH THIS ONE. FOR FINANCIAL ASSIS-
tance, I'd like to thank Jody Carlson, John Van Gossen of the
Wyoming State Vocational Rehabilitation Department, and
Jim Clark of the University of North Carolina at Greensboro.
Musical know-how came from Shelley Clark and Kelly
Rubrecht. Special thanks and affection go to Caleb, Lonicera,
Matt, Ben, and Douglas. Tell your mothers to write. Tracy
Bernstein tracked down the song permissions for me and Marian
Wood took care of everything else.

# PROLOGUE

*Loren held the sewing needle under hot running water. Twirling the eye end between his fingers, he hummed a song to himself—an old song written by a former governor of Louisiana. It was called "You Are My Sunshine" and Loren liked the words because he understood them.*

*He shut off the water with his left hand, and still humming and twirling the needle between his thumb and index finger, he walked into his room and sat on the edge of the bed, on the Daffy Duck king-size bedspread. Loren looked at the needle. "Simple enough," he said.*

*His humming broke into words, "You make me happy, when skies are gray. You'll never know, dear, how much I love you..." Loren lifted the needle and jabbed it into his left palm.*

*Blood flowed out of his hand, filling the cup made by lifting his thumb and little finger. "Please don't take my sunshine away."*

*Leaning forward, he dribbled blood into his typewriter keyboard, starting at the Q and moving slowly down and to the right to the ?, then up past the P and O and back across to Z.*

*Lana Sue came through the door carrying a handful of folded socks and humming a song of her own, one he didn't recognize. She opened the bottom drawer of his chest and dropped in the socks.*

*"What the hell are you doing, Loren?"*

*"I'm starting a new novel."*

"By bleeding into the typewriter?"

"It's symbolic."

Talking over her shoulder as she walked into the bathroom, Lana Sue asked, "Of what?"

"I don't have to explain my symbols."

She came back with a wad of toilet paper which she placed in Loren's hand. "Make a fist." She clenched Loren's hand around the toilet paper. "I suppose you want to cleanse the crap. Prove to the reader that you're giving your all this time."

"More of an offering to New York City."

Lana Sue sat beside Loren on the bed and held his bleeding over the floor so none of the drip stained her bedspread. "Elevate this," she said. "It'll stop in a minute. What's this one going to be about?"

"The book?"

"Yes, Loren. What's the book about?"

"Children abandoning their parents, mostly."

"I've read that one."

"Also true love, God, and the difference between good and bad."

"You know the difference between good and bad?"

"Sure. I've been listening to your Hank Williams and Patsy Cline albums."

Lana Sue looked at the mess on the typewriter. "You're compromising."

"I haven't even started. How can I be compromising?"

"You bled all over the old Royal portable. You'll write the book on the electric Remington."

"Blood would gum up the Remington. I wouldn't get to write at all."

"It doesn't work if you bleed into the wrong machine, Loren."

"It doesn't?" Loren's hand started to throb.

Lana Sue shook her head. "Nope, sorry."

"Do we have any Band-Aids?"

# Part One

# 1

Sometimes I have these gaps which are amazingly like being dead except that they don't last, and I have an awful feeling that being dead lasts.

I shot through a gap to find the sun warm on my back. I was sitting in the dirt between two rocks on the spine of a dark green ridge. The rock on my left had a shape like a small foreign car, a hatchbacked Saab from the early seventies. The other rock, on my right, was smaller, more rounded, and pockmarked with lichen. My fingers held a lower larkspur, twisting it slowly counterclockwise.

One of the rules I made many years ago, back when I used to make rules: A good time is not worth having if you can't remember it. That's why the gaps are like death. Death is not a good time.

———

It was the quiet hot of midday, the sky fairly buzzing with color, light blue across the canyon, darker blue to the north over Yellowstone, shading to silver and blinding near the sun. The carpet of brown lodgepole pine needles rustled and boiled around me. Each needle was sliced in half and connected at the base. I knew they were lodgepoles because spruce and fir aren't sliced and limber pine needles are cut in fives.

My stomach hurt from a lack of food. One of my eyes itched like crazy, and I knew enough not to rub it and make it worse, but I didn't know enough to solve the problem by dropping the larkspur. A male Barrow's goldeneye made a neck-out landing on the cirque pond far below me. Above, a jet messed up the scene by leaving a white trail across an otherwise faultless sky. The roar came from the back end of the vapor, as if the sound had been left behind.

I now reached into my left front shirt pocket and withdrew a three-by-five-inch card, pink line above a series of blue lines. I read, *Your name is Loren Paul.*

Oh.

———

The goldeneye and a mate I hadn't noticed earlier skipped across the pond, rose in a three-quarter circle over a budding chokecherry, and flew west toward lower altitudes where they belonged. In their wake, they left a V pattern on the water punctuated by expanding doughnuts made by their wingtips on the takeoff. I thought about how I might word it to Lana Sue when I saw her in a few days. We could sit at the kitchen table and drink coffee while I diagrammed the design of V and dots. She would ask with some skepticism how I knew the ducks were Barrow's goldeneyes and which one was the male.

If I saw Lana Sue in a few days. Our last contact had ended with her Toyota spitting gravel into my face.

The chokecherry exploded and burst into flames.

Indian boys used to not eat for four days and stray into the woods in search of a Vision. Jesus fasted forty and met Satan, who gave him a ride to the mountaintop. Mohammed, Joseph Smith, Max Brand, Martin Luther King, and the Son of Sam all had Visions. I'd gone three long, foodless days in hopes of seeing just such an occurrence as a spontaneous fireball, but now that it was actually happening, I had trouble buying the bit.

I looked at the sky. Still blue. A raven wheeled far up above the peaks. No, two ravens, one barely a dot. I wondered if they saw the fire. Far to the west, over by the Tetons, a stringy cloud crept across the horizon. Taking out the card, I read my name again. *Loren Paul*. I already knew that. The flames didn't spread, in fact they appeared to be dying a brown smoky death. If somebody wanted to attract my attention and reveal the Purpose, He wasn't being awfully patient about the whole thing.

My own religious preferences run closer to the Cheyenne Medicine Wheel than the Presbyterian Whitebeard, and this was just the kind of trick Father Coyote liked to pull in the stories, so I figured I better shimmy down the cliff face for a reality check.

Father Coyote? I was beginning to think like a *Peanuts* character who hauls a blanket around to fight off stage-four anxiety attacks.

This wasn't really a valley or a canyon. My hero, Max Brand, would call it a coulee—not a term you hear that often in conversation. I look the face by a friction descent, scraping both hands raw on rock, loose sand, and sticky greasewood. My daypack and canteen lay in the dirt up top, a mistake because a terrible dry mouth came on halfway down the slope.

The chokecherry bush smoldered next to an empty gallon of Coleman fuel. I touched the black branch, jerking back in quick pain. The fire was definite. The hallucination theory was dead. Which pissed me off. Neither God nor Father Coyote has to resort to Coleman fuel to ignite a chokeberry bush. So far as I know, there's not a single believed-in deity on earth would even need a match.

Therefore, somebody was fucking with my head.

Since Lana Sue yelled "I'm not going down with you, Loren," and left in a huff, Marcie VanHorn was the only person with any notion of my whereabouts. Marcie was sixteen and lived in a tube top. No one in a tube top would do this to me.

The blackened branch leaped aside and a shot echoed through the canyon. I dived, down and right, rolled onto my feet and hit dirt next to a Volkswagen-sized boulder. The dry mouth took on a hot aluminum taste. My throat closed. Since the shot could have come from anywhere, there was no way to tell if I was hiding behind cover or in front of it.

The rock next to my ear splintered. Another shot rang up the hill. I crab-scrambled to the back side of the boulder, then belly-slid over to another, smaller rock.

The secret seemed to be to resist panic, to breathe slowly and use my skittering brain. The hiding spot was a good choice so long as whoever was firing stayed put. I had no reason to think he would. Nothing on earth could have stopped this character from walking across the clearing, stepping around the boulder, and blowing my crotch into the creek.

The third shot skipped off my rock and over my head. I flattened, face pressed into gravel. The scene felt almost unreal. I mean, I was once a late sixties South Texas longhair, so I know about drug wars, peace marches gone bad, redneck insurrection—all that love generation jive—but, at thirty-five, I had never been shot at before. Everyone should be shot at once. It fosters humility.

Surprisingly enough, I didn't wet my leg. My theory is that modern American life—TV, movies, the few of us who read books—prepares us for violence. We go out each day fully expecting to be shot. I know I do. Or it could be the absence of booze and food undid my survival instinct.

Instead of screaming, I crouched in the fetal position of a breech baby, remembering Buggie. I thought of a story he once told me about a white rabbit who could speak English even after it had been killed, skinned, and cooked. The rabbit said, "If you eat me you'll get a hare caught in your throat."

I suddenly got the joke.

Another shot cracked the rock. I lay my ear against the ground and imagined the slap-slap of hunting boots coming to finish me off. It appeared I would discover what happens after we die by the same method as everyone else. Would he blast me from several feet away or hold the barrel flush against my temple so I could feel the cold metal before my brains scattered?

Whenever I'm someplace and I don't know the proper course of action, I always ask myself, "What would Jimmy Stewart do if he was here?" This is a fine way to make decisions because Jimmy always knew right from wrong and bravery from chicken-shit. I tried Cary Grant or Max Brand, but ran into situations where they didn't apply. Jimmy Stewart always applies.

However, the Stewart Standard had never come up in a crisis of physical danger—I'm rarely in real physical danger. One thing for certain, Jimmy never cowered behind a rock waiting for death. He acted—either attack or evade, depending on the reel—but never did he wait while others romped all over him.

Attacking didn't seem feasible because I was unarmed. I own a rifle—a 7 mm Ruger Magnum I bought to scare snowmobilers and dirt bikers off our land. I've never shot it at anything more mobile than "Listen to the Warm" by Rod McKuen. Besides, it was back home in a cottonwood-post gun rack. Who thinks to take a rifle along when he's searching for God?

That left the Jimmy Stewart method of evasion. I raised my head to scan the immediate area. Grass, a few larkspur and balsam root, pond upstream, meadow down—nothing to stop a bullet. Fifteen feet from my rock a line of willows ran along both sides of the creek, stretching downstream to the edge of the clearing and beyond. If I made the thicket, I could snake around, maybe even slide into the water, and lose the sniper.

Of course, the sniper would know that also and have his sights trained on that side of the rock. One budge toward the creek and he could nail me. But aiming a rifle barrel at one spot for minutes on end is not that easy. Sooner or later, he'd have to relax and that would be the moment to make my dive.

I tried to picture the guy. Did he know me? Or was the whole thing a random ambush—some retard with khaki pants and a long-bore rifle, slobbering on himself, snarling, "I'm gonna set these chokecherries on fire and shoot anyone that comes by." The guy probably rhymed *fire* with *jar* and drew faces in the dirt when he peed.

Jimmy Stewart wouldn't wait long and neither could I. I edged my knees up under my chest, raised onto my toes, and hesitated a moment to see if he'd shoot my ass off. When he didn't, I said a little prayer to God knows who and took off.

# 2

THE SUMMER I TURNED FOURTEEN, I DECIDED DOGS AND CATS were agents of God, angels who spied on us and reported unclean thoughts and screwups to the man up top. Actually, dogs reported to cats, who spoke directly to God. Dogs can't talk to God. Just cats.

The episode was discovered when I attached notes to Him onto neighborhood dog and cat collars. *I know what you're doing, but it's okay. You can trust me not to tell anyone. Please let me go.*

Neighbors complained to Mom and my stepdad, who sent me to a county extension analyst, who said the problem was artificial flavors and coloring and if I ate better I still wouldn't be happy, but at least I wouldn't bother anyone.

We—Lana Sue and I—own two dogs and two cats now: Rocky, Josie, Fitz, and Zelda. I still won't do anything in front of the animals that I don't want God or Lana Sue to know about.

———

My mother is a beehive hairdo cocktail waitress in a jukebox and bingo club in Victoria, Texas. She wears fake gold earrings shaped like the Texas A&M logo. She keeps Coronet facial tissues between the cups in her bra. She chews three sticks of Trident at once and fries everything she eats.

Mom royally botched the job of raising me and my two brothers. Patrick grew into a real estate magnate in Corpus Christi. He's a swamp drainer. Garret is a Jesus freak serving ten to twenty-five on a heroin charge in the Georgia State pen in Reidsville. There was also a baby sister, Kathy, who got herself killed by a Texas Ranger during a race riot in Houston. They caught her looting a Woolworth's department store. She died with her arms full of Barbie dolls.

My stepfather, Don, works on an offshore rig in the Gulf, bowls in the low 200s, and has worn white socks every day of his life. He sleeps in the same underwear he bowls in. Mom told me my real dad was an evangelist for the Southern Ministry, but I don't believe her. I doubt if she knew.

If I ever sell another book, I'm going to a plastic surgeon to have my navel smoothed over. I don't want any reminders that I was ever connected to that woman.

---

Writing books is what I do—or did. Lately, I've been thinking there may be more to life than pretending I'm somebody else. In ten years of almost daily typing I sold two formula Westerns and one of those sentimental novels where you make the readers like a character, then you kill him. After I met Lana Sue, I wrote a vaguely true, mostly lies book called *The Yeast Infection*. All the carefully veiled characters recognized themselves and I found myself embroiled in two lawsuits and a fistfight. I won the lawsuits. Would have won the fistfight, but Jimmy Stewart doesn't hit women.

Movie rights sold, amazingly enough, and Lana Sue and I suddenly arrived in Temporary Fat City. Lana Sue'd been raised upper tax bracket, so she handled it okay. I went nuts—Super Bowl tickets, eighty-dollar bottles of sherry, Nautilus machines, personalized license plates on the Chevelle. After a quick trip to Carano, Italy, in search of Max Brand's first grave—he had two—I still maintained enough cash to support us without hourly work at least through the summer.

A summer in Jackson Hole without money thoughts is the gift of a lifetime and gifts should not be pissed away on idleness. I decided that in order to stay with Lana Sue I had to resolve my past and in order to do that I had to give up Buggie.

Lana Sue said, "Loren, no disembodied voice up in the mountains is waiting to tell you where Buggie is."

"I'll force it out of him."

"Out of who?"

"Whoever's up there."

"Wave bye-bye, Loren, 'cause I won't be here when you come back down."

Lana Sue's daddy was a gynecologist and her grandma committed suicide. Her former husband was a country music promoter who used to fake epileptic fits whenever she wouldn't go down on him, so Lana Sue was well acquainted with insanity before she came to me and she doesn't care to get involved with purposeful psychosis.

"You're getting heavy," she said.

"Don't you ever wonder about the purpose of life?"

"I wonder about the price of Tony Lamas or how many calories are in frozen yogurt. The purpose of life doesn't matter, Loren."

"Does to me."

As America goes lightweight—light beer, light cigarettes, light margarine—being "heavy" is the last great sin. It replaced saying "fuck" on television.

Lana Sue sang in one of her hub's bands before I spirited her away to the Wyoming wilderness. She wasn't good enough to be in the band without balling somebody, and she knew it, and the husband, Ace, reminded her of this fact every night.

Ace said, "You could never be in this band if you weren't screwing me," which made her resent him, naturally. Ace is the title character in *The Yeast Infection*. I came, fell into the picture, and told her I wouldn't give her anything at all if she slept with me, so she did. I lied, though, because after the last book came out, we got our picture in the *Casper Star Tribune's* Sunday Supplement. I have the picture in a frame on my desk. Lana Sue and I are standing by the greenhouse, petting our dog, Rocky, who has just ripped the heart out of a marmot that's not in the picture. Lana Sue is wearing a dark wool shirt and tight jeans. Her hair is the best part of the picture. I love Lana Sue's hair.

My face looks like I just woke up with a bad schnapps hangover. The back of my jeans hangs down loose was if my ass has been surgically removed. Even in the grainy newspaper picture, my glasses are noticeably dirty. The caption says Lana Sue and I are a "vibrant young Wyoming couple." Lana Sue is vibrant. I don't label well.

———

I fell in love with Lana Sue because she fell in love with me. Also, because she sings on the toilet. The morning after our first night, I woke up fuzzy and heard the chorus of "Jambalaya" coming from the bathroom. The song is a list of interesting Louisiana foods. Hank Williams wrote it.

Figuring it was safe, I did my usual blind morning stumble into the can and there sat a beautiful woman, the beautiful woman, my adolescent fantasy woman, with panties around her ankles.

"Nobody sings on the toilet," I said.

"I do."

"You're supposed to sing in the shower."

"I sing anywhere I want."

"My God." I backed out, closed the door, and leaned my forehead on the cool paint of the frame. Seven-thirty on a Sunday morning and she's singing Hank Williams on the crapper. I decided to marry her and have children.

———

Lana Sue is the most self-confident person I've ever known. She's so smooth and…adaptable. And cheerful—how many cheerful people do you meet who aren't unrealistic to the point of retarded?

More remarkable than that, Lana Sue thinks I'm "hot stuff." She said so. She said I'm a prize she got for not going nuts or settling for anything less. Isn't that remarkable, a woman of balance and perspective, not to mention beautiful as the sun rising over the Tetons, swept off her feet by a manic-depressive soul searcher with no ass? There's no accounting for tastes.

The only thing that worries me is, Lana Sue seems too good to be true, and too good to be true almost always isn't—true. But so far, up until I obsessed out on this search, Lana Sue has walked that narrow writer's wife line between taking my artistic temperament seriously and treating me like a learning-deficient cousin. She even listens with a straight face when I babble on about emanations from dead novelists.

"I read Flannery O'Connor a chapter of Erica Jong and she rolled over in her grave," I said, and Lana Sue answered, "Uh-huh," and not a question about how I knew without digging her up.

Or one day I said, "Scott Fitzgerald is calling. He wants to explain the ending of *The Last Tycoon*," and Lana Sue answered, "Take the Toyota, it's gassed up."

Nine days later when I pulled back in the driveway, she asked, "What's the ending?" and didn't laugh or anything when I told her Scott changed his mind. God only knows the woman was patient. She put up with an unholy amount of metaphysical fufaw before driving out of my life.

———

How long? Four days ago, five maybe, the day before Lana Sue left, I sat out by the creek behind our cabin, inspecting minute plant life. The whole week had been spent either up on a ridge top screaming, "*Behold, the Universe*," or down on my hands and knees, gaping in amazement at the infinite detail of a spider's front legs. My blind spot was the middle view—people, trees.

An aspen leaf with a tiny bug in it fell into my hands. The bug had burrowed a maze around the inside of the leaf, eating every bit of chlorophyll, leaving behind a sort of Pac-Man game with tracers. He had traveled as extensively in one leaf as anyone could ever hope to.

"Neat," I said. I like to share special things with Lana Sue. That's one reason I live with her. So, holding the leaf gently in my palm, I walked into the cabin.

"Look what I found," I said.

Lana Sue sat at the kitchen table. Her hair wasn't as wavy as usual. Maybe it was dirty, I don't know. She had on a white T-shirt and a pair of shorts that made her legs look heavy. She held a teaspoon with her fist like a kid would and she was eating sugar straight from the bowl.

I must have surprised her because Lana Sue jerked and her face wasn't her at all. It was red and torn-looking, a cross between panic and despair, nothing like she ever looked before.

"Yuck," I said. "You're eating white sugar."

The spoon sailed across the room and bounced off my chest. Lana Sue ran out the front door, crying.

Lana Sue never cries. I didn't think tears were in her. I stood in the middle of the kitchen floor, next to the wood stove, looking at the design in the yellow leaf. The next day, she left.

# 3

I SLITHERED AROUND THE WILLOWS FOR AN HOUR OR SO, camouflaging myself as a snake. At first I heaved rocks way upstream in hopes of drawing fire, but nothing came of it. No shots, no sounds other than the whisper in the creek—the gunman seemed to have disappeared. Or never existed. Truly bizarre events always seem unreal afterwards, especially if you haven't eaten in three days, so I finally wound up creeping back to the empty Coleman fuel can just to prove I wasn't lost in a dream sequence.

It was real all right. The chokecherry still smoked. My nose caught a wet seaweed odor, not something you'd imagine on your own.

The forest line on both sides of the coulee showed no signs of a sniper. Up on the ridge I'd come down, a deer lowered her head, then raised it, chewing, calmly looking down at me—a standard all-clear signal to any Max Brand reader. I stood up for a better view. The deer was pretty, all innocent and brown and noble, the way wild animals are supposed to be. She stared at me with soft, wet doe-eyes. If I'd had my Ruger I could have nailed her dead.

One thing I decided for certain: Starvation is for people who don't have food. Half this country is fasting for health or religious purposes, and I saw no reason why I should follow the crowd. If thousands of rich, beautiful Californians can't find God on clear juice and bottled water, I wasn't going to find him hungry. I'm too skinny to miss a meal.

———

Sunday morning, before setting out on my Quest, I drove to the Safeway in Jackson and drifted up and down the aisles, admiring the food, saying my good-byes, so to speak. Some was canned, some frozen, some more chemicals than dead plant or animal matter, but it was all admirable. Like freedom or electricity or legs, no one appreciates food who hasn't unwillingly gone without it.

I pushed a basket up and down the maze of aisles, searching for the perfect post-Vision snack, something light but with nutrition, something that would jump-start my empty system. Cookies lacked substance, jerky was too much, I don't really care for fresh fruit.

Then I saw the red and clear cellophane of the Fig Newton display and Divine Inspiration said, "*Look no more.*" My Divine Inspiration sounds like the guy who used to narrate the Disney nature flicks, the voice of a northeast Texan on Darvons.

He also told me to pick up a Spell-Write notebook and two Bic Clics. With my memory what it's been lately, God might tell me what happens after we die and I'd forget.

At the checkout counter, I saw a forty-eight-point Gothic headline on the *National Star*, SCIENTISTS FIND DEFINITE PROOF OF LIFE AFTER DEATH. I showed the checker girl.

"How about that," she said.

"Do you believe it?"

"Naw, if the proof was definite, it'd be in *USA Today*."

"I suppose so."

———

My daypack is brown nylon with green strings and leather stitched along the bottom. It has two pockets, the big one at the top and a flat one on the back for easy access. A pair of straps hang down for securing my 100 percent fiberfill sleeping bag. I like my daypack. I bought it when I sold the first Western.

Chest heaving like an old man, sweat trickling down my forehead draining dirt into my eyes, I untied the cord around the top pocket and dumped all my stuff on the ground. An army canteen landed on top of the pile and it didn't take long to sort out the Fig Newtons.

I sat next to the empty pack and twisted open the canteen top. As I sucked down water, a gray jay glided in and landed on two hops about eight feet up the trail.

"Hello," I said.

The jay cocked its head right and hopped toward me.

"How's your karmatic input-output ratio?" I asked the jay. Inside the cellophane wrapper, two lines of fig-filled pastry lay sealed in more cellophane. "Want some Fig Newton? I bet you never ate a fig." The jay hopped a couple hops closer.

"Watch for seeds." I stuck a whole cookie in my mouth, tore another one in half, and threw one of the halves at the jay—almost caught him in the beak. He flew into a tree and made a shrill "*Jeeah, jeeah*" sound.

"What's the problem?" I threw the other half farther off the trail. The Fig Newton tasted good, so I had another and washed it down with canteen water. Since I hadn't eaten in three days and my stomach felt odd, I figured it wouldn't be wise to stuff myself right off. Four would be the limit now, then four more later.

The jay flew back and hopped to the farthest piece of Fig Newton. He pecked at it a couple times, then picked up the whole chunk with his bill and flew into a different tree.

Sitting up on my knees, I arranged all the stuff in a line. Normally, whatever Loren carried would have been whatever Lana Sue packed, but this time I was pretty sure he put the things in the daypack himself. Lana Sue hadn't been in the mood. The only other possibility was Marcie VanHorn, but that didn't seem likely because my relationship with her hadn't reached the helpless stage yet. I generally have to sleep with a woman before she starts treating me like a child.

The gray jay swooped down and landed next to the other half Newton. I watched him a minute while chewing another one myself. By then I'd lost count and couldn't remember if I'd eaten three or four, so I ate two more.

Okay—far left of the lineup. Neat's-foot oil. That showed Loren wasn't particularly practical because I wore running shoes—Adidas three stripers. The bottle had a picture of a bearded man on the front. I assumed he was Mr. Neat.

Two fishing lures. One green and white, the other red and white with an imprint of a devil figure stamped on the gold back.

Toilet paper. Good sign. Toothbrush—red, but no toothpaste. The possibility began to dawn on me that, as Loren walked out of the cabin, he picked up the old daypack and put it, and whatever happened to be in it, on his back.

Three paperback books. *Black Elk Speaks, Panama* by Tom McGuane, and a phone directory for all the Holiday Inns in America. Waiting for a sign, I flipped through *Panama,* stopped and read an italicized sentence. *This time the pus is everywhere.*

Because of its bugles and groans, the Sioux Indians thought the elk was the sex animal. In their religion, the color black symbolized wisdom. Black Elk literally translates as Wise Fuck. I'd love to publish a book under that pen name: *Wise Fuck Speaks.* It'd be a lock for a book club selection.

I found no message in the Holiday Inn directory. There was also a comic book put out by the Jehovah's Witnesses and the

Spell-Write spiral notebook. The comic book showed a sinner who was outraged at waking up and finding himself in Hell. The flames looked tacky and lacked credibility. The sinner hoped to do life over again from the perspective of knowing what Hell was like, but God, or a Jehovah's Witness spokesman, said, "Nope, you should have listened when I knocked on your door." All God's lines were footnoted.

I flipped open the notebook and read, *Being happy is nicer,* and *Outer circumstances are irrelevant to inner peace.* On the second page it said, *Nothing matters but loss* and *Love is a train. It may be jumped, but not chased.*

All these sayings were in my handwriting, but someone else must have written them because I don't remember and, if I'm ever deep in a clairvoyant trance, I hope I can do better than that. I didn't starve, drive myself manic, and lose Lana Sue to come up with *Being happy is nicer.*

I pulled a pen from my back pocket and, turning to page 3, wrote, *Nothing worth knowing can be expressed in words.*

To the notebook's right lay a USGS quadmap of Sleeping Indian Mountain. This was the most important piece of evidence yet because, hopefully, I was squatting somewhere on the backside of the Sleeping Indian, and if so, Loren had planned ahead. Together with the toilet paper, the map showed foresight.

I tore off a piece of Fig Newton and threw it to the gray jay. Slipping the rest into my mouth, I continued the inventory: Boy Scout knife, three blades—long, short, and can opener. Matches wrapped in a plastic bag. A tiny pencil sharpener shaped like the Washington Monument. An unopened letter from Kearney, Nebraska—Christmas seal on the back. A plastic first aid kit—empty. An army canteen—metal liner with a green cloth cover, U.S. ARMY stenciled on one side, DO NOT HOLD NEAR FLAME on the other. A card for a drug rehabilitation clinic in Houston. A phone number on a slip of yellow-lined paper—no name or identifying characteristic. An aspirin. A blue Trojan-Enz prophylactic.

Lana Sue was protected by a copper coil, which makes me wonder what Loren had in mind.

A Sierra Club cup. And last, on the far right of this mess, one row of a double-row pack of Fig Newtons. What did it all mean? When you're on a Search everything means something. There's no such thing as a medium without a message.

I opened the letter from Kearney, Nebraska.

*Dear Stoolhead,* it read.

*I spent $4.95 on that book of yours,* Disappearance, *and I want my money back. You should be in jail. You're so smug, so frigging perfect. You should be sent to Russia. I hope your father is ashamed.*

*I hate you,*
*Patsy Holt*

I tried to picture Patsy Holt. I decided she was fifty-six and parted her iron-black hair down the middle and ate frozen dinners every night. Probably drank buttermilk by the gallon. Maybe I should move to Nebraska and meet her and not tell her who I am. We could fall in love and have oral sex orgasms and later, after we married, I'd pull out the letter and we'd have a big laugh.

The jay cried "*Jeeah*" as the sun dipped behind a cloud. An awful lot of clouds had drifted in while I was wallowing around the willow thicket. The breeze on my face suddenly felt cooler. Starting on the right, I began stuffing items into the daypack. I was sure Loren's—my—crux lay in that pile of junk some-where, but it was beyond me to figure where. He carried an unneeded rubber and wasn't popular in Nebraska. Not much to go on when the goal is perfect truth.

Time to move up the mountain. Packed, fed, and anxious to hit the trail, I stood on the side of the coulee to look one last time at the burned chokecherry next to the bubbling creek. It was real. I wasn't paranoid.

———

Confession time. I have this semidisgusting personality flaw in that, at times, many times, I act stupider than I am. For years I blamed the habit on Mom—as she took my clunkiness for granted, I grew into it—but Mom's over fifteen years back down the road so the rationale should have petered out by now.

My ignorance of the unused rubber is just the sort of false innocence that drives Lana Sue nuts. I know damn well the intentions of that condom—Marcie VanHorn. I'd like a witness here that the offending item lay snuggled in my daypack, still sealed in aluminum foil. Although unfulfillment won't help much if Lana Sue catches on. She's as likely to kick ass over what I wanted to do as what I did.

Marcie VanHorn and her father, Lee, are our closest neighbors. They live a half mile down the town road in a barn they've converted into a house next to a house they've converted into a barn. Marcie is a winner. At sixteen, with a ripe body, high energy, and a trust fund, what could you expect? She's the image of those teenage girls in the JC Penney catalog who model shortie nighties in poses of slumber-party pillow fights— tight butt, long legs, small breasts, eyes that challenge.

Things would have remained totally theoretical if Lee VanHorn hadn't organized a welcome-to-the-valley pack trip the summer we moved to Jackson Hole. Lana Sue hated her horse, didn't like the mosquitoes, and missed her cigarettes, all of which got taken out on me. Meanwhile,

Marcie read *Yeast Infection*, bought the sensitive-poet-at-heart inference, and fell into instant, if temporary, adoration. I eat up adoration.

Even then, things could have stayed on a level of a guilt-inducing wet dream, but the second night out, Lana Sue didn't hobble the hated horse properly and he gimped off up the canyon. Lee discovered the escape and he and Lana Sue gave chase, which left Marcie and me tending the fire. There, in the orange flicker of the campsite, the little hardbody offered herself to me.

Side by side, we sat on stumps, staring into the burning coals. Marcie touched my hand with fingers hot from holding a cup of fresh-made instant cocoa. "Virginity is too big a deal," she said. "It's awful pressure, but I can't see cracking it with a boy from school. He might get all hung up."

I sipped chocolate with my free hand. "I see your problem, Marcie."

"I need an older man, someone experienced, who would be gentle and teaching, then afterwards, not bother me anymore."

"Maybe if we think hard, we'll come up with someone." False stupidity again. I knew Marcie's bottom line.

She looked at me with those pale, pale eyes and that blossoming sixteen-year-old body. "Will you make love to me, Loren?"

I sipped and stared into the fire. She was a child, Lana Sue and I had only been married two months, Lee had a room full of guns and every right to use one. But then, look at the trust in her eyes and the promise in those tangerine breasts. Yes or no, I would live to regret the answer.

"No."

Marcie sighed. "Wish we had some schnapps for the chocolate."

"Not that I wouldn't be honored. Maybe someday, after I've been married longer."

She smiled. "You know where I live."

Two years later, ten minutes after Lana Sue called the marriage quits, I grabbed fifty cents off her bureau and drove the Chevelle to the Cowboy Joe Service Station MEN's room.

*4*

ONCE, AGAIN, I FOUND MYSELF TRUDGING THROUGH RED dust with a U-shaped canyon on the left and dense Doug fir on the right. Far to the right, above where the Tetons would be if I could see through the trees, silent lightning flashed once, then again a few seconds later. With luck, I might see a distant storm if I made the top of the Indian by nightfall. God likes to reveal secrets in bad weather.

The trail took a hard right where a dry side canyon came in to join the main creek. The elbow of the ridge overlooked one of those scenic vistas you see on a Friends of the Earth calendar. The kind with a photo of a lone hiker wearing two thousand dollars worth of equipment and standing with his toes over the edge, gazing out at the wondrous glory of the wild. I never stand with my toes over the edge.

A huge old quaking aspen jutted through the rocks on the other side, the forested non-edge side of the trail. Compared to pine, aspen are a snap to climb. The leaves don't hurt. The branches are spaced like playground equipment. Though the view from twelve feet off the ground was basically the same as the one seen standing on it, once I settled myself and the day-pack into an almost comfortable niche, I felt more secure, in control. I've always felt safe in trees. No memories can get you—no lions, or tigers, or bears.

The afternoon sun did nice glittery things to the rocks across the canyon, making them sparkle and pulsate slightly. Way down there, flowing toward my pond and burnt chokecherry, the stream changed colors from green to blue to silver-gray. I saw a coyote. Imagine that. Shaggy tail and all, I saw a coyote who didn't see me.

I pulled out the notebook and pen—God might want me to take notes—then fluffed the pack into a respectable tree pillow. I hummed a low song—theme from *The Andy Griffith Show*—in hopes of driving all thoughts from my mind. First rule of the mystic business: You must think of nothing in order to think of anything new. The server cannot pour hot coffee into a full cup. So to speak.

The sun moved. The aspen leaves quaked. Wispy clouds formed themselves into faces and puppies and soft, white cow-flops. An ant crawled across my thumb and I massacred him. My eyes itched. I developed an intense erection.

Opening the notebook, I sucked the pen a moment, then wrote, *There's no aphrodisiac as strong as belief in death.*

This made me think of Lana Sue. I wondered where she was and who she was under. Lana Sue wasn't a self-analyzing deep spirit like me. She enjoyed things she liked and avoided things she didn't. Great attitude if you can get away with it.

I don't know why Lana Sue went for my line and I don't care to know. By now I've learned if you're unpretentiously extreme enough, some woman somewhere is going to be impressed. Only normal men grow old alone.

I stole Lana Sue from a low-quality music agent who stole her from a pedal steel guitar player named Mickey who stole her from an oral surgeon named Ron. To my limited knowledge, Lana Sue never spent a night alone since her first honeymoon over twenty-one years ago. I asked her about it on our wedding night.

"How long was there between Ron and Mickey?" I asked.

Lana Sue sat in a chair next to the bed, reading a six-month-old *Rolling Stone* and wearing a long red T-shirt with nothing on underneath.

She licked a finger to flip the page. "What do you mean?"

"Ron was your first mate. Then Mickey was. How long was the time between them?"

She raised her eyes from the paper. "How long does it take to drive from Houston to Lubbock?"

"Eight or nine hours."

"Eight or nine hours, then."

I lay on the bed, looking at brochures for Jackson Hole. Since *Yeast Infection* sold, we were thinking of moving out of Denver. The pictures of mountains, log cabins, and healthy, fulfilled people made Jackson Hole look like a better neighborhood. Besides, I had hidden motivation: Buggie might still be there.

"How about Mickey and Ace?"

"How about Mickey and Ace?"

"How long was that gap?"

"We were in a motel. Ace had a room three doors down." She watched now to see if this affected me.

I pretended to study a picture of a nice cabin with a couple of outbuildings. A rock chimney rose from each end of the shingled roof. A Saint Bernard stood next to the front door, staring glassy-eyed at the photographer. Oddly enough, three months later we bought the place.

"You packed your stuff and moved three doors down?"

"Ace and I flew out that afternoon, so Mickey never had to listen to the bedsprings or anything."

Her legs were crossed at the thighs and her feet lay propped on mine on the bed. The whole scene felt real comfortable and domestic. I didn't want to be an irritant.

"When was the last night you slept alone?" I asked.

"I don't remember."

"Think about it. Can you remember a single time where you slept all night without a man in the bed?"

Lana Sue cocked her head off to one side and looked at me. "No."

"Doesn't that strike you as strange?"

Pulling her feet off mine, she stood and walked to the door and switched off the light, "No."

———

Following the theory that you lose 'em the way you get 'em, I knew right from the beginning that I would outlive my marriage. Lana Sue doesn't have the attention span to stay with anyone forever. I can accept that.

However, the wise husband does not leave a beautiful woman who has never slept alone alone. I have several times now—the Flannery O'Connor trip to Georgia, another drive to Maryland, a couple of solitary backpacking ventures—but, so far as I know, she stayed true through it all. So far as I know. I don't think she would hide it from me if she did sleep with someone. Lana Sue's not that kind of woman.

The day before my Search, when Lana Sue hit me in the ear with the vacuum cleaner and screamed, "That's it, Loren. Crack. You lose," she'd been mad enough and self-righteous enough to guiltlessly hump every cowboy in northwest Wyoming.

———

A person invaded. Right there, trotting down the trail in *my* wilderness—light blue Bill Rogers running suit, Nike shoes featuring the patented *swoosh,* hair blond as a manila envelope— it was an off-road jogger. On *my* mountain.

I threw a jar of neat's-foot oil at his head. Unfortunately, I missed.

He stopped and said, "Shit."

"What the hell are you doing?"

His words came in a rush as he tried to control his breathing. "Running. What are you doing?"

"I'm looking for my son."

"In a tree?"

I didn't owe this guy any explanations. "Everyone looks like you in San Diego. You should run there."

"It's a free mountain."

"You hear that on Donahue or Letterman?"

The jogger had stopped moving forward, but he hadn't stopped moving. He kept shifting from one foot to the other in a kind of toe spring. He held his hands in front of his ribs like a squirrel.

"Have you seen anyone with a rifle?" I asked.

"A rifle?"

"Might be a woman from Nebraska."

His eyes squinted because the sun was right above my head. He had to look into it to see me. "No, no women at all."

"How about anyone with a rifle?"

"I've run this trail three times a week all summer, and you're the first person I've seen up here."

"Why?"

He stopped running in place and leaned one hand on my tree. "Why what?"

"Why have you run this trail three times a week all summer?"

"I'm entered in the hill climb in August. This trail's about as steep as the one in the race."

I looked up and down the trail to see if this was true. "What month is it now?"

"Are you some kind of nut?"

"I don't know."

"It's late July. July twenty-fifth, to be exact. You want the day of the week?"

I shook my head. "That'd be too much." He looked up at me and waited. Maybe he expected me to do something, jump and break my ankles or something. Maybe I was just an excuse for a rest stop. "How far have you run?" I asked.

"Nine miles so far. It's another seven from here to my car on the road, but they're all downhill."

"Seven miles. I haven't come very far."

"I've got to go," he said, but he didn't go.

"If you see anyone with a rifle, tell them I changed my mind and went to town."

He nodded. "What if I see your son?"

"You won't."

He stared at me a moment, then his hands came up and he started running in place again. "Is that all?"

"Isn't that enough?"

The blond man jogged down the hill and off my mountain.

———

Another time, another tree, ridged trunk, narrow flat leaves like a willow only it wasn't a willow. My brain fried. I'd driven the Toyota straight through from Jackson to Rockville, Maryland, living on black coffee and orange peels, hurling the pulps onto shoulders for the mice and birds and creatures my mind created out of yellow spots that grew between the eyelid and the eye.

Scott and Zelda Fitzgerald lay a couple of hundred yards down the slope, near a more immediate funeral where serious women poured from a hearse and a couple of limousines. It seemed to be an all-girl funeral. I wondered what was the sex of the body in the casket. I wondered what sex it had been before it died. One of the women saw me in the tree and stared for a moment, then turned back to the awning and the box.

I'd always idolized him, tried to write like him, drink like him, find a consuming woman like he did. I root for the Princeton football team. My first dog was Gatsby and the cats we live with now are Fitz and Zelda. Scott was the best and could have been the greatest. I felt underwater.

The women lined up, facing away, all in black. One woman stood profile to me and said the words you say at these things—fertilizer to fertilizer/blank tape to blank tape—whatever they say.

Nothing came across as solid. A line of telephone poles, the Toyota, the white building behind me with its pillars and steps, all shimmered as if seen through the top part of flames. The horizons breathed. The only spot in focus was the line of black and the woman turned sideways, looking down at something that used to be someone.

I went to sleep and didn't fall from the tree until after midnight.

———

The Fig Newtons were acting up in my empty stomach, causing problems not easily dealt with in a tree, and the sun pushed the shadows longer by the minute. Besides, the top of the mountain called. What an anthropomorphic thought.

A man walked down the trail from the same direction as the jogger. He was an older man in gray khakis, a red wool shirt, and hiking boots. I couldn't see his face because he kept it down, looking at the ground, but a rifle hung from his right hand.

I decided to stay put.

The man knelt and studied something on the trail—the neat's-foot oil—then he squinted at the sun before moving toward my tree. He limped a little, taking shorter steps with his left foot than he did with the right.

Hunting season is in October, and this guy was no hunter anyway. He carried the rifle like a putter. His face was deep-tanned across the forehead, nothing at all like a hunter's tan.

He stopped below my perch and touched the dust where the jogger had run in place. Turning his head, he looked down along the trail, then over at the canyon, then behind himself, up the hill. I wondered who he was. The face seemed familiar, but way out of context, like someone from an old television commercial.

He stood back up and leaned one hand against the aspen. Had I been Jimmy Stewart, I would have leaped from the tree, landed on his back, wrestled the rifle from his grasp, and demanded to know why he'd shot at me. Then I would have had Henry Fonda blow his face off. But I'm not Jimmy Stewart. I'm a writer and writers don't leap from trees. They create people to jump for them.

Besides which, this would-be killer was tracking a jogger who ran to the road, got in his car, and drove away. He would probably follow all the way into town and forget me. I hoped. Couldn't be much of a tracker if he didn't know a Nike sole from an Adidas. The man coughed twice, then limped slowly on down the trail.

———

Down the tree and into the woods. I walked backwards so the tracks would lead out of the forest instead of in—a cheap Max Brand trick that anyone who'd ever read a Western would catch, but this old fart didn't look like the type to waste his time on category fiction. More likely he subscribed to *Omni* and *Smithsonian,* maybe even *Dynamic Jazz Reports.*

Soon though, I fell backwards over a root. Forward again, I pushed into the deepest, darkest, most forbidding part of the forest. Afternoon suddenly turned into evening. An owl whooshed by my ear. The bushes blended together to form shadows that made strange sounds. I ducked into a westward-running gully that smelled of angry grizzlies, salivating with desire to rip the entrails from innocent intruders.

On a narrow shelf that jutted up beside the gully floor, I unloaded the pack, built a small fire, and sat cross-legged in the dirt, watching the tops of the fir and spruce grow dark against the stars. If the old man had followed, he'd have an easy kill with me outlined by the fire, but I was pretty sure he hadn't. Most assassins and all hit men come from cities, and no city boy, not even a killer, would follow a local into the unknown darkness. That was the theory anyway.

——

A coyote howled a five-note pattern, three the same tone, then down, then up, more or less. Then silence. Then the first three again, down, back up for a hold. I tossed a chunk of green pine onto the fire. The log would smoke like crazy and mark my position, but I always feel safe when coyotes howl. Silence would mean something out there has them nervous, and whatever scares a coyote scares me.

I draped one arm over the woodpile as if it was a loyal, tired dog keeping me company. With the other hand, I drank. Canteen water tasted better than the Fig Newtons. My fiberfill bag lay stretched on the back side of the fire. Flame-strobe action gave it an occupied look, like a woman tossing in her sleep, wishing I would come to bed and warm her bare feet. I pretended it was Lana Sue. Then I imagined Marcie VanHorn. Then Debra Winger. The Debra Winger fantasy worked pretty well, so I let it float awhile.

A campfire is the only thing on earth that looks the same as it did a thousand years ago. Everything else, the land, the water, even the color of the sunset has changed this century. The only way to communicate with people from ages gone by is to gaze into the coals of a campfire. That's why people write books and have babies. We want to communicate.

I considered masturbation. Lana Sue had been gone four

days now, and she hadn't exactly been eager for mounting all last week. But I've never been comfortable with wilderness whack-offs because of my glasses. On, I feel formal, and off, I'm exposed.

Another coyote answered, five notes, same pattern. Down the gully an owl nailed a rabbit or something. For ten seconds the night filled with screams. I jumped to look, but, naturally, I'd been staring into the coals and couldn't see diddly for a full minute. The screams passed over my head and into the black. As they did, an entire set of coyotes went off like fire alarms up the ridge. I've always wondered if there's not some Darwinistic reason why coyotes and crying babies sound so much alike.

"More damn noise here than in Jackson." I threw a stack of wood on the fire. Built myself a roaring pep-rally of a bonfire so hot I had to scoot back to the corner of the ledge where anything with claws could reach out from the depths of the gully and grab my ass.

Every time I tried to consider the purpose of the Search, I either got horny or spooked. Time to concentrate. I drank more water, wishing it was Canadian whiskey. I think better on whiskey.

I considered death: If my span of self-awareness is forty, fifty, at tops eighty years, with frigging eternity stretched out both before and after, then the odds against me sitting in front of this campfire are at least infinity to one. The chance of me being in this moment when the number of moments there are is considered—these odds are much lower than the odds that God lives in a centigrade thermometer in Joplin, Missouri. Any religion, no matter how farfetched, impractical, or flat bizarre, is more likely to be true, if you play the percentages, than the belief that my sixty-year portion of infinity just *came up*.

Bring it down to the issues at hand. I was hungry. Some asshole shot at me. I was no closer to resolving the past and future than I'd been at home couch-potatoed by beer and TV baseball. Only now my Search had lost me the reason I started it—Lana Sue.

I didn't want to lose Lana Sue. She's my partner. If I saw a three-legged cat, Lana Sue would be the one I would tell. There'd be no use in finding truth or even a good ice-cream cone if I couldn't go say to Lana Sue, "Hey, guess what I found today?" Lana Sue thinks the people in *Doonesbury* are real. We had an argument about it once. She cares about the children of roadkill prairie dogs. She anticipates joy—no matter how bothered she gets by life, death, guilt, and grief, I can never picture Lana Sue losing her love of lunch.

And purposely, consciously, just three days ago, I said, "Sorry, honey, this thing is more important than you," and *walked* away from her.

What is this *thing* that was worth starvation, solitude, confusion—now I'm being shot at, for Chrissake? What is all this in the name of? *Truth.* Am I a murderer? Where does a family go when it dies? Where will I go?

Hell, let's capitalize the whole fucking thing. TRUTH. THE SEARCH. GOD. *Ta-da,* "Loren Paul looks into his campfire *and figures it all out.*" If it was as simple as driving yourself nuts and wandering into the mountains, wouldn't someone else have pulled the trick by now?

Jesus Christ. And, in the process, I'd chased away my only shot at legitimate communication. And love. "Shit," I said. "Next time I bring whiskey."

# Part Two

# 5

YOU ONLY HAVE TO TALK TO LOREN PAUL FOR TWO MINUTES to realize that his socks don't match. I met him when I was seventeen and nauseatingly normal. Loren was fifteen, but he's never passed for normal in his life. I was walking alone that day, which I know is rare for a girl of seventeen, but twenty minutes before Loren threw his first pass, I sat in a doctor's office full of artsy mood posters being told I was pregnant.

I held hands with myself and stared at a poster showing two beautiful people on the beach, arms around each other, gazing at the waves. The people, the sand, the sunset, all looked very fine and pure. The caption read, LOVE IS…BEAUTIFUL.

Young Dr. Betts smiled and pulled his chair close to mine and touched my knee. He had the teeth of a television preacher, lots of turquoise jewelry around his neck, and hair as long as anyone in Houston in 1964.

"Your tests are positive," he smiled, putting pressure on my knee.

"You mean I'm knocked up?"

"Yes, Lana Sue, you are knocked up."

"Oh, fuck."

Walking down Bissonnet Road, I crossed the tracks and dazed my way up fast-food row. Pizza, burgers, roast beef slices, and ice cream, the franchise system was off and running in southwest Houston.

The father's name was Ron and the problem was that I liked him. He was kind of sexy, and he treated me nice. He always paid for everything we did. I just didn't know if I wanted to have a baby by or with him. I wanted to be a country-western singer, and a kid would slow me down. They weren't even allowed in places where country singers sing.

My plan was to move fast. Patsy Cline died the March before, and no new supersexy superstar had stepped forward to take her place. Everyone was talking about the funny-dressing longhairs from England—Dave Clark Five and the Beatles—but I knew they wouldn't last. Girls just liked the accents. No one could hit it big in music without fiddles.

The music scene was ripe for a new champion—me. Only I couldn't tour pregnant.

At that time, women in Texas did not go in much for early termination. It was illegal, expensive, somewhat dangerous, and hard to pull off. Hell, I didn't know anyone who had ever had one.

Six years later, I didn't know many who hadn't, but at seventeen I was no trendsetter. I lived with my parents and wore cotton panties.

This skinny, short kid stepped up beside me and said, "You look dejected."

"I am dejected." I'd seen him before. He was several grades behind me in school, which made a lot of difference. Normally, I'd have run across the street before someone saw me talking to a little boy and told Ron, but I suppose impregnation mixed me up. I didn't tell him to get lost.

"You're Lana Sue Goodwin," he said.

"I know."

"I'm Loren Paul."

I kept walking.

"I'm a Leo with my Venus in Scorpio," he added.

"What the fuck's that mean?" Dr. Betts was the first adult I'd ever said "fuck" to. The power made me reckless.

"It's astrology. It means I'm sexy."

"You're five feet two and your voice squeaks. That's not sexy. I wouldn't even talk to you if I wasn't dejected."

He stuck both hands in his pockets and walked looking at the ground. I could tell he might cry at any moment.

"I'm sorry," I said. "I'm just upset right now. I would rather be alone."

"Lana Sue," he said, not looking at me, "I think you have the nicest ass in Bellaire High School."

He was on my outside when we reached the corner and I did it on purpose. The twerp asked for it, playing the wounded little boy and not watching where he walked. I passed just to the left of a stop sign and Loren walked into the pole, knocking himself silly.

Cute, huh? A nice how-I-met-Grandpa story to amuse the grandkids with on a rainy afternoon. Prove to them that Granny was once young and interesting. But there's more. One extra bit that sets Loren apart from the thousands to millions of fifteen-year-old nerds who vow undying, unwanted love for the first girl who's polite to them.

Loren caught a cab downtown that night and had Lana Sue tattooed on his lower back. Directly over the kidney.

Then, the little bastard never told me. What's the use of mutilating yourself over someone if you don't tell them? Eighteen years later, two husbands for me, a wife for Loren, three children between us, and enough frustration, boredom, grief, and nausea for six families, we met again and completed the pass in an eight-dollar-a-night motor court on the south side of Denver.

The sex wasn't that good. We were both blotto drunk and Loren took forever in coming. I found myself listening to Dick

Cavett interview a pretentious Gore Vidal on the TV in the next room. To be fair, Loren took so long because he made sure I got off before letting himself turn loose, and I wasn't easy to arouse. I finally managed it, though, and twenty minutes later, so did he.

Lightning didn't strike and the earth didn't shake, but I wasn't looking for lightning and quakes. I was looking to forget Ace and what a mess I'd made of my life. I sure as hell wasn't looking for a new husband.

Loren relaxed me, and at the time I needed relaxation more than passion.

Afterwards, he mumbled something like, "Gee, thanks," and rolled over to sleep. I thought that was odd, but all men are odd, so I answered, "You're welcome." I was wide awake. Wide awake, alone, and drunk in a sleazebag motel bed after making sweaty sex with a virtual stranger, knowing my husband was probably in the same situation, and not caring.

How's that for a depressing scenario—American as Valium and ancient as recreational love.

Time for postcoital nicotine. I groped around the night stand for cigarettes and matches. To me, afterglow means the coal moving up and down in the darkness beside a snoring man. Making love depresses me sometimes.

One-handed, I lit a match and there it was, my own name staring at me from the back of what I thought was a one-night painkiller.

The match burnt my finger. With two hands this time, I lit another and cupped it close to his skin—LANA SUE in faded red with what had long ago been a black outline.

I hit him on the ass. "Hey."

Loren raised his head. "Whassamattah?"

"My name's on your back."

He lowered his head again. "Oh, yeah, I forgot."

"What's my name doing on your body?"

"I paid a black man fifteen dollars to put it there."

The match went out. I could burn him with the smoking stub or go to sleep and ignore everything.

Loren sighed and rolled over and slid his arm around my shoulders. I dropped the unlit cigarette and cuddled close with my hands under my chin. It felt nice.

He said, "Remember that day you walked me into the pole on Bissonnet?"

"Sure. I had a lot on my mind that day."

"Well, you hurt my feelings. I knelt on the sidewalk, holding my bleeding nose and watching your beautiful ass swish away, and I swore that someday I'd get you."

"That's dumb."

"I swore I'd seduce you and you wouldn't be such a high-and-mighty senior who humiliates freshmen just because they have feelings."

"So you carved my name on your back?"

"A black artist drew your name on my back. Years and years from then, when I conquered your body, I wanted you to find that tattoo and know I'd been lying in wait for you all that time. I wanted you to know Loren Paul is something special."

"That's hard to deny."

"Yeah, I'm not like other guys."

Hell, after that I had to marry Loren just to get back at him for what he did to get back at me.


I know what you're thinking. I thought it too. The night Loren returned from his Flannery O'Connor grave trip, he drank himself comatose and I searched his entire body, hair roots to toe jamb. I'm the only name on it.

––––

Once I asked Loren what his first wife thought of the tattoo.

"I told her it was a birthmark."

"And she believed you?"

He shrugged. "She wanted to."

Loren's first wife, Ann, committed suicide while he was writing a book. Loren finished the book, which is why we're rich and don't have to do things we don't want to do.

———

Before Loren, I'd been rich enough not to do the things I don't want to do three times. All three times, I walked away from the man who came with the money. Being rich isn't necessary. I also left a poor man, but I kind of regret that one.

The decision to go or stay never tears me apart or anything. I don't think about it at all. One day, I'm fine, the next, I'm unhappy, the next, I'm gone. None of my formers ever suspects trouble because I don't dream of leaving until the Crack. That's what I call it—the Crack.

The Crack is the moment the situation turns impossible and I go from satisfied to dissatisfied. Dissatisfied to out the door takes about an hour. Sometimes I don't want to go. Lord knows, I wanted to stay with Loren. I think. I just don't have much control over my life.

Take my pal and ex-true love, Mickey Thunder. Way back in 1963—the morning after our last gig in an awful low-ceilinged club full of drunken soldiers in Fort Smith, Arkansas—my daddy and a hired investigator kicked in an unlocked door at the Fox Box Motel and found Mickey passed out on me and four other band members in stages of degeneracy on the floor. A week's worth of beer cans, apple cores, butts, and slut magazines lay scattered around like we'd forgotten our upbringing. None of us wore any clothes. It was a real unpleasant scene and completely out of Daddy's background.

Daddy was shocked. Screaming, *"Statutory," "Whore,"* and *"Oh my God,"* he dragged me out of bed, out the door, then back in the door to throw a blanket over my body.

Mickey said, "Aw, Christ."

Choosie said, "Tell him to fuck off, Lannie."

I didn't say anything. The fun was over.

But the second time, sixteen years later, after Ron and the twins and God knows how many dinner parties, tennis lessons, and charitable functions, I ran away with Mickey again.

This time I knew Mickey was the one for life. He's such a drunk, I didn't figure *for life* meant for my life, but I loved him and sure never figured on leaving him unburied.

I lasted fourteen months. One morning in a slum shack of a motel in Brigham City, Utah, life with Mickey wasn't fun.

The room could have been the Fox Box held in a museum for future generations. That's how much Mickey's life had progressed. Mine too, come to think of it. The only difference was, the band members slept next door. Not much growth for all those years.

Mickey woke up with his usual hangover and his usual breath. He wasn't as appetizing as he'd been at twenty. The long, bony face had become a waxy color—corpselike. His hand shook when he poured the first Jim Beam of the day.

"Are we going to make that album for Ace?" I asked.

"No."

"Why not?"

"I've made albums."

"I haven't."

"It's not something you want to do."

"You got something against success?"

"Yep." He lay back, covering his face with one arm. "Lannie, you're not that good. You're fine for our band and what we do, but Ace would throw you to that Nashville zoo, he'd have you dressing like Daisy Mae and bending over on *Hee Haw.* That's not our style."

"I am, too, good."

He opened his eyes at me. "For you to make it in this business, you're gonna have to suck some dicks, and I don't want to be around to watch."

Hell of a thing to say.

Mickey staggered into the bathroom to throw up. I followed and sat on the edge of the tub, pulling Mickey's hair behind his ears so he wouldn't puke on it.

He didn't care I kept puke out of his hair because he didn't care if he puked on it. I looked at his sharp nose and high cheekbones, the dent at his temple. Mickey hadn't gained a pound of flesh since the first time I held his hair back while he hugged a toilet. Still looked like a death's mask. Nothing changes but me.

*Crack.* I didn't want to be there anymore. "I'll do the album without you," I said.

Mickey dry-heaved a couple of times and pulled himself up to the sink. He drank from the cold water tap before looking over at me. "That mean the partnership is over?"

"I suppose so."

"Suit yourself." He stood, facing the mirror. "I have to hit you now."

"Why?" The man could hardly stand without help. In a fair fight, I'd have knocked his lights out.

"So you won't be tempted to come back if you get lonely."

"Okay." Mickey hit me, though not very hard. He's hit me a lot harder when we were making love.

That was that. I closed my suitcase and left.

———

More to the point, I didn't want to leave Loren. I never *want* to leave, but I have no patience with insanity. Daddy burned me out on sensitive men. I could have handled the eccentric-novelist act, the buttoning-his-shirt-and-zipping-him-up-before-we-went-out-the-door routine. I could even have handled the silly fantasy with Marcie. Someday he'd luck out with her and I'd catch him and he'd spend the next twenty years paying the debt. One transgression makes a powerful weapon in the hands of a true bitch—which is what I suppose I am.

But to turn himself paranoid, depressive, neurotic, and an asshole *on purpose*. And it was on purpose. Loren knew he was slipping into compulsive fixation.

"To obsess, you have to ignore something," I said. "And you're ignoring me."

"I cannot live in the present until I know what happened before. God better come up with some answers or else."

Which seemed okay. He'd always been a little abstracted by that Buggie thing. I figured to let him wallow in it until he got bored with misery and realized I counted for something.

Only I never expected the side effects—the amazing amount of energy, the total lack of a need for sleep. He developed an awesome sex drive. I wouldn't have minded that one so much, except, when we made love, he acted like he didn't know who he was with. Twice he jumped me without saying a word before, during, or after. I can't stand being ignored, especially when I'm fucking.

I caught him in the bathroom, whispering to Zelda. He put a padlock on his shorts drawer. I walked into the study while he was typing and Loren lurched forward, covering the page with his whole upper body.

At dinner that night, he babbled over an hour about his little sister that the Rangers killed. Sometimes he called her Kathy. Sometimes he called her Debby. He couldn't remember.

He said, "They killed her for collecting Barbie dolls."

Loren began to affect my peace of mind. I started waking

up at three in the morning, unable to get back to sleep. I took four showers a day. As his sex drive soared, mine zilched, which upset me a lot because I've always been proud of my sex drive and I hate to lose something I'm proud of.

"Let's sit naked in the creek," Loren said.

"I'm not in the mood."

"I'll borrow a horse from the VanHorns and we can make it at full gallop."

"I hate horses."

"I think I'll go watch the moon rise."

"Go right ahead."

Loren went out to lie on his back in the yard and discuss life with the moon and I reached for a Milky Way.

———

I couldn't have been more than seven when I became aware of Daddy's dark clouds. Sometimes, for no reason, he quit talking to me, quit loving me as far as I could see, and I felt so awful that I took comfort in candy. Or maybe I punished myself for letting him down, I don't know. All I know is, every few months Daddy sat in his chair with no intention of ever doing anything again, and I stuffed myself with cupcakes, soda pop, Hershey bars, anything sweet I could find. I was sneaky about it, hid Ding Dongs in my bottom drawer and chocolate kisses in my dollhouse.

All through junior high and high school, I remember periodic nightmares of long silences and junk-food blues.

Now, whenever I feel rejected, I gorge. Who knows why? But the day Loren caught me spooning down white sugar, I knew something was terribly wrong.

———

The next day I found a gray hair in my brush, scalded myself on the morning coffee, and my six-hundred-dollar, fourteen-attachment, will-pick-up-anything-from-tenpenny-nails-to-carpet-patterns vacuum cleaner broke. Midway through my own room, it made a clattering sound, smelled like burning rubber, and stopped sucking.

Even sane, Loren can't fix a drink, and in his infinite purity, he'd decided mechanical devices were beneath the dignity of him and his buddy God.

"My mind must be free to roam the skies of enlightenment," he said the time I asked him to light the oven for dinner.

So, I had to take the vacuum cleaner apart, figure out the problem, and put it all back together again. Major decisions are ninety percent timing, you realize that? Three hours earlier, before the gray hair and the vacuum trauma, I wouldn't have left Loren. I'd have brained him, but I wouldn't have left. There's no use talking that way, though, because you can't change timing.

None of the damn pieces fit. I sat in the center of a dirty rug, surrounded by long tilings and tiny things and clumps of floor crud, right on the narrow edge of screaming and hurling the drapes attachment through the window, when Loren wandered in the door from the kitchen and walked through my nuts-and-washers-and-doodads-that-don't-go-anywhere pile.

"Listen to this," he said. *"A one-eyed man is able to see, a lame man is able to tread. He treads on the tail of a tiger. The tiger bites the man."*

"Loren, you're kicking my nuts."

"What do you think that means, Lana Sue? It sounds like if everything isn't perfect and you keep going anyway, you'll get bit by a tiger. Does that mean handicapped people should just sit down and never move?"

"What book is that?"

Loren turned it around to show the cover. "The *I Ching*."

"The whole damn house is falling apart and you're reading the *I Ching*?"

"It seems relevant."

I picked up a hollow, lightweight metal tube, usually used for vacuuming under things, and swung it as hard as I could into Loren's temple.

"That's it. *Crack.* You're off the list, Loren. I hope God can cook, clean, and fuck 'cause you can't and I won't."

Loren raised his hand to his head, feeling the place I'd whacked. "I don't understand."

"That's the first truth you've found all day. You don't understand anything and you're understanding less by the minute."

"Why did you hit me?"

I turned and headed for the door.

"Lana Sue, are you leaving?"

Whirling, "I'm not going down with you, Loren. You want to go insane, that's your business, but don't expect me to go with you. And don't expect me to be here when you come back."

He just looked at me, fingering the lump on his head.

Since Loren wouldn't argue with me, all the way out to the truck I argued with myself. "Lana, what are you doing? You love this one. Don't blow it."

"I don't have to put up with this crap anymore. There's no excuse for living with a metaphysical boogieman."

"Sure there is. Kick the vacuum pieces in the closet. They don't matter."

"I'm not killing my marriage so I won't have to put a vacuum cleaner back together."

"Bullshit."

———

I stopped in Jackson long enough to gas up the Toyota before heading south. South is the secure way to head in a crisis. It's warm all year in the South. Daddy lives there.

Rolling down all the windows, I jammed an Emmylou tape in the deck and cranked the truck up to 80.

Life wasn't fair all of a sudden. I'd married one man who turned into someone else who forced me to do something I didn't want to do.

I screamed into the wind, *"My husband's an idiot."*

"The others were idiots," another voice said—a voice from a part of me I don't see too often. "Loren's good. Nothing good ever happened to you before. Don't throw it away."

"Fuck off, who asked you anyway?"

"You always talk like a slut when you're upset."

"Look what's happened, I'm talking out loud to something that calls me a slut. This doesn't happen to me...*I'm normal."* I turned Emmylou up loud, hoping to drown the conversation, but inner voices are persistent suckers.

"Don't shout when you're alone, Lana Sue."

"Shut up, creep."

"Loren accepts you. He doesn't judge or want anything from you. He doesn't force anything on you."

"He reads the *I Ching* out loud. He talks to the moon and it talks back. Do you want to live with a man who talks to the moon?"

"Do you want to live without him?"

I cranked the truck up to the 95-100 range, which scared me and my voices into shutting up. Wyoming flew past like it was on a video screen and nothing was real. I imagined if the Toyota crashed, a light would flash, a buzzer would honk, and I'd have to put in another quarter—not a good pretend game to play when you're driving. A stray antelope could have turned the Lana Sue story into a tragedy without even knowing what hit him.

Emmylou sang a fast song about a pinball machine in Amarillo, Texas. I hummed along, picking the guitar breaks on the steering wheel. Our band played Amarillo several times—I even sang at the Golden Sandies Homecoming Dance way back in another life. I've had so many lives and sometimes they don't connect.

The high-speed emotionalism wasn't safe, and I'm not stupid—at least not for more than ten minutes—so I backed off on the accelerator, watching the sagebrush slow to a dull blur. Digging through the glove compartment, I replaced Emmylou with Bru Hau.

> *I got a hole in my boot, I got a hole in my coat, there's a hole in my fancy shirt, I got a hole in my life, where my baby walked out.*

The main attraction, and drawback, to country music is that if you've just left a husband, wife, or love of some kind, or even worse, been left by a husband, wife, or love of some kind, every single one of those syrupy, corny, otherwise trite songs touches you. Sometimes I don't want to be touched.

Sure, it's all been said before, but as I try to explain to Loren, all real emotions have been felt millions of times. Nothing sincere is original. Trite is basic, and if your emotions are basic, you relate to trite.

> *There was a hole in our love and she walked right through it,*
> *To get a better point of view you might say that I blew it.*

As Bru Hau's heartbreak song got to me, the Toyota moved slower. I saw less and less of the high desert and more and more of what used to be. I slid into memories.

> *You work me too hard and your jokes ain't funny*
> *I can't live in your life full of dreams and no money*

More than slid. Skimming along Highway 89, rolling south away from Loren, I got down and mud-wrestled with my past. Slime might be a better term than mud.

# 6

DADDY WAS A GYNECOLOGIST. GRANDMA COMMITTED SUICIDE.

I come from a long line of moody people on my father's side and social climbers on Mom's. Dad's family was wealthy and wanted to be normal, were desperate to be normal. Mom's family was normal and wanted to be wealthy. The two lines culminated in me, Lana Sue Goodwin Potts Roe Paul, the moodiest social climber.

My sister Dessie once said, "Daddy fell in love with Mom because her mom served dinner at exactly the same time every night and all the furniture in the living room was wrapped in plastic. He figured anyone that normal couldn't put out crazy kids."

He figured wrong, of course. Dessie turned gay at eleven. I caught her going down on the baby-sitter the night Mom and Dad drove downtown to see *The King and I*. I thought she was playing hide-and-seek from me and had found a really dumb place to hide. Dessie lives in New York City now with a famous lesbian magazine editor. My sister never was cute like me. Maybe she got the wrong hormones.

Dessie won't go to Houston to visit Mom and Dad anymore, says they're provincial and have bad taste.

"I do not care to associate myself with anyone who serves

Riunite on ice with a salmon loaf," Dessie says, "even if they are my parents."

From the earliest I remember, especially after Daddy started having sad spells, much was made of "Grandma's blood." When Dessie sat in the middle of Wildwood Way and refused to budge, Mom said, "Grandma's blood." When I threw the veal piccata into the living room knickknack shelf, it was "Grandma's blood." I never found out what Grandma's sin was, other than killing herself while her sons were off on Iwo Jima wasting Japs, but she sure got blamed for a lot of grief fifteen years later.

Once every seven or eight months I'd come home from school and Mom would meet me at the door, whispering, "Grandma's blood is in your father again. Why don't you go to Roxanne's for the night?"

"Why do I have to leave?"

"For one night. You can come back tomorrow."

"Daddy won't be any better tomorrow."

"Yes, he will. He just needs some rest. You'll be fine at Roxanne's."

"Sure, Mom. We got any candy bars? I'm hungry."

I packed off to my cousin Roxanne's with my toothbrush, a rolled-up nightie, and an overnight case full of junk food, which I finished off by bedtime. The next day I would walk home to find Daddy sitting in his overstuffed Naugahyde recliner, staring at his hand on his knee. He usually sat about a week, sometimes a week and a half or two, not talking, not even blinking as far as Dessie and I could tell. Each night around bedtime he'd exhale a sigh that tore my spine from bottom to top.

I reached a time where I could handle the catatonic daddy routine by pretending he wasn't really there, that man in the chair was a visiting plant, but I never got used to the sighs. I still remember how terrible the nightly wait was and how much I hated myself when it came.

Then one morning I'd wake up and Daddy would be in the kitchen, teasing, rumpling hair, flipping pancakes, full of energy and projects. His favorite project was the garden. Daddy spent hundreds of hours piddling over strains of saffron, trying to find one that flourished in Houston's climate. I don't think gynecology was all that important to him. He only put in enough time at it to finance his real interests, like saffron.

Poor Mama married the wrong money. She didn't want a family of temperamental neurotics. She wanted a television commercial life. A household where the biggest problems were choosing a feminine spray and stains in the toilet bowl. She wanted two large American-made automobiles and a separate family room away from the dining and living room combination—a bathroom of her very own.

Lord only knows what Daddy wanted—to get through it all, I suppose, to grow old with a presentable wife, plenty of insurance, virgin daughters, and enough money to bury himself with dignity.

That was the problem right there—virgin daughters. His spells coincided with my first period, my first date, my first C in school. Any excuse from me and Daddy's eyes filmed over and he shuffled around the house like an old man for a day, then he moaned out loud and sat down and I got sent to Roxanne's for another night.

Mom knew who to blame, all right. Daddy had a spell just before I ran away with Mickey. It started on Christmas Eve, midway through Perry Como.

Perry sat on a three-legged stool, singing about the bells of Saint Somebody while Mom hummed along. She had set up a card table for stringing cranberries and popcorn. Mom just couldn't accept the fact that we were not a regular, wholesome

American family like the ones on Donna Reed and "My Three Sons." Daddy leaned back in his recliner, smoking a cigar. Dessie was upstairs with her best friend, Brenda.

I sat on the couch, eating a TV dinner and wondering how Mom would feel if I told her Dessie wasn't upstairs gossiping about boys. Wouldn't it be neat at sixteen to surprise your complacent *Better Homes and Gardens* mother with, "My sister's up in her room licking Brenda's clit, Ma." I'd love it. She could never act so damn self-righteous around me again.

But, I didn't. It would be too much like stepping on a puppy's head. Instead, I silently chewed Salisbury steak and watched Perry Como and my mother fake the Christmas spirit.

Daddy leaned over and took off his left slipper and threw it at the television. Mom and I stopped in midhum and chew, staring at the slipper on the floor.

Daddy groaned, "Jesus Christ."

He didn't say another word clear through *The Tonight Show*—just sat there with one slipper on his foot and one slipper on the rug.

Before bed, Mom caught me in the hall and pulled me into her and Daddy's bathroom with the fuzzy toilet seat cover. The towels were red and green, used only during the holiday season.

"Grandma's blood is acting up in your father again," she whispered loudly. "What did you do?"

"I didn't do anything, Mama," I said, though I knew better. I didn't know what awful injustice I'd committed, but I knew Daddy's depression was my fault. It was never Dessie who caused him to stop talking. Always me, I was older.

"You're so pretty and sweet," Mom said, touching my hair. "You have all the advantages, Lannie. Don't break your father's heart."

A week later, I ran off to get laid and become a country star, but if someone says you're breaking their heart before you've done anything, you might as well do something. You get blamed either way.

A couple of years after the twins were born, I took a course in psychology at Rice. The course gave me just enough under-graduate ammunition to try defending myself.

"Daddy's manic," I shouted at Mom. "It's bad chemicals he inherited from Grandma or too much salt or something. I don't cause these episodes. They just happen."

Mom looked at herself in the lavatory mirror, holding her narrow chin up and to the right. Every serious talk I ever had with her took place in the bathroom. It's like the woman can't express herself more than three feet from a douche bag.

"If only you hadn't run off with that musician."

"The spells were as bad before I left as they are now."

"That's not true, Lannie. Your father has never been happy since that first night you didn't come home."

"My father's never been happy since the day I was born. I can't vouch for earlier."

Mom's lip quivered and she blinked quickly. "Don't say that. We were happy when we were young. I remember."

"I'm sorry, Mama."

She opened the cabinet and reached in for another blue Valium. "You must be careful, Lannie. Your father loves you more than anything on earth. I hate to think what he might do to himself if you ever pulled another stunt like that."

Translation: Disappoint Daddy and he'll kill himself and it will be your fault.

———

Daddy was a gynecologist in Houston, which means we never had to do without. He chose Houston because of the humidity. A gynecologist's dreamland, he called it. We lived in Bellaire, which is a reasonably upper-middle part of the city—mostly white people, mostly with money. I was typical to the point of nausea. Skirts to the knees, socks to the knees, hair usually straight, though flipped up during a Doris Day stage and page-boyed when Patty Duke pageboyed hers.

I had a boyfriend, Ron, who played basketball and ate pizza. He drove a huge '55 Oldsmobile with bad springs that rode like a ship in heavy weather. We went out four times before he kissed me, seven times before he felt my left breast, thirteen before he felt my right.

Most of our "dates" were spent sprawled on the floor in the family room, reading DC comics and drinking 7-Ups. Sometimes we played Ping-Pong in the garage with another couple. Passion didn't come up too often.

I don't remember school. I don't think it was important. I never stopped to think about myself or whether everyone was like me, or I was like anyone. I do remember the summers. We circled from the A&W to the Sonic endlessly, singing along with the Rhondelles, beating out Ventures drum solos on the dashboard.

Ron and I French-kissed a couple of times at the drive-in *(Son of Flubber),* I giggled about how weird it felt later with the girls at a slumber party where we each smoked a Lark cigarette and I threw up in the kitchen sink because someone else was throwing up in the bathroom.

Most of the summer of '62 was spent in a one-piece bathing suit at the country club, though I don't remember swimming that much, mostly just lying around the pool, watching the boys show off. I had a good tan by August. I remember that tan. Happiness was not an issue. Who thinks, *Am I happy?* when they're fifteen? Loren probably did, but he's peculiar.

School started. I was a junior. Football season, Thanksgiving, basketball season, Christmas. The high point came on my birthday in October when I got a driver's license. Because

I was going with the captain of the basketball team, I had a fairly good shot at Queen in February. I didn't worry about it much. I was more worried about keeping my weight down and my teeth straight—braces terrified me. I also stood in front of the mirror most nights, searching for boobs that never came. Other girls had boobs. I knew all the kids thought I was a squirrel for not having any.

I asked Daddy for a car for Christmas, but he gave me a watch instead. What did I need a watch for? What I needed was wheels of my own. With wheels I could be popular without knockers.

All this life based on growing up in the American dream ended on New Year's Eve. It was my cousin Roxanne's fault. Roxy is my favorite hell-raising relative. She's a year and then some younger than me, but her daddy wasn't a manic gynecologist, so Roxanne started her smoking, drinking, life-in-the-fast-lane period way before Dessie or me. Not only did Roxanne get lucky at fourteen, but she claims she had regular orgasms. I doubt it.

The reason I doubt it is because Roxanne's supposed Big Os came off rodeo cowboys. Even older women complain about short rides and losses of concentration on the rodeo circuit. Bull riders and calf ropers are just too horny. I can't conceive of a kid cowboy lasting more than eight seconds, but I guess that shows a prejudicial viewpoint picked up later after several years of working honky-tonks.

Looking back, I find Roxanne's pastime really amazing. I mean, knowing her rich and easy background, hanging out with cowboys was a lot more rebellious than the early sex, but then, Roxanne didn't give a damn what anyone thought of her cowboy fetish. She said a limp turned her on.

Rox's cowboy that winter was an older, browner guy named Neb—which I think was short for Nebraska. Neb had a face like a muddy teardrop and knees farther apart than his shoulders. He chewed and spit. I thought he was repulsive, though I never have figured out Roxanne's tastes in butt.

Along about Thanksgiving, Neb gave Roxanne two tickets to a New Year's Eve concert by something called Conway Twitty and the Twitty Birds, his obvious plan being that I should drive Roxanne to the concert so he could get her drunk and hump her. I didn't cooperate.

"No."

Roxy pleaded. "Every Christmas Ron gets drug off to his grandma's in Wichita Falls and every New Year's Eve you sit home watching TV. It's time you had some fun, Lannie."

"I can't stand hillbilly music. Twitty sounds like twang and twang stinks."

"I bet you never even heard any real country music."

"I heard it and I hate it. No."

"Maybe Neb can bring a friend for you."

"I'm not going to pop my cherry with a smelly cowboy in a pickup truck. Besides I'm going steady. Why should I screw a stranger if I won't screw Ron?"

"Because Ron doesn't know how."

"That's possible."

"You don't have to screw Neb's friend. Just pretend you might and he'll buy you some drinks."

"Forget it."

Roxanne bothered me the whole week after Christmas. Part of her problem was that I was sixteen and could drive and she was fifteen and couldn't. If Neb picked her up at home, they were afraid her parents would call the police.

I finally gave in. You can ask Loren. Or Ron, Ace, or Mickey. Persistence is my weakness. I'll give in to anyone who's willing to beg awhile.

We told Mom and Dad we were going to a slumber party

at Brenda's with Dessie. Dessie and Brenda were glad to cover for us. It made them look less suspicious also. I wore my pink sweater and jeans. Roxanne wore a skirt and cowboy boots. She looked like Dale Evans pretending to be a teenage hooker.

We ate Mama Burgers at the A&W before driving downtown, but the night almost collapsed right there because Roxanne tried to steal her root beer mug and we got caught and the man threatened to call the cops. He only let us go because she cried.

We each drank a beer while I drove Daddy's car downtown. Roxanne had taken us two apiece from her parents' refrigerator. I said they'd find out, but she said they wouldn't. Her parents were throwing a New Year's Eve party and they'd never miss four Lone Stars.

"Here," she said, handing me a straw from the A&W. "You get drunk quicker if you suck it up."

"Why?"

"I don't know why, but everyone says it works."

The concert was in the old Baxter Hall on Second Street. We got there early and sat in the car, drinking beer out of straws and looking at all the people on the sidewalk.

"Where's Neb?" I asked.

Roxanne smoked a cigarette, a Lucky Strike. Her long fingernails were painted bright brown to go with her eyes and brown hair. Even back at fifteen, Roxanne fit like a comfortable cat into the sophisticated world of beer, cigarettes, and easy sex. "He said he'd meet us at the door. I talked to him this afternoon and he's bringing a friend for you like I figured."

"I never knew a real cowboy before."

"They're the same as those jocks you go out with, only their peckers are pointed like their boots."

This got us both to laughing with mouthfuls of beer, which got beer all over the front seat of Daddy's car.

"Can I try a cigarette?" I asked, opening my other Lone Star.

"Sure"—Roxanne handed me the pack—"but only if you inhale. I'm sick and tired of butt beggars who hold the smoke in their mouths and try to look cool."

I lit up, but I didn't inhale. "I saw Ron's pecker once."

Roxanne seemed to think this was about the funniest thing she'd ever heard. I suppose she'd seen dozens by then. "What did it look like?" she giggled.

"I don't know, like they're supposed to, I guess. It was dark. He pulled it out in the parking lot after the Brownsville game. Ron wanted me to touch it, but I didn't."

"Was it hard and stiff?"

"I don't think so. It looked kind of gross."

This sent us into more giggles and more beerspit in Daddy's car. I tried to wipe some off the seat with a Kleenex.

"Jesus, Daddy'll kill me."

"Too late now. Look at that." Roxanne pointed at a big woman with a bigger cowboy going into the hall. The woman wore a huge, blond sparkly wig and a belt buckle with blue rocks on it. As she passed, the back of the belt read IMOGENE.

"How do you figure she got those pants on?" I asked.

"A long time ago, then she grew into 'em. Check out this guy." The original rhinestone urban asshole strutted past. "Maybe he's a pimp for horses," Roxanne said.

Three couples spilled, laughing, out of a pickup truck beside us. The women were all thin and chewed gum. Two had chrome silver hair and the other had dyed hers an unbelievable zit red. Obviously, all three had spent a lot of time and money making themselves look like they looked.

"Where did all these hicks and freaks come from?" I asked.

"Houston."

"I need some air."

Sixteen years old, half-drunk on two beers, walking in to

hear something called the Twitty Birds, I started to think. It wasn't easy. I'm sure I was the first girl in my class at Bellaire to think a thought someone hadn't told her first.

These people around me, some even touching me, all had real faces, open to good and bad and love and pain. These people seemed to believe in their own legitimacy, but they weren't like me or my parents or any of my parents' friends. I'd never in my life met an unmarried adult. Or a black person. We had a maid named Bobbie who I took for granted was poor, but I'd never actually talked to her.

These people on both sides of me didn't give a damn about getting into a good college.

That thought staggered me. Here were grown women who weren't bums or degenerates, but most of them obviously hadn't been Sub Debs and had never even thought about what they were missing. I bet not one of those three women with the aluminum hairdos knew the difference between a Lucky Circle Girl and a Jolly Jill. I bet they didn't care. And their dates probably didn't consider themselves washed-up, skid-row hoboes even though they didn't hold membership in a restricted country club.

These people didn't dress like me, talk like me, wear their hair like me, or want the things I'd been told I wanted, yet none of them looked miserable because of it.

Suddenly, in a white flash of teen enlightenment, I realized that people completely unlike me outnumber people like me. KaBoom. Second insight. They were not worth less than people like me.

I stopped in the middle of the sidewalk on Second Street. "Roxanne," I said, "the people not like us outnumber the people like us."

"Of course. There's Neb. Wow, his friend is cute, we may have to trade."

"And the people not like us are just as good as we are."

"Whoever said they weren't? Hey, Neb, over here."

———

Neb's friend was kind of a nice guy, in an angular sort of way. His face wasn't scarred and all his teeth seemed to line up right. I didn't catch whether his name was Mel or Del. The face matched either one.

"So you're Hot Rox's cousin," he said with a grin that might have been a leer.

"I'm not a bit like her."

"Oh." Mel or Del looked disappointed.

Roxanne laughed hysterically at something Neb said and he put his arm around her shoulders as we walked through the double doors.

The Baxter is a wonderful place for a concert. I'd love to sing there sometime. Hardwood floors, high, dark ceiling, small tables scattered around like a real ballroom. We sat toward the front on the right. No one checked our IDs or anything. It was great—my first experience at being treated like a grown-up.

A waitress in a low-cut blouse and square-dancing skirt gave us each a funny hat and a toy that clicked when you spun it or unrolled when you blew in it. The guys grabbed up the toys you blew in and started zipping us in the ears and tits.

Roxanne jumped right into the spirit, but I hung back some, it all seemed a bit stupid to me.

Without even asking, Neb ordered four tequila sunrises. I caught him winking at Mel or Del.

"Why did you wink?" I asked.

"Got sawdust in my eye."

I didn't see any sawdust, but what the hell, why push it? If Roxanne wanted to be hustled, that was her business. What pisses me off is a man thinking he can seduce someone who doesn't want to be seduced. All the charm and tequila in Houston wouldn't trick me into doing something I didn't think up first.

Roxanne laughed every time Neb opened his mouth whether he meant to be funny or not. And whenever she laughed, she touched him—on the arm, the hair, the side of the face, somewhere. It grated my stomach. The laugh she used around boys was nothing like her girl laugh. It was all shriek and no sincerity. There are certain women that I like fine until you get them around men and then I can't stand to be anywhere near the bitches. Roxanne is one.

As soon as the lights dimmed, my date—sure wish I knew his name—grabbed my hand and held it between both of his. He didn't intertwine fingers, but held on like a double handshake.

The first band was called Thunder Road, and Mickey was in it. He sat behind a flat thing that looked like an electric bicycle rack, grinning, chewing gum, scanning the audience with this self-satisfied look. The band broke into a fast instrumental, sort of a Texas polka. I liked it.

"What's that thing the guy is sitting behind?" I asked.

Mel or Del stopped gazing at me long enough to check the stage. "The drummer?"

"No, the other guy."

"That's a pedal steel. You never saw a pedal steel before?"

"Uh-uh. What's it do?"

"Like a guitar strung across an ironing board. You play it with your hands, knees, and feet."

"All at the same time?"

I sometimes wonder why I chose Mickey. He seemed so worldly, leaning over his steel, nodding his head more to the chewing gum than the music. Maybe not worldly, but Houstonly. I'd just discovered a huge mass of people with a value system different from mine, and Mickey looked like he understood them.

Even sitting down, I could tell he was real tall. His face was all ridges, his cheekbones, chin, and nose stuck out as if he'd recently starved to death—a chewing, smiling skull.

The waitress brought our sunrises just as the song ended, so I was the only one at the table to applaud. The others were digging for money or oohing over the orange and red colors or some foolishness.

"Clap," I said.

Mel or Del just looked at me with his billfold in one hand and two dollars in the other.

The fiddle player stepped up to a microphone and said they were happy to be in Houston and he hoped everyone has a wonderful New Year's and gets drunk and laid. The rest of the table came round long enough to applaud and cheer that one.

Then the fiddler said, "Since this is the tenth anniversary of the death of country music's greatest legend, Hank Williams, we'd like to play a few of his songs for you."

Mickey leaned forward, and closing his eyes, moved into the introduction of "I'm So Lonesome I Could Cry." I didn't breathe. His fingers made the most beautiful, saddest sounds I'd ever heard, like he touched my insides, casually picking up all the vital organs and squeezing.

The steel *wept,* not the quiet tears or uncontrolled sobbing like a woman's crying, but the deep, helpless grief of a man at the end of himself. I couldn't believe the sounds, the pain, the hopelessness of each slowly bending note, and all the while, Mickey smiling, looking down at his hands as if he wasn't even connected to the wails coming from the speakers.

I'd be embarrassed if it happened now, but I was moved, forced to feel strong emotion. Imagine that, Lana Sue feeling strongly. Maybe it was more the steel than the man. Maybe I'd have fallen in love with the first pedal steel player I heard, no matter who it was, but Mickey got the nod that night.

Oh, shit. Let's get as corny as we can here. I was sixteen and semidrunk and the occasion called for corn. *The set ended with my sunrise untouched and my heart stomped on.* Let's see Loren get mushier than that.

As Mickey stood up, he smiled and nodded and looked at me. I know he did.

Wrestling my hand free of Mel or Del's double grip, I said, "I've got to go to the ladies' room."

Roxanne glanced over. "You want me to go with you, honey?"

"No, I can make it alone."

She frowned. "You okay, Lannie?"

"Sure, the beer just went right through. I'll be back in a second."

——

It took some time, but I found Mickey backstage. He sat alone in a dressing room, his long legs propped on a guitar case, a fifth of Wild Turkey tucked between them.

"Hi," I said.

He looked me up and down, slowly, calmly. Later I realized that was the same look he gave porterhouse steaks or cases of beer, but at the time, the look made me tremble and go tin-mouthed.

He didn't say anything, so I jumped right in, talking as fast as possible. "You don't know me, but my name is Lana Sue Goodwin and I'm a virgin but that doesn't really matter because I admire your music and, just watching, I think you could teach me about the world, you know, the people in the world that you sing about. You see, I've led an awfully sheltered life, and I don't know anything about anything, like why people do what they do and how you play that beautiful machine of yours, and you seem to know. Maybe you don't, maybe I'm just being a squirrel, but I don't think so and Christ, you have to grow up sometime."

Mickey stuck two fingers in his mouth, pulled out his gum, and rubbed it into the bottom of his chair. He opened the fifth and drank. I counted. His Adam's apple rose and fell three times. He grunted once and handed me the bottle.

"Thank you," I said. I tried to rub his cooties off the bottle mouth without him seeing.

"You a cocktease?" he asked.

"Of course not." I didn't even know what the word meant. I took a sip and handled it real well—no gasp, no shudder, no gag. I felt real grown-up. "This is certainly smooth whiskey."

"Certainly?"

"Certainly is."

Mickey reached for the bottle and took another swig. "You hungry?"

"Sure." This wasn't exactly what I expected and I wasn't hungry, but I figured I'd better be agreeable or he wouldn't talk to me.

"I need a hamburger." He stood up about a foot taller than me. "What's your name again?"

"Lana Sue. What's yours?"

"Mickey Thunder."

"Really?"

"Naw, that's my stage name. Real name is Michael Rossitelli." We walked across the street to a hotel coffee shop and ate hamburgers and french fries and talked. He told me about growing up poor, playing music, and being on the road all the time. I told him about Pep Club. I asked a lot of questions about his steel guitar. Mickey drew me a diagram of all the strings and their notes and what each of the eight foot pedals and four knee pedals did.

"Why do some make tones go up and some make tones go down and some do both?" I asked.

"Because that's how you play it."

"But it's so complicated, moving your fingers, feet and knees all at the same time."

"That's why most steel players don't sing. I can't sing for shit."

"Is that why you chose steel?"

"Naw, you get to play sitting down. I hate standing up."

"I want to hear you play some more."

"Let's have a drink first."

A couple of hours later—after the Twitty Birds and Roxanne, Neb, and whoever I was with were all gone, after everyone was gone—Mickey and I stumbled blind drunk onto the stage so he could play a song on his pedal steel. I was very drunk. I'd never been very drunk before. A teenager's first drunk is a bizarre, spinning experience that no amount of Coca-Cola and aspirin can prepare you for. God, was I drunk.

Mickey was only his usual every-night-stinking drunk. Halfway across the stage, he lurched into me and we fell over a drum and rolled under his instrument.

Virginity was a big deal back then. Maybe it should still be a big deal. I mean, there are three things that you only do once. You're born, you lose your virginity, and you die. Life's like that. Everything else can be repeated. Of those, losing virginity is the only one you have any control over. It's also the only one that's supposed to be fun and the only one you can reflect back on later.

I kind of wasted my once-in-a-lifetime loss because I was too drunk and don't remember much. We rolled around onstage, all tangled together with cords and wires and each other. His fingers went everywhere at once. His breath wasn't pleasant, but his fingers sure were.

Mickey said some dirty words.

I grunted around some.

The next thing it was light and some guys were laughing and I was lying on a dusty stage without clothes on.

Imagine kerplunking your typical American adolescent down in western Pakistan. He's lost, right? Everything he sees and touches is new and bizarre and he has no way of knowing what is normal for western Pakistan and what is considered strange even there. If his guide says everyone eats monkeys' feet or shaves their chests or prays five times a day or gives away all their money on the new moon, this theoretical typical kid has no way of knowing if he's being fed truth or dog manure.

Now—there is a large difference between the life of a doctor's daughter and the life of a groupie, snuff queen, or whatever you want to call a girl on the road with a second-rate country band. The two styles have no common points. Every detail  the food, the hours, the lack of privacy, especially the people—was unlike anything from my past, and Mickey was my only connection to reality. So when Mickey said all musicians drink Wild Turkey all day and all night, who was I to question? He told me working-class women give their men blow jobs before breakfast. I'd never met a working-class woman, how should I know better? You've got to trust your guide in these situations and I drew Mickey Thunder as my guide.

Not that I didn't eat up every minute of it. For ten glorious weeks we wheeled around Texas, Oklahoma, and Arkansas, singing, playing, driving, and screwing our way across America's Heartland. We were Thunder Road, hottest Western band in a five-state area—at least the ads said so and, like Mickey, I had no reason to think they lied.

I truly loved the traveling band life, all those EAT HERE cafes with "guaranteed" steaks and "famous" apple pie, the grime of gas station bathrooms, practically existing on Peanut Planks and Orange Crushes. We slept in the cheapest motels on earth, disgusting little boxes with stained sheets and rusted iron bathtubs where you showered with A-200 instead of soap. If only Roxanne could have seen me sleeping six in a bed with five horny, drunk musicians. Wet dreams fell like rain.

The time was evenly split between the van, the motels, and the bars. I liked the bars best because that's where I met the people. Country bars back then all had black floors carpeted with cigarette butts and spilled beer. The air was unbreathable by today's standards. None of the tables had four equal legs, none of the bartenders had clean teeth, and all the waitresses were overweight with ratted-up hair and tight jeans. At least that's how I remember it, twenty-two years down the line.

The bars blur together, but the customers don't. I liked the country bar customers. They acted like they felt. If a cowboy felt drunk, he acted drunk. If he felt lonesome or mean, he acted lonesome or mean. Amazing. Dancing, fighting, crying, I saw more raw emotion in a country bar in one night than I've seen in all my country clubs put together.

Poor people treat you like anybody else, like you're as good or bad, weak or stupid, as them. They take sixteen-year-old girls seriously.

The second night out we played in a county-line bar outside of Beaumont filled mostly with black farmers and Gulf workers. They were nice to me. I couldn't believe it. They acted like I was as regular as they were. One of the wives asked me what I thought of the new disposable diapers. I told her they sounded great.

The women spend a lot of their time pregnant. Every blacktop-highway cafe had at least one stuck-out waitress who called me honey and asked how many young'uns I had. They seemed disappointed when I said none. In Texarkana, I met a girl named Jamey that I liked because she had the exact same birthday as me. Jamey had two boys, both down with a rural pox of some kind, a car with a busted oil pan, and a husband who had run off to Shreveport with her younger sister and refused to pay child support. A couple of days before I came along she'd had to shoot the family dog because she couldn't afford to take him to the vet, and, just to make it all country song material, she'd skipped her last two periods.

I listened to this story with all the respect of Mary Magdalene listening to Jesus. I admired that girl so much, but Jamey acted like she was nothing out of the ordinary. *She was cheerful.* The heaviest decision of my life was whether or not to tease my hair like Kitty Wells's. Only two weeks ago I'd cried my eyes out because Daddy didn't buy me a Chevy for Christmas, and here was a girl *my age* raising two boys without money or hope.

"You must be worried sick," I said.

"Why?"

———

Choosie played fiddle. He was older, twenty-six, and only slept with fat girls. He lived on cashews and Dr Pepper. Would drink half a 10-2-4 bottle of Dr Pepper and fill it back up with whiskey or tequila. Or wine or beer. Mickey always said Choosie wasn't. Then he'd funnel in a pack of cashews and a couple of pills and drink the whole mix in one pull. I like to threw up watching the first time.

Lined up between Mick and Choosie stood Paul Bob, Butch Bob, and Bob Bob, bass, drums, and lead guitar. The Bobs were thin, long-fingered embarrassed boys with dirty jeans and a never-ending supply of toothpicks.

We got along well, but I made the boys nervous. They were at that woman-craving age and cramped quarters caused them to see a good deal of my body. All the boys, except maybe

Choosie, wasted a lot of time fantasizing about what it would feel like to hump me.

"Come on, Lannie," Bob Bob whined. "One quick romp or I'll bust." I didn't mention he'd busted all over my arm in his sleep last night.

"You mind?" I asked Mickey.

"Wouldn't want the boy to explode. Have to find a new guitar player."

Much to everyone's disappointment, including Mickey, even mine, I suppose, I never did. Middle-class morality flowed too deep for me to rationalize the term "Gang Bang Queen," no matter what the circumstances. We all draw the line somewhere.

After a while they let me sing a few songs onstage, mostly slow, mostly sad, Patsy Cline and Loretta Lynn material. The rush beat sex all to pieces. I stood, fingertips touching the mike stand, face upturned a tad, moaning "I've Got the Memories But She's Got You," pretending to be the spurned woman. Not pretending, I *felt* the heartbreak, I *was* that woman, sitting alone with her pictures and memories, feeling the ache as her soul broke up and floated away. Though I'd never been unhappy in my life, I could click right into pain as if it was the natural state of being me.

At the end of a song, I wrenched myself back into the present and looked down through the tears and smoke at those men and they stared up at me with their mouths open, Pearl beers poised above the table—and I found the power. Those men wanted me. Me, sixteen-year-old Lana Sue Goodwin, student council representative at Bellaire High. I had the *power*.

It didn't matter if they were married or alone, too old to get it up or too young to get in, I could take any one of them I wanted.

Mickey knew it too. "You sure turn on horny drunks," he said.

"It's my charisma."

"It's your twat."

We traveled mainly on two-lane state highways. Mickey and I drove the van full of equipment while the others followed in Choosie's '54 Studebaker station wagon, which was nice because driving was the closest Mick and I ever came to privacy.

The van was an old Dodge deathmobile with no lights, springs, or brakes to brag about—not a car really, but a condemned roller coaster with a built-in bar. I sat on a milk crate between the front seats, Mickey on one side and an amp on the other. That way we could grab each other without a bunch of scooting and shifting.

Mickey constantly fooled with the radio, searching out Arkansas hillbilly stations, and when he found one, he'd turn the volume up so loud the speakers crackled and I couldn't understand any of the words.

He banged his fist on the dash and jumped around in his seat, swerving all over both lanes, hollering stuff like, *"Aw right,"* *"Sing it, baby,"* and *"God, Lannie Sue, I love miserable people."*

"Why's that, Mickey?"

His head dipped with the song. "They're the only ones real, the only ones worth fooling with. You show me a happy person, I'll show you a fake and a liar. Listen to this."

That day he cranked up Patti Page on "Tennessee Waltz." The sound came through as if they'd recorded her from the far side of a crowded roller rink, but, on the last note, I looked over at the tears on Mickey's face.

"You sure are emotional."

"You gotta be emotional or you might as well be dead, Lana Sue. Emotions are like muscles or brains. If you don't use 'em, you lose 'em. Man that don't cry regular won't be able when he needs to later."

I snuggled up on one arm. "How'd you get so smart?"

Mickey rolled down the window so nothing stood between his smile and the wheat fields. "Pussy and booze," he said. "Pussy and booze."

———

Lost virginity and extended school skipping were only secondary goals of what is known in the Goodwin family as "Lannie's fling." My plan, right from the beginning, was to learn about the "real" world. Given that Daddy's system of money, Cadillacs, charge cards, and shoes made from dead animals was fake, was Mickey's alternative "real"?

I had to know. Are sex, drugs, and alcohol any more sincere than pep clubs, braces, and plastic furniture? Or maybe the third group, our customers—the farmers, waitresses, and mechanics— had found a legitimate way of getting by. Is a crop duster closer to honesty than a public relations expert specializing in Republican candidates from Southern California?

I still haven't decided. The battle between wealthy hypocrisy and poverty-stricken down-homeness has raged around and in me for thirty-eight years now, and I still don't know if a wood stove shows more integrity than a microwave oven.

Mickey taught me how to drink. We drank a lot. He taught me how to slide around fakes, rapists, and nose breakers, how to spot if someone wants something from you or wants to give something to you. Mickey showed me how to cut loose, ignore everything negative, and have one hell of a good time. Most people can't do that.

We lived an excessive life, working, drinking, crying, fighting, and screwing much too much. I enjoyed it then. Stability tends to wear away the extremes of life. Everyone needs to see the highest highs and lowest lows at least once. It's worth cleaning up the mess.

Mickey's most important lessons dealt with sex. He lived for sex, was obsessed with sex, and gave almost all his energy to sex, and Mickey expected no less from his partner. I couldn't lean over an amp without him trying to stick something in somewhere. Mickey taught me the joy of oral. The joy of anal. The joy of nonstop. A month after losing my virginity, I knew every position I've seen, heard about, or tried in the twenty-two years since.

I learned that shame or shyness only obstructs the fun. Without embarrassment, we made love in a bed full of people pretending they were asleep. Or on his lap in a moving van. We used to catch quickies in the men's bathroom stall during the break between sets.

Mickey claimed "real" isn't polyester versus rags. When analysis comes down to it, the difference between loving and wishing you loved, living and putting up a pretty good front, is the Regular Orgasm. If you can find an RO in a flaming sun, you're living an honest, sincere, productive life. If not, you're fooling somebody and it might be you.

That last is a line of bull I didn't buy even at sixteen, much less thirty-eight.

———

Sending Daddy a postcard was a serious error, of course, on the order of looking at your watch while making love, but you've got to remember these were pre-Runaway Hotline days. What was a girl on the road to do? Worry the poor manic crotch doctor to death? Even flighty heartbreakers follow certain lines of loyalty.

Daddy and the Christian Detective Agency didn't catch us until mid-March, and, even then, we might have resisted the rescue had Patsy Cline's sudden death not broken Mickey's will to be obnoxious. Halfway between Memphis and Nashville, Mickey's riotous-living act cracked and crumbled and the alcohol turned depressant as opposed to fire.

"I may grow up," he said.

"Aw, shit."

The country music system stagnated. By the time Daddy and his religious dick arrived, I didn't really care who carried me off.

———

Patsy Cline's death was so important to us, such a turning point, that I find it hard to believe all America didn't screech to a halt and hang its head in mourning, but I've come to realize lately that most people didn't even know who Patsy was. Country-western music wasn't considered legitimate back then.

I asked Loren where he was the day Patsy Cline died, and he said, "Oh, is she dead?" What an ignoramus.

She didn't make the "Deaths" column in *Time* magazine. Some 1920s playboy made the list, but the greatest female country singer of all time was left off. Shows America's priorities.

For me, it was one of those scenes where you always remember where you were and exactly what you were doing—like prominent assassinations or marriage proposals you accept or the beginnings of wars back when wars had definable beginnings.

The long booth in the Confederate Truck Stop on the Arkansas side of West Memphis at 8:30 on a rainy Wednesday morning. We'd been up all night celebrating Butch Bob's birthday. Somewhere in there, all of us except Mickey had eaten black capsules so we could talk faster, only they made my grits look and smell like something put out by a sick cat. My jaws were grinding my back molars into dust.

Bob Bob and I argued about the blond girl who played Elly May on *The Beverly Hillbillies*. Bob Bob said a shark in South America bit off her legs and I said it wasn't true.

"A cocktail waitress told me last night," Bob Bob whined.

"You believe everything a cocktail waitress tells you?"

"Yes."

Choosie's hands were under the table, pouring Jack Black into a Dr Pepper bottle. Next to the wall, Mickey turned the jukebox selector wheel, even though the WHO *Early Bird Show* blared from a radio next to the cereal pyramid behind the counter. Flatt and Scruggs were playing "T for Texas." I listened to the banjo break, thinking it would sound better with a steel behind it.

"How do you figure this works with the buttons at every booth and the jukebox way down there?" Butch Bob asked.

"Electricity," Choosie said.

Paul Bob snorted. "You're not as smart as people give you credit for."

Butch Bob was real dazed. He'd just turned twenty-one, which meant last night was his first legal drunk and he'd taken advantage of the fact.

The song ended and the announcement came on. "Benton County Sheriffs Department announced that the crash site of a single-engine Cessna Cherokee was found early today near Camden, Tennessee. The Federal Aviation Administration has been called in to investigate the accident which killed country singers Patsy Cline, Lloyd 'Cowboy' Copas, Hawkshaw Hawkins, and their pilot, Randy Hughes."

Just like that. There was no one to deny it to. The disc jockey came on all choked up and said something nice about Patsy, then he played "Leavin' on Your Mind."

I looked at Mickey. We all looked at Mickey, waiting for a sign, waiting for him to show us how to feel.

*If you've got leavin' on your mind,*
*Tell me now, get it over,*
*Hurt me now, get it over,*
*If you've got leavin' on your mind.*

I listened to the voice I'd discovered just two months ago. I sang her songs, I wanted to be Patsy Cline. She was country music's center, our role model, and now her voice was silent. Not silent—dead.

Mickey didn't move, just stared at a point somewhere on the wheel while Patsy filled the booth, creating a sort of stop-action spell that held us stuck in the moment, no one wanting to go on to the next moment where she didn't exist.

*If there's a new love in your heart,*
*Tell me now, get it over,*
*Hurt me now, get it over,*
*If there's a new love in your heart.*

I was more worried about how it affected Mickey than how it affected me. Death made the getting drunk and fucking game seem pretty worthless and Mickey wasn't the type to handle realizing the things he thought mattered were worthless. He blinked once, listening to her sing. I reached over and touched his hand, but I don't think he felt me.

Six of us, not thinking but feeling, hardly even breathing, sat through the end of the song and into a few seconds of dead air.

"That was the late great Patsy Cline, and here's a word from the men who keep those trucks on the road," and the radio went into a Texaco jingle.

"You through here, honey?"

I nodded.

The waitress leaned across Bob Bob and took my untouched plate of grits and eggs. "Shame about Patsy, ain't it?"

"Shame," Mickey said.

"You want more coffee?" and the spell was broken.

# 7

A STORM BLEW UP TO THE SOUTHWEST. AS I SKIMMED THE last couple of miles between Pinedale and Rock Springs, the sun dropped below the clouds and sent American Rose-colored spires forking across the high desert. Deserts look real nice in some light shade other than bright white. The rocks come off as a soft stark that I like a lot.

*However*, the explosion with Loren and three hours of past wallowing had pretty much exhausted my sunset-appreciation abilities. What my body and mind craved more than beauty was a modern relaxant. Like scotch. Sunsets take some viewing effort to make you feel the way you want to feel, whereas with scotch all you do is swallow.

I pulled left on the north edge of town into the Outlaw Inn and parked across from the drive-in, walk-up liquor store. Turning off Hank Snow, I leaned back, breathed, and felt the highway vibration drain from my hands to the steering wheel. Wind blew trash across the parking lot and around the corner of the inn. Like a filmy black nightgown, the rain line slid down the bare ridge on the other side of town, turning all the shapes into gray blurs. Men hurried in and out of the motel and liquor store, trying to beat the rain. They wore boots and hats of some kind, a few cowboy hats, but mostly redneck work caps. Their sleeves were rolled up just below the elbows, and everyone I saw had thick wrists.

The men seemed real sure about what they were doing outside the Outlaw Inn in Rock Springs, Wyoming. I was the only one sitting, waiting, but then, I was the only woman. All the other women had already gone wherever they wanted to go. I was the last.

It wasn't one of those rains where a few drops spatter your windshield, then it picks up a little, then a five-second lull before someone turns on the shower. This thing came across town like a waterfall on the march. I watched it jump the Interstate, then a Mobil station disappeared. Men hurried to and from their trucks, racing the deadline. The rain swept across the parking lot, and just as the Toyota went under, I thought maybe I should have gone inside sooner.

Too late, I wanted my scotch. After scotch, I wanted to hear a familiar voice. Locking the door, I walked across the gap and into the inn. Not running, I refused to run. Running in a storm is admitting the world can beat you.

The Outlaw Bar is a long, low Naugahyde and shadows affair with no room for a decent band. I'd been there once before. The night we drove up from Denver, Loren and I drank an incredible amount of tequila while some pale kid with a JC Penney guitar, a Mr. Microphone amp, and a drums-in-a-box machine sang Beatles songs, reading the words off a notebook paperclipped to an iron music stand.

That's the kind of place I chose as sanctuary from the storm and my botched-up life. My crises never have any class.

I ordered a double Red Label and demanded the change from my one and only twenty in quarters.

The bartender complained, "That'll clean me out."

"So?" I'd had it with men who didn't like what I wanted.

Scotch in the right hand, change clutched in the left, I dribbled rain back into the lobby and a bank of pay phones.

The band was supposed to be playing an almost uptown lounge near Clovis, New Mexico. With luck, I could catch him before the first set. The manager or whoever answered didn't feel much like looking for anyone, but I was rude, and five minutes and another round of quarters later, Mickey's high twang drifted over the lines from New Mexico.

"Yo."

"Mickey, it's me, Lana Sue."

"Hey, Lannie." The voice moved away. "It's Lana Sue." Then back again: "Did you get the postcard from San Antonio? You should of been there, Lannie. The club thought they'd booked a New Wave act, whatever the hell that is, and we showed up drinking Turkey and chewin' Hawken. They like to shit. No one in the joint had ever seen a pedal steel. We played one night before they bought up the rest of the week. Weirdest crowd you ever saw."

"Mickey, I left Loren."

There was a pause. "Think it's for good?"

I drained a swallow of scotch. "I suppose. Hell, I don't know."

"Another one bites the dust, huh?"

"Looks that way."

There was another pause while he covered the phone mouthpiece and said something to someone near. Mickey came back. "Where are you?"

"Rock Springs."

He whistled low. "That's no place for anyone carryin' a cunt, Lana Sue. Why don't you come down here awhile? Sing some unhappy songs. Or we'll be up in Cody Monday after next. You could meet us there and drink heavy for a couple weeks."

I laughed—sort of—and took another gulp. "Maybe, but I doubt it. Getting wasted, not sleeping, and smelling bad never did much for me."

"Makes me younger."

"How do you know, Mick? It's the only way you've lived for twenty years."

"Only way I feel comfortable. How's old Loren taking it?"

"I don't know. I left."

"Anyone ever hear anything about that boy of his?"

"Nope." I waited for a subtle Loren's-had-enough-trouble-without-you jab, but none came. Maybe it was implied by the silence.

Mickey made a high rattle sound with this throat. "Say, Lana Sue, you be insulted if I gave some advice, in a friendly spirit, I mean?"

I threw a couple ounces of scotch into my system. It helped. "In a friendly spirit?"

"Lana Sue, you're not so young anymore. There's gonna come a time when good looks and a wet crotch won't be enough, and I think you oughta consider and stop leaving ever' one that cares for you. You might think about settling for somethin' less than perfect."

Washed-up old alcoholics leave themselves wide open to cruel put-downs, and I came within a real shade of using one on Mickey, but he meant right, in his own disgusting way. Besides, over the years I've cut Mickey with every cruel word possible and nothing I ever said affected him one way or the other. He's a prick, but he's not a bad prick. What I said was, "That's your advice?"

"In a friendly spirit."

"Listen, friendly spirit, is Cassie around? I'd like to talk to her."

"She's right here. Lana Sue, Cassie gets better-looking and sings stronger ever' day. You may have royally fucked your own life, but you done good by her."

How many ways could I take that? "Just put her on, Mick." I switched the phone over to my other ear and sucked on the empty scotch glass a moment. Sometimes being best buddies with a former lover isn't all that satisfying. I mean, I know I can turn to Mickey whenever the S hits the F, but I also suspect the well-meaning brotherly bit is a cover-up and he secretly loves to see me down enough to need him. Something of a "she left me then, but look where she runs in times of stress" attitude.

"Mama?"

"Cassie, how're you doing?"

"Great, Mama. We like to filled the place last night, and when I sung 'Stand By Your Man,' a whole bunch of people stood up and cheered. It was wonderful."

"Sang."

"What?"

"You sang 'Stand By Your Man.' Not sung it."

I shouldn't have said that. After a moment of breathing, Cassie said, "Heard you and Loren split up."

"I'm afraid so."

"Any special reason?"

I couldn't think of a special reason. "Naw," I said. "Just something that had to be done."

Cassie giggled. "My old love 'em and leave 'em Mama."

"Yeah." No one spoke a moment. "Is Mickey treating you good?"

"Hell, Mama, you know Mickey."

I never know if Cassie is putting me on. "You hear from Connie any?"

"Got a letter the other day. Skipper's been offered a junior partnership, only he doesn't know it's on the condition that she plays friendly with the boss."

"What's she gonna do?"

"Play friendly. She wants Skipper to get that partnership real bad so they can get a big-screen TV."

"She say anything about me?"

"Mama, you know Connie hates the ground you walk on."

Set myself up for that one. Tilting the glass to pop an ice cube in my mouth, I asked, "How about your daddy?"

"Aw, he don't write much. Guess him and Wanda are happy as ducks down there in Houston, making all that money and buying all that stuff."

"He always did enjoy that."

"Yep."

Nobody said anything for a while, so I figured it was time to end it. I felt kind of emotional. It's funny, I never cry in front of anyone, or hardly ever, but stick a phone in my ear and I'll go puddle-eyed every time.

"I've got to go, I'm running out of quarters."

"Mama, you take care of yourself, okay?"

"Yeah, you take care of yourself. Watch out for Mickey."

"Aw, he don't take much watching out for. He only wants two things. Give him those and he's happy as pie."

"Booze and pussy," I said.

"You got it. Booze and pussy."

———

Since I left Loren in a spontaneous snit, I wound up in Rock Springs with the shirt on my back, the jeans I was wearing, and one twenty-dollar bill that wasn't going to last long. I'd have landed barefoot if I hadn't found a pair of sandals on the truck floor. Separation should be thought out, I know, but planning ahead is not the Lana Sue style. "Packing a few things" takes the edge off the drama. Better to buy a new wardrobe.

My billfold was in the glove compartment, so the problem wasn't anything challenging. Wood and dirt may be real, and plastic fake, but my cousin Roxanne has a saying: "A Visa card will get you through times of no money better than money will get you through times of no Visa card."

I slapped plastic on the counter, signed my name, and a nice man gave me the key to a big, clean room overlooking the indoor pool.

Given a choice in these matters, I'd live in a motel room every day of my life. They're so clean and pure and sterile. Houses reek of memories. Every spot and every object in a house carries associations with someone or something emotional.

A motel room holds no past. The only true rest I've found came while standing on a paper shower mat or sleeping between sheets I've never slept between or making it with some man I've known less than an hour. Pure happiness cannot be linked to the past because the past isn't pure.

Jesus, I'm starting to talk like Loren.

Anyway, I found myself in a beautifully noncomplicated room, took an hour-long bath so hot I turned red from the neck down, and dried myself with a towel I've never seen before or since. Flipping on the television for background noise, I lay naked on the bed and stretched. I do like my body. Unlike Loren, all my parts work fine. Every nerve can feel great. Every joint knows the joy of full rotation. My body contains the highest quality hair, teeth, eyes, breasts, feet and hands. The skin fits perfectly, neither too loose nor too tight, each pore working properly.

Due to a lifelong diet between sugar binges, I carry no excess fat. All right, that depends on your definition of excess. Most men like my shape, but most women in my shape would think about losing five pounds. I'd call myself tightly packed without any overhangs. Sometimes I get nervous internally, my digestive tract shuts down or over-works, but that is a small problem fixed by roughage, prunes, or chalky pills. I'll never giggle uncontrollably again, and the thought of two days without sleep turns me to trash, but on the whole, without making aging a battle or an obsession,

I've held together real well for thirty-eight years. I'm quite proud of me.

I don't have a whole lot else to be proud of, but a good body is something—a lot more than some people can brag about. My sister for instance, looks formidable. Half the time Roxanne could pass for a San Antonio hooker. And Mom, poor Mom, spent thousands of dollars fighting gravity and lost. Even that hero-worshiping, possibly husband-chasing little sixteen-year-old down the road pops a pimple every time she drinks a Pepsi.

Mickey shouldn't have said that about good looks and a wet crotch not being enough. I'm not old. Good looks and a wet crotch will always be enough.

———

I am thirty-eight years old. How odd. Sometimes, when I first wake up in the morning, I lie in bed, staring at the ceiling, and I say it aloud. "I am thirty-eight years old."

Where did it go? No matter how old you are, you never can pin down where it went. I don't feel thirty-eight. When I was eighteen, I didn't think thirty-eight-year-olds had emotions or problems, and I never dreamed they had sex. I figured they just sat around waiting to die.

Now, I suppose I feel that way about eighty-year-olds—and when I'm eighty, I bet I'll say aloud, *"I am eighty years old,"* and I won't know where it went.

I hate to think about things without answers, like where it went. I never solve anything and after a while I feel worn out and confused. I don't see how Loren does it.

———

An hour later I sat on the end barstool, smoking a low-tar concoction and contemplating another double Red Label. As a habit, I don't smoke. I mean, I used to. With Ace I smoked like a flaming snow tire, and I never officially quit. Living in our mountain cabin next to a clear, unpolluted stream, I started liking the idea of putting clean stuff in myself and, after a while, I started not liking the idea of putting in scuz, so I gradually tapered on down to nonsmokerdom.

Now, I smoke cigarettes on three occasions. Make that four occasions. Sugar binges, which happen once in six months or so; extreme drunks, which happen even less; on the make for a man, something that hadn't happened since I married Loren; and the day before my period. I smoke a full pack during the PMSs.

The cigarette in the Outlaw Bar was caused by condition three—on the make for a man. Lord knows, there were enough of them around, the bar was three-fourths full and seven out of eight customers were single men, but I was picky. I wanted a certain kind of man. Pleasant, unassuming, nice-looking with a reasonable body, yet no one I was likely to feel any emotion for. The last thing I wanted was emotion.

Loren always makes me feel something—love, hate, disgust, warmth, frustration, passion, sick. He's so damn intense, and I don't always like intense. Feeling all the time burns me out. Every so often I like sex that's all sweat and no emotions.

Unless he was a total loser, I figured on taking the third pass. Number three must be a little daring to take a shot after seeing one and two strike out, but he wouldn't be too cocky or he'd try sooner. Three is a safe number.

Knowing that, I still managed to screw up.

"Hi there."

"Hello."

"Care to meet a nice guy with charm and personality?"

"No."

"How about me. I'm a jerk."

"That was rehearsed. Go away."

"How about I buy you a drink instead?"

"You're caller number one."

"Huh?"

"I never pick number one. They're always inadequate."

"Hey, nobody calls me inadequate."

"Not in that way. Desperate, insecure. You've got a flaw, I can feel it. Sorry, but I like to think I can do better."

"Nobody else'll try."

"Wanna bet?"

Snappy patter is a delicate art form. We can't all be Neil Simon and Marsha Mason. Still, I try to keep it above astrology, where are you from, and insinuating eye contact. The goal with a possible sex object is to score a few points without overpowering the poor schmuck while testing him for some sign of intelligence and quickness. It helps if both parties have the same end in mind.

This kid, number one, showed a certain persistence and a winning smile, but he looked too young to trust. I wanted a man who could take my mind off me for an hour, not a cute charmer with clear eyes. Certainly not a cowboy—a typical, thin, side-burned, dressed-up-to-go-to-town kid cowboy. I figured his age at twenty-two, only one year older than my daughters. Confidence practically oozed from under his huge felt hat. I don't care much for men with that kind of seducing confidence. They intrigue me, but I don't like them.

Maybe the kid sensed this or maybe he only knew one approach and that happened to be the winning line.

He smiled. "You left your husband today, right?" The thirty points for intuition light must have flashed because the boy pressed on.

"You're looking for a fast, meaningless good time. No strings. No aftershocks. A basic quickie." Brains in a cowboy always shock me. I know they're no dumber than anyone else, but they usually act like they are and it throws me off when they aren't.

I nodded. "Something like that."

"Look no farther. Nobody gets hung up over me and I get hung up over nobody."

Further might have been better than farther, but I wasn't certain. Besides, his chin was cute. "I can get that from my fingers."

"I'm better than fingers. I weigh more."

"Okay."

"Okay what?"

"You can buy me a drink. But I'm warning you. I don't like you so far and I'm not stuck on this stool. If I see a better offer, you're out of luck."

———

Wyoming cowboys are real strange people. They dress funny. You see a character in town made out like a complete dude, jeans tucked inside knee-high Tony Lamas, three silk handkerchiefs around his neck, bandanna out the back pocket, cowboy hat the size of a Karmann Ghia with a little string pulled tight under his neck, that character almost surely works with cows. The tough, macho cowboys you run into on the street probably drive trucks or sack groceries at Safeway. They dress up like a real cowboy at work, and a real cowboy come to town decks out like Tom Mix in *The Border Bandito*.

The kid, whose name turned out to be Billy G, worked with cows. His jeans weren't jammed into his boots, thank God, but he wore a side-button, black cavalry shirt and a belt with a giant bronze buckle that said COORS. His hat was a dark brown umbrella with a peacock eye feather stuck in front. He offered me a pinch of wintergreen snuff. I refused.

———

Billy G bought a few drinks which turned into dinner which turned into your usual modern system of verbal foreplay. The boy had a certain smoothness, I'll have to give him that. Whether instincts or experience, he paced us through the various levels of enticement, never pushing at any crucial moments which would have allowed me to make a decision. Some eye contact, a touch to the hair, a hand on the knee, another round of scotch, and suddenly I was a little drunk and being steered by the elbow into a restaurant full of Billy G's buddies.

"The whole damn spread's here," he said.

"Spread?"

We wasted ten minutes on slapping shoulders, waving across the tables, and answering *What's going down, You're growing uglier by the minute, Gettin' any lately,* and *Don't do anything I wouldn't do.* Not a man in the place spoke a sentence he hadn't spoken at least three hundred times. Billy G showed me off—"Look what I got, guys"—like a mounted elk.

Well, I wasn't mounted yet. Reading the cute menu (Buffalo Bill Burgers and Calamity Jane Steaks) I began to feel misgivings. Loren needed me to remind him when to eat. Also, I had meant to pack his Vision Quest bag that night, even saved a Twinkie surprise to hide under his spare socks. Now he wouldn't remember the spare socks.

I knew exactly what would happen. Loren would realize he was helpless without me and trot off down the road for salvation from pimply Marcie. For months now she'd been waiting to save his tortured artistic soul—which was my job. Marcie couldn't handle Loren. He'd convince her that saving a tortured soul meant sitting on it.

The waitress had bloodred fingernails, blue hair, and chewed gum, naturally.

"Can I getcha another drink?"

"Scotch."

"Whatcha eatin'?"

"I'll have the Bridger cut prime rib and a baked potato. Russian dressing on the salad."

"All we got's French and Thousand Island, honey."

"Thousand Island, then."

Billy G was born in Chicago, but turned cowboy when he hit thirteen.

"How long ago was that?"

"A lifetime."

"Mine or yours?"

He cowboyed at the Flying Fist Ranch, which he called the Flying Fuck, FF for short, and seemed to think I was totally uneducated because I never heard of it.

"Big as Delaware but worth more," he said. "Thorne Axel's private kingdom."

"Who's Thorne Axel?"

Billy G was aghast. "You never heard of Thorne Axel?"

"Well, shit, I'm sorry."

"He owns the Flying Fist. Everybody knows Thorne Axel."

"I don't."

"You'll have to meet him."

Supper came and Billy G lost the train of thought. He cut up his entire steak before taking the first bite. I found that odd. My prime was a bit rare for my tastes, I don't suck blood as a rule, but it tasted fine and Billy G was paying, so I didn't complain. If I am a bitch, which is hard to deny, I'm a better bitch than most. I almost never complain. Nobody likes a complainer, but everyone loves a bitch.

Ten minutes of silent chewing later, Billy G's mind came back from his stomach. "Thorne's on a drunk."

I'd been thinking of calling Loren to remind him about the socks, so I missed it. "What?"

"Thorne's been drunk three days. The whole crew came

to town to cheer him up. I saw him around here sometime yesterday."

"Why's Thorne on a drunk?"

Billy G put his right hand over his liver like a half-mast pledge of allegiance and belched, not loudly, but still enough to antagonize my romantic interests. "Wife left him again. Kid's a dope dealer. Daughter turned dramatic and shot up a herd of yearlings. It was a mess."

"Why'd she shoot the yearlings?"

"Who can figure the mind of a crazy woman? You want the potato skin?"

"No."

"Vitamins're in the skin. I always eat the skin." Billy G speared my potato leavings with his steak knife. "That's the trouble with E.T."

"Who?"

"Thorne's hippie son. He's a vegetarian, but he don't eat potato skins. No protein'll make your brains dry out."

"His real name is E.T.?"

"Ain't it a shame." Billy G lowered his voice. "He sits with his legs crossed above his knees, like a girl."

I whispered back, "Maybe E.T.'s a fag."

"Naw, Thorne'd kill him if he sucked wienie. Probably just a lack of potato skins."

"I don't eat potato skins."

He pointed with his knife. "You cross your legs above the knees."

———

Given that Billy G belched after supper, said "crazywoman" as if the two went together, and wore a black shirt, which ever since Johnny Cash I have found obscene, I wonder why I went ahead and slept with him.

I knew I was going to sleep with somebody. The sleeping—nice word for sex, isn't it—came from a personal need caused by anxiety at leaving Loren. Some people get drunk. Some people go for long walks and cry. I fuck. Perhaps it's Grandma's blood again. She's easy to blame. She's dead. More likely, though, I just need to feel another man's butt every now and then. The marriage with Ron lagged along for fifteen reasonably good years, but once every eight or ten months, the pressure of mediocrity became pain and, without premeditation, I drove to some country bar on the southeast side of Houston and picked up a stranger.

I get off with strangers and I didn't with Ron. He wasn't bad in bed, he lasted as long as most, but with Ron I had a past and future. I can't get off if I'm worried about past and future. Same with Ace and sometimes, but not always, Mickey and Loren.

Anyway, Billy G was my first transgression against Loren, and since we'd split up that morning, I didn't count him as a technical fool-around.

However, Billy G wasn't the usual type I chose for morphine sex. I generally pick guys who need me as much as I need them. Lost souls, nerds, and salesmen. These guys appreciate me. The Billy Gs of the world look at it as conquering me—another notch on the bedpost. I'd rather find a man with an active fantasy life and make all his dreams come true. While satisfying my own itch, of course. The pain lays have nothing in common with the true loves. That's a whole different thing.

Roxanne says my attitude toward sex is practically male.

I chose Billy G because he didn't agree that his boss's son was probably gay. That seemed almost noble of him. Every man I ever met would jump all over an insinuation about another man's heteroness. Each confirmed queer means one less competitor, I suppose. You try it. Say, "I think that guy's a fag," to any man about any man and he'll agree with you every time.

Thorne's son was a hippie, a vegetarian, and a drug dealer, all causes for manhood suspicion, but Billy G dismissed my fag label. I liked that. So I took him upstairs and fucked his brains out.

———

Women have chosen lovers for less.

That's why it's all right for me to move on Billy G, but it's not all right for Loren to stick one in little Marcie. This is no double standard here, I don't buy that crap. This is truth. Loren can't make love without falling in it. Look what happened with me and that mouse of a wife of his. One hump and he's ready to get married.

I use my extramarital sex for medicinal purposes. There's a lot of pressure in being me, and a six-hour frenzy session with a stranger releases that pressure. It damn sure beats drinking and crying.

———

Besides, I'm not the coldhearted man eater my daughters and almost everyone else thinks I am. Leaving Loren caused me considerable distress. If it hadn't, I wouldn't have kept Billy G awake all night, but every time we collapsed in a heap of sweat and exhaustion, I'd stop and think of poor Loren—Loren reading, or Loren walking in the woods alone, or Loren sitting at his typewriter.

The only way to block the tears and nausea was to shove Billy G in and go at it. After five or six hours, even that didn't help, so I let the wasted kid go to sleep. He wasn't worth much by then anyway. Billy G must have thought he'd gotten hold of God's own nympho.

I mean, I loved Loren. I married the creep. Personal extravaganzas should be fair. True love overcomes circumstances. That's what I'd always been taught and that's what I believed. I wanted to be loved. Is that asking too much? I wanted a man I could talk to and count on. I wanted two lawn chairs on a sun deck, and a piano, and a greenhouse for my vegetables. I wanted another baby. I didn't want to drink twelve shots of scotch and suck a cowboy's dick, for Chrissake. I wanted to be normal.

Things just never worked out the way I wanted.

Around dawn, I slid out of bed and knelt on the bathroom tile and threw up everything.

# Part Three

# 8

GIVEN LIFE TO LIVE ALL OVER AGAIN, I WOULDN'T HAVE crawled into my bag and fallen asleep next to the dying fire that third night of the Vision Quest.

I've had these dreams for a couple of years now, they're like reverse nightmares, but much worse than a nightmare because with a nightmare, waking up is relief. In my dreams, something good happens, something very good that feels so real, and I know is real. I'm happy. Often I'm so happy I say, "Thank God, this isn't a dream, the waiting is over," only it is a dream. The happiness carries over for a couple of seconds after I awaken, then recognition rolls in and my stomach contracts like I've been hit. A day that begins with one of these dreams is a hard day to finish.

We were all together, Buggie, Ann, and I in the Alice Street duplex—in our tiny kitchen with the cartoons held to the refrigerator by strawberry magnets and the herb chart on the wall surrounded by Buggie's preschool drawings of eagles and elephants. Buggie looked around five, maybe. His blond hair hung down in his eyes and over his collar. Ann never would cut his hair. She always made me do it, then she would pick at his head for a week, sighing and saying I'd cut too much.

Ann stood next to the double sink, backlit by the sun pouring in our kitchen window. I couldn't see her face clearly, but she wore an old Denver Broncos football jersey she'd picked up at a yard sale, faded jeans, and sandals she bought from a hippie store up by the capitol. They were supposed to do something good for her feet, something to do with the natural slope of the arch.

The Bug wanted to go outside and dig a hole. He sat at the breakfast table, ignoring cold Zoom, banging his plastic bucket with his plastic shovel. The handle of the shovel was wood, but the scoop part was plastic.

I quizzed him on *Walden*. *"Rather than love, than money, than fame, give me truth,"* I read. "What do you think Thoreau meant by that?"

Buggie looked down at his little blue pail. "I dunno."

"You knew yesterday. Did you forget already?"

Ann turned on water at the sink. "Don't you think that's a little abstract for a kindergartner?"

"You're never too young for *Walden*. What do you think he meant by truth, Buggie?"

Buggie squirmed in the chair and banged the shovel from side to side in the bucket. He twisted his mouth around, thinking. I taught Buggie to always twist his mouth around when he was thinking.

"Truth is knowing what happens," he said.

I beamed at Ann. "Aha," I said, "too young to understand, huh?"

Buggie continued: "The man says it's better to know what's happening than to be famous or rich or those other things."

"Right. Now do you think that's proper?"

"Mary wants to go outside. The worms leave if we're not there early."

"Do you think it's better to know what's happening than to have love, money, or fame?"

He slid out of his chair. "I'd rather be loved."

Hell, it was only a dream. I think.

It would be just like Buggie to say, "I'd rather be loved." He was a real earnest boy with melting brown eyes and a straight mouth. As a baby, he hardly ever cried, but he didn't laugh much either. Buggie never acted the way I would expect a kid to act. He didn't demand the attention other kids crave, and he never put out precocious sayings we could write down and send to his grandparents—which was probably for the best, since none of his grandparents could stand us.

Mostly he pushed soldiers or trucks around his room or the backyard. Soldier pushing was serious business to Buggie. He was much too intense to "play."

As I recall, Buggie rode his bike a lot. A red Western Auto Flyer with pedals he had to stand on to reach. The details still come to mind, his hands, for instance, and those filthy off-white tennis shoes he was so proud of. I can remember every crack on that plastic shovel with the wooden handle, but I can't seem to remember what Buggie was like. I can't see his face anymore.

———

Ann and Buggie. Where did the woman leave off and the child begin? How was I supposed to see a difference? Maybe that jumbled-together feeling, my inability to separate one from the other, was why I let Ann down so badly the last couple of years. I like to think there was a reason other than me being me.

It's just that nothing in my background prepared me for the emotions of fatherhood. Before Buggie, I stuck children in a category with geography, motorcycles, and corporate structures—things I'd never thought about, had an opinion of or any curiosity for. Buggie was the first child I ever looked at up close.

Ann, too, was something I'd never experienced. She was a nonstudent who'd been taking care of herself for so long she knew what she was doing. At the time, I thought that was kind of unique, though now I realize there're a lot more single moms in the world than there are students.

I don't know what I was emotionally prepared for back then—smoking pot, I suppose. Watching TV. Fantasizing a rich and creative sex life based mainly on female English professors and graveyard-shift waitresses.

The spring of my junior year at DU, I used the one-two punch of marijuana and daytime television to, for all purposes, lobotomize my sensibility. I slept fourteen hours a night, ate no hot food, made it through school by putting in just enough effort to keep from losing my Guaranteed Student Loan. The problem was my attitude, of course. What other problem is there? I wanted to be a writer and refused to be anything else. I thought life was meaningless unless I was a writer and the fact that I hadn't written anything longer than the dedications to my first three novels depressed me into becoming an apathetic, make that pathetic, wreck. That Ann saw anything salvageable in me is one of those mysteries that reinforces my belief in Unexplainable Shit.

But women are always falling in love with potential instead of fact. Men aren't like that.

———

The joint I was smoking had a runner, a little line of fire that crept down to my finger and threatened to cut off the burning end, dumping hot coal in my lap. Besides the uncontrolled runner, my attention was split pretty evenly between a half-finished essay on "Dryden's Use of Romantic Imagery" and *Gilligan's Island* on the TV. All three confused me somewhat, which is nothing new.

On the one hand, Dryden said his girlfriend could raise the dead, which didn't make sense unless he was personifying his prick, while on the other hand, the Captain beat Gilligan across the head and shoulders with a navy cap. Even high, I didn't find this funny, but evidently I was supposed to because all these people in the TV audience were cracking up. This upset me on account of I've always been proud of my ability to see humor in any situation, and if most people thought one man beating another with a cap was funny, I was slipping away from most people. And on the third hand, if I had three hands, the joint had to be dealt with immediately. I spit on my finger and studied the joint carefully, working out a repair plan, when a woman carried a baby into my living room.

"I knocked on the door, but you didn't answer," she said.

What to do with the finger wad of spit? I must have looked peculiar, sitting there pointing a foamy noogie at the ceiling, but I couldn't stick it back in my mouth or under the end table. The woman was kind of pretty, I didn't want to disgust her in the first three seconds of our relationship.

"I didn't think you would mind if I came on in, it's sort of an emergency."

The coal finally released into my lap, I jumped up, slapping at myself and stomping on the carpet. In the confusion of the moment, I stealthily scraped my finger clean on an empty Cheetos bag. I don't think she noticed.

Standing, I saw the woman was shorter than me by a couple of inches, and a little skinnier. Her dusty-blond hair hung straight across her shoulders to about the elbow level. The diapered boy sat perched on her right hip where he concentrated on pulling a dangly gold-colored earring out of her lobe. The baby looked especially clean.

"My baby swallowed a tube of Krazy Glue and I've got to get him to a doctor."

"You need a ride?"

"No, no, I have a car, but I run a day-care center in my place. Nine kids are waiting down there."

I set Dryden and the empty roach paper on the pile of books, notebooks, food wrappers, marijuana-smoking paraphernalia, and about a dozen dirty coffee cups that hid my end table. Here was something interesting. So long as the kid didn't die from glue poisoning, this might turn into something fun to watch myself handle.

The baby didn't look on the edge of death. He leaned forward and reached for me, making a gurgling sound in his throat. I didn't know whether babies gurgle as a rule, or that was glue eating his stomach, but he didn't seem to be feeling any pain, and the woman stood there looking concerned and expectant, but certainly nowhere near panic.

"What can I do to help?"

"Would you watch the kids while we're gone? Dr. Karnes is just a couple of blocks down Anders Street. It shouldn't take long."

"An entire tube of Krazy Glue?"

"The top was off. You don't have to do anything, just be there and watch so they don't hurt themselves."

The baby and I looked in each other's eyes and he smiled. I was amazed. "Okay."

———

That's how I came to be sitting in a kitchen chair, more or less surrounded by nine little people: six boys, three Jesses, a Jason, Justin, and Jeremiah; and three girls, Heather, Heather, and Thamu Kamala. The kitchen was an exact copy of mine only clean and filled with cribs and baby beds. They were stacked on top of each other. Someone had tacked a picture of the Rocky Mountains over the sink and framed it with red curtains so it would look like a window instead of a picture. On top of the refrigerator I spotted *Betty Crocker's Cookbook, Be Here Now,* and Joan Baez's book about her husband the draft dodger.

Six or seven of the little rug rats stood in a rough semicircle, sucking on thumbs and blankets and earless bears and staring at me. On the whole, they were a pretty cute bunch—all mammals are cute at the toddler stage, why should people be different—except most of their noses dripped and one of the Jesses was ugly as a hobbit.

"Can any of you blink?" I asked.

They all stared.

"Watch this." With both hands, I pointed at my eyes and blinked several times in succession.

Justin sniffed, but no one else seemed to understand. How old does a kid have to be to learn blinking anyway?

Deep from my memory came a game I remember my brother Patrick playing with Kathy when she was about this age. I pushed on my nose and popped out my tongue. Then I pulled on my left ear, sliding my tongue to the right corner of my mouth, then pulled on my right ear, sliding my tongue to the left corner. This trick makes for an interesting cause-and-effect illusion if you do it right.

The oldest girl, Thamu Kamala, said, "Jason pooped his pants."

"He should change them."

"He's too little."

"Which one's Jason?"

She pointed to an oversize baby curled in the fetal position under a crib. Looked like crib death to me.

"Is he dead?"

"What's dead?"

I walked into the bathroom and found a hand mirror on a shelf above a line of five porta-potties. Back in the kitchen, I knelt and held the mirror in front of Jason's little nose.

"He's alive."

"His diaper stinks."

"Do you know how to change it?"

"Course not."

"Me either. Where's the TV?"

For three hours, the kids stared at me while I sat on the couch and watched reruns. *Andy Griffith, Petticoat Junction, The Beverly Hillbillies, Dark Shadows,* and *I Love Lucy* twice. A couple of the younger boys curled up next to me and slept with their fists in their mouths. Ugly Jesse looked much cuter asleep than he had awake, more like a troll doll than a hobbit. I considered putting him and the other sleeper in cribs—the living room was even more littered with cribs, baby beds, and bassinets than the kitchen—but the couch felt comfortable, and most of the cribs were crammed with toys, jackets, coloring books, all kinds of kiddie junk. Not stuff I'd want to sleep on.

Thamu Kamala put her hands on her hips. "You aren't going to change any diapers?"

"Diapers are outside my frame of reference."

"Are you going to read stories and put the little ones down for naps?"

"I only brought this one book." I showed Thamu Kamala the Dryden volume. "Would you like a reading of *Satire Upon the True-Blue Protestant Poet T.S.*"?

"That's all you got?"

"You have something against Dryden?"

She considered a moment, pretending to review all the Dryden she knew. I say pretending because I don't think Thamu Kamala knew any Dryden.

"Okay, let's try it."

*"All human things are subject to decay,"* I read.

Another Jesse fell asleep around line 89, then I lost a Heather to *Petticoat Junction* on line 120. Thamu Kamala soon joined her and by the bitter end, all but one little Heather were asleep or lined up on the floor, staring openmouthed at the TV.

"How did you like the poem?" I asked Heather. She would have been a regular-looking kid except Heather's hair flew out in a mass of red curls, like Orphan Annie mated with Bozo the Clown.

"Did you understand the part about Sir Formal's oration?"

Heather didn't move and, of course, she didn't blink.

"Cat got your tongue? That sometimes happens to me too. Just toss away your inhibitions and speak what's on your mind. Pop it right on out."

Thamu Kamala sat up and gave me a look of extreme disgust. I've been on the receiving end of looks of disgust from some of the finest women around, but who would have expected such intense disgust from a preschooler? Thamu Kamala was the youngest person yet to actively hate me.

One hand went to her hip. I'd seen that gesture before. "Heather's deaf, dummy."

"Oh." She didn't look deaf. "Can she read lips?"

"She's two years old."

"Oh." I slid Heather onto my lap and together we watched the end of *Petticoat Junction*. Three pretty girls named Betty Jo, Bobby Jo, and Billy Jo tried to pull Fred Ziffel's pig, Arnold, out of a bathtub while Uncle Joe stalled a couple of city-slicker guests downstairs. I imagined I was in the tub and Billy Jo found me alluring.

Just as I spun into a complex, group-sex fantasy, the woman and baby came through the apartment door. She was all apologies and reports on the baby's condition.

"Dr. Karnes says it'll pass right through, no problem. They X-rayed and you should see it, a little metal tube floating around in Buggie's tummy."

"He'll dump a tube of Krazy Glue?"

"Probably not till tomorrow."

Thamu Kamala ratted on me. "He let everyone sit in poop all afternoon." I'd hate to marry Thamu Kamala someday.

"I'm sure Loren did just fine." The woman swept around the room tossing toys and rags and general kid clutter into the cribs. She seemed small and efficient at what she did, like someone who'd carried a heavy burden so long she didn't know it was a burden and everyone else didn't have to carry it. I liked her lips. They were thin and plum-colored.

"What's your name?" I asked.

Her hand jumped to cover her mouth. "Oh God, I forgot, I mean, I told you the kids' names, but not mine."

"You were in a hurry."

She stepped forward with her hand out. "I'm Ann Smith and this is Buggie."

"I'm Loren Paul."

"I know, it's on your mailbox." She looked straight at my eyes. "You're a student, aren't you? I've seen you come and go with big piles of books."

I nodded. "I never met anyone really named Smith before."

Ann laughed, a nice laugh—gentle, subdued. "There's plenty of us." She broke the handshake. "I'm throwing together spaghetti later, you want some? The least I can do is feed you."

I watched Buggie climb an orange baby bed. "Are you married?"

"No, what's that got to do with spaghetti?"

"I don't know. Sure, I'll come down. What time?"

We talked a couple of minutes, exchanging livelihoods and hometowns. Every now and then she pulled Buggie off something he was climbing or kept one of the little girls from beating up one of the little boys. Thamu Kamala kept interrupting to tell her about somebody's diaper. Ugly Jesse woke up and crawled into her lap and fell back asleep. I can't claim

I was swept away by instant, undying love for Ann. I liked her, I liked her voice and the easy way she handled the kids. I liked her hands, but the liking was more on a possible-sex-object level than as a future partner.

Ann wasn't the kind of woman who knocks a man over and possesses his soul on the first meeting. She took her life seriously and expected more good to come of it than bad. I could see that much. Realistic optimism might be the term for Ann's attitude. I never believed much in realism or optimism myself, but I was depressed and Ann wasn't, so who was I to go judging attitudes?

When I stood to leave, Buggie crawled across the rug and looked up at me. He raised one hand to shoulder level and made a fist, then opened it, then made a fist again, gurgling something that might have been words.

Ann smiled proudly. "That's bye-bye in Buggie talk."

I waved down to the little person on the floor. "Bye-bye, Buggie."

———

You can always tell what a man expects from a relationship by the kind of condom he buys before the first date. Take a guy who sneaks into a PATRONS ONLY bathroom at a gas station and drops a quarter in the rainbow-colors, for-prevention-of-disease-only machine; that guy isn't expecting a whole lot. Mostly, he's arming himself against an "I can't go through with this, I have no protection" defense. Then there's the one who goes to a well-lit pharmacy and buys a box of three moderately priced, individually tested, rolled, and sealed, lubricated with a non-petroleum jelly condoms—which is what I did between the wineshop and Ann's apartment that night—this guy is thoughtful, yet practical, expectant, yet experienced. He doesn't run into the drugstore screaming, "I've got a hot date tonight. Gimme some insurance." He cares about the woman and he cares about himself.

At the top extreme we have the overkill joker who gets himself fitted and pays eight dollars for two dozen all-natural lambskins with extra-large end reservoirs. He's probably gay.

Most men, of course, don't buy anything. They either don't care or don't dream. Or else they use the same superstitious logic that makes a fisherman go fishing without a stringer and women stop wearing underwear when their period is overdue.

Nineteen out of twenty rubbers I ever bought stayed in the sterile packets. Broken down statistically: Eighteen times I struck out, my one winner was with a woman on the pill, and the last date before Ann, this young-to-the-point-of-statutory girl begged me to unroll it on my finger because she said she'd never seen one. When I did, she laughed hysterically, jumped from the car, and disappeared out of my life forever.

I kept walking into drugstores and buying the things anyway. No one can call me an irresponsible lay.

———

Ann met me at the door with Buggie propped in his usual right hip position. Buggie had on blue overalls buttoned up the inseam and a red pullover jersey. Ann wore a long flowered skirt with a rose-colored ruffly top. She looked dressed up, as if she'd thought about what to wear and decided on something nice. Her hair was pulled back behind her ears.

"How's Buggie?" I asked.

"No Krazy Glue tube yet," she said. "I wonder if it'll hurt when he poops it." How about that? I was on a date with a woman who called shit poop.

We stood around the doorway a moment, imagining what it would feel like to pass a tube. I imagined it coming out sideways and she imagined it coming out end to end, which shows a basic difference between the ways Ann and I planned our futures.

"The spaghetti's about ready," she said. "Can I get you something to drink? Buggie has apple juice and I'm sipping wine in the kitchen."

I held out my bottle of Blue Nun. I know wine connoisseurs think you're a tasteless chump for drinking white wine with spaghetti, but I generally bought Blue Nun no matter what was for dinner because it complemented pot so well.

"Let's finish my bottle first, then go on to yours," Ann said.

"Sounds fine to me."

She disappeared into the kitchen, then came back with a glass of rosé. Tasted like Mateus, but I'm not certain.

"You and Buggie get acquainted while I work on supper. There's appetizers on the TV table." Ann's eyes held a gleam I hadn't noticed in the afternoon. They sparkled with little brown flecks that seemed to travel around the center of the whitest eye-whites I've ever seen. She looked cheerful and pretty. I was almost certain Ann had expectations of the evening—you don't look cheerful without expectations—but I wasn't sure what the expectations involved.

Buggie sat next to me on the couch while I looked over a plate of bite-sized chunks of cauliflower, broccoli, and fresh mushrooms. I dunked a cauliflower into the creamy dip and held it for Buggie to lick. Instead, he reached for my glasses and almost pulled them off before I caught his little hand.

Buggie's brow puckered up, his eyes watered, and he let out a howl.

Ann's voice came from the kitchen. "Throw him in a crib if he bothers you."

"We're just playing. He's having a great time." Buggie howled louder. "Which crib is his?"

"Any that you can find the bottom."

Facing Buggie, I made a duck sound I'd learned in grade school and hadn't practiced since. The sound involves loading saliva under your tongue and then squishing it out the sides while you talk. This takes some skill and not everyone can do it.

With one sniff, Buggie stopped crying. He grabbed my lower lip and pulled.

"*Awoww.*" Buggie pulled me down to his level and stared into my eyes. His pupils were darker and deeper than Ann's— fiercer. He stared at me with this look, I swear it was a threat. A mess-with-my-mama-and-you'll-answer-to-me threat. He meant it too.

Possibly Buggie didn't threaten me at all. He was only a kid. Possibly I saw in his eyes what I thought I deserved. Every time a new woman enters my life, my first reaction is confusion and guilt. I doubt my motives. Do I really like the woman or have I staked her out as someone to sleep with? Am I okay or a selfish jerk? Would I want to get involved with me if I was her? The answer to that last one is, hell, no.

Looking up, I saw Ann watching us from the kitchen doorway. She held a large wooden bowl with both hands. I doubt if Ann saw the threat or the guilt, whichever it was, because her face still glowed with cheerful expectations. I decided right then to love her.

"You mind Roquefort dressing?" she asked.

"It's my favorite, that or blue cheese," I said as best I could with Buggie pulling on my lip. "How do I get him to let go?"

"You say, 'Let go, Buggie.' I did and it worked. Ann set the salad down. "He can be a nuisance if you let him, but we get along, don't we, shortcake?" She poked him in the belly and Buggie gurgled again, just like in the afternoon.

I looked in his eyes one last time. The kid and I understood each other, we'd made a connection.

The spaghetti turned out great. Ann had tossed some sliced

mushrooms into the sauce right before pulling it off the heat, so they weren't quite soft. That impressed me. The spaghetti itself was a touch overboiled, but, Lord knows, the dinner beat the oranges, grapes, Cheetos, and coffee diet I was used to.

Ann bounced up and down about eight times while we ate, going after Parmesan and more wine and napkins to wipe Buggie's face. She anticipated everything either one of us wanted, and some things I didn't want. I doubt if Ann was accustomed to adult company, so she tried especially hard to please me. Someone wishing to please me was a new concept, but I adjusted in about three minutes.

All through the meal Buggie was the model of babyhood, happy, laughing, playful when I wanted playful, quiet when I wanted quiet. Ann gave him a bowl of spaghetti and sauce which he turned into the most endearing mess I ever saw. You'd think he was a trained boy.

"Is Buggie his real name?"

"Fred."

"Fred?"

"Fred Blue Smith."

"No wonder you call him Buggie. How old is he?"

"A year next week. The day-care kids are giving him a party, aren't they, my little Bugaroo?" Buggie slapped his hand into the spaghetti bowl.

I drank some wine, wondering how I got so far into life without seeing this side of things. They seemed to fit so easily and comfortably together, playing at eating, watching each other for signs of mood. Will he eat another bite if I pretend the spoon is an airplane? Will she be mad if I throw my cup overboard?

———

We talked about Denver and my school and her day care and what Krazy Glue does if you eat it. She told me she'd never married Buggie's father. Never even thought about it. I told her I was going to write a book someday. We finished her bottle and opened mine. For once, I found a woman I could relax around without worrying whether or not she wanted to be somewhere else. Ann seemed content to sit at the table drinking wine and talking.

After supper, Buggie and I went back to the couch to play funny sounds while Ann cleared the dishes.

"I'll just soak them," she said. "I don't feel like washing right now."

"I never feel like washing dishes."

Ann put a Joni Mitchell album on the cheap stereo and we sat on the couch, holding hands, while Buggie crawled around, exploring under all the cribs and baby beds.

"You want to smoke a joint?" I asked.

"Wine's fine for me, but you go ahead."

"That's okay, I'll drink and sit here with you."

"Don't let me stop you."

We talked some more and I found myself explaining why John Steinbeck wrote good books on the West Coast and bad books on the East Coast. The theory was pretty weak and I don't know how I got started on it, but Ann acted interested. At least she nodded her head at pertinent points and asked reasonable questions. I talked a good deal more than I generally do, but even as I raved on like an imbecile, I was thinking that anyone interested in this drivel must be my perfect match. Or so starved for human contact she'd listen to anything. Right in the middle of my comparison of *The Winter of Our Discontent* to *Of Mice and Men,* Ann leaned over and kissed me.

"What's that for?"

"You had it coming."

Buggie crawled over and up on Ann's lap, where he collapsed. One second he was reaching for her wineglass, gurgling his little heart out, the next second he nestled into her breasts and fell asleep. I followed Ann to one of the cribs, where she lay Buggie down and undressed him like a rag doll. Ann stuck her finger in his diaper. "You sure are cooperating tonight," she said to the sleeping Buggie.

"No Krazy Glue?"

"No nothing. Dry as the desert."

She pulled a blue blanket up to Buggie's chin, then stood back to admire her creation. I put my arm around her and together we watched him sleep. With Ann so small against me, I felt protective—as if I was a piece of something that mattered. There's nothing more emotional than a sleeping child being watched by his mother.

Ann turned over the Joni Mitchell and we retired to the couch, where I kissed her. "That feels nice," she murmured, kissing back. The kissing and hugging felt natural, not frenzied, nobody pushed the ritual or turned animal or anything. We held each other awhile, then kissed awhile, then lay back to relax and think about it awhile. The best thing was the lack of paranoia. Am I getting into something I can't handle? Does she want what I want? Will there be aftereffects? None of that meant anything compared to feeling good with Ann on the couch.

The album ended and Ann got up to put on another one, a jazzy instrumental I wasn't familiar with.

Back next to me, Ann mumbled again, "This sure feels nice."

"Yeah."

"I don't usually…"

"Yeah."

My hands roved and explored, we started kissing more than relaxing and thinking, clothes hit the floor one at a time, and soon we reached the point where it's very difficult to turn back.

"Do you need, uh?"

"I have an IUD."

"Yeah?"

Buggie woke with a scream.

I stopped. "You think he crapped the tube?"

"No, Buggie doesn't like men to touch me. Don't worry, he's okay."

"But he's yelling his head off."

"Loren, please don't stop. Buggie just feels threatened. He's got to learn there's more to my life than him." Ann squirmed under me, pulling me into her.

I entered for about two seconds and Buggie's screaming doubled. "He sounds hurt."

"He's fine. Lie still and he'll go back to sleep." I lay on Ann, in Ann, not moving. After a bit, the Bug quietened down some and she risked a few timid hip thrusts. As soon as I moved, though, the crying rose with a wail. Buggie stood in his crib, holding the side, tears streaming down his red face.

"I don't think I can continue."

Ann grabbed my back. "You can't stop now."

"But he's going to rupture something."

"Hold on." She pushed me off and ran naked to the crib. "No tube," she said. Picking up the baby, she scampered back and settled into the couch next to me. "He won't feel threatened if I hold him."

"Is there room for all three of us?"

"Sure, put your legs here. You'll have to prop on your elbows some. There. If he cries, pet him and tell him it's okay. It'll work. He likes you."

"Pet Buggie while I'm pumping you?"

"It'll work. I've done this before."

So. Buggie sat on Ann's chest between her breasts, facing me, looking quite serious about the business. Ann pulled me back in and we were off. The position worked so long as my eyes stayed open and on Buggie. Whenever I got a little carried away and picked up the tempo or touched Ann with one of my hands, his eyes filled with tears and his little mouth popped open. I slowed down and stroked him and said, "Good baby. It's okay. I'm not hurting your mama. Everything's fine."

Buggie's face held a mixture of trust and fear, that look I was to see a thousand times in the years to come. I can still see it in front of me. His brows are down and his mouth spreads in a line. His eyes turn pitiful. Imagine the look of a puppy right before your father drowns it.

Meanwhile, down under the menfolk, Ann writhed and moaned and had wonderful sex. She came a few times, I popped with an *"Ugh,"* and Buggie leaned forward and pulled on my ear.

Over a period of time, until the wedding actually, we faced this crisis two or three times a week. Sometimes, if we stayed real quiet, Buggie slept through it. Once we hired a baby-sitter and fooled around upstairs in my place, but, on the whole, sex with Ann involved fucking her body while looking in Buggie's eyes. God only knows what this did to the stepfather-baby relationship.

I know I didn't feel perverted or incestuous or anything else distasteful, at least not at the time. From Buggie's point of view, I don't know what it did. He was very young and couldn't have remembered this strange form of love later when he grew old enough to be scarred by grown-ups. I don't know, though. He must have been affected in some way.

———

The next morning the silver Krazy Glue tube appeared in Buggie's pamper. "Looks like a Cracker Jack prize," I said. "He digested the paint. You think the glue still sticks?"

"Don't see why not."

"I'll hide it somewhere safer this time."

I decided to take Ann and Buggie to the Oak Avenue

Cemetery for a picnic. A poet named Peter Pym had died of alcohol abuse the month before and I wanted to check his emanations, though I didn't mention to Ann that the purpose of the picnic was to stand on a grave.

What I said was, "It's a beautiful day, let's go walk around the cemetery."

Not missing a beat, Ann answered, "Should I pack some food? Buggie gets hungry if he doesn't eat every two hours. How do you feel about cucumbers?"

Normally I don't care much for poets, dead or alive. They're a little pithy for me—all sensitivity and no attention span. However, Peter Pym was the Western Shakespeare, only poet ever elected to the Cowboy Hall of Fame. He was rumored to have appeared in four Tom Mix movies and been narrowly edged out of the original Sons of the Pioneers.

It was Peter Pym who wrote "The Cowboy's Melody."

*With a ten-dollar horse and a forty-dollar saddle*
*I'll soon be down in Texas a-punchin' on the cattle.*

Without saying why, I dragged Ann and Buggie back and forth across the cemetery three times before I found the marker, and then he put out all the aura of a fresh cow patty on a cold day. Personally, I don't think Peter Pym wrote "The Cowboy's Melody." I think he stole it.

We spread the quilt between Peter and Mary Louise Wolfe (1904-1972). Some interesting vibes rose from Mary's dirt, along the lines of a faithful sixty-year diary keeper, but I figured I better not investigate until later. Finding and standing over Peter Pym had been plenty for Ann to witness before lunch.

Ann had packed a real picnic basket with cucumber sand-wiches and hard-boiled eggs with the yolks pulled out, then spiced up, and somehow crammed back in again. She'd made a spinach salad with vinegar and oil dressing and an apricot mush thing for Buggie. We drank iced Mellow Mint tea and ate strawberries dipped in brown sugar for dessert. I'd never been on a picnic with a picnic basket before. In Texas we used brown paper sacks.

Winter in Denver is long and cold, followed by a spring short and slushy. That Saturday in the cemetery was the first dry, clear day since October. Maybe being with Ann and Buggie made me notice more than I'd been noticing lately, but it seemed as if the trees were greener and the telephone poles higher than I remembered. The gravestones reflected light so brightly I wished I'd brought my clip-on sunglasses. Mostly, though, I didn't look at the gravestones. Mostly, I looked at Ann and Buggie.

The grass fascinated Buggie. Imagine discovering lawns for the first time—what it must have felt like to sit on the corner of the quilt and lean over to touch the giant green carpet that seemed to cover the world. At first, he didn't trust it. He stared at the grass, then at Ann, then back at the grass. Finally, he tipped over onto his hands and knees and edged forward a bit. When Buggie completely cleared the blanket, he stopped and looked at Ann and smiled.

"Go for it," she said.

Buggie muttered some baby language and took off at a fast crawl.

Ann lay sideways on the blanket, kind of simmering in the sunshine. Every time I looked at her I saw something new that I liked. First, the hips, they were nice, not fat, but the perfect size for balancing babies. Then I noticed the little double dimple that appeared on her chin when she smiled. Those dents raised Ann above cute to pretty.

We held hands and watched a man on a backhoe dig a grave

down the hill a ways. What the man was doing didn't seem to have any connection to anything we'd ever do. Ann rolled onto her stomach, propped on her arms, facing Buggie. "He's going to walk any day now," she said. "The principles are down, all he needs is balance."

The kid was close. He clutched the side of Mary Louise Wolfe and pulled himself upright. Releasing his hold, Buggie stood alone, swaying, but unsupported.

"Come on, Buggie," Ann said. "Come to Mama."

"You can do it, Bug," I said. "Let's see you dance."

Carefully he put one foot out, lurched forward a step, wavered, and crashed on his face, laughing. I moved to go help, but Ann touched my arm. "Let him do it."

Buggie crawled back to the gravestone and pulled himself up again. We gave encouragement again, "Come on, Buggie. You can do it, Buggie," and he crashed again. You've got to give credit to the little guy, falling on his face didn't dampen his enthusiasm.

While Buggie tottered off among the plots, I got Ann to talking some and she told me her life's story so far.

"It's not very original," she said.

"I bet it's nothing like mine."

She was raised in a big frame house in Coos Bay, Oregon, where it rains all the time, in a family of seven kids. When she was about nine, her mom developed colon cancer and took five miserable years in dying, so Ann couldn't remember much about her except the helplessness.

"They kept her so doped on painkillers she used to pass out in the lawn chair and my little brother and I had to carry her in," Ann said. "Toward the end, her hair fell out and she lost a lot of weight. She crapped through a hole over her hip. It was kind of sad."

What could I say? All my tragedies had been self-inflicted. I couldn't comprehend what it would feel like to have something bad happen.

Ann's father dropped off the deep end after her mom's death. He drank too much, lost his sales job, and took to blaming his tragic life on government bureaucracy and ethnic minorities— especially Jews. He kept a pistol in the glove compartment. Once when Ann was with him, he fired at a Cadillac driver who cut him off on the freeway.

He never forgave Ann for growing up, or maybe he was mad because she lived and her mom didn't, Ann wasn't sure. All she knew was her father became very angry and stopped talking to her about the time she went through puberty. In Ann's mind, her father's hatred and the menstrual cycle were somehow connected. Her periods always brought on guilt.

"Didn't all this screw you up?" I asked.

She watched Buggie pull plastic flowers from the base of a stone. "I don't think so. Everybody comes from a weird past. That doesn't give you an excuse to be crazy."

"Does me."

Sickness, anger, and depression made dreary surroundings for a teenage girl, so when Ann met a group of smiling, serene religious fanatics chanting on the beach, she took off and joined the sect.

"They were happy and all I wanted was to be happy."

Buggie crawled back, dragging a plastic flower between his legs. He handed it to Ann, who was so pleased she wiped off most of the dirt and stuck the flower in her hair above her ear. It was a blue flower with yellow spots in the center.

"I dropped out of high school to follow the guru to Boulder," she said. "He put me to work in the Divine Light Mission Day Care Center. That's where I found out how much I enjoy taking care of kids."

"You were in a cult?"

"Almost two years. It wasn't bad. I was too young to deal with drugs and easy sex. Religion was the healthy alternative."

"Did you eat brown rice and tofu?"

Ann laughed, and Buggie looked up to see the cause. "Constantly. I still can't stand the smell of soy sauce."

"I'm liking you more all the time. Why'd you leave the cult?"

Ann shrugged. Her hair fell across her shoulders and glinted off her breasts. I like what sunshine does to clean hair. "Grew up, I guess. I got disenchanted with the Maharaj Ji. He was supposed to be fourteen, but he drove a yellow Rolls-Royce. He watched cartoons on a big-screen color TV all day and ate like a pig. I can't see worshiping a fat little boy." She touched my shoulder. "That's why I liked you when I first saw you carrying those stacks of books to your car. I go for thin."

"I'm not thin on purpose."

"Buggie's wet. Hand me that bag."

"You going to change his diaper?"

"That's what you do when the baby gets wet." On his back, Buggie squirmed like an upside-down turtle, his legs and arms thrashing the air. Ann leaned way over so he could play with her hair while she tore open the sticky tabs.

"I need a diaper lesson. Thamu Kamala gave me a hard time yesterday because I couldn't change Jason or Jesse or somebody."

"Thamu Kamala gives everyone a hard time. Her mom's a sect dropout like me, but her dad still wears purple robes and carries an invisible torch whenever he leaves the ashram. They split her every other week. I think Thamu Kamala's growing up confused."

Ann pulled the dirty diaper off Buggie and stuffed it into a plastic bag. Lifting his feet, she went to work on his bottom with a washcloth.

"What happened after you left the cult?"

"Nothing much, I drifted here to Denver and hung around the freaks in Cheeseman Park. Lived a couple of years with a guy who made turquoise jewelry and sold barbiturates. That one ended badly."

"What happened?"

"See, you slip the diaper under him quickly and flip this part up. Otherwise, you'll get a face full of pee."

"What happened to the downs seller?"

"One night he felt frustrated and ate too many of his own barbs. You know what that means."

"He beat you up."

"I moved into the apartment I have now and opened my own day care. Rebounded around some and wound up pregnant."

Her hands zoomed over Buggie, tucking, straightening folds. Just like that, he was dry, freshly diapered, rolled back onto his hands and knees, and ready to take on the world again. Smiling, Ann watched him scoot off across the lawn.

"Where's Buggie's father?"

"Chuck got himself killed the day Buggie was born. It's real freaky. He called the hospital and said he would be right over, he still wanted me to marry him. He kept thinking when I actually saw the baby I'd break down and say yes, but I wouldn't have. Chuck was a nice enough guy, but not somebody to marry. You've got to be in love to get married, you know."

"Got to?"

Ann gave me meaningful eye contact. "I would never marry anyone without both of us being in love." She let me think about this a minute before continuing: "Anyway, he never showed up and the next day I read in the paper he'd been shot dead in the hospital parking lot. Isn't that weird? In broad daylight, in South Denver."

The story made me nervous. Death and grief were experiences I'd managed to miss up to that point, and here, lying next to me on an old quilt, sipping iced herbal tea and watching her child toddle, was a true death and grief authority. We'd made love, after a fashion. I liked her. It was too late to avoid involvement even if I wanted to, and I didn't want to—I didn't think—but there's something disheartening about initiating a relationship with a woman who's been surrounded by disaster all her life. That stuff wears off on people.

"Sounds like you haven't had a lot of breaks," I said.

"Why?"

"All those terrible things that happened to you. Don't you ever feel cheated by life?"

Ann looked at me strangely, as if she'd never thought about it on those terms. "I've been real fortunate," she said. "I'm healthy and I have Buggie. I love the day-care kids." She smiled again. "Now, if you stick around a while, life will be pretty much complete."

I thought about me sticking around a while as a means of making her life complete. I'd only known Ann one day and hadn't dwelt on the future yet, but the longer I watched Ann watch Buggie, the better the idea sounded. Loren Paul and his family. What an interesting phrase.

# 9

My romances tend to move with speed. Ann and I met on a Friday afternoon, by Saturday night we were "going steady" as she put it, Sunday I moved my toothbrush and hookah downstairs, and on Monday morning Ann poured cream in my coffee without being asked and told me to pick up formula on my way home from school. One moment we were blitzed by that first rush of new love, and the next time I looked around, we were sunk belly deep in a comfortable rut. Or stability, depending on how you look at it.

The new life felt considerably better than the old one had, so I stayed with it, never stopping long enough to wonder if there might be more than just this way or that way. Throughout the years, both before and after Ann, I've never been able to see more than two choices at a time. This simplifies decision making, but Lana Sue says my narrowness of options causes me to make mistakes. I think I would make mistakes no matter how many choices I was given.

I know exactly why I felt better with the new life than I had with the old one. We're coming up on an important point here: Pre-Ann and Buggie, I had a poor outlook. I thought people are born, we hang around a few years pretending it will last forever, either we breed or we don't, we consume more than we create or we don't. Mostly we're miserable and every once in a while we aren't, but whether it's a tenth-week termination or 106 years down the line, sooner or later we all disappear. *So what?*

With that attitude it's no wonder I watched *I Love Lucy* and smoked dope all day. The little I managed to pull off was motivated by the unpleasantness of the alternatives. School beat work, so I stayed in school. Being alive put off the disappearance, so I did what had to be done to stay alive.

And then—*drum roll*—Buggie swallowed a tube of Krazy Glue. Suddenly something mattered. *Something has to matter.* Otherwise, a person's life will be miserable and empty. Am I the last one to figure that out? The what that matters is unimportant—God, Coke-bottle collecting, track and field—all are equally useful in staving off the uselessness. For my stepfather, Don, bowling matters. Napoleon wanted to conquer Russia. Lana Sue's mom thinks the quality of her life is directly dependent on the meat prices at Kroger's. Career and love life may be a little trite, but they seem to work as well as anything.

To someone on the outside, your basis may look like a joke, but if you know it's important, really know and go on knowing, you'll never fall into despair.

After all those years of neoexistential pouting, I awoke Monday morning caring about something. Driving in to class on the I-45 loop, I seriously worried about Buggie's diet, Ann's reproductive organs, my future. Within a week, I started writing a book. No matter what Sartre, Camus, or Vonnegut says, a man with no future does not write a book.

I enjoyed making love in the glow of TV light and the wave that swept over me when I awoke early and watched Ann's face asleep on the pillow next to me. Those first few weeks were an orgy of touching, meaningful moments that made me sick with love. However, it was the smaller rushes, the day-to-day routines, that gave me the powerful something-matters feeling I had always wanted—pushing Buggie in a grocery cart down the aisles in Food Lion, sorting socks next to Ann at the Laundromat, holding Buggie while she swabbed his ear with a warmed Bermuda onion when he had an infection—that's when I felt life was worth the trouble even if it has to end.

Another rule: A woman who makes laundry day fun is a woman to keep.

The semester ended in a flurry of B minuses and C pluses. Summer loomed as a long, easy three months of warmth, family, and regular sex—or the summer would have loomed if I'd had any money. The only job I could find was breakfast-lunch dishwasher at the Hard Wok Cafe on East Colfax. I like Chinese people. Remember that. My body does not contain a single ethnically prejudiced bone, but Jesus Christ, it's unnatural to expect someone to eat rice and bok choy before 8:00 a.m. Our breakfast special was jellied lamb loaf. Try jellied lamb loaf with your first cup of coffee some morning and see if you don't resent our little Oriental brothers.

And all the cooks, waiters, and busboys spoke nothing to each other but Chinese. Fast Chinese, like they'd gone to the Ho Chi School of Speed Speaking. They had so much energy and, at that time of day, I had so little, I felt like a 33⅓ man in a 78 world.

I wrote my first Western in the Hard Wok kitchen. Professional dishwashing is a great job for mental retards or soaring philosophers because you must be either so far below the work that it constitutes a challenge, or so far above it that the drama is all in your brain and your bodily actions can be ignored. To those hyper cooks banging wok tools and singing "At the Copa" in Chinese unison, I may have appeared to be scraping, spraying, shoving, sorting, and stacking, but in actuality my Jackson Sterilizer dishmachine and I were in 1882

Bitter Creek, Wyoming, defending goodness and fistfighting bad men with livid facial scars.

Except that they drank, fought, and chased women endlessly, all my characters were stolen directly from *Andy Griffith* TV show reruns. Usually I played Andy's parts and the Jackson Sterilizer was Barney, but sometimes we'd switch and he'd be Gomer while I played Opie. The garbage disposal played the role of Ernest T. Bass. We blocked out every scene, experimenting with dialogue, going over the fights and shootouts one instant at a time.

At 2:30, I sped home, took the stairs to my apartment two steps at a bound, and typed furiously for an hour before my mind wandered and I lost the lines that sounded so bright and clear in the steam of my Sterilizer. The book was about a sheriff with bad manners and good intentions and a woman the other way around. The sympathetic whore with the heart of gold acted suspiciously like Aunt Bee, and Floyd shot himself every time he picked up a gun, but, as a cheap Western, I thought the book worked, sort of.

Typing done, I reread the previous day's work, fixing blatant inconsistencies, like the heroine's eyes that kept changing color and the bad guys whose names were never the same two chapters in a row. After that, I watched a real *Andy Griffith* rerun, taking notes of course, and waited for the moms in their Volkswagen bugs and buses to carry away all the little Jesses and Heathers downstairs. Around 5:30, Ann knocked on the ceiling twice with a mop handle and I answered with a hiking boot. Then I trotted downstairs for an evening of quiet domesticity.

———

I decided it would be fun if Buggie's first words were multi-syllabled and significant. His biographer would love me for it.

For two weeks, I debated between "environmental action" and "Spare change, mister," finally opting for "transcendental."

"Transcendental," I said seven thousand times.

"Agwahk," Buggie answered.

My job was to sit Buggie in his high chair and feed him supper while Ann worked on our own dinner, which by then had become the big event of the day.

"Open up," I quacked in my duck voice, shoveling in what I could from a Flintstones bowl of lentil-barley soup. I cleanly shaved the spit-out off his chin with the spoon. In two months, I'd become a whiz at the father skills. I cleaned, fed, entertained, and when I wanted, ignored the baby as well as any sperm daddy around. Didn't even retch at peeling off a diarrhea-filled diaper. I call that commitment.

"Transcendental," I said.

Buggie reached for the soup bowl, but I saved it. "Transcendental," I said again.

"He's not a parrot," Ann said.

"Transcendental."

Ann moved around the stove, throwing vegetables and spices into a Dutch oven on one of the burners. "I wish you wouldn't treat him like a pet."

"He's a genius. Did you see him playing baby in a coma the other night?" Buggie shook his head from side to side, daring me to stick soup in his mouth.

"I saw you feeding him chocolate kisses when he got it right. The sugar kept him up all night."

"Transcendental," I said. I reached over and pinched Buggie's little nostrils together. After a moment's resistance, his mouth opened and I popped in a spoonful of soup.

Ann stirred whatever it was with a ladle. I loved suppertime best of all—the three of us together, doing small important jobs. My kind of peaceful.

"He's not a dog," Ann said.

"I know. He can't learn to bark. Transcendental."

"I mean it, Loren."

Buggie spit out the mouthful of soup he'd been saving. I've seen that kid hold stuff in his mouth for hours before blabbing it out at an inappropriate moment.

"I just want the Bug to know the things that were important to me as a boy. I didn't have a dad to teach me tricks."

"Such as?"

"Such as…I want to show Buggie how to hitchhike and panhandle in parks."

"Loren."

"Real soon I'm going to teach him to roll reefers. He'll be the best year-old reefer roller in Colorado."

"You better be kidding."

"Buggie'll be the hit of every party. I'll buy a home movie camera and film him and send it off to Hollywood."

Ann turned clear around. "Loren, Fred is my son. Not yours."

"I forget sometimes."

"Write it down. He's my son and he's a person, not a pet."

"A person, not a pet."

Buggie lunged forward, arms at full extension, and pushed the soup onto the floor. The bowl landed right side up and spun around and round, showing first Dino, then Barney, then Pebbles.

I said, "Transcendental."

———

A week later, in the parking lot at Wendy's, Buggie made a fist at a Jeep CJ5 and said, *"Car,"* just plain as could be.

Another couple of weeks, he learned *Mama, TV, me,* and *trouble.* I don't remember the little punk ever saying "transcendental."

———

After supper we usually sat around and read or watched television until bedtime. The first couple of weeks I lay on the couch a lot, smoking pot, but that gradually lost its charm. Getting stoned alone with someone is different from getting stoned alone alone. There isn't much use. I had more fun chasing Buggie around the living room. Once he learned to walk, Buggie moved quickly on to running, then constant running.

He ran like a monkey, with both hands over his head, but not like a kid because he didn't squeal and shout. Whoever heard of a child playing tag without making noise? I'd chase him left around a baby bed, then cut back right to head him off, and he'd scoot under the bed and over an arm of the couch. Buggie wasn't very fast—he was only one—but he had the concentration of an athlete, say a pole-vaulter or a gymnast. I almost hated to end the game by catching him.

When bedtime finally arrived, I would grab him around the waist and, as I carried Buggie upside down to his baby bed under the mobile of plastic farm animals, he always looked up at me over his bottom lip with that what-did-I-do-to-get-treated-this-way face. Maybe he thought night-night was punishment for allowing me to catch him.

While Buggie and I played, Ann busied around, scissoring figures for the felt board storytime or glueing glitter and poking holes in poster paper. Most nights she practiced songs from a book that showed hand signal accompaniments. *Itsy bitsy spider went up the water spout,* that sort of thing. To me, it takes at least two grown-ups to handle one child. Four—divorced real parents and new stepmoms and -dads—works even better. But Ann took care of ten. And me. Imagine that.

She didn't talk much about her business. In fact, Ann didn't talk much about anything, and because of that, I took a long time getting to know her. We never worked out those subtle signals that husbands and wives who have lived together for years use to get across what they really mean in spite of what they say.

"Would you care to leave the party, dear?"

"Oh, I don't care, honey, it's up to you."

A long-term mate should know whether that particular "I don't care" means yes, no, or I don't care, but with Ann, I never knew for certain what she meant, so I had to act on the literal value. Acting on the literal value can cause a lot of misunderstanding.

Another thing I couldn't catch on to was her thought process. How she chose a movie or why she decided on waffles one morning and oatmeal the next. Ann told me she was satisfied with us and that was all that counted for her, but I wanted to know why she was satisfied so I could do something to keep her that way.

What Ann and I did mostly that summer was make each other happy. Which is a lot to claim. We went from not being together to being together so fast, it's hard to believe that real love was involved. I felt like I loved her, believed I loved her, but how real can love be with someone you hardly know? Love or not, we caused happiness in each other, and I don't think either Ann or I had been happy for as long as a summer before. Besides, look at all the loving couples out there who feel miserable most of the time. Given a choice between love and happiness, I go with happiness. Love might come along later.

———

For my birthday in August, Thamu Kamala and her mom, Joyce, came over to sit with Buggie so Ann could take me out to dinner. Buggie and I were playing crocodile and the kid when Thamu Kamala marched through the door. Crocodile and the kid involves me slithering around on the rug while Buggie throws couch cushions at my head.

"Mom's parking the car," Thamu Kamala said.

"Come on in, we're playing a game."

She stood in the doorway, glaring at me on the floor. "Look at you, wallowing like an animal. Buggie must think he's trapped with a fool."

I sat up. "That's some vocabulary for a five-year-old kid."

Thamu Kamala went into her familiar hands on the hips routine. "I have an IQ of one-sixty-one, which makes me a genius. So there."

"Okay, genius, let's work out a truce. We both like Ann, right? We both spend a lot of time in her apartment. I think we should try to be friends."

Thamu Kamala tossed her hair as contemptuously as a woman twenty years her senior. "I'd *rather* be dead."

"That's a possibility."

"What's a possibility?" Ann asked, coming in from the bedroom. She wore her best long skirt and a white blouse with strings tied around the sleeves. Her earrings were gold dangles that I hadn't seen before.

"Your boyfriend threatened to kill me."

"Don't threaten to kill Thamu Kamala." Ann bent to pluck Buggie from the couch. She held him high and swung him around and across her shoulder. Every time I saw those two together I turned all emotional inside.

Joyce came in the door dressed like a Gypsy fortune-teller. "Who'd you threaten to kill, Loren?" Her eye makeup was excessive and the black fingernail polish overstated the style a bit, but I liked Joyce. I admire any single mother who's cheerful.

Thamu Kamala hid behind her mother's sparkly, full skirt. "He threatened to kill me. We should call the police and have Loren hauled away."

"I didn't threaten to kill your daughter."

Joyce smiled, open and friendly, as if she believed me instead of Thamu Kamala. "Her father's been reading her a book on child abuse among the nonspiritual," she said.

"That explains everything."

Joyce laughed and turned to Ann. "You sure look pretty tonight, that's a beautiful skirt."

Ann straightened the waistline. "You really think so? I've been deciding what to wear all week. Every stitch I own is clean and ironed in case I change my mind at the last minute."

I wished I'd been the one to say Ann looked nice, but by then it was too late. My only recourse was to play the efficient young family man. "We'll be home by two at the latest. Numbers are next to the phone. If he cries give him juice, bedtime is seven-thirty, and…and…" I ran out of instructions.

Joyce looked impressed. "My, my," she said to Ann, "you've trained this one well. Thamu Kamala's father was too cosmic to be bothered by bedtime."

Ann came up and put her arm around me. "I've got a winner, all right. Pop's in the refrigerator, cookies in the cookie jar."

"We'll be fine. Where are you two lovebirds planning to dine?"

Ann smiled at the word lovebirds. "Los Gatos. I heard they have a band. Wouldn't that be nice? Live music makes a place feel so fancy."

Single moms will talk all night if someone doesn't put a stop to it. I looked at my wrist, pretending I wore a watch. "Ann, hon, my birthday will be over soon."

As we walked out the door, I heard Thamu Kamala say, "Jesus, that guy's got the astral aura of a goat."

———

All the way across town Ann worried that I didn't like Mexican food and was just being polite to humor her.

"Why would I do that?" I asked.

"You always sacrifice what you want in order not to hurt my feelings. Are you sure you wouldn't rather try the Grinning Greek downtown? I don't mind. I like them both."

"I have never sacrificed anything not to hurt feelings, and how do you know you like them both if you haven't eaten in either one, and it's my birthday. If I didn't like Mexican food, believe me, I'd say so."

Ann twisted a button on her peasant blouse. "I wish I could be sure."

"Be sure. I'm exactly where I want to be, doing exactly what I want to do with exactly who I want to do it with."

Ann sighed and reached under the gearshift to put her hand on my upper leg. "You're sweet, Loren. You treat me so good."

I wasn't aware of that. We passed a billboard that showed a seductive woman lying on a black satin sheet, wishing someone would ply her with Cutty Sark. I fantasized what it would be like to ply the woman. It made a nice fantasy that I revised several times in the next few miles.

"Do you think Buggie will be all right with Joyce?" Ann asked.

From the Interstate, Los Gatos looked like a big, stuccoed armory under attack by a twenty-foot neon tower. As we swung into the parking lot, "The Lonely Bull" by Herb Alpert and the Tijuana Brass blared from speakers mounted on top of the building. I circled the lot twice, passing empty spaces in hopes of getting closer, then when I gave up and returned, the spaces were taken. We ended up parking a quarter mile from the restaurant. Before I killed the engine, Ann jumped from the car, ran around, and when I stepped out, she grabbed and kissed me.

"This is going to be far-out," she said.

"I never heard you use that term before."

"Far-out's what the Maharaj Ji used to say about Mexican food."

———

I held Ann's hand as we threaded through a cluster of concerned-looking people bunched up in front of the shiny blond hostess. "We'd like a table near the orchestra."

The hostess had the cheekbones of a Comanche warrior. "What orchestra? Name."

"I heard you have a band."

"We have a band. No orchestra. Name."

"Loren."

She glanced behind me at Ann. "Two?"

I nodded. The hostess wrote *Loren* and *(2)* at the bottom of a long line of names. "It'll be an hour. You can wait in the bar."

"Where's that?"

The blond woman stood up and kept going, up and up, way over my head, I couldn't believe it. She was the tallest blond woman I've ever seen. "Through that curtain." She pointed. If I owned a restaurant, I'd put a hostess out front who smiled now and then, but I hate to judge personalities.

Rooster piñatas and bunches of dried peppers hung from the bar's ceiling. Much of the wall behind our table was covered by a weaving of the sunrise over an extinct volcano with a little mud hut and a profiled donkey standing at the base. All the colors used in the weaving were shades found naturally in the desert.

Ann couldn't let herself relax. "Did you see a phone? I forgot to tell Joyce Buggie likes a glass of kefir at bedtime."

"I told her he'd drink apple juice."

"Loren, that's all wrong. He drinks apple juice in the afternoon and kefir at night. Now I have to call her."

I knew better than to disagree. "I saw a phone in the waiting room." Ann left, searching for a dime and a telephone.

The customers all looked either drunk or bored—which I guess is what you get when you sit in a bar for an hour, hoping a table will open up. My entire adult life has been dedicated to the policy that it's better to be drunk than bored, so I waved the cocktail waitress over and ordered a pitcher of margaritas. The waitress was cute, in a young and restless sort of way, but I wouldn't say she had any characteristics of Spanish blood. She looked more Colorado Presbyterian sorority sister, the sort of woman who drove a Mustang 2+2, permed her hair, and thought sex was a sin but committed it anyway.

The bartender now, he was authentic—swarthy, dark mustache and sideburns, purple ruffled shirt, sneer. Sex wasn't sinful to the bartender.

Ann arrived moments behind the Presbyterian waitress with our pitcher. "Joyce says Buggie's okay. He's helping Thamu Kamala put a puzzle together." Ann sat and poured herself a drink. "You don't think Joyce would lie, do you?"

I used the cocktail napkin to wipe salt off my glass rim. "Why would she lie?"

"I don't know, but she sounded odd. She said Buggie didn't want to talk to me."

"He can barely talk."

"She said he was having too much fun throwing puzzle pieces." Ann sipped and made a face. "What is this?"

"Margarita, it's good."

She sipped once more. "Is it tequila? I don't think I like tequila."

For someone drinking something she didn't like, Ann sure polished off that pitcher in record time. Whenever I drink or smoke pot or have sex or anything relaxing, I like to think about something other than what I'm doing. Who wants to think, I will now chug this tequila before chugging tequila? It takes away the spontaneity. I'd rather dream about fishing or dead writers or what deeds of valor I would perform if a small plane crashed through the ceiling and cut the bartender in half. But when Ann drank, which didn't happen often, she forced as much alcohol as possible into her body in as short a time as possible. The only way I could keep up was to concentrate on not daydreaming and pay attention to the rise and fall of margarita in the glass. Every few minutes the shiny blond woman came through the curtain and everyone perked up until she called the name. On the average, though, more waiting people came in the bar than called people went out. Two costumed Mexicans carrying an accordion and a guitar pushed through the crowd, singing, "Girl from Ipanema."

Ann was shocked. "That's the band?"

I was mystified. "Isn't Ipanema in France?"

"California."

"Are you sure?"

Ann nodded. "Suburb of West Covina. One of my sisters lives there."

"I didn't know West Covina had suburbs."

Ann laughed, not her normal laugh, this laugh was definitely tequila-inspired. "That makes my sister the girl from Ipanema."

One glass into the second pitcher and Ann started to talk. Her diction came out fine, no slurs, no stutters to speak of. I only knew she was drunk because her eyes glassed over and she talked more than usual about things she didn't normally talk about.

"My dad would really hate you," she said. "If the two of you ever met, I think he would shoot you with his pistol." Every father of every girl I so much as took on a Coke date has hated me.

Ann tossed down half a glass of margarita. "Whoa," she said, "that really slakes the thirst."

"Slakes?"

"He would shoot you because you smoke drugs and wash dishes instead of working. But mostly he would shoot you because you have a penis." At the word *penis,* Ann had a giggle fit. She scrunched down and checked out the neighboring tables to see if any eavesdroppers showed offense.

"Does your father hate everyone with a penis?"

"Only the ones who know me." She stared into her glass a moment. "Or maybe he hates me because I don't have one." As Ann's mind temporarily dropped into a remembrance trance, I took the opportunity to catch up on my drink and look at the cocktail waitress again. She wore a short skirt and bloodred hose. Her posture seemed contrived to accentuate the bust area.

I wondered what my mom would think of me if I weren't related to her and Kathy brought me home. She'd probably give me instant iced tea and Wheat Thins and ask me what my parents did for a living. She'd talk about her younger years, then, as I stood up to leave, she'd smile and say, "Hurry back." Afterwards Mom would scream at Kathy and take away her phone privileges until she promised never to see me again.

Ann came back with a jolt. "Dad mails out a family newsletter every Christmas. It's mimeographed with a list of where all us kids are and what we're doing, who we've married, how many children, that kind of thing, but after my sister told him about Freedom, he stopped sending me the letter. Isn't that sad?"

I hadn't followed the sequence properly. "What's Freedom?"

"A hippie I cohabited with. He made turquoise jewelry and sold barbiturates."

"I've heard of him."

"Did I ever tell you I used to take barbiturates sometimes." Ann giggled again. "I may not act it now, but I was one wild little teenybopper."

I tried to picture Ann as wild or a teenybopper, but neither concept would flesh out. To me, she had always been a young mother who had to be drunk to say *penis*.

"I didn't shave my legs or pits for four years," she said, as if to prove her decadent youth.

"Neither did I." The giant hostess pushed through the curtain and called a name. The people sitting at the next table stood and followed her away.

"Didn't those people come in after us?" I asked.

"When Daddy found out about Buggie, he took my name completely out of the newsletter. Someone reading it now wouldn't even know I exist."

"I could have sworn those people came in after we did. I think the frigid beanpole skipped us."

"When your own dad denies your existence, it's hard to believe in it yourself," Ann said. She looked ready to cry. I'd never seen Ann's entire alcohol progression, so I didn't know what to expect. Most women slide smoothly from happy to thoughtful to sad to playful to sexy, but every now and then I'd met one who went happy-thoughtful-sad-hysterical-angry-unconscious. That's the type you don't want to take into a fancy restaurant.

"*Loren.*" The blond tower clamped a hand onto my shoulder. "I called your party three times. Once more and I give away the table."

"I'm sorry, we were talking and didn't hear. Ann, you take the glasses, I'll carry the pitcher." I never seem to go anywhere without apologizing to somebody about something.

The hostess led us through two or three dining rooms, past the roving Mexican duet who still played "Girl from Ipanema," to a small, round table under a gory bullfighting painting.

"Here," she said. "The special is chicken tacos. Your waitress's name is Toni."

"Miss," I asked politely, "I don't mean to pry, but do you have a personal problem that is affecting your attitude toward me?"

That was a mistake. Her lower lip trembled, then her

forehead wrinkled. The lake-blue eyes filled with tears and, as the hostess folded into the chair she had intended for me, she broke into mournful sobs.

Ann said, "Now look what you've done."

The hostess lay her head on the table and wept—loudly. I never know how to act around crying strangers. Everywhere I turned diners stared accusingly back at me. A few even muttered ugly comments. The only comment loud enough to understand came from a cowboy two tables down. "Hostessing is tough enough without assholes giving her a bunch of shit." He wore a fringe jacket and a gray felt hat, obviously a man who ate meat three times a day and thought anyone who doesn't chew is a sissy.

"Hey, I didn't give her shit. I asked if she had a personal problem."

The cowboy pushed back his chair and stood. "That's not giving her shit?"

"Nothing like the shit you're giving me."

"I'll show you shit." He stepped around the table toward me. The whole dining room drew in its breath, poised on the edge of a disgusting scene, and, from the sound of the general buzz, public opinion ran with the cowboy.

As usual in these situations, I was saved by the intervention of a woman. The hostess stepped between me and the cowboy, leaving me with a view of the bra line on her back. She sniffed a couple of times. "It's okay. It's not his fault. I shouldn't have come to work tonight." Her back quivered a second. "I just thought work might be good for me. I thought I could make it through the shift, but I was wrong. I shouldn't have tried."

The cowboy was out of sight in front of the hostess, but from the expression on Ann's face, I gathered he wasn't going to stomp me after all. That was nice. Getting stomped would have messed up my birthday.

While Ann and the hostess hem-hawed around, apologizing

to each other, I poured myself a margarita and considered the implications. Two of my primary goals are to complete life without hurting anyone or pissing anyone off, yet I seem doomed to fail at every turn. In fact, I hurt more often than I help. How do people manage inoffensiveness? Do people manage it or are my goals automatic failures?

"That sobered me up," Ann said. "Let's order another pitcher."

———

We finished the second pitcher before the waitress took our orders, so I don't recall what I ate. Ann had the chicken tacos and I think I ordered something green and stuffed. Like magic, more margaritas appeared in front of my plate. The way this kind of restaurant works is they make you wait for a table so long that by the time the food arrives, you're too drunk to know if it's any good. The rest of my birthday evening was like trying to watch two television shows on one television. Awareness came in, went out, came in again, but the plot kept moving right along whether I was there or not.

I did come around for some important information. From the blur, Ann's voice said, "I've been offered the assistant directorship of a community day-care center, a hundred and twenty kids, eleven teachers, fenced-in play area, a cook who fixes lunch and snack, then cleans up the mess. What do you think?"

"I thought you loved your own kids?"

Ann nodded. "I do, but Thamu Kamala leaves for kindergarten in three weeks, and the Wilderness Society is transferring Jesse's dad to San Francisco, something to do with whales. The other kids could probably come with me."

I dropped my fork. I don't know whether someone picked it up or gave me a new one, or maybe I picked it up myself, although I doubt that. All I know is my hand soon held a fork that looked and felt similar to the one I dropped.

At some point, the cowboy stood over me, breathing like a tired bear. His hands were clenched, so I didn't look any higher. I concentrated on my refried beans, pretending they so engrossed me that I couldn't notice anything else. He didn't say anything that I remember. Later, I raised my head and he was gone.

Ann was still talking, but I'm not sure if I missed a little or a lot. "I'm tired of doing all the work myself, and it would be nice to be around other women. At the big center I'll earn vacations so we can travel and go camping. I really miss camping. I haven't been once since Buggie was born."

"I didn't know you liked outdoors." Every time I felt certain about Ann's values and opinions, she'd say something new and I'd have to start all over.

"Besides," Ann said, "with the kids gone you could move into my apartment. Or we could rent a house together. Wouldn't that be neat?"

"You mean live together full time? Leave my place? All my books are there."

I have a feeling this conversation lasted clear through whatever we ate, but my brain switched to another channel and didn't come back until I found myself pressed against Ann as she leaned back on the car hood.

I heard myself saying, "Let's go to my apartment and make love."

Ann glowed. "Loren, I'm so happy. We're going to have the most wonderful life together, you wait and see. All my dreams are coming true."

"Or would you rather do it on the car?"

She kissed me a long time. Finally Ann pulled back and looked full into my face. "Don't you love being happy? I never thought it could be so much fun."

The drive home has left my memory banks, thank God. The next awareness wave caught us in bed in my apartment. I wanted to slow down so I could enjoy the prospect of sex without a child between us, but Ann was in too big a hurry to enjoy prospects. She never was big on foreplay. I think Ann got most of her foreplay in her imagination during the daytime, so when our bodies came together, she didn't have to waste any time.

I lay there wishing I wasn't so drunk and likely to switch channels in the middle of something nice. This was my chance to writhe around, make all the noise I wanted, and actually think of myself during sex for a change. But somehow I didn't feel like you're supposed to feel when you make love on your birthday. I felt like I was listening to the sound track of a dirty movie.

My mood must have rubbed off on Ann because after a while she lay still with her face in my shoulder hollow.

I said, "I love you," to see how it sounded, but again, the words came out like in a movie.

Ann cried a few minutes, either out of happiness or misery, I have trouble telling the difference. Then I woke up alone in a room full of light.

———

The sweat-soaked sheets twisted around my legs, making my first thoughts run to tequila paralysis. Then, when I shook the sheets off and tried raising myself into the hands-and-knees sick-dog position, I discovered I'd slept with my faceless alarm clock as a pillow. The hands had been circling for hours, tying hair and clock into a solid, immovable tangle stuck to the side of my head. Every ticktock boomed in my ear like bombs marching into Hanoi.

I leaned over the edge of the bed and spit some very old-tasting saliva into the wastepaper basket. I said aloud, "This won't do."

The pounding clock on my head and the dropping-through-space stomach were awful, waking up alone in my own bed was disorienting, but the bad news was the room full of light. Brightness meant I was horribly late for work. One hand on the clock so its weight wouldn't rip out my roots, I stumbled across a pile of dirty clothes to the phone and called the Hard Wok.

What I should have done first is put on my boxer shorts because the Chinese gentleman I spoke with fired me and I don't handle adversity well naked. Who does? A person would have to maintain an almost egomaniacal self-image not to be affected when he's standing naked and sick with a clock hanging off his head while a short foreigner fires him from the scummiest job on earth. The man said he'd been waiting for an excuse to get rid of me. He said the kitchen crew refused to work any longer with a spook who argues with himself in funny voices and slow-motion fistfights the dishmachine. That was his exact word for me—spook. Maybe it means something different in Chinese.

Midway through the conversation, the green, stuffed thing unexpectedly came back up. I returned as soon as possible, but the phone line was dead. I found my boxers and put them on and sat, watching *Guiding Light* and feeling sorry for myself because I couldn't hold a job I didn't want anyway. I've never been good at doing things I don't want to do. Soon the room stopped lurching and I staggered downstairs to see if Ann could cut the alarm clock out of my hair.

———

My firing brought a quick end to the separate apartments debate before it even began. The Guaranteed Student Loan wouldn't pay off until school started in mid-September, two weeks after rent was due. Moving in with a woman out of economic distress is generally a major error, but, in this case, I probably would have taken the plunge anyway—eventually. Besides, there wasn't a whole lot of choice.

We boxed up the books, plants, TV, underwear, and posters of famous (dead) writers, carted the load downstairs, and stuffed it into two vacant baby beds. Ann was tickled pink.

"It was all on purpose, you know."

"What was on purpose?"

"I got you drunk and seduced you on your birthday just so you'd oversleep and lose your job and move in with Buggie and me."

"Seduce means to persuade somebody to do something they don't want to do. I've never been seduced in my life."

"Well, I did it on purpose anyway. I want you stuck with us forever."

I have to doubt that Ann got me drunk so she could get me fired. Ann was incapable of harboring an ulterior motive.

Before I lost the dishwashing job, I didn't realize the amazing amount of difference between living with a woman and staying with her every night. Bathroom privileges, for instance, or the fact that *Exercise with Jeanie* came on opposite *Andy Griffith*. Or dishes. Whenever I washed the dishes before my books moved downstairs, I was rewarded with deep appreciation and love. Suddenly I was *expected* to do my part. No more "Oh, Loren, you're so sweet, you don't have to clean up this mess." Instead, Tuesday, Thursday, and Saturday nights, and every other Sunday, she flopped on the couch with Buggie and said, "Your turn, pal." Same with laundry, trash, and dirty diapers.

Even worse, I lost my safety valve. When Buggie decided he hated everyone and everything, or when Ann played her Rod McKuen albums about the earth and the sky, or when I simply felt like being by myself for a while, I could no longer say, "See you later, honey," and go home. I considered taking up smoking so I could run out to the 7-Eleven once a day, but that idea seemed stupid even for me.

Another thing—a person who lives alone for many years tends to develop disgusting habits. Thoughtless nose probing, for example. Talking to myself at meals, leaving notebooks and socks wherever they drop, drinking straight from the milk carton, leaving the toilet seat up, scratching whenever and whatever itched. Overnight I had to start watching myself. I hate watching myself.

———

Another main difference between living alone and living with a woman and her child is that you're forced to pay attention to holidays. Holidays are a time set aside for feeling secure and smug, and they tend to be depressing if you aren't. Secure and smug. The year before Ann, my junior year at DU, I beat the holiday manics by reading *The Grapes of Wrath* clear through Thanksgiving weekend. Christmas—the biggie—I settled into bed with a family-size bag of Doritos and a notebook and spent the day listing 101 offbeat ways a person can get himself killed. Easter was easier. Good Friday I ate a half ounce of psychedelic cacti and dry-heaved from the Passion to the Resurrection.

But people with children actually look forward to the holiday season, at least they pretend to. They use holidays to mark the passage of time, bring out the cameras, record growth. Holidays become bribes: "No bubble blower now, maybe if you're a good boy Santa will bring you one," or deadlines: "If this kid isn't out of diapers by Labor Day I'll scream." When a couple gets old, they fondly look back on the Easter Dobie wet his pants in church or the summer vacation they packed four kids and two dogs into the station wagon and drove to Knott's Berry Farm.

I can't really say what it felt like or what I thought about on a day-to-day basis that first year. The routines are fuzzy, but each holiday is stored on tape somewhere in my cerebral cortex to be replayed whenever the nostalgia impulse overcomes common sense.

There's Halloween. I dressed up as Aunt Jemima, black face, boobs, the works. Buggie took one look and cried for three hours. Thanksgiving we ate fresh pineapple and trout a la Hemingway for breakfast, then drove down to Colorado Springs to visit Garden of the Gods Park. Buggie said a five-word sentence and that night Ann and I made love on the couch while *Casablanca* played on the Channel 11 holiday movie.

Buggie was still too young to understand Santa Claus theory—the strange fat man who brought free stuff in the night—but he liked to open boxes. Ann individually wrapped all kinds of stocking stuffers, and Christmas morning while we sat on the couch, warming our hands around mugs of hot coffee and rum, Buggie tore through package after package. Colored felt-tip pens, tiny race cars, bags of gummy bears, pop-up books, a pretend telephone that rang when you twisted the dial—Buggie pulled each one out of its colored paper, glanced at it a moment, then tossed the present toward us, the paper toward the tree, and moved on to another box.

"He'd be just as happy if I'd wrapped forty empty boxes," Ann said.

I leaned back, faked a yawn, and slid my arm around Ann. The feeling of family was almost spine-tingling. Why hadn't anyone ever told me what Christmas morning with a loving woman and a young child would be like? I'd have run off and married at fourteen.

Ann shifted into my arm. "I hope he likes the turtle." She'd spent weeks choosing between a stuffed giraffe and a cow, and, as the stores closed Christmas Eve, ditched both for a giant green turtle with half-closed eyelids and a striped baseball cap that I objected to on the grounds of unrealism. A turtle can't pull a baseball cap into its shell.

"I bet he loves it."

"You always bet he loves anything, Loren. Do you realize how important presents are at his age? That turtle could affect Buggie's whole life?"

My present for Buggie was a twelve-volume set of O. Henry short stories that I'd found at a yard sale across from campus. The plan was to read Buggie one story every night at bedtime— all 241 of them over and over—until he was old enough to read by himself. I thought an O. Henry story a night for several years would affect Buggie's later life more than a turtle with a baseball cap, but Ann had been so proud when she brought the turtle home from the Target Store that I didn't say what I thought.

Buggie's present-opening method was more or less unique to my experience. He didn't tear on the ends or seams. Instead, he clawed right at the middle of the package until he'd gouged a hole, then he ripped the wrapping paper into strips. The floor looked like refuse from a New York City ticker tape parade before he finally dug his way into the next-to-last box and pulled the turtle out by one of its ears. He sat back, staring at the turtle seriously.

"I didn't know turtles have ears," Ann said.

"I didn't know they have baseball caps."

"Eekle," Buggie said.

Ann laughed, warm and at home. "No, it's a turtle. Turtle like in the rabbit and turtle story."

Buggie looked over at us. "Eekle."

Ann set down her coffee mug and leaned forward. I could tell she was pleased with Buggie's reaction to the turtle. At least he hadn't thrown it into the pile and gone on to the next unwrapping job. "What should we name him?" she asked.

Buggie held the turtle to his chest, "Hawiet."

"Harriet," I said. "That's a girl's name. Why would you name a boy turtle a girl's name?"

"He can name her anything he likes."

"Hawiet."

While Buggie crawled toward the big O. Henry package, Ann took our cups to the kitchen for more coffee and rum. I watched Buggie drag Harriet around the big box, muttering to her or him, whatever the turtle was, in some language that runs between babies and stuffed animals. I couldn't help but wonder if my mom felt this together-with-a-spot-in-the-world glow on my second Christmas. Or Garret's. Or Patrick's. It seemed impossible not to feel worthwhile and loving under these conditions, but if Mom had felt something good then, I wondered what happened later. Could the same thing ever happen between Buggie and Ann that had happened between my mom and me? Or Ann and her dad? This was a depressing line of wondering. How could something so simple as a parent's love for a child get so complicated? The worst things in life are always the best things gone bad.

"Here," Ann said. She handed me a package.

"What's this?"

"Your present, silly."

"What is it?"

"Open it and find out." I daresay those five lines were being repeated in six million homes across America at that very instant. There's something nice about tradition. It doesn't have to be original.

I held off on my gift a few minutes, savoring the feeling. Besides, Buggie was on the edge of discovering literature. He tore straight through the top of the paper, completely unwrapping the box before lifting the top flap. Then he reached in and right-hand-threw the first book at the television. The second was left-handed into the tree. Once all the books lay scattered around on the floor, Buggie tipped the box sideways and crawled in. He sat in the box, holding Harriet by a flipper and looking out at us with those melting panda bear eyes. I could have cried from love.

Ann sighed. "Oh, look, don't you wish we had a camera."

I smiled because deep in my sock crib was a Kodak Pocket Instamatic I hadn't had time to wrap. "Maybe Santa will bring one next year," I said.

"Next year he'll be too big."

"For what?"

Ann's present to me was a pair of woollysock slippers with leather soles and a red monkey head on the front. While Ann looked proud, I kicked off my flip-flops and tried them on. They felt real comfortable and warm, but I wasn't completely happy about the monkey heads.

I hugged Ann. "Thanks, darlin'."

"Loren, this is the best Christmas of my life."

We kissed a long time until I started to get excited and slid a hand down to her breast. Ann had very sensitive breasts, I guess because she'd nursed Buggie for so long. I could almost always get her wet by touching her breasts.

"Maybe we ought to go back to bed while he plays with his toys," I murmured.

Before Ann could answer, Buggie took off up the Christmas tree. I heard a sound like a *pop* and opened my eyes in time to glimpse a shaking tree; then it fell, breaking bulbs, shorting out lights, knocking a philodendron into the turntable, crashing both to the floor. I jumped the end table and waded into the mess, knee-deep in branches, pine needles, and wrapping paper. I couldn't find Buggie. I couldn't hear Buggie. He should have been screaming his little head off, but, when I froze for a moment, I couldn't hear a thing.

Ann was on her knees beside me, digging through the branches, her eyes jittering around, all whites like a wild horse when it's scared. I jumped from the pile and lifted the whole tree up by the four-legged base. Buggie lay on his back, covered with needles, looking up at us with that expression on his face. That Buggie's-been-betrayed-again expression.

Ann scooped him up and hugged and cried and ran around the room until Buggie got the idea and started crying also. He looked okay to me, just a little surprised. I think Ann's carrying on affected him more than the fall. Ann circled the room three or four times, too worked up to settle in one spot. Finally she stopped and glared at me. "Don't you ever kiss me in front of Buggie again."

That seemed like an odd thing to say. "You think Buggie climbed the tree because we were kissing?"

"Why else? Every time I start to feel good, something bad happens. I'm not going to feel good anymore."

"Ann, that's not rational."

"Who says I'm supposed to be rational?"

All day, Ann concentrated on feeling as depressed as possible so nothing bad would happen to us. She didn't even perk up when I gave her the unwrapped camera. To watch her fussing around the apartment, roaming from place to place, yet never letting Buggie leave her sight, you'd think this wasn't Christmas and we weren't all together.

———

Maybe her "act the opposite of how you feel" logic worked because the day before New Year's Eve, something good happened. We found a two-bedroom duplex on the same block as Ann's day-care center. The duplex was blue with a big fenced-in backyard, a single garage, and a private patio next to a rock garden with some prickly plants that weren't dead. Ann and I talked in plurals about the duplex. *Our* bathroom. *Our* broken oven. *We* should find a set of chairs for *our* kitchen. For the first time, I didn't feel as if I was living in someone else's place.

Ann had been poor for so long, she'd become a real pro at secondhand-store shopping. Not that I hadn't been poor as long as Ann, it's just that I don't have standards when it comes to my surroundings. A foam rubber pad on the floor and a phone company cable spool were good enough for me. I never had the patience for the secondhand circuit.

Ann had plenty of patience for both of us. We made all the rounds; found a beautiful iron bed frame at the Salvation Army, an overstuffed rocker and love seat at the St. Vincent de Paul Store, a firm mattress and springs at a garage sale in Aurora, and best of all, two long chests of drawers with most of the paint and some of the knobs still like new. No more baby bed storage.

"We can get rid of the cribs now," I said, though I should have known better. No woman has fourteen places for babies to sleep unless she wants them.

Tears formed. "I like my cribs. Some of these have been with me since the Divine Light. Look, see this spot? Buggie knocked a tooth out right there, and Joyce gave me that one on Thamu Kamala's third birthday. Jesse swallowed a peach pit and almost died in that one. I saved him. How could I throw out the crib Jesse was in when I saved his life?"

"We don't need them anymore."

"We don't need your desk either."

Ann and I compromised. We carried all the various bits of baby paraphernalia out to the garage except for three especially meaningful pieces. I had a hell of a time getting them all in, had to pile the frames and little mattresses two deep, baby beds on bottom, cribs, cradles, and bassinets on top. You'd think Ann was having her cat put to sleep. She said bye-bye to each piece.

"The beds will still be here when you need them."

"It's not the same, Loren."

I shut the garage door and, so far as I know, neither one of us saw those cribs again for four years.

She shouldn't have threatened my desk. It was a beautiful desk I found sitting next to a Goodwill Industries dumpster in the Cinderella City parking lot. Like to never fit it in the backseat of my car. My desk was a slightly larger version of the one I sat behind in the second grade—chair welded permanently to the desk legs, pen trough on the far side of the sloping top. The lid flapped open so if I wanted anything from inside, I had to clear the top and stack all my papers and typewriter on the floor.

I loved that desk. Loved typing at a fifteen-degree angle and doodling Charlie Brown pictures on the wood. For authenticity, I ruined a steak knife carving ᴎᴎA ꙅƎVOꙆ ᴎƎЯOꙆ and 8ᘓ' ꙅЯOIᴎƎꙅ on my chair, so when I typed a long time and stood up, you could read LOREN LOVES ANN and SENIORS '68 on my butt—if you could see my butt.

The desk didn't see much use that spring, though. I finished the Western in October, and by January, schoolwork had lost its charm. This was the last semester of my senior year and all my classes were required subjects I'd been avoiding since high school. Geometry. Botany. Ethics. What does an English major need with ethics? Even my English classes bored me silly. "Jonathan Yardley's Place in the History of Literary Criticism" and "Major Colorado Poets." Like any writer, in fact like anybody I've ever met, including critics, I think the literary critic belongs in the same category as the blowfly. And Jonathan Yardley is to literary criticism what belladonna is to the dry mouth. As to "Major Colorado Poets," the quality drops off dramatically after Peter Pym, the Western Shakespeare.

My New Year's resolution was to survive the semester and graduate. Within a couple of weeks, I realized I'd set my sights too high and modified the goal to survival until Easter vacation.

By Lincoln's birthday it was survive until Friday afternoon. The ethics class was the worst. Ethics must be my tragic deficiency.

———

Spring break we drove across Idaho to visit Ernest Hemingway. Ann wanted to see Zion National Park, but I had something important to discuss and Hemingway was the closest dead writer of major magnitude. I promised her Zion in the summer, a false promise because events came up that summer and Ann never made it to Zion. I feel kind of bad about that.

The trip was a disappointment. Buggie caught the croup, or what Ann called croup, the cabin we rented came without hot water, the Chevelle threw a radiator hose, and, the real disappointment, Hemingway didn't provide any answers. The bum hardly provided any waves, just a few weak hisses, more like swamp gas than immortality. I've always suspected that macho woman-bull-lion-killer act hid a shallow personality. Maybe his heroes showed no emotions because Hemingway had none himself. I don't see any use in admiring a person without emotions.

Almost a foot of slushy snow covered the grave, but that's no excuse. If emanations can pierce the coffin and six feet of dirt, snow should be child's play. A dead greeting card designer could vibe through a foot of snow. It may be that Hemingway used up his creativity in life—I can respect that. What good does creativity do a dead man? Still, you'd think something would be left, a few inventive ashes or something. Of course, I'm not Hemingway's type. It could be that way down in the ground, he sensed an antihero overhead, a wimp who likes women and thinks bullfights and wars are silly, and he decided not to emit while I was in the vicinity. Figures the self-idolizer would turn into a snobby corpse.

Still, I was disappointed. I loved my family, they made being alive mean something, but we'd been together a year and that first rush of mattering was slacking off a bit. With graduation looming in the near future, I needed some reassurance that life was more than a personal adventure. I'd decided happiness meant a lot, but I wanted something else—something bigger than love between two mortal people.

Hemingway never was big on reassurance in his life and writing. I guess I was asking too much to expect it from him after his death.

# *10*

BUGGIE AND I LAY ON THE FLOOR, COLORING A BULLWINKLE coloring book, watching *The Life and Times of Grizzly Adams.* On the show, a mountain lion protected a French domestic rabbit because it was pregnant. I'm not sure what the mountain lion protected the rabbit from.

"Mine," said Buggie, taking my crayon.

"Okay," I said. Neither one of us colored inside the lines very well, but I did better than the Bug. Ann sat on the couch, sewing patches in my new jeans. Neil Young wore patches on his jeans, so I wanted some on mine.

"Why does the rabbit have such huge ears?" Ann asked.

"It's French," I said. "See, the guy in the balloon is French, so the rabbit must be French too."

"What is a French guy in a balloon doing in the mountains?"

"They didn't explain that."

Buggie reached his hand toward a grizzly bear whose name was Ben, or, a least, the people on the show called him Ben. Buggie made clutching movements with his little fist and said, "My bet."

"It's a bear, Buggie. Bears don't make good pets."

"My bet."

Ann spoke through a needle between her teeth. "Friday

was pet day at the day care. All the big kids brought animals. You should have seen Heather's pet lima bean plant. She had a ribbon tied through its leaves."

Buggie looked at Ann. "Bet."

"Maybe we should buy him a dog," I said. "A beagle, beagles handle kid abuse well. They'll put up with anything and not bite."

"I'd rather have a cat."

"Cats don't like children." This rapidly deteriorated into a stock cats versus dogs discussion with neither side offering an opinion less than five hundred years old. Most family debates could be recorded by actors and actresses, sold in stores, and played in the tape deck whenever a disagreement occurs. That way the debaters wouldn't have to actually participate and could use their time watching television.

Buggie decided to ignore us and go back to coloring Bullwinkle. He grabbed my new crayon. "Mine."

"Hey, I get this one. You've got enough."

"Mine."

Ann leaned down and took my crayon. "Let him color, Loren," she said, handing the crayon to Buggie.

That left me with white. Who can color a white page with a white Crayola? "Look, Buggie. Don't color the sky blue. Try green or red."

"Why shouldn't he color the sky blue? The sky is blue."

I stole the blue crayon and Buggie started to cry. "Someone will see the drawing and think we made him color the sky blue."

"So?"

"They'll think we're overstructuring Buggie's education. Forcing him to deal with reality."

"Give him the crayon, Loren."

"But—"

"The pictures all end up in the trash anyway. Who's to see we have a structured kid?"

Little did Ann know I stashed all Buggies's drawings in my file box behind the unsold Western, four short stories, and my brand-new, probably never-to-be-used college diploma. I saved hundreds of Buggie's childhood scrawlings for posterity.

The phone rang and Ann and I looked at each other, waiting to see if the other one would get up to answer it. I won. Ann set her sewing on the end of the couch, out of Buggie's and my reach, and went into the kitchen. I gave Buggie back the blue crayon so he'd stop crying and I could listen in on the call.

Ann didn't talk long, in fact, she talked hardly at all; mostly she listened. Twice I heard, "Don't you want to talk to him?" and once, "When are you planning to do that?"

Buggie colored the sky blue and I colored Bullwinkle's feet white. On the TV, a tame grizzly bear tracked down the rabbit while four humans stood in a semicircle and discussed the importance of individual expression. Something in Ann's tone on "Don't you want to talk to him?" gave me an intense goose pimply feeling, like the pattern of the last year was turning on its head and there was nothing I could do to stop it. I always feel the change right before it happens and I never try to stop it.

Ann came back in the living room, but she didn't sit down. I knew the goose pimply feeling was right because she held both hands together above her elbows. Ann's hands usually hung down, relaxed.

"That was your stepfather," she said.

"Don?"

"Is that your stepfather's name?"

"Yes."

Ann hesitated, "Your sister was killed last night."

I looked at Buggie. He sat, watching Ann and chewing on the crayon.

Ann continued: "In Houston, in some kind of a race riot. He wasn't sure of the details, but I guess a policeman accidentally shot her."

"Her name is Kathy."

"That's what your stepfather said."

"Why didn't he tell me himself?"

"He didn't say."

Ann came back to the couch and sat where she could touch my shoulders. I reached over and took the crayon out of Buggie's mouth. "Your tongue's blue," I said.

"Mine," Buggie answered.

We sat awhile, no one doing anything. *Grizzly Adams* came to a happy conclusion, the rabbit had her babies. A commercial about a mother and daughter with equally soft hands took its place.

"The funeral is Wednesday morning," Ann said. "Your stepfather didn't think you'd want to go."

"I'd like to be there."

She looked at me closely, "Do you want me to come?"

I met Ann's eyes and made a decision. "We'll get married in Texas."

"Married?"

"I mean, do you want to? I'd kind of like to get married..."

Buggie got up and walked across the coloring book and stood between Ann's legs, balancing himself by holding onto my hair.

"You want to go to your sister's funeral and, afterwards, marry me?"

"We could get married before the funeral."

"Why?" She picked up the Bug and sat him in her lap. He looked at me seriously.

"What?"

"Why now? You never mentioned marriage before. You never even mentioned having a sister before."

"Her name is Kathy."

"You said that." Ann waited, her mouth a line, her eyes looking directly in my face. I wanted badly to read the expression, but it was ridiculous to try. Better to keep talking.

"I suppose it's a matter of balance. Losing one next of kin means I should add another."

"That's an odd reason for getting married."

I touched her. "I love you and the Bug."

"Which do you love most?"

Buggie seemed to be following the conversation closely, his mouth set in the same line. I realized where he came by the famous Buggie look.

"Between you and Buggie?" Ann nodded. "That's not a fair question. You're one and the same to me."

"If Fred wasn't here, would you still love me?"

The question was so unthinkable that I hesitated too long. "Of course."

Ann nodded again. She stared at me a couple of minutes, then said, "I'll marry you anyway."

———

That night Buggie went climbing again. I was in the rocker, reading aloud to Buggie from a Flannery O'Connor short story book—the story about the guy who steals the ape suit so he can be somebody. Ann was washing the dishes, which may sound odd since it was my night, but I got out of the job on account of Kathy being dead. Aren't the consequences of an action amazing? The temperature rises to 110 in Houston, so some black kids break into a True Value Hardware to steal an air conditioner, the break-in escalates into a riot, and a Texas Ranger kills my sister, and because of all this, two days later, I get out of doing the dishes.

"You okay?" Ann asked from the kitchen.

"Did you know that when she was five years old, Flannery O'Connor taught a chicken to walk backwards?"

"I thought all chickens walk backwards."

"The Pathé News Agency filmed the trick and showed it as a short subject before movies all across America. Flannery was more famous then than when she died thirty-four years later as the greatest woman writer of all time."

Ann's voice came through the sound of running water. "Was Flannery O'Connor the greatest woman writer of all time?"

"Of course." I was all set to launch into the standard O'Connor-versus-everyone-else rap when Buggie chose that moment to scream, "*Medago*," and scamper up the living room drapes. He made about a foot and a half up the wall before the whole shebang fell on his head. Ann ran in from the kitchen, Buggie cried like his world was canceled, I stood around, hoping Ann wouldn't blame me and say Buggie climbed the drapes to get attention because she was washing dishes. Be just like her to swear off housework so as not to threaten the kid.

Ann's only comment was "Jeez Louise, Loren, keep an eye on him."

"I was reading, he went up in a flash."

Buggie quit howling and picked up the curtain rod. He swung it back over his head like a baseball bat, then forward until it pointed at my desk. *"Biggin,"* he said. He patiently watched the end of the rod awhile, then swung it again, making a *boosh* gurgly sound in the back of his mouth.

"Where'd he learn how to fish?" Ann asked.

"Is he fishing?"

"Didn't you hear him?"

Buggie looked at me seriously and said, "Biggin."

To quote Buggie phonetically, most of his sentences would read like *Igawdoepahrum*. No one except Ann and I understood a word he said, and I faked it much of the time. When Buggie cooed, "Burwazzahassie," I nodded and smiled and said things like "Is that so, then what happened?" I always figured Ann did the same, but now I don't know. Maybe she understood all those grunts and slurs.

I tied a four-foot length of curtain cord onto the end of the rod and Buggie went "biggin" all evening. The kid had a tremendous attention span. It's like he was born to obsession.

All the way to Texas, Buggie sat in his safety chair in back and fished over the front seat between Ann and me. About every five minutes, he hollered, "Biggin," and hit me in the right ear with the rod or cord. He never hit Ann, only me.

Buggie's technique caused our first real argument. He didn't reel in the line—just sat watching the rod for several minutes before pepping me in the ear on the backswing. North of Raton, New Mexico, I decided this was all wrong. Pulling onto the shoulder, I turned to face Buggie in the backseat.

"You're casting like a bait fisherman."

Ann was working a crossword puzzle and didn't understand why we stopped. "What?"

I took the rod from Buggie's hand. "Here, wave it back and forth. Pretend it's a floating, double-tapered line with a barbless size twelve Royal Humpy on a 4X leader. Two false casts, then let it down easy."

Considering we were in a '63 Chevelle, I showed pretty good form. "See," I said.

The Bug's lower lip shot out and his eyes watered.

"Give him the fishing pole," Ann said.

"We must establish proper habits," I said. "He's casting like a bait fisherman."

"What's wrong with that?"

"Only germs use worms. Now, Buggie, you try it." I handed the rod back to the kid. He howled and threw it on the floor.

Ann blamed me, of course. "Jesus." She twisted around

and reached over the backseat floor. "Look what you've done, Loren. He was perfectly fine. Do you know how hard it is to keep a two-year-old perfectly fine on a long trip?"

Buggie howled louder.

"My brother will be at the funeral. Do you want him to think I'm raising a worm watcher?"

"I don't give a shit what he thinks." Ann pulled up the rod and stuck it in Buggie's hands. He stuck out his lower lip, then threw the rod back on the floor.

"You don't care?" Ann hardly ever said *shit,* so when she did, the word carried a lot of power.

Ann turned from Buggie to look at me. "Oh, Loren, of course I want your brother to like us, but if he bases his like or dislike on how Buggie swings a curtain rod, there's not much I can do."

Buggie suddenly stopped crying. He didn't sniffle twice or suck air or any of the regular signs of stopping crying. He went from full-blast screamer to quiet all in one instant.

"Okay," I said, "I won't make a big thing."

"You already did."

"Do you mind if we camp by a river tonight so I can show him a few casts? Is that all right?"

In mid-nod, Ann remembered something, "Brother? We're together over a year without you mentioning a sister, now there's a brother? How big is this family anyway?"

"Two brothers and a sister—well, she's dead, so I guess I shouldn't count her anymore. Also a mom and a stepdad." That made four left if I counted Don. "Garrett won't be at the funeral. He's in jail in Reidsville, Georgia."

Ann reached down on the backseat floor and retrieved the fishing pole again. "Why's that?" Buggie looked at the pole a moment, torn between his principles and his toys. The toy won; he took the curtain rod.

"He was in Vietnam and came back dependent. One week it's heroin, the next week Jesus, sometimes both at once. He got caught in a heroin phase and sent to prison for twelve years."

"Which side is he on now?"

"Jesus, last I heard, but that was awhile back."

As I turned to start the Chevelle, Buggie swung the rod side-armed and caught me full in the temple. "Digaloot—fishin,'" he said.

———

I didn't tell Ann the story of my other brother, Patrick. He's the oldest. Patrick enrolled in a special school to learn how to win friends and influence people. He used to stand on a chair and shout, "*I'm enthusiastic.*" Whenever he met someone he would repeat their name three times in conversation so he knew the names of everyone he knew.

Patrick met a girl from El Paso named Libby. The weekend Patrick and Libby announced their engagement, they went water-skiing on Lake Texhoma and Libby skied into a big ball of water moccasins. While Patrick watched, the snakes wrapped around her arms and legs and life preserver and killed her.

When I left Victoria, Patrick was selling real estate for a company that was draining a swamp where the last whooping cranes on earth used to lay their eggs. He drank often and watched professional sports on TV. He never stood on a chair, shouting, "*I'm enthusiastic,*" anymore.

———

Ann and I were married by a justice of the peace in Borger, Texas, on August 5, 1976. The JP's face looked like an aerial photograph of a Panhandle dirt farm. His wife, the witness, had hair the color and texture of a brand new S.O.S. pad. She pronounced Ann with two syllables and Loren with one.

Before the ceremony, she licked a Tennessee Ernie Ford spiritual album clean, set it on pearl-colored monaural record player, and played "The Old Rugged Cross." I liked the sound.

Ann wore a white blouse and new jeans and carried Buggie on her right hip. Buggie wore Pampers. He carried his fishing pole in both hands, casting it occasionally at the JP. I forget what I wore, probably whatever I had on when we pulled into town. My lip was all swollen from a giant canker sore that Ann said broke out because I wasn't releasing the pain of Kathy's death.

"Stop internalizing," she said. "Let the emotion flow. Holding back only causes ulcers and strokes."

"I can't decide what emotion I feel."

"Pick one and let it out."

I picked anger and let it out by shaking my fist at the back of the first Texas Ranger who drove past, but the canker sore only spread.

The judge acted as if I was peculiar because I didn't have a ring to give Ann. Ann didn't seem to mind. She smiled and cheek-kissed the judge and his wife after the ceremony. Ann's lips came away from the woman's cheek light blue and dusted with something chalky.

We honeymooned outside Borger on brown Lake Meredith so Buggie could throw his cord in the water and I could visit the Texas Panhandle Pueblo Culture National Monument. I wanted to see what kind of waves emitted from people who had been dead several thousand years. None of those Pueblos must have been creative writers because I didn't feel a thing but hot.

They couldn't have been too awfully smart. Imagine being the first people around with the whole of North and South America to choose for a home and picking the Texas Panhandle. Just proves Aggies come from an ancient heritage.

———

I've only been married twice, but I think wedding night sex is about the best there is. Worth having a wedding for. I mean, on the wedding night, even though the couple has lived together for years, the partners should feel especially pleasant toward one another.

It may not surprise the rest of the world, but it did me. Sex is a good deal better when the partners feel pleasant toward one another.

I'm almost certain Ann loved me that day. She wasn't blind in love or anything, Ann knew my faults, but she did marry me and I did marry her. Considering the aftereffects, the fact that Ann and I married on purpose should be stressed.

———

I swung the Chevelle into the driveway where I'd played basketball and Red Rover, Red Rover all those years ago. The yard looked the same—unwatered yellow. Someone had painted the garage, but the house was still the peeling off-white I remembered.

Ann turned the rearview mirror to herself. She'd spent the last hundred miles trying to make herself and Buggie look like they hadn't been stuck in a baking car for three days. "I failed," she said. "What do you think of a headband? Maybe a headband would hide the dirt."

"You look fine. When we get in there, keep Buggie from climbing anything. Mom's not too good with kids."

"You should of phoned from Borger. She might want to change sheets or plan menus or something. My mom about worked me to death when company was coming. I had to clean house and dig out the guest towels. Cook extra food. Jeez, I hated company."

"My family is different."

I wondered how different my family would prove to be. The last contact had ended on a misunderstanding. I forgot what brought on the misunderstanding, but I remembered we parted with sour feelings on both sides, so the upcoming reunion was causing some nervousness, which I hadn't mentioned to Ann. Reunions always contain the possibility of accusations, berations, and painful regrets, and this particular reunion contained more possibilities than most.

Barging in didn't seem right—I no longer lived there—so I rang the doorbell and stood in the heat, waiting. The thing I was most torn about was my hands. Should they be in my pockets or out ready to hug? What if I set myself up for a hug and no one offered? Footsteps sounded inside, moving toward the door.

"Let me have Buggie."

"What?"

I took him from Ann. "It'll look better if I'm holding him."

"Loren."

The door swung open on a short-haired woman with sturdy calves and a rayon print dress. I noticed her calves right away. "They moved and didn't tell me," I said.

"You're Loren, aren't you? I've seen pictures of you from way back. Of course, you're older now, but I recognize the glasses. Isn't it awful about Kathy?"

"Could we come in?"

Other than the strange woman, stepping into the living room was like breaking the wax on a time capsule. Maybe they kept everything exactly as it was the day I left as a memorial. Or so I wouldn't be disoriented if I returned in the night. Nothing had moved or aged—same ratty hooked rug, same nearly matching sofa and chairs, same pocked Motorola. There was the painting of Jesus done all in shades of brown. I spotted the hole I accidentally shot in Jesus' neck with a new .22 Don bought me on my sixteenth birthday.

"Look everyone," the short-haired woman announced. "It's Loren."

"Figures." Mom stood in her slip and electric curlers, ironing something black. A cigarette hung from lips that sagged more than I recalled, and her hair around the rollers was more silver-blond where it had been a deeper yellow-blond. "You always was more interested in dead family than live," she said.

"I'm glad to see you, Mama."

"Hey, Spunky." Don gave me a mock salute from the over-stuffed recliner in front of the Motorola. "Ain't it a shame."

His calling me Spunky was one of several reasons I couldn't stand my stepfather.

"Sure is." I took for granted, "Ain't it a shame," referred to Kathy, but he could have meant the game he was watching or the heat or something unrelated to anything I'd ever heard about. It is to Ann's everlasting credit that, after hearing Don, she never once called me Spunky. Not even in teasing.

"Look, Patrick, it's your brother." The woman must have figured Patrick needed more introduction than Mom or Don.

Patrick sat at the kitchen table, staring at me over a Macintosh Scotch bottle and a tinted Coca-Cola glass. He raised the glass as if to toast. "Kathy's dead," he said.

"That's why we came down." In my absence, Patrick's hair had fallen out except around the sides and his face had changed to gray.

Mom flipped an ash into a plastic ashtray on the ironing board. "He was nuts over dead animals. It got so the backyard stunk from all the armadillos and possums he buried out there. And birds, hundreds of stinking birds in his drawers and closet." I think she was talking to the strange woman, but Mom kept glancing at the ceiling as if she was talking to someone up there. "The police brought him home after they caught him in Grumbach's Funeral Parlor, touching the bodies. Millie Grumbach thought he was disgusting."

"Aw, Mom, I was just a kid."

"You better not touch Kathy today. I got friends coming from the bar. I won't have you pawing your dead sister."

The hostility confused me. I don't know how I expected Mom to behave, but this wasn't it. I touched Ann's shoulder. "Folks, I'd like you to meet my wife, Ann, and this is our son, Buggie...Fred."

Caught them off guard with that one. They'd been all worked into an attitude and now they had to adjust. Mom stubbed out her cigarette, eyeing Buggie. Patrick more like leered at Ann. Don kept his eyes on the game, but he must have been paying attention. The Cubs led the Mets nine to two, and that couldn't have been as interesting as the long-lost son appearing with wife and child.

"What a beautiful baby," Mom said. "Is he legitimate?"

"Was I?"

*All right.* Get those hostilities out where everyone can see. To hell with polite conversation in suburbia. Buggie squirmed in my arms. A cat sauntered in from the direction of my old room. He sat in the doorway and yawned, watching. Somewhere in the back of the house, a washing machine went into an off-balance spin cycle.

"I'm real pleased to meet you, Mrs. Paul," Ann said. "Loren's told me all about you."

Patrick spoke. "How long have you and my brother been married?"

"Since yesterday." Ann reached over like she wanted Buggie, but I pretended not to see.

Patrick drained his glass and clicked it down with some finality. "You're in it now."

"What do you mean by that?" I asked.

The cat turned and walked back toward my old room.

"Guess he didn't mention my name," Mom said, lighting another cigarette. Ann forcibly removed Buggie from my arms. I didn't mind. The moment for a spontaneous hug was past.

"Name's Mrs. Buttercott. Deela Buttercott. I've been Mrs. Buttercott fifteen years, but he ain't heard yet."

Driving down from Colorado, I'd daydreamed a number of possible receptions and how I would graciously handle each. I would comfort the grief-stricken, bolster the bewildered and lost, show humility if praised for my collegiate degree or the taste displayed by my marriage. But I hadn't made any plans based on festered resentments. In spite of Kathy's funeral, I'd hoped for a cheerful welcome.

There's a short story in the Bible, I think Jesus wrote it, about a prodigal son who comes home after more or less going off to college and blowing his daddy's trust fund on women and whiskey and never writing or calling collect on Mother's Day, never so much as a Christmas card. If he was anything like me, he used his mom's self-addressed, stamped envelopes to store marijuana. The money runs out, the kid comes home, and his dad goes apeshit with joy. Buys him all new clothes, throws a king-hell of a party, kills the fatted calf. The kid's brother resents all this, understandably, because he stayed home and didn't get any whiskey or women and the dad never gave a hoot one way or another.

I had hoped for something along the lines of the Bible story. Not the new clothes or the king-hell party—after all, we were gathering for a funeral—but "Gee, it's good to see you," or "You've stayed away too long, son," would have been nice. My sister was dead. In any normal family, that alone would have been cause for forgiveness and drawing together. My old mama, though, she didn't draw together for anybody.

The short-haired woman came over and shook Ann's hand. "I'm Jennifer, I'm married to him." She pointed at Patrick. "We've only been married a year, but we separated last month because he's an alcoholic. Don't you just hate alcoholics? The only thing in the world worse than being an alcoholic is being married to one. He talked me into coming back for a few days because Kathy got killed. Did you know Kathy?"

"No." Ann kept glancing around, looking for a place to sit or run, I'm not sure which. Her pupils were so dilated that her eyes showed only black and white. She didn't seem to notice Buggie squirming. I guided her to the plastic divan and motioned her to sit.

"You okay?"

Ann nodded. I sat next to her. The plastic on the couch was light brown with dark brown splotches. I think it was supposed to look like cowhide.

"My own mother has ankylosis spondylitis," Jennifer continued. "She can't raise her head above her waist anymore, but you should talk to her. Mind sharp as a tack. She gets up and dresses herself every day. Isn't that remarkable?"

I couldn't understand why this woman was telling me about her mother. I held down one side of the room, Mom and Patrick the other, daring each other to draw first so we could open fire with old crimes neither forgotten nor forgiven—*She gave away my puppy; he tore up my second-grade art project; she married a man who calls me Spunky; he's ashamed of his family; my real love died and his didn't; ignorant, unsophisticated hick; ingrate*— unspoken bullets flew around the room, while, oblivious to the crossfire, this woman with fat legs talked about her mother who was shaped like a horseshoe.

"Is the boy hungry? Mrs. Howell from next door brought over a bucket of chicken and some coleslaw and chocolate cake. The cake's Winn-Dixie, but the coleslaw tastes homemade.

Your baby must be hungry after the ride. Long drives are so hard on children."

"No thanks," I answered.

"Thank you for offering," Ann said.

"Just trying to be polite."

"We appreciate it."

Jennifer sat on the couch next to Ann, and for some reason, took her hand. "Kathy was such a pretty girl. So nice. She was a twirler in junior high, you know."

"I didn't know."

"The last few years she got a little wild sometimes, and she was always woozy on drugs, but I know for a fact Kathy never used a needle. She used to say to me, 'Jenny,' she called me Jenny even though no one else does. 'Jenny, I love being hammered, but I'll never use a needle. Needles are going too far.' I think she would have grown out of drugs eventually. She was a good girl, deep inside. It was those boys got her to do it. Kathy just wanted to be popular. She'd have grown out of it, wouldn't she, Patrick?"

Patrick's look was nasty. "How the hell should I know. She's dead."

Something shifted and Mom, Patrick, and I turned our attention to Jennifer. My theory on what happened is that all the disarrayed anger and bitterness flying around the room united into one blazing, pure column of hatred aimed at this brainless outsider who had the *gall* to explain Kathy to us. Her own family.

"When the riots started, Kathy and her little friends drove over to Houston. They said they wanted to watch the cops and niggers shoot each other, but what they really wanted was to loot drugstores."

"Shut up." Patrick spit.

I threw in my opinion. "Oh, yeah?"

But Mama was the one to let the emotions flow. No internalizing-caused canker sore for Mama. At least, not on her lips. "To hell with you, Jennifer. Kathy didn't take drugs and she wasn't no tramp. They killed her coming out of Woolworth's with five Barbie dolls and two Kens. Kathy loved Barbie and Ken."

"Why, Deela, I never said Kathy was a tramp. You know how much Kathy and I cared for each other. We were like sisters."

"Same as Loren and I are like brothers," Patrick said, which I thought was a cheap shot.

Mom pointed the iron at Jennifer like an outstretched pistol.

"You always thought Kathy was a whore and a heroin addict and you hate your husband. What are you doing here?"

Jennifer paled. "I came to help you. In times of grief we must forget past differences and support each other."

"*Bullshit.*" The iron sailed past Patrick and out the kitchen window. Glass sprayed the sink and windowsill. Mom shouted over Buggie's surprised wail, "You think we're getting what we deserve and you came for a front-row seat, you bitch." Mom appeared ready to spring around the ironing board. "Maybe Kathy was a tramp, and I've got one boy in prison, Pat always drunk, and that son of a bitch who don't even write in four years, but my baby's dead and I'll be damned if I'll be a side-show for you."

The violence drained from Mom's face and tears came. She bent over so I could see the scalp furrows between her electric curlers. A tear clung to the bottom of her cigarette. Others dripped onto her black dress. She lifted one hand to her face and emitted a choked sort of sob.

I put my finger in Buggie's fist and rocked it up and down, watching him cry. Ann, too, concentrated on soothing Buggie. Jennifer sat straight, looking at the broken window and squeezing her left hand with her right. Patrick stared into his empty glass.

Twenty seconds passed. Maybe thirty. The volume of Mom's crying sank from anger to grief to despair to a sniffly lost kind of resignation. Don leaned over and turned up the sound on the ball game. Not looking at Mom, he said, "Quitcher bitchin', Deela. Bad things happen to ever'body. You're not special."

————

High-school funerals always play to a full house. This is because so few teenagers believe in death, and when one of their kind jams the fact home, they stream toward the body, drawn by the irresistibility of all repulsive objects.

The Victoria Bible Baptist Church was packing them in. All young, all stunned. Except for those strange men who make a profession of funerals, I didn't see a single grown-up outside the family pew. Twisting in my seat, I watched the young faces. A few wept, some showed anger and resentment, as if Kathy's death was a colossal gyp, but most wore the lost, lethargic looks of small children—say, a month old baby. Their egos had not yet deflected the truth, and in that short gap of vulnerability, they seemed almost human.

Buggie pushed a truck along the pew between Ann and me. Patrick and Jennifer sat between us and Mom, with Don on the inside aisle. Mom was through crying. Her eyes stayed away from Kathy, seeming to focus on a chart plotting the figures for last week's Sunday school attendance—DOWN FOUR. Her crossed hands never moved.

Kathy's death affected me a good deal more than her life had. I hardly remembered her life. She was thirteen when I last knew her. She wore a pink cashmere sweater with Kinney Casual tennis shoes and she talked on the phone. She hated cheese in any form. I can't recall her voice.

The people who coordinate these functions had placed a rose across Kathy's breast. I hadn't seen her breasts before. They looked cosmetic. Her neck was longer and her cheekbones higher than I recalled. She'd grown her hair out to where it swept across the side of her face and over her shoulders. This dead Kathy wasn't old enough to legally vote, drink, or make love. She'd never been out of South Texas. I wondered if the Ranger who killed her felt any regret.

The preacher was younger than me. Tanned, self-assured, he stood up there like a golf pro—a fourth-generation country club sophisticate. He prayed awhile, then he compared Kathy's life to the flight of an arrow. *"It's not how far you fly, it's how straight."* I felt like saying "crap," but everyone else seemed to buy the Kathy-as-straight-arrow metaphor, who was I to push for realism?

I should face something here. Ever since I boxed up a squashed mole for Show 'n' Tell in the first grade, I've been a pseudodeath obsessive. I think about death, talk about death, write about death, play little games with it. I figure flow charts on the possibilities of heaven, reincarnation, transmigration, the void; does the spirit inhabit rocks? Are snow crystals unborn babies? However, in spite of a daily diet of the stuff, I have no idea what really happens when people disappear. I'm an expert without an opinion. Religious and antireligious beliefs all strike me as bizarre.

The one image of death I hold to came from a *Twilight Zone* I saw years ago. I must have been very young; I remember watching the show in my rocking horse jammies and my brother Garret spilling a purple Fizzies drink on the rug. *The Twilight Zone* was about an old woman who was frightened of death and would never open her door for fear it would get her. Robert Redford played a charming young man who tricks his way into her apartment, convinces her that death is neat, and leads the old lady away into a fog bank. Ever since, I've pictured dying as being led into a fog bank by Robert

Redford. According to my odds chart, this has the same degree of possibility as heaven.

The element I hadn't expected from Kathy was the wash of creative energy. Rose-colored, smoky waves flowed from the casket, pressing me into the wood of the pew. Trapped in her dead body was all the creativity of another Emily Dickinson or Tennessee Williams. Or Agatha Christie. Exploding potential... I couldn't understand how that much potential could go unrealized. I mean, I understood how—a hollow-point bullet through the spine—but why? Nature, God, blind chance, Whoever is so thriftless. Sitting next to Buggie, I thought, *If someone is in charge of this world, He, She, or It doesn't know His, Her, or Its ass from a hole in the dirt.*

Ann touched my hand. "Don't think that."

Had I spoken? Or was Ann's intuition getting out of control?

"It's time to go," she said.

"What?"

"We have to leave first. Get Buggie's truck."

———

"Didn't Mom say people from her bar would be there? I didn't see anyone old enough to work in a bar."

"There was an old guy sitting back by himself. That one." Ann pointed out a small brown man coming through the church door. He walked slowly, like something was the matter with his legs, and a number of teenagers shuffled behind him, trying to get around and out into the sun.

"He looks like a teacher or school janitor," I said. "He doesn't move like someone who works in a bar." Ann, Buggie, and I waited in the unstarted Chevelle, watching Kathy's friends and classmates. I balanced my hands on the steering wheel while Ann twisted around to strap Buggie into his safety seat.

"There, all cozy and secure like a good little Bug," she

cooed. Ann settled back into the front seat. "That was kind of sad. Your sister was very pretty."

"I can't believe this heat. How can people live here?"

"Was Texas always this hot when you were growing up?"

"In August. Did you hear that minister, 'how straight the arrow flies'? I almost got up and said something."

"What?"

"I don't know, something."

Two girls Kathy's age walked past the Chevelle and got into a Datsun 240Z. One of the girls was very tall and skinny and when she smiled her mouth glittered from braces. As the door shut, I heard laughter. The effects of death were already wearing off.

"We're supposed to pull in line after Patrick," Ann said. "I hope he can drive."

"Jennifer's behind the wheel." I looked at my hands. "God, it's hot." Carloads of Texans swept by on the avenue to our left. Across the street, people moved in and out of a Burger King next to a bowling alley. There wasn't a dog or bird or cat in sight. In front of the church, one scrawny juniper hung on in a circle of dirt surrounded by concrete sidewalk.

Ann looked out her side window. "We had a storm at Mama's funeral. A creek rose and flooded the cemetery, filled up her hole so they had to bring out a sump pump before they buried her. Dad fried a salmon for supper. I rolled up some hush puppies. Larry kept asking when Mama'd be home."

"Who's Larry?"

"My littlest brother. He was only eight and someone told him Mama went to heaven but he'd see her again real soon. I thought Dad would sock him if he didn't shut up, but he kept asking and asking, wouldn't let it go."

The hearse pulled out slowly, followed by Mom and Don, then Jennifer and Patrick. "We're next," Ann said.

I looked across the street, thinking about William Faulkner. A little boy coming from the Burger King dropped a white sack and his mother swatted him on the rear. A man in a Buick LeSabre pulled up to the drive-away window. What would William Faulkner make of this, I wondered. That death and Burger King coexist?

Buggie gurgled, "Foonral."

"They're going without us," Ann said.

"Would you mind if we skipped the cemetery?"

"Go straight back to your mom's?"

"Let's just sit here a minute."

Ann reached across and took my hand. That felt nice. I really loved Ann and Buggie. I tried to picture us in South Texas, driving down this busy street, pulling into the Burger King, wearing shorts and T-shirts ten months a year. I could see Texas and I could see us, but the two pictures wouldn't come together. Those kids at the funeral hadn't looked like anyone I'd ever seen in Denver. Texas suddenly felt like the wrong place to be.

I pushed in the clutch. "Let's leave town," I said. "I don't really care to see the family again today."

"Where do you want to go?"

The engine kicked on with a rumble, then idled down to quiet. "This is no way to spend a honeymoon. Let's drive along the coast and up across Mississippi."

"Won't your mom be hurt?"

She had said one in prison, one drunk, and that son of a bitch. Why was I the son of a bitch? I had a college education and a wife and child. What more could she want?

"I don't see how I could hurt her any more than I already have. We're just starting life. I think we ought to stay away from my relatives awhile."

I made a U-turn, heading the opposite direction from

Kathy, Mom, and Patrick. Cracking the side vent, I leaned forward so my shirt wouldn't stick to the car seat. There comes a time, even when it's closest and most real, when you must say *Fuck death. This heavy crap is a bore,* and get on with your life. Even if life ends, it's still out there and has to be somehow handled.

"Why Mississippi?" Ann asked.

"I've never been there."

She smiled. "Which dead writer are we going to happen to be near?"

"No dead writers. I'd just like to see a swamp for a change. Don't you ever get tired of the Rockies?"

———

I told her at supper that night.

"William Faulkner."

"I knew we'd find a dead writer before the honeymoon ended."

"We're not going just to see Faulkner. He's along the way."

Ann laughed like I'd delighted her again. "That's why I love you, Loren. Only you would think Mississippi is along the way between Texas and Colorado."

"That's a typical thing to say."

Ann rolled clam linguini around her fork. "Have you ever read his books?"

"I started *Sound and the Fury* once. Faulkner was so creative most people don't know what he's talking about." We ate in a dark place with booths, just across the Louisiana line from Beaumont. I think it was called Neptune's Cavern. We stopped there because of an old RECOMMENDED BY DUNCAN HINES sign above the door.

"Do you know what he's talking about? Buggie, sit up. Loren, pull Buggie up before he falls." Buggie had managed to slide down between his booster seat and the table. Another six inches and he would drop, conking his head and causing a scene.

I pulled Buggie upright by his armpits. "I'll know after I see the grave." He held a cracker out over the carpet and mashed a fistful of cracker crumbs.

"How will you know?"

"He'll tell me." I tried to distract Buggie with a french fry, but he turned his head with a "Yish," and kept crumbling crackers onto the floor.

"The french fry has ketchup on it," Ann said. I knew that.

"Yish," Buggie said.

"He won't eat ketchup anymore." Buggie's picky food habits changed by the day. For six months once he lived on macaroni and cheese. Then he switched to a peanut butter and jelly period. Ann came around the table and knelt to brush Buggie's crumbs from the floor onto her paper napkin.

"You don't have to do that."

"It'll only take a second. He's making a mess." Buggie squeezed another cracker. Some of the crumbs floated into Ann's long hair.

I grabbed his hand, "Cool it, Bug. C'mon, Ann, the waitress has a special cracker tool—a crumb vacuum or something."

"She might get mad if she sees what we let him do."

"What do you care if the waitress gets mad? She's paid to put up with kids and we'll never see her again."

Ann looked up from her napkin of bread crumbs. "I just don't want to make anyone mad."

I shut up and ate my fried shrimp. Usually I prefer shrimp sautéed or boiled, but death in the family makes people do things a little differently. I couldn't get over Mom calling me a son of a bitch. What kind of an attitude is that? Son of a bitch. You'd think I grew up to be a hit man or something.

Back in her side of the booth, Ann folded the crumby napkin in a square and pressed it into the table next to a box of white and pink sugar packets. "Your mother was angry with you."

"No kidding."

"I wasn't comfortable around her. I mean, she broke a window and scared Buggie. My mother never broke a window."

"She was angry with everyone. It must be tough, losing a kid like that—even for my mother."

Ann knocked on the bottom of the table. "She seemed especially angry with you."

"I don't blame her. Look at the breading on this shrimp, must be a half inch thick. You wade through all this breading to find a tiny little shrimp under there."

Ann looked sympathetically at my shrimp. "I don't see how they get away with that." It was a small shrimp. "Here, have some linguini." She shoved her plate across the table. I shook my head, so she offered Buggie a bite. He held both hands over his mouth.

"Why didn't you write her all those years?" Ann asked.

"Are you saying I'm a bad person? 'Cause if you are, I can't disagree." Ann hardly ever criticized me. She didn't have the self-confidence.

"Of course not, Loren. You're a good person. Nobody is saying you're bad. I just wonder why you didn't stay in touch when you left home. I'd be hurt if Buggie treated me like you treated your mother."

I spit out a shrimp tail. For some reason I've always put the whole last bite of shrimp in my mouth and sucked on the tail, then spit it out. Like a cherry and a cherry pit. "I wanted to forget all that."

Buggie reached into Ann's linguini and pulled out a clam.

"Bet," he said.

Ann took the clam. "That's not a pet, Buggie, it's a clam."

Buggie let out a howl that made the other customers turn. I could see the looks—*child abusers. Baby beaters.* A kid turns into a pitiless blackmailer the second you take him out in public.

Ann gave in. "So keep the clam already." Buggie grasped it with both hands and smiled, which in Buggie was rare enough to make us both stop eating.

"Forget all what?" Ann asked.

How to explain? "She's a cocktail waitress in an oil-field bar," I started.

"Buggie, it's a shell. You can't keep it."

"She buys records and kitchen utensils from ads on TV. She eats frozen chicken potpies—the kind with no bottom crust. And white bread. She cuts coupons from the Sunday paper. All that Chiclet chewing." I shuddered. "None of Steinbeck's women chewed gum. No one in *Siddhartha* even went to the bathroom."

Ann was paying more attention to Buggie than to me. "It's dead, Buggie. Put it down." Buggie clutched the greasy clam to his heart.

"My bet."

Ann turned back to me. "You hate your mom for chewing gum and going to the bathroom?"

I wanted to explain something complex and Neptune's Cavern wasn't the time or place. "It's a matter of class. I was real short in high school. Didn't start growing until I was almost twenty."

"What's that got to do with Chiclets?"

"People treated me like a spook and I was miserable."

"Make Buggie put down the clam."

"I kind of like his pet." Buggie studied the clam closely, muttering sounds that I couldn't understand. "Nobody thought I was neat. Women ran from me for fear I'd get attached. Don only liked Patrick. Mom kept telling me I would always fail at everything. What's its name, Buggie?"

"Don't encourage him. Your mom didn't really tell you you would fail at everything."

"All pets have a name."

Buggie looked at me seriously. "Mary."

"Mary the clam. She's a good pet. Here, you eat her insides." I reached into Mary, fingered out her meat, and popped it in my mouth. She was a tad gritty. "Now she won't stink. You can keep a glass of salt water by the bed for her to sleep in at night."

"He can't keep a clam." Ann tried to look severe, but she could never really be too severe with either of us. Together we had her swamped.

Buggie didn't seem to mind or notice the loss of Mary's insides. He ran his finger around the fan contour of her shell and said, "Mary."

I ate another doughy shrimp and drank some red wine, thinking of my youth. I hardly ever think of my youth. "I started reading books," I said. "The writers treated me with respect I didn't get at home and the characters had a class I thought everyone except the people around me had. Book characters never curl their hair or use Kleenex. Books became real and real became something to ignore."

Ann's index finger rolled around her wineglass rim. "When Mom was sick, I used to pretend I was Nancy Drew. Nancy never had to change her mom's colostomy bag."

Buggie held the clam like a puppet and made the two halves move up and down like lips. "Hewo, will you play with me?" *Play* came out *pway,* which could have two meanings.

"Oh God," Ann sighed. "All we need now is an imaginary friend."

"I think it's great. Shows imagination and adaptability that he can find friendship in a shell."

"You still should write your mother."

Buggie held the clam over his glass of Sprite. "I'm firsty."

"Tell Mary what you did today," I said.

"Foonral."

# 11

FOR THE NEXT THREE YEARS, MARY WAS BUGGIE'S ONLY friend and companion. They talked together, played together, slept together. My glass of salt water by the bed didn't go over. Buggie said she would drown. He didn't seem to connect that Mary once lived undersea. After months of handling, she didn't even look like a clam anymore. The ridges wore flat and smooth and Buggie's grubby thumbprint appeared at the base of each half. I thought the imaginary pal obsession would peter out when Mary's hinges fell apart, but Buggie acted as if he didn't notice. He carried both halves in his pocket and slept with them under the pillow same as ever.

"He loves that clam more than me," Ann said.

"At least he's not lonely."

"But a clam."

Thinking of those three years is like thinking about a book I liked years ago, but haven't read since. I wasn't me. I was a comfortable minor character, eating, sleeping, walking from over here to over there. I stopped examining myself—which is very strange for me. I found a job cleaning bricks. The construction company I worked for would buy an old building and flatten it, then send my crew in with gloves and hammers and we'd knock all the chinking off the bricks and stack them in a truck. Most of the crew were college graduates who couldn't find jobs in their chosen field—English and sociology majors mostly. We used to discuss the whale symbolism in *Moby Dick* over our thermos bottles and plastic-wrapped sandwiches at lunch.

The best thing about a career in brick cleaning—at least in Denver—is every December the temperature drops so cold a brick shatters when you hammer it. That meant company layoffs and four months of collecting unemployment checks while I wrote Westerns. State employment commissions are the new art patrons of modern America.

In a blazing example of Unexplainable Shit, Berkley Publishing bought my first Western. I called it *Barney Runs Amok* and used Kelly Palamino as my pen name. I thought Palamino sounded like a cross between an Italian and a horse. They gave me five hundred dollars and twelve complimentary copies. I signed eight of the books and sent them to Victoria to Mom. One went to Ann's father.

Meanwhile, Ann kept the steady income flowing from her day-care job. She was very sober about her work, much more sober than I was about brick cleaning or writing. Ann thought she affected the futures of her kids. She was scared to death one would grow up to be a rapist or a suicide and it would be her fault.

Buggie grew like those crystals that explode when you drop them in water. He grew too fast. I liked him at three, I wanted him to stay three forever. Then I liked him at four, but he wouldn't stop there either. His face thinned as he aged, giving him that grown-up head on a child's body that was so popular in TV commercials back then. He demanded independence, wouldn't let Ann or me do anything for him. I remember mornings we all sat in a circle for forty-five minutes while Buggie struggled with his shoes. Just when I thought he had them on and tied, Buggie would decide the socks weren't perfect. He'd yank everything off and start all over.

Ann taught Buggie necessary stuff like colors and numbers, traffic signs, the seasons, the four food groups, but the more vital aspects of his education were in my hands. Every night after our romp, Buggie bathed and climbed into his jammies and sat on the edge of his bed with Mary perched on the night-stand, waiting for my reading of Important Works.

Being a parent is an amazing project—you're given this beautiful, fertile, empty mind and told to fill it up with any ideas you want. What power. What responsibility. No one cares if you're paranoid or racist or live in fantasyland, whatever you think matters is what you dump into this little person, where it germinates and flourishes. I chose to fill Buggie with the most noble thoughts from all the hundreds of generations who have searched for Truth. He would grow up to be the sum total of the human experience—a goal which I admit put a lot of weight on the little fellow's shoulders.

After one round of O. Henry, I spent a year on the classics—*Jason and the Argonauts*, *The Aeneid*, *The Odyssey*. I read him *Walden* and *Sand County Almanac* and *Bury My Heart at Wounded Knee*. He loved *Slaughterhouse Five*, though he claimed it made Mary cry. By kindergarten, Buggie had already heard every book Fitzgerald wrote. He was conversant with Bellow's *Adventures of Augie March*. He told his teacher he would laugh her out of the classroom if she pulled that Dick and Jane crap on him.

Which, of course, was ridiculous. By his fifth birthday, Buggie had stopped laughing. Stopped crying also. He didn't do anything emotional—never acted frustrated or craved hugs. He accepted what we gave him and asked for nothing else. I asked Ann if Buggie was abnormal.

"What do you mean, 'abnormal'?"

"You're around kids all day. Are they all as isolated as Buggie?"

"Fred is not isolated, he's shy."

"Shy is when you're afraid of people. Buggie ignores people. He ignores us."

Ann didn't like that. "Bull, Loren. He doesn't ignore me. Buggie's just better than the other kids. He's special."

"Then he's not normal."

"He's special."

We made weekend camping trips into the mountains above Boulder every summer. Winter nights we popped Jiffy Pop and played Candyland and Scrabble. The second year we installed cable TV. There was even talk of a microwave oven. What I'm trying to prove here is that I was once a regular guy. I didn't set out to wander crazed through the Wilderness, attempting to contact God. I once kept up with garbage pickup day and wrote down the mileage whenever I changed the oil in the car. For three years I behaved as I was expected to behave.

———

Then, one June morning when it was too pretty outside for me to clean bricks, the postman brought news that my second Western had sold. I kissed the mailbox. I ran around the yard, yee-hawing in my bathrobe until the neighbor's dog howled. The contract with its enclosed thousand-dollar check called for a significant gesture of celebration—a cake. Fireworks. Loud music and alcohol. It called for an entire day with nothing constructive attempted.

I spent most of the afternoon gathering materials, even missed my *Andy Griffith* rerun, but by 4:30 Ann's surprise was all set. I'd made a little flagpole out of three straws and taped the check to the top. This was stuck in a Safeway angel food cake and surrounded by sparklers. I peeled the outer seal on a bottle of cold duck and loosened the plastic top so one good thumb-push would pop it. Laura Nyro's "Dancin' in the Streets" circled round and round on the turntable, awaiting only my release of the tone arm to blast my secondhand speakers into pieces of crackling junk. The anticipation was so thick I had to drink a beer not to be overwhelmed.

Finally, Ann and Buggie bumped through the door and I hit it with the sparklers and Laura Nyro. The champagne bottle put up a struggle before it *banged* and foamed over onto the kitchen table, but the overall effect was one of good fortune. Ann acted properly impressed. She hugged me and admired the check and said the regular things about champagne bubbling up her nose. Only a writer's wife has to act happy when her husband earns a thousand dollars for three years' work. Buggie sat on the floor, pretending the plastic champagne top was a raft and the rug was an ocean. He swayed back and forth and made castaways-on-the-sea sounds.

"Let's spend the money quickly," I said.

"We could put a down payment on a car."

"I don't want a new car. I want to blow the thousand on extravagance. You and Buggie deserve some foolish fun for a change."

Ann sipped champagne from a tumbler with *Dukes of Hazzard* characters painted on the side. "We haven't had a real vacation since our honeymoon when you got in the argument with that dead writer."

"Faulkner."

"Yeah, Faulkner. We could take a vacation. God knows I need one."

"Okay, vacation time, where would you like to go?"

"Me? It's your book, Loren, you choose the place."

"Nope, I'm giving you a dream vacation…for a thousand dollars. Name the spot."

"I couldn't, Loren. You decide."

Selling the Western made me feel magnanimous. Ann hardly ever got to make a decision, this seemed like the time. Besides, I was pretty sure she'd choose Zion and that's where I wanted to go, only I wanted her to say it. I'd recently read an article about an environmental writer named Everet Reuss who walked into the desert in 1934 and didn't come back—yet. Someone claimed to have seen him around 1950, but it didn't seem possible he could have lived this long. The article said Everet was the subject of much speculation and mythmaking among desert lovers. If he was dead, I figured maybe I could find him from his emanations the way a horse smells out water. I might become well-known as a Western writer and mystery solver.

"Name the spot," I said. "This vacation is a present to you."

Ann smiled. "Wyoming."

"Wyoming? I thought you wanted to tour Zion and ride a mule down the Grand Canyon."

"Deserts are too hot in the summer. I saw a picture of the Tetons in *Cosmo* last month. It was in an article called 'Vacation-lands of the Stars.' John Travolta skied there last winter."

"Well, we better see the place John Travolta skied."

"You don't like Wyoming?"

"Sure, I like Wyoming. I just thought you wanted Zion."

"Would you rather see Zion, I really don't care. We could go to Zion if you'd rather."

"You chose Wyoming, we'll go to Wyoming."

"Are you sure you really want to?"

"I really want to. Buggie'll like Yellowstone. He's never seen a bear."

Ann smiled at Buggie on the floor. "Have you ever seen a bear?"

"Me? No, I haven't seen a bear either."

Buggie turned the champagne top on its side and made gurgling, sinking noises in his throat. He looked up at us and said, "Everbody drownded."

———

"All right, flip her there where the creek runs into the lake. The current will take it out a ways."

Buggie's face scrunched into a mask of concentration. He cast with all his might, hurtling the nymph into the dirt at his feet.

"Almost," I said. "Don't swing so hard this time and let go of the button a little sooner."

Wordlessly, Buggie reeled in. He planted both feet and swung the rod as hard as he could. The lure shot out a couple of feet and slapped down on the water like a flattened palm.

"Let the line out, let it out. Now, watch the bobber." Okay. I admit Buggie was fishing with a little weight and a bobber, which is bait fishing without bait. Maybe in those last three years I'd begun to compromise my strict moral standards, but, hell, Buggie was only five years old. He was too short to cast a fly line. And anyhow, the nymph was hand-tied from artificial materials. It was so tiny whoever tied it must have used a magnifying glass. Any pro will testify there's no shame in fishing with a nymph the size of a thumbnail.

"Gonna catcht a fish," Buggie said. His alert eyes never left the red bobber as it bobbed out into Jackson Lake. I settled onto the ground and leaned back into the warm bank, fairly bursting with pride. Here I was alive and saying the ancient words—"A man's calling is to provide sustenance for women, my son. Observe, learn the skills my father passed to me as his father passed them to him, the skills you shall pass on to your son." Lying there, watching the sun glitter on the Tetons, I felt like a bead in the necklace of history. A frame in the film of life. Hot damn for tradition.

Not that Don ever took me fishing.

"Keep the line tight," I said, "so you can set the hook if you get a bite." Buggie scowled, ignoring my advice.

I yawned and stretched, smug as a Siamese cat. An osprey

floated low over the perfect blue water. The mountains sprang from the far side of the lake as if they'd been washed clean last night and hung up to sparkle for my enjoyment. So far the vacation had been a tremendous success. More than I could have hoped for. The Chevelle was running like a champ. The weather couldn't have been improved by God Himself. We were camped in a place called Lizard Creek Campground, a spot so perfect you'd think Disney studios hired an exterior decorator to place the stones and trees. Best of all, with the responsibility of guiding kids to normalcy off Ann's shoulders, she was relaxed and happy. I loved to see Ann happy.

That morning, for the first time ever, she stayed in bed after I got up. She lay on her back with her arms thrown over her head, almost exposing her breasts, but not quite. It was the pose of a seductress. I leaned down and kissed her awake.

"You two fish," she murmured. "I feel like more sleep." Ann was my best friend and partner, but it had been a long time since I thought of her as a seductress. Maybe I never had. Instead of fishing with Buggie, I had a strong wish to crawl back into the sleeping bags and hold Ann and tell her she was beautiful.

"Have fun, take care of Buggie," she said in her near sleep.

"*Loren.*" I must have dozed off in the sun because Buggie was kicking my foot and saying, "Loren, Loren." He clutched the rod tight, holding it straight over his head. His face held a cross between excitement and fear that could only mean he had a fish. A couple of feet from the bank, the bobber moved down, then up, then back down again. With a jerk of the rod, it sank.

"You got one. Hell's bells, Buggie, set the hook. Reel him in slow, don't loosen the line, slow, nice and easy."

Buggie didn't reel at all. He turned and ran up the bank with the rod, dragging a little four-inch trout across the sand

and rocks, then over a sagebrush, finally bouncing him into a willow bush.

"You got him, Bug. You caught a fish. Gee, it's a beauty."

Buggie dropped his rod and crept down the bank, staring open-mouthed at his trout. The fish lay on its side, sucking air, the hook clear through its tongue. "It's a cutthroat," I said. "A nice one."

"Is it alive?"

"Won't be for long after that ride over the rocks."

"Should I name him?"

"God, no, Buggie. Never name anything you're going to eat."

Buggie's eyes grew big. I saw him swallow. "We're gonna eat him?"

The trout fit in my hand lengthwise, its eye turned up with an expression eerily like Buggie's betrayed look. "Of course we're going to eat it. That's why people fish. We don't kill animals just for fun."

"I don't want to kill it. Could we put it back?"

As if to answer his question, the trout's gills quivered and bled. It died. "Too late," I said. "Wave bye-bye to the trout spirit."

After waving bye-bye, Buggie stood next to me with a hand on my shoulder while I cleaned the fish. I slit the belly and ran my little finger through the cavity, flipping the heart, intestines, liver, and fluorescent pink floater bag into the lake. The fish was almost too small to slide onto the stringer.

"He in heaven?"

"Yep, the spirit rises through the sky to fish heaven. It's a place like this only with no people. Pretty soon he'll find a new mama and come back again."

"Will he still be a fish?"

"Probably, but if he was a good fish, he might come back as something better, a frog or a horny toad or something."

"Is he alive in heaven?"

"No, he's dead. He has to die so we can eat. But he'll be back again soon." I felt funny, laying reincarnation on the boy. To me, reincarnation shows more imagination than heaven or the Elysian fields, but it's still basic wishful thinking. At the time, I didn't believe in wishful thinking. However, the alternative was to have Buggie feel like a murderer. I had hoped to protect him from guilt until he was at least six or seven.

"I could have had oatmeal," Buggie said.

———

Buggie carried the trout as we walked up the trail through patches of lupine and Indian paintbrush. I could see he was mumbling something over and over to himself—or maybe to Mary in his pocket. From the anguished look on his face, I think Buggie was in conflict over whether to feel pride or shame in what he had done. All I heard in the general mutter was "dead fish" a couple of times.

When we reached the campground, three little boys from the pickup camper parked next to us ran up, demanding to see the trout, fingering him, poking at his gills. They were obviously so impressed at Buggie's catch that he decided to be proud. I mean, if people admire what you've done, you must have done good. Right?

"I catcht him all by myself," Buggie said. "Gonna eat him up."

Ann busied around the Coleman stove, making coffee and eggs and home fried potatoes. She looked sparkly clean and awake in her jeans and Denver University sweatshirt, her hair back in a pony tail. I winked at her, knowing she felt wicked for staying in bed after I got up.

"Buggie caught a whale."

"All by myself."

Ann set down her spatula and held the trout up to the light.

"All by yourself? Buggie, I'm so proud of you." Same tone as when I sold the Western and lit sparklers all over the angel food cake.

"I catcht him and Loren cut out his guts."

"Caught," I said. "Do you believe a kid who's heard *The Great Gatsby* start to finish and still says catcht?"

Ann kissed me under the ear. "If Buggie wants to say catcht, he can say catcht."

I held her close a moment. "Did anyone ever tell you that you smell just like a patch of Colorado columbines growing next to a bubbling mountain brook?"

Ann laughed, which was the purpose of the compliment. "Why, yes, a man at the gas station mentioned that just yesterday."

I nuzzled her neck, following a tendon down into her collarbone. "What say you and me discuss this privately?"

Ann pulled back in mock horror. "Didn't you get enough discussion last night?"

"I'll never get enough discussion."

"What about little ears?"

"We'll send him out to play in the forest."

"Can you cook him?" Buggie asked.

Ann broke off the hug. "Only if you men cut off the head. I don't do heads."

It's nice to be with someone you can nuzzle and say stupid nonsense to before breakfast. I've had long periods in my life when I couldn't. Or didn't. Sometime, even when I was married and doing fine, I'd start stewing about God or Truth or how to write meaningful shit—that's a lie, I can't blame higher purposes; it takes almost nothing to sidetrack me. I can get lost cleaning bricks. One day I'm blown away by the difference between happiness and misery, I'm appreciative as all hell, then a week later I read the newspaper at breakfast, watch *M\*A\*S\*H* reruns during supper, and answer interested questions with a pig grunt. I wander around in this daze until a last vacation or a spray of gravel in the chest from a woman making her exit wakes me up enough to figure out the obvious. But by then it can be too late.

———

Buggie's trout fried down to one midsized bite apiece. The grapefruit-pink meat would have been good if I'd deboned him properly. The bones were so tiny, though, they couldn't stick sideways in the throat or splinter through the stomach lining or anything else awful. We just chewed a little longer than usual. Buggie cut his bite into fourths. Bending over his plate, he picked at each section, extricating hairlike bones and wiping them off on his pants' leg. When he was satisfied with one quarter, he popped the meat into his mouth and moved on to the next piece.

Ann ate and hummed at the same time. The song she hummed was called "Sunshine Superman" and had been recorded by a boy named Donovan back in our younger days. "Sunshine Superman" was a sure sign of a good mood. A little footsie under the table gained me a playful kick in the knee.

"Stop that." Ann laughed.

"Stop what? Wasn't me, must have been a squirrel running up your leg."

"Let's go on a hike today, Loren. How about you, Bugger? Want to see a waterfall?"

Buggie looked up from his last tiny piece of fish. "How does the trout find a new mama if it's dead?"

"What have you been telling him?"

"He felt bad about killing the trout so I explained heaven and coming back."

"His spirit is in trout heaven, looking for a new mama. I wanted to name him, but Loren wouldn't let me."

Ann poked her eggs with a fork. Because of our flirting around, they'd fried up hard as silicone breast implants. "Loren did something right for a change. All Mary doesn't need is a fish sidekick."

"But how does the trout find a new mama?"

Ann looked at me. "You started this, you tell him."

"God assigns moms. It's like when you pick teams for a game."

"Oh." Buggie thought a minute. "Can I keep the head?"

"No," Ann said. "I don't think Buggie should hear strange religious theories. He's too young."

I dumped my cold coffee on the ground and went to the Coleman stove for a fresh cup. "Better now than when he's old and impressionable. I never met a religious fanatic or a cultie yet who was exposed to it as a child."

"How many culties besides me have you met?"

Buggie jumped from the picnic bench. "Can Mary and I go play with those kids? They have a dump truck."

"You want to play with other kids?"

"A wheel turns round and the back goes high and the dirt falls out. We're makin' a road."

"Okay, but if their mom says to go home you come straight back, hear?"

I waited until Ann started the dishes to make my move. Then I stole up behind her, circling my arms around her waist and pushing my belt buckle into the base of her spine. I kissed her earlobe. "You smell good this morning," I said. "God knows I tried, but I can't keep my hands off your body." With a practiced touch, I ran my fingers from her waist to the flesh beneath her breasts.

Ann shivered. "Loren, it's broad daylight. What will the neighbors think?"

"The neighbors can fuck each other, I'll take care of you."

"Loren."

I turned Ann around and kissed her. Soapy hands slid up the back of my neck.

"It's daytime, Loren."

"I didn't notice."

We kissed awhile longer with Ann whispering, "But, but," every few kisses and me whispering, "Of course we can." Soon, her body pressed harder against mine, her breathing deepened, and she stopped the "but, buts." Seduction always works when the woman is washing dishes. Hot, sudsy water must be an aphrodisiac.

"Where's Buggie?" she whispered.

I ran my fingers down the muscles of her back. "He's okay. He's next door loading a dump truck."

"That feels good. Touch there. Yeah, are you sure he'll be okay?"

"He's in kid heaven over there."

I took Ann's hand and led her to the tent. Before lifting the flap, we looked over at Buggie playing with three little boys on a mound of dirt beside a pair of lodgepole pines. Buggie leaned forward, smoothing the earth with a piece of bark.

"He's getting filthy," Ann said.

"He's fine. Buggie needs to play with other boys more."

"I hope he doesn't ruin his new tennis shoes."

The sex that last time was warm, slow, and emotional—no intricate positions, no intense thrashing about—just basic easy lovemaking. I kept my eyes open, watching the levels of passion flit across Ann's face. With my finger, I traced the lines across her forehead, the pink on the inside of her barely parted lips. I felt her breasts and stomach and legs against me. She concentrated on what she felt right then; her harmony with the immediate moment was so great, I felt a little saddened that I could never lose myself so completely as Ann. I remember the gasp she made when she came. And the softness in her eyes when she looked at me afterwards.

Later, Ann pulled a sleeping bag over us and we lay next to each other, watching the canvas roof breathe in the wind. She relaxed into the hollow between my shoulder and ribs. I draped her dark blond hair across my chest. "Where should we hike?"

She snuggled closer. "Somewhere flat for Buggie."

"Mountains aren't usually flat."

"How about around a lake?"

"Sounds good." It didn't matter to me where we hiked. I could have stayed in the tent all day.

Ann covered her mouth and yawned. "You think I should get Buggie's eyes checked?"

"Is he acting like he can't see?"

"Some guy from county health came around the day care last week. He said all kids should have their eyes checked before starting kindergarten."

"Did his father wear glasses?"

Ann looked up at me. "Jeez, I don't remember. I don't think so."

"You don't remember if he wore glasses or not?"

"It was a long time ago and I barely knew the guy. I don't notice things like glasses." Ann ran her fingernails across my stomach. She knew I liked that. "You want chicken or burritos for supper?"

"Doesn't matter much to me. Burritos sound good."

"Okay, burritos. We'll have to pick up salsa from the store at Signal Mountain." Ann felt along the edge of the tent until she found a towel. "You mind dragging the Bug away from the dump truck? I want to clean up some before we leave."

"Don't suppose you're ready for seconds?"

Ann laughed. "Once is enough before lunch."

No kids were playing on the dirt mound, but I went over to see their work. Little roads wound up and around, one road dead-ended on both ends and was lined with white stones. I figured that one to be Buggie's. The next-door neighbors sat inside their camper, eating breakfast, the parents on one side of the table, facing the redheaded boys who might have been triplets. They all looked the same age.

"Have you seen Buggie?"

The mother chewed and swallowed before she spoke. "Who?"

"The little boy who was helping build roads out here a while ago."

"Oh, him, he's cute. Doesn't smile much." She looked behind me toward the mound. "He was there when I called the boys in."

"How long ago was that?"

"Five minutes, he couldn't have gone far."

As I crossed back to our camp, Ann came through the tent flap, buttoning her shirt. "Got the Bug?"

"Can't find him. The kids he was playing with went in five minutes ago. Their mother said he was still digging when she saw him."

"Jeez, Loren, I knew this would happen if we fooled around. You don't think he heard us, do you?"

I checked under the picnic table where we'd stashed the fishing equipment. "Pole's still here, he didn't go fishing."

"Oh, hell, I hate it when I don't know where he is."

"Couldn't have wandered far. Maybe he climbed something. You look up in the trees, I'll walk down by the creek and the lake. That's the only direction where he could hurt himself."

This is all we need, I thought, walking back down through the campground and along the creek. Buggie probably heard us making love. He was too young to know what he was hearing, but he'd know it was something he was excluded from. Be just like the kid, hiding to punish us for having fun without him.

Every thirty feet or so I stopped to call. My main concern was to find him before Ann started worrying. Good moods in Ann were fragile. One hint of guilt and she'd mope the rest of vacation.

The trail ran downhill with purple lupine lining both sides. I hoped Buggie hadn't fallen in the creek. It certainly wasn't deep enough to drown anyone, but we'd have to dry him off and change his clothes and go through a long "Why did you go away alone?" speech. It'd be afternoon by the time we started the hike.

I stopped to look at a couple of Indian paintbrush. One was a brilliant red, almost an unnatural color. A shell lay pressed into the dirt at its base. I walked a couple of steps before it sunk in that the shell was out of place. On my knees, I dug the shell up and turned it over. Mary.

I tore through the lupine until I found her other half just off the trail. When I picked it up, the shell broke and the part with Buggie's thumbprint shook off my hand and into the creek. I leaned over the water, feeling among the rocks and mud. For a moment, one finger touched the shell, breaking it free of the bottom, tumbling it along in the current. I lunged into the creek and crawled downstream after Mary, but my hands and knees roiled up the streambed and I couldn't follow where she went.

I called, *"Buggie."*

I staggered out of the creek and ran to the lake. *"Buggie."*

I ran back to the paintbrush and searched the ground again, this time hunting for a footprint or a button or something. Anything. I called again, *"Buggie."*

And again.

# 12

I'D RATHER NOT TALK ABOUT THIS. EVERYONE KEPT SAYING, "logical explanation." The other campers, then the park rangers and county deputy-sheriffs. I was ready to scream the next time I heard, "Just you wait, he'll come back and there'll be a logical explanation." There was no logical explanation. Buggie went up in smoke. No amount of tragedy rehearsal even grazes the horror of a worst nightmare come true.

The police insinuated Buggie either ran away or was stolen by his grandparents. The reporters pushed us and demanded articulate answers. "Mrs. Paul, how does it feel when your son disappears?" Ann stared through them, not seeing or hearing. It was as if the rest of the world ceased to exist. While search parties pored over maps and divided up the area, Ann wandered randomly through the woods and along the shore, calling Buggie in a voice that was more prayer than beckoning.

We camped at Lizard Creek all summer until the snows came in November. I went over every inch of that area a hundred times. "He's not here," I said to Ann.

"I know he's still alive somewhere. Maybe if we go home he'll come back there."

Back in Denver we mailed posters to kindergartens, day-care centers, and grade schools. We handled leads and religious cranks and well-wishers. We cried. We hated ourselves. I stopped eating. Ann stopped sleeping. Every child on the street caused an emotional explosion.

Jesus, I'd rather not talk about this.

Ann and I both did what we had to do to survive each day. Remembering past insanities, I made an appointment at the county mental health center and found someone to talk to. Ann went back to Buggie's pediatrician for tranquilizers and sleeping pills. He was the only doctor she'd ever known. Ann told me once she used to take barbiturates, so I guess she was reverting to her past also.

Since I was supposed to be a writer, the therapist at county mental health suggested I try a form of grief therapy called implosion. It's when you dwell on the cause of your grief until you beat it to death. Then, according to the theory, you let it go. Implosion therapy is a little like cutting an arrowhead out of your chest with a sterilized Bowie knife. My Bowie knife was my typewriter. I started with the first time I saw Buggie and wrote down everything I could remember, every conversation, every look in his eyes, every morning wake-up and good-night kiss.

The book about Buggie became my obsession while Ann's obsession was Buggie himself. There's quite a bit of difference. While I re-created his speech patterns, Ann washed and ironed his shirts and baked brownies just in case he came back suddenly. Every day Ann expected Buggie to walk through the door, and every day he didn't, she withdrew a little further.

———

The second rainy October after Buggie disappeared I drove downtown to check out some photographs of a murdered boy at the police station. I didn't bother to tell Ann where I was going. We'd been through the emotional rip of identifying dead children so often by then—praying it's not Buggie because there's a chance he's still alive, knowing that if it is him the wait will be over, but a new grief just as bad will take its place. The rising gorge of guilt, hope, and fear as we slide the pictures from their manila envelopes, then relief and a sick drop in the stomach when it's not Buggie. The revulsion at our own emotions for being glad someone else's son is dead. Finally, nausea at the pictures of white, silent little boys that could have been Buggie. No wonder Ann needed more and more sleeping pills to close her eyes.

It wasn't Buggie this time either. I sat at a wide desk with a gray top, shuffling through photos of a little boy about four years old. Blond hair. He'd been found in the well of a farm outside Roanoke, Virginia. I could see the trachial membrane inside a gash that showed from one side of the jaw to the other. He couldn't have been in the well for long. The Winnie-the-Pooh Collection label was still readable on his T-shirt. He wore OshKosh shorts. His left hand had been cut off.

"No, this isn't Buggie," I said.

The lieutenant didn't look up from the papers he was reading, "Well, thanks for coming down. We'll just have to keep looking."

"Sure."

Later, I sat in the car and shook. A song called "Wasted Away Again in Margaritaville" played on the radio. I looked at the rain on the station steps and imagined Buggie's face on the body in the photograph, Buggie's neck slashed, Buggie's hand cut off. I imagined Buggie as dead and rotting. I screamed. Something had to change. I had to dump some pain even if it meant giving up hope. Even if it meant forgetting Buggie.

Driving home on the Interstate, I said, "He's not coming back," several times to see how it sounded. Could I believe it? "Buggie is dead." The words came out all scrambled, like

I was speaking backwards or something. They didn't relate to anything I knew about.

Two teenage girls from down the street stood on the wet sidewalk in front of our duplex, watching my garage. I waved as I pulled into the driveway, but they didn't wave back.

Smoke seeped from the crack under the garage door. I ran through the side entrance and found Ann pressed against the wall, her eyes gone animal. The smoke came from a great wad of white paper stuffed under the pile of baby beds, cradles, and bassinets. She had gone after the beds with my ax before setting the fire.

"Come on," I said, pulling Ann toward the door.

"I don't have to."

The open side door provided enough oxygen to burst the pile of beds into flames.

I pulled harder, yelling, "It's okay, let's go in the house and talk."

"Buggie knows every move you make."

I leaned down and picked up one of the papers she'd used to start the fire. It was page 148 of my *Disappearance* manuscript.

"Please come outside, Ann."

"Why?"

I forced her out into the air and shut the door. Together, we stumbled across the yard through the rain, stopping next to the Chevelle.

"Why?" I asked.

Ann looked at me. "I miss Fred."

We turned to watch the flames through the garage door windows. The fire was pretty, all oranges and pink, little lines creeping like cancer up the dry wall and under the rafters of the roof. The two teenage girls came over and stood near us.

One said, "Look at her go."

The other said, "Should we try to put it out?"

Through the window I saw the pile of broken beds and cradles collapse, sinking into the flames. Ann held her hand up at shoulder level, whispering, "Bye-bye."

———

Someone called the fire department and soon a group of men in yellow slickers and fire hats stood around watching the garage glow. They pulled out a hose to cool the side of the duplex next to the fire, but the rain did all the real work. After a while the firemen turned the hose off and loitered around the front yard with our neighbors and their children.

Ann sat on the street curb, her back to the garage. Her dirty blond hair reflected the fire. Once every revolution the blue firetruck light flashed on her face, showing her straight mouth and sunken eyes. I knelt at Ann's side and touched her shoulder. Her head turned and in the next flash I saw Buggie staring at me, accusing me, never forgiving me. Then the dark came, and when the light circled back, Buggie had been replaced by a mask.

———

Three months later while I was typing at the kitchen table, Ann sat on the edge of Buggie's bed and swallowed a large number of pills. She washed the pills down with apple juice. I was working on a scene in which he learned to ice skate and I needed to know what color to make his sweater. I went into the bedroom to search his drawers and found Ann dead on top of the blankets.

# Part Four

# *13*

Phone ringing. God, I hate phone ringing. Consciousness fought sleep for ten or twelve jolts, almost lost, then floated to the surface. I moaned and knocked the phone off the nightstand onto the floor. The ringing died; a tiny voice came from under the bed.

"Billy. Billy G. goddammit. I know you're in there. It's important, Billy. Answer the damn phone."

Billy? Some nuisances are easier dealt with than ignored. I slid half off the bed so my head hung down near the voice. Blood swept into my ears and the headache of a lifetime roared into the backs of my eyes.

"Huh?"

"Put Billy G Tanker on the phone. It's an emergency."

"No Billy here. I'm sleep." I moved to hang up.

"He must be in there. We all saw him go in."

"No Billy."

"Listen, lady, this isn't funny."

Twisting my head, I saw yellow translucent shapes swimming around an unfamiliar room. No Billy in sight. My tongue tasted like old tinfoil. My skin stunk. When I raised myself back to bed level, the yellow spots turned black.

Bedroom was wrong. Walls puke green instead of logs. No cats. Loren should be making coffee. Jesus, my crotch hurt.

A body next to me rolled over with its mouth open.

Self-revulsion tidal-waved through my chest. The broken vacuum, Loren's face when I hit him, the asphalt highway to Rock Springs, a marching storm, Mickey and Cassie on the phone, scotch, quarts of scotch—the bad dream was true.

I closed my eyes in hopes it would go away. "Jesus, what did I do this time?"

The voice on the phone begged, "Please, this is an emergency. Put Billy G on."

The body was still there when my eyes opened. It chewed and mumbled in its sleep. Must be Billy G. I wondered where I got him. Or why. He was kind of cute, in a cleft-chin sort of way, but what a baby face. He couldn't be young as he looked, my crotch hurt too much for that, but this Billy G was definitely a young one. Reminded me of a boyfriend Cassie or Connie had in the eighth grade. Son of a pawing psychoanalyst.

I shook the hairy arm draped over his forehead. "Are you Billy G?"

Both eyes popped open, staring at the ceiling. Green eyes, dazed green eyes.

"Phone's for you," I said.

"Phone?"

"Telephone."

Naked, I slid from the bed into the bathroom. There's no place like a bathroom for staring in the mirror and hating yourself in the morning. Weight on the palms of my hands, I leaned over the sink and looked at the slimy woman I'd turned into. Bruise-colored bags wilted under my eyes. Lines cracked from the edge of my mouth to saggy jawbones. My hair looked exhausted.

Yesterday, I lived in a cabin in the mountains, a cabin with a room all my own and a husband who knew what that meant. Today, I'm a hussy.

What would Loren think? What would Daddy think? I knew what Daddy would think. He'd tell Mama I finally reached my potential.

Not that this was the first time I'd ever woken up in the wicked woman position—motel room, dead bottle on the floor, hairy stranger in bed, awful odors. But it was the first time since that night in south Denver with Loren.

"You swore off meaningless one-nighters," I said to the mirror. "You left Loren yesterday," the mirror said back.

Hanging my head, I looked down at the dark drain, my hair draping onto the white porcelain of the sink.

Obviously, the situation called for one of two choices: I could wallow in self-hatred for days punishing myself with sugar suicide, or I could sit on the can, take my morning leak, and get on with life. Neither choice changed the past, so after-the-fact regrets seemed pretty much pointless. My eyes lifted back to stare at themselves in the mirror.

"Piss and get on with it."

I left the bathroom to a full moon shot of Billy G's backside. His voice came from under the bed. "Can't find my boot."

My jeans and shirt lay crumpled beneath a chair. Panties were nowhere in sight. "Your boot's on the TV."

Billy G pulled his pants on by hopping up and down on his right foot. "Thorne's gone crazy in the bar. He's screaming and shooting out windows."

"Who's shooting windows?"

"Thorne Axel. My boss, remember, I told you about him at dinner."

"Dinner?"

"He owns the Flying Fist. I've got to help him."

Vaguely, I recalled something about a hippie son and a cow-killer daughter. "He's the one who's been drunk for two days?"

"Three. Hurry it up, Lana Sue, we've got to save him."

We? I sat in the angular motel chair and shrugged on my shirt. A wild man shooting windows sounded like just the sort of thing I should avoid, another version of Daddy and Loren, but I've always been intrigued by men going off the deep end. It couldn't hurt to go down and add more male dramatics to my memory banks. At the very least, it put off for a while any decisions about returning to Loren or heading for Houston.

———

Shattered glass sparkled in the soft darkness of the bar, but it wasn't from shot-out windows because the bar didn't have windows. As Billy G and I stood in the entrance, a crack came from the far end of the room and a row of Cutty Sark bottles exploded over the bartender's head.

A voice boomed from the dark. "Out, slime. All you parasites stay the hell away from me."

A remarkably thin cowboy knelt behind the first table to our left. Another one had himself snaked in between the barstools and the bar. His hat had fallen off and rolled into the aisle.

"He cut himself, Billy, says he's gonna die and he'll shoot anyone tries to stop him." I recognized the skinny cowboy as the voice on the phone.

"We could rush him when he reloads," the hatless one said without conviction.

As my eyes grew accustomed to the dark I made out Thorne at the back table by the one-person bandstand. He was smoking a fat cigar that alternately lit bright and dimmed. For every one beat of the cigar, blood spurted twice in a high arc a couple feet over his outstretched left arm. The right hand moved from some kind of pistol to a bottle and back.

I turned to Billy G. "He's not too close to death. Look at that blood pressure."

Billy G had gone a cooked-lasagna-noodle color. "What happened?"

The hatless cowboy crammed against the bar wore silver spurs on filthy roach-killer boots and spoke in a natural whine common to men I generally can't stand. "We drank shots all night, then Thorne went crazy and run off with that forty-five of his'n. We come back he was bleedin' and wouldn't let no one near him."

I swung around to the bartender. He had three-inch sideburns and fuzzy hair that glimmered from his glass shower. "That bleedings got to be stopped or he'll hurt himself. You got any bar towels?"

The bartender blinked once like an owl.

I shouted at him. "Bar towels, you know, rags to wipe up the mess."

He looked down at the glass carpet. "You'll never clean up this mess."

"Jesus." I looked at Billy G, but he was just a boy. Probably never even seen any real blood. Neither had I—not cut artery type blood—but somebody had to move or the old man would drain and keel over dead.

I peeled off my shirt and walked into the bar.

Billy G came to life. "Lana Sue, you're naked."

I wasn't naked, but I was topless and that fact seemed to confuse Thorne. He pointed the pistol at my belly, then set the gun down long enough for a quick suck on the bottle, then pointed the pistol at my belly again.

"One more step and I'll blow your tits off."

"Bullshit." The key in a showdown is self-confidence. Make the other guy think you aren't scared silly. I walked right up, sat in the center of the blood spray, and pressed my shirt into the slash. He'd gone deep and made a mess out of the crook of his arm. On the table next to a half fifth of Ten High lay what looked like a set of brass knuckles with a razor blade on the back and a hook blade coming out the little finger side.

Thorne waved his gun at something behind me and growled, "Get back." Whoever had followed me got back. Thorne looked at my hands on his arm. "You're screwing up my death."

When I shifted, a pump of blood spray got me right up the chest and into my face and mouth. I spit blood on the bandstand.

"Come on, Thorne, you aren't committing suicide. This is a baby play for attention."

Thorne put the pistol barrel in his mouth.

"Oh God," I said, "please don't."

He took the pistol out again. "This isn't what I expected."

"Me either."

"Just my luck. I'm killing myself and a beautiful woman with her tits hanging out walks in and saves me. We'll have to get married now."

"I'm already married."

"So am I."

My shirt was pretty much blood soaked by then. I rewadded it, pulling both sleeves over the flow. "I think you should go to the hospital."

"No. That's my crew back there. They'll think I don't know how to kill myself."

I looked up at his face. The eyes were dark with heavy gray flecks, same as his hair and mustache. The skin showed rough brown and lined as if he'd spent his life outdoors. "Get through this as easily as possible," I said. "In a week you'll look back and be nothing but embarrassed."

Thorne didn't answer. Behind us I heard more and more people pushing through the door with *What happened? Who's that? Why's she half naked?* Without setting down the pistol, Thorne picked up the Ten High and swallowed.

"Mind if I have a poke at that bottle? My nerves are a little ragged this morning and you aren't helping any."

He glanced at me. "Suit yourself."

"I don't usually drink Ten High. There's less calories in scotch." I grabbed the bottle with my right hand and took a swig. My hand shook so the effect wasn't quite what I'd intended.

My intention was to come on decisive and tough. Not that I felt that way, I felt on the verge of vomit, but suicides are anything but decisive. They waver—*I want to die, I want to live, I'm confused*—so they'll generally follow any order they're given. I figured between my tough act and boobs, I'd shock the old man into cooperation.

Thorne kept his tired eyes and the pistol aimed at the crowd behind me. "My wife left," he said.

"I'm sorry."

"My kids are both spineless, useless brats."

"I have two daughters myself."

"Do they hate you?"

"One does. The other sleeps with my old boyfriend."

"Both my kids hate me. And my wife."

We each took another drink. I thought the blood might be clotting. Or he might be empty, the red stain had stopped spreading in my shirt. Way off, I heard a siren.

"You ever leave your husband?" Thorne asked.

"Yesterday."

"Janey and I were married twenty-six years. I worked my tail off to give her what she wanted. I'm rich, did you know that? I'm richer'n shit."

"Billy told me."

"Who's Billy?"

"Billy G, he works for you."

"Seven or eight Billys work for me."

The siren stopped out front. Thorne seemed to sag from exhaustion and lack of blood. "I wasted my life," he said.

"It's time to go to the hospital now."

He smiled. It was a tired smile, weak with the lips pressed together, the smile of an unhappy person who still maintained a sense of the silliness of desperation. "Tell you what. I won't kill myself if you'll sleep with me tonight."

"Nope."

"No?"

"No, I won't do it."

"You'd rather see me dead?:

"I'd rather see you alive, but I won't sleep with you. I don't save men."

He thought a minute. "What's your name?"

"Lana Sue Paul."

"Will you come to the hospital and talk to me? All I wanted was someone to talk to."

Why not? "Okay."

Thorne threw the gun over the bar, breaking some bottles and a mirror. Spectators moved in for the aftermath.

———

I won't be blackmailed into sex ever again.

Ron said I owed it to him because he married me when I was pregnant and the pressures of his career made him nervous.

Mickey said if I didn't screw him whenever he wanted, he'd just find someone who would.

Worst of all were those fake epileptic fits of Ace's. I'm still not completely sure they were fake. He claimed frustration triggered a chemical reaction in his medulla oblongata. Hell, I don't know.

Only Loren never demanded anything from me. He never threatened me with adultery. Never acted little boy hurt or put upon when I wasn't in the mood. Loren seemed to realize my personal happiness was not solely dependent on him. Factors other than a mate can cause depression or distraction. Why can't anyone else see that?

Maybe Loren wasn't so wise, maybe he was thinking about God or something and didn't notice me enough to get hurt. I don't like to think so.

One thing for certain. I don't sleep with anyone who holds suicide over my head as the if-you-don't. Give in to that one and you're fair game for every pitiful man on earth.

———

First I drove to McDonald's for Chicken McNuggets and coffee. The girl at the drive-up window played it straight, as if serving bloody ax murderers was part of the training.

When she smiled, silver braces glittered in the sunlight. "Here's your change, ma'am, have a nice day."

I held out a gory hand. "Thanks."

Billy G met me in the emergency waiting room at the hospital. The only other person in sight was a long-haired kid handcuffed to a pastel chair.

"Where'd you get that shirt?" Billy G asked.

"Bartender gave it to me. They sew up Thorne yet?"

"Your tits still show."

"Blood makes the cotton sticky. You like it?" I held my arms out and turned.

"Looks majestic," the longhair said. This wasn't your average scuzball hippie. The kid's hair hung way down his back, straight and golden blond. When he moved his head, it shimmered and rippled like a clean sheet you snap out a time or two before settling onto a queen-size bed. He even had dimples.

"You get a kick out of flashing your boobs at strangers? Is that it, a born cocktease?"

"Wait a minute."

"Sit right there, woman, and don't move. I'll see what's

happening with Thorne." Billy G wheeled and stalked away, leaving me too shocked to run hit him.

The arrogance of the little punk. The macho cowboy prickitude. There are women who enjoy being called woman. They think it shows more respect than girl or lady, but every time I've heard a man use the word it was in the directive—*sit, woman*—or possessive—*my woman*—and nobody directs or possesses Lana Sue Potts Paul.

As I steamed, all primed to lash out at the next male who got in my way, I became aware that the pretty longhair wanted to speak. He leaned as far forward as the cuffs would allow, watching with blue-eyed anticipation.

I stared at him. "What do you want?"

"You seem brought down, sister." Same tone inflection as Jesus on *The Books of the Bible on Cassette* Mom listens to during soaps she isn't interested in. When I didn't speak, he continued: "The intensity of your vibrations is washing away my inner peace. That's a lot of self to lay on another soul."

Why is it the prettiest ones always turn out to be dopes? "Don't talk to me anymore."

The boy sat back and considered this a moment. "I respect your stance," he said, "but I have a major problem and you're my only means of salvation."

Another one. Everywhere I turn, some man is calling me his means of salvation. "Do I look like a saint?" I held out bloody hands. "Huh? I left my husband yesterday and let an asshole rut on me all night and then a man I never even met spurts blood in my mouth. I don't have any panties, my vacuum's broke, I have a hangover that would kill a bull. I ate at McDonald's for breakfast. I'm in no mood to be the salvation for some frybrain from a time capsule. No one talks like you, buddy. Your type got jobs ten years ago."

Words stampeded from my mouth. In ninety seconds of

continuous blather, I told the hippie about Loren's search for God, Cassie running off with Mickey, my failure as a singer in Nashville, sugar, Roxanne, Daddy's saffron obsession, Connie's hatred, my problem with orgasms and strangers. I ended with Loren's boy and how guilty I felt for replacing his first wife. I'd never told anybody that one before.

Talk about your captive audience. I felt so bad for this poor handcuffed love child that, out of breath, I ended with, "Okay, what can I do for you?"

He smiled like an angel. "I wasn't certain you'd stop in time. If you make haste, you can save me from many years in prison."

With his looks, he'd be dead in two weeks of prison. "Tell me what to do."

The hippie spoke quickly. "These peace officers heavied out on me in the parking lot at the Minit Stop. They threatened a body search, so I swallowed an unopened pack of Freedent sugarless gum. They're out finding a doctor and a stomach pump."

"Why swallow all that gum?"

"I hoped to postpone the search. There's an ounce of cocala in my back pocket."

I never heard anyone say that before. "Cocaine?"

"The Andes call it cocala. I prefer the Indian word. Cocaine sounds unhealthy—like Coca-Cola."

"How're you going to dump the coke with your hands cuffed?"

"I prayed to Lord Caitanya that you might take it."

This was interesting. "They'd put me in jail."

"Why should anyone suspect you?" Other than a quart of blood down my front, I looked law-abiding. "Please, you'll be saving me twenty to fifty years of imprisonment."

"What do I do with an ounce of coke?" A stupid question, I admit.

"Snort it, flush it, sell it, I don't care. Just hurry, I mean, make haste."

So I did. I walked over, reached into the pretty hippie's back pocket, pulled out a plastic Baggie full of sparkly white stuff, and stuck it into my front pocket. With time to spare. Five minutes later when a policeman came to lead him away, I sat on the other side of the room, thumbing through a copy of *Country Living*.

As he stood, the longhair looked at me and smiled like an angel again. "Peace be with you, sister. We shall meet once more in the astral."

"Sure."

———

Billy G, Thorne, and the skinny cowboy shuffled into the waiting room. Thorne's left arm bulged from bandages and his face looked a bad gray—like when you put milk in old coffee.

The skinny cowboy grinned at my tits. "Twenty-one stitches and two pints of the red stuff. He's good as new."

"No, I'm not," Thorne said. "I'm tired. Killing yourself is hard work."

I stood. "They give you tranquilizers?"

"A few, but I'm not supposed to take them till I sober up."

"How do you feel?"

"Sober."

Billy G spoke: "Lana Sue, can't you find another shirt?"

I said, "Shut up."

Thorne glanced from me to Billy, but he didn't say anything; I guess he was too worn out from his own melodrama to worry much about ours. "You have a car here?" he asked me.

"Out front."

"Billy, drive my truck back to the ranch. I'll ride with Mrs. Paul." Thorne moved past me toward the door.

I said, "But—"

Billy G said, "But—"

Thorne stopped shuffling and turned on us. "Move it, I don't have all day."

*Don't have all day* struck me as odd words to come from a man who'd just tried to die.

———

That's how I found myself miles from anywhere I'd ever heard of, neck deep in a Cadillac-sized bathtub, being attended by an honest-to-God live-in maid. In Houston, our maid rode the bus over from the ghetto. She'd have walked off the job if I ever ordered her to draw a bath.

Maria was either amazingly tactful or preinformed. Had my boss come home wearing ten pounds of bandages and helped by a blood-caked stranger, I would have asked questions.

All Maria said was "Would you care for a bath, ma'am?"

"Yes, thank you."

Thorne stood at the bottom of a wide hardwood staircase. He nodded a couple of times, focusing on me for the first time since we left the hospital. "See if any of Janey's clothes fit her, Maria. There's a closetful of old stuff from before the kids were born somewhere."

"I know just where to find them," Maria said.

Thorne started up the stairs. "I imagine she's hungry too. Find something to feed her."

"Will that be all?"

"You might fix me a drink." Without speaking to me, Thorne clomped up the stairs.

I held out my hand to Maria. "I'm Lana Sue."

"I know." Maria was short, under five feet, but she wasn't misproportioned like a dwarf or a midget, and her posture made me feel like a slouch. She led me into this bathroom straight out of a steaming ABC miniseries.

"You shouldn't treat Thorne like you're a slave and he's Genghis Khan," I said.

"Mr. Axel is my boss."

"He'll forget that if you don't remind him."

She laughed, high like a starling. "Why would I want Thorne to forget he's my boss?"

"Be a woman instead of a servant. He'll wonder what you want."

That's my method. Five minutes in the house and I was restraining the maid and, in my head, throwing out the stuffed animals on the walls and retiling the John floor. It was some John too. Sinks and mirrors and lights, little stools so you could poke at your face without standing up. The bathtub was a round, ceramic thing with steps and a handrail. It had a phone and a tape deck and a television with a VCR on top and a round mirror on the ceiling.

A dial between the tap and a cigarette lighter said I was soaking at 101 degrees Fahrenheit. Nice of someone to let me know. The bottom of the tub contoured itself around my back and neck, soothing away the killer hangover.

Maria brought in some clothes, a plaid shirt large enough for a logger and some green work pants with pockets down to the knees. "Do you mind eating supper in the kitchen?" Maria asked. "Mr. Axel isn't having any and on Sundays we don't make much fuss."

"Sunday?"

"Today is Sunday."

Christ, Loren was wearing off on me. I never forgot the day until he came along. If I'd stayed with him much longer, he'd have me right alongside, hanging out with dead writers and talking to the moon. Snuggling deeper into the tub, I raised the temperature to 103 and punched the whirlpool button.

"This is some bathroom," I said to Maria. "I'm a John

connoisseur and this is the fanciest yet. My mom would go nuts in here."

Maria held up my shirt, eyeing the bloody stain. She was dark and self-contained-looking. I figured Maria for around Cassie and Connie's age. "You should see the master bathroom upstairs. It has a built-in microwave oven."

"Why?"

"Janey and Thorne lived out here six years in a cabin with only an outhouse over on the hill. When she was pregnant with E.T. her bladder distended or something and made the colon spastic. They pitched a tent for her up by the outhouse, then winter came and she carried a slop jar around the cabin. Now Janey doesn't like going more than a few steps from a flush toilet."

Maria hid her mouth with her hand as she giggled. "There are six in the house and two more in the barn."

"I'd like to meet this woman."

A frown jumped to Maria's face. "I do not think so. The meeting would not be pleasant."

That added a dimension to the arrangement. "Is she expected back soon?"

"She filled her handbag with credit cards and flew to Paris, France. The last thing I heard her say was that she'd never again play second fiddle to a steer. Can I bring you anything?"

"Is there any Grand Marnier around? I like Grand Marnier with a hot bath."

"Of course, Mrs. Paul."

"Call me Lana Sue." I snuggled deeper into the tub. This was comfortable. I wondered if Thorne could work out a deal with someone at the nearest airport so we'd get a call should his wife decide to appear without notice. Surely she would arrive by plane.

The only tape in sight was the Sons of the Pioneers, *Tumbling*

*Tumbleweeds*. I always was a sucker for simplicity and corn, so I plugged the tape in and closed my eyes to avoid the ceiling mirror. That mirror would be the first thing to come down if I chose to stick around.

If I chose to stick around—the idea was interesting. So far, I liked Thorne a lot. He was the Western authoritative innocent, straightforward and sincere, a king of the range type like Ben Cartwright, who'd suddenly realized good intentions, hard work, and sacrifice for tomorrow don't make for a loving family. Without half trying, I could give him a pleasure jolt that would keep him going for years. The man deserved a little happiness. And while I was giving Thorne something to look back on in his old age, I could work in one hell of a vacation for myself. I could be matriarch of the prairies, queen of a ranch bigger than Delaware. Then, after a month or so—if Janey didn't appear—I might go back and forgive Loren or go to Texas and let Daddy forgive me, or stay put and not have anybody forgive anything.

My nonfussy supper turned out to be a beautiful steak with asparagus tips, homemade french fries, and a four-color salad. I've always felt you can trust a person who calls the evening chowdown supper instead of dinner. They fall into my real category.

While I ate, Maria whipped together a batch of brownies. She was admirable all the way around, Maria.

"Mrs. Axel's clothes don't fit you well." When she smiled, I could see brownie frosting on Maria's front teeth.

"She must be a large woman."

"Janey is very strong. My clothes might do better. Maybe you should try them."

"You're tiny, Maria. I'd rip the seams out of anything you wear."

Her chin went up. "I'm bigger than I look."

"Nobody can hide six inches of height."

"Well, my boyfriend gave me his football jersey before he

went out on the rigs. He was a fullback in high school. Second string."

"If I can't make it to town tomorrow, we'll check this jersey out."

A twenty-fiveish-looking girl walked in as I spoke. She was layered-flesh fat with short rat-brown hair and skin the texture and color of a used golf ball. She barked, "You're moving in, then."

"Thorne asked me to stay a few days until he gets better. Who're you?"

The girl sneered. "What's the matter with Daddy? He stub his little toe and can't walk to the bar without help from a hooker? Mom's been gone four days and the vultures are landing."

In the silence, Maria said, "Can I fix you something, Darlene?"

"No. Why doesn't she have clothes of her own? Daddy picking them up naked now? I suppose it cuts down on small talk." She stalked to the refrigerator.

I chose to be pleasant. "Your father tried to kill himself. I helped him, but he bled on my clothes."

Darlene blinked a couple times and the scowl softened for a moment. "Tried to kill himself?"

"We were in time."

"How hard did he try to kill himself?"

"Couple of pints."

"Let me guess. He cut himself in public, probably a bar. Good, safe place to drum up pity."

"Something like that."

Darlene returned to the table with a quart of mayonnaise. "I'm gay," she said. She seemed to watch me, waiting for an effect.

"I don't think so."

"You calling me a liar?"

"My sister's gay. Her friends are all nice to me, at first anyway. I don't think you're gay."

"Latently, I am." She opened the jar and spooned mayonnaise into her slit of a mouth. "He didn't really try to kill himself. It was a show."

"Aren't you the one who shoots calves?"

"Yearlings."

"Why would you want your father to kill himself?"

White glop flowed from spoon to face. "'Cause I'm miserable and it's his fault."

"Why don't you leave?"

Darlene's mouthful of mayonnaise reminded me of a pimple joke we all told in junior high. She said, "Don't be stupid."

———

I found Thorne lying on the far end of a long leather couch that had spurs carved in the wood frame. Holding a glass in one hand, he stared at a soundless television screen.

"*60 Minutes.*" I recognized Mike Wallace.

"You feeling okay?" I settled into a high-back chair that matched the couch.

"I'm still here," he answered, which didn't exactly relate to my question. "You eat?" Thorne had an exhausted Roman senator look. The combination of weight, pride, and alcohol involved in holding together a dynasty does odd things to a man's face and shoulders.

"Maria fed me." I slouched into my favorite position—right leg over right chair arm, back against left chair arm, left foot dragging on the floor—and watched Mike interview an Arab. The Arab had a wide gap in his front teeth, which made him look sneaky.

"Ain't Maria a doll?"

"You're a fortunate man to have her."

"You bet." Thorne didn't act too interested in whether I sat with him or not. I've never dealt well with being ignored.

"I met your daughter."

He blinked and drank from the glass.

"She seems to resent my presence. I guess it's because her mom just left."

"Darlene hates Janey more than she hates me. Shot her in the back once with a twenty-two. Said Janey read her diary." He paused for a drink. "What could be there to read, anyway?"

"Did it hurt Mrs. Axel?"

"Getting shot? Naw, Janey's real strong. I cut the bullet out myself." Thorne smiled, I suppose thinking of his wife's back as he cut her open.

"Could I have a drink?"

"Bar's over there."

"You want a refresher?"

"Thanks, Jim Beam blends real nice with my new pills. I'm hardly miserable at all."

As I poured the drinks, I thought about poor, fat Darlene shooting her mother. I tried to picture Daddy in our living room back home, cutting a bullet out of Mom's back. Daddy would wear his doctor's mask and sterilize a steak knife. Mom would cover all the furniture with newspapers.

"Does Darlene have a skin disease?" I asked.

"She's coyote ugly, ain't she?"

"You shouldn't talk that way about your daughter. Maybe she's sick." I walked back to the couch and handed Thorne his glass, then sat on the end and propped his feet in my lap. While Thorne talked, I took off his boots. He wasn't wearing socks.

"That ain't sickness. It's lack of sun. She eats and sleeps all day and wanders around the ranch all night. The hands are scared of her."

"Why is Darlene so unhappy?"

Thorne drank awhile, considering the question. *60 Minutes* ended and *Murder, She Wrote* came on, still without sound.

"Hell if I know," Thorne said.

"Have you ever asked her?"

"No."

"Lot of people talk if you ask questions."

Thorne set his glass on the end table with a clink. He pulled his head up so he could see me better. "Listen here, Lana Ann."

"Lana Sue."

"Lana Sue, the complications surrounding this household took many years to build into the mess you see today. This ain't no movie. You can't waltz in here with folksy wisdom and common sense and make everybody dandy."

"I'm sorry."

"My wife didn't just leave on the spur of the moment. I didn't try to kill myself because I was drunk. Those aren't phases my children are going through. You dropped from the sky into a fucked-up situation."

"I'm sorry."

Thorne settled back down into the couch. "All right. It's not your fault. You're the first good thing to come along in years. Just don't think you can solve all our problems after two hours of hanging around."

"Okay."

"Christ, if it was that easy, I would kill myself."

Thorne finished his drink and fell asleep. I sat, sucking ice cubes and watching the old lady solve the murder, which was about a rock star electrocuted on a hot mike. Even without sound, I knew who did it by the second commercial. The show went boring after that and I started to wonder about my own fucked-up situations with Loren, Cassie, and Daddy. Did I want to throw off all those complications and take on another, just as screwed-up set?

It's like my mom. Mama watched every single episode of *Guiding Light* for eighteen years. Then, one Tuesday while

Alan and Hope were discovering who Phillip's real father was, she switched to *Another World*—without knowing any of the characters or their past and present loves or anything. Mom never went back.

Maybe some of Mama rubbed off on me after all. I never thought so before.

I smoked a couple of cigarettes and watched Thorne sleep. As he breathed, the ends of his mustache quivered a bit. A white scar creased his leathery tan from the bottom of one ear to his cheekbone. To me, Thorne looked strong and whole, a man in control of what happens to him. Nothing like a person who would grieve to the point of suicide. Suicides are supposed to be pale and meek—like Ann or my grandmother.

The arm must have hurt because Thorne rolled over a couple times trying it in different positions. Loren sleeps spread all over the bed, sometimes using me as a pillow. Ace always curled on his left side with his right leg thrown across my hip. I guess to keep me pinned down.

When I first ran away with Mickey he slept on his back, but after Jimi Hendrix died from choking on his own vomit Mickey rolled over. He was the only one of the bunch who snored much.

I hate to think it, but I don't remember how Ron slept. Fourteen years together and I can't picture the guy in bed.

*Murder, She Wrote* was followed by a detective show whose name I missed. Someone chased someone until a car exploded. I crawled along the couch and snuggled up next to Thorne's body. His breathing shifted a moment, then his good arm came around my shoulders. As I drifted into sleep, I felt Maria cover us with a blanket. Loren would have almost approved.

# 14

Way back in March of '63 when Daddy and the Christian Detective Agency dragged me, uncomplaining, back to Bellaire High, it was as if I'd slept those three months. My friends treated me like I'd been ill, Ron acted as if I never left. One of Daddy's doctor buddies checked me over and announced the family's fears were true, I had violated the sacred trust of virginity.

The funny thing was that Daddy didn't go into a week-long silence. I guess he wasted so much depression on my bad grades and minor disappointments that manic catatonia just wasn't appropriate for something as big as being found naked in a motel room with five likewise naked country musicians. My sins were so outrageous it was either forgive and forget or send me to detention hall for life. So everyone forgot—or pretended to. Daddy even bought me a used Chevy. I almost forgot myself. The days turned hot and life focused down to the country club pool in the afternoons and Pizza Hut at night.

Between the two, I circled Houston's fast-food strips endlessly in his Oldsmobile with Ron or my Chevy with Roxanne. Gas was cheap. We put on a couple hundred miles a day in a five-mile circuit, looking at other teenagers who looked at us. I remember honking the horn a lot.

Because of my long absence, they made me take two credits of summer school—which I couldn't stand. Everyone in town but me got to sleep late and drink Pepsis in front of the soap operas until time to drive over to the pool. I spent my mornings daydreaming away Texan History and Home Ec. Who knows what I daydreamed about; not Mickey, and probably not Ron. Maybe I didn't daydream at all but turned my brain into a white noise channel. That can happen when you're bored in hot weather.

I know I worried more about my tan than the economic class of real people. I listened to Top 40 all summer—"Wipe Out," "Tie Me Kangaroo Down," "Frankie and Johnny." Roxanne taught me breast development exercises, but I could still look down my nightgown and see my feet. It was as if Mickey and singing onstage and my discovery of dignified poverty were only dreams.

There was one element of my fling that I couldn't forget and that was how relaxing and fun sex can be—Mickey's Regular Orgasm theory of mental health. I fought the urge, tried to ignore the urge, self-abused myself through the urge, but the honest truth is that, as summer turned into what passes for fall in Houston, my frustration grew to the point of out of hand.

"So get laid," Roxanne said.

"I don't know."

"It's fun, you know it's fun. Keep the fun you learned from Mickey and forget the stupid."

"I promised Daddy I wouldn't."

Roxanne pretended to choke on her hamburger. We were in a booth at McDonald's, waiting for Ron and Roxanne's newest cowboy, who was really a drywall hanger faking it as a cowboy on weekends. "Why in hell did you promise not to get laid?"

I sipped Sprite through a straw. "When I first came back,

Daddy was going to ship me to a psychiatrist. Then he said Mom would die if I ever had sex again. Then he said it would end his career."

"You believed all of that?"

"Then he bought me the Chevy."

Roxanne collapsed into hysteria. She shouted loud enough so all the customers and the girls behind the counter turned to stare at me. "Your father gave you a car if you promised not to fuck?" I tried to shush her, but she wouldn't let it go. "A car for a pure ass, what kind of a deal is that?"

"It's a used car."

"Why drive around if you can't fuck anybody?"

"Shut up, Roxanne. I promised for his peace of mind. And Mama's. The Chevy was just a bonus."

Roxanne laughed so much I got mad and decided to wait for Ron outside. As I slid from the booth she caught my arm. "You're getting the crappy end of the deal," she laughed. "That car doesn't have a tape deck. Tell him you won't give feel-ups for a tape deck."

"To hell with you," I said, though that made her laugh even more.

The truth is I made a stupid deal and I knew it was stupid at the time, but the Chevy (a '61 Impala painted bright red) wasn't the only reason I gave up sex—not that it was a bad reason. Somehow, though, from a distance of a few months, I suffered an antifling backlash. What I'd done with Mickey and the boys came to seem tacky and dumb. I mean, if Mickey loved me he should have done something to keep me around. Not that he ever said he loved me.

My mistake was I started comparing. I lined up Choosie and the black-toothed bartenders and all the truck-stop waitresses against Mom and Dad and their friends in their Grand Prix and Mercedes. I forgot how real and sincere I thought the waitresses were and only remembered that none of the women in Mom's golf foursome had to work. If one of the neighbors got sick they could go to the doctor and be taken care of. If a car broke, it could be fixed. That didn't seem to be giving up the sincere life for money.

So my values pendulum swung too far back the other way. I decided being rich was better than being poor and the symptoms I connected with poverty were whiskey, country music, and sex. For a few months anyway, I became a snotty teenager again. I reverted to typical.

However, once found, country music and regular sex aren't something that can be walked away from. By fall, I was listening to Loretta Lynn again, and this new guy named Merle Haggard. I was following the steel breaks in Buck Owens and Ernest Tubb.

Late at night I slid into my white nightgown and turned off all the lights in my room, then, using the glow from the dial, I tuned WBAP Country on my portable Westinghouse radio. I waited for Kitty Wells or Sammi Smith to come on crooning a heartbreak song, then I ran my fingers across my stomach into the gap between my legs. I pretended my fingers were Mickey's on his steel. I tried to remember what it was like to stand onstage next to him, closing my eyes and singing about sadness and pain, giving the customers part of myself. Then I pretended Mickey was in me.

The sound was so low I could hardly hear Sammi's depression. I was afraid Daddy would wake up and bust through the door. I don't know which would have upset him the most, me listening to country music or playing with myself.

———

Every Friday night through October and November, usually after a football game, Ron and I cruised his Oldsmobile out to a fresh housing development and parked along the newly laid-out streets. Houston neighborhoods sprung up so fast in those days we had to change tracts every few weeks to stay ahead of the houses.

Some Fridays after we parked, we argued so long over leaving the radio on Top 40 or country that nothing happened. Usually, though, one of us would give in and Ron would take his watch off and set it on the dash, then he'd slide his long arms over my shoulders and we'd put in an hour or so of adolescent window steaming. After maybe a month and a half of this, Ron realized—or became conditioned to the fact—that I went further and sweated steamier to country than I did to the Singing Nun. That put an end to the radio arguments.

Our frustration came about because Ron wanted to go "all the way"—he was desperate to go "all the way"—but he didn't know squat about technique. I had sworn not to cross the forbidden line, but I knew how much fun even coming close could be with proper finger and tongue work.

I tried being patient with Ron and his social background. He really didn't know much past basketball, Southern Baptist summer camps, and Pat Boone's *Twixt Twelve and Twenty*. He kissed with too much pressure, groped like a blind baby, whined if things didn't go his way; whenever he blundered into an erogenous zone, he poked at it with one fingernail.

One correct touch and I would have been so wet and frothy all the promises in Texas couldn't hold me back, but my Daddy-induced code kept me from showing Ron how it was done. Sometimes I prayed his fingers would accidentally brush the right spots and I could lose control without guilt.

———

Thanksgiving night we parked out past Deer Park in a new luxury development along Galveston Bay. A norther had blown in and Ron wanted to run the engine and the heater, but I was afraid we'd asphyxiate from carbon monoxide like the kids in Beaumont did while they were screwing in her parents' garage. Ron said we weren't in a garage and we wouldn't die if we got warm. I sat with my arms crossed and the window down all the way until he relented and turned off the engine. Then Ron sulked awhile. He was a big kid, not as tall as Mickey, but at least forty pounds heavier. Ron was an only child—his father worked sixteen hours a day so he would never have to hear his wife's constant grating babble. As Ron's mom talked, she scampered around like a squirrel, doing every conceivable suck-up task in the house. Ron had never washed dishes or made a bed or mowed a lawn. He never did anything he didn't want to do, which is a great situation for an adult, but leads to sulkiness in children, especially sports heroes.

However, that night I felt friendly toward Ron. He'd given up watching the Texas-Texas A&M game on my parents' TV to take me out for a Coke. That's what kids all told their moms and dads back then when they wanted to go park for hours and whip themselves into a sexual frenzy.

"We're going out for a Coke," I told Mom.

"Don't be late," she trilled from her usual post in the bathroom. Daddy was studying a saffron catalog and didn't look up.

I didn't want Ron to sulk, I wanted him to be happy, I just didn't care to die from necking in an Oldsmobile. Since Ron wouldn't come to me, I slid across the plastic seat covers, reached across and pulled his watch off for him. Then I leaned up and swabbed his ear with my tongue. Ron played tough for about twenty seconds before he fell sideways on top of me. In the confusion of teeth, elbows, and my left foot in the ashtray, Ron slid his big hand down the front of my panties.

Of course, no one in church camp had told him it works better with the girl's jeans unbuttoned, so Ron's hand cramped up against my bladder and stuck. I waited awhile, kissed awhile, smelled the after-shave he'd sprinkled behind his ears, but Ron seemed satisfied with an abdomen grip.

What was I supposed to do, work on wrestling holds with the dunce? His hand pressed so hard it nearly made me pee. Leaning back against the door handle, I went into one of my internal conversations that always get me in trouble.

"God," I said to myself, "I can't expect him to know everything."

"What about the Chevy?" I answered.

"Remember what Roxanne said, 'You can't fuck a car, Lana Sue.'"

So I reached down and unbuttoned my jeans—even slid the zipper down a ways.

Ron stopped in midkiss. His whole body went rigid. I think the sudden freedom shocked his hand into paralysis. Then his fingers plunged into what back then was called a "finger fuck." Who knows what it's called now, but in 1963 a high-school boy's wildest ambition was a finger fuck.

I tingled some and was all set to tingle more, only Ron was way too low; and his fingers didn't move, they froze as far in me as he could reach. I looked at his face up next to mine. The eyes were wide open and unsure of what was real—like a little kid seeing the ocean for the first time. His breath came in gasps. A picture flashed of Ron hyperventilating and passing out with his hand up my crotch. It wouldn't have felt much different if he had fainted.

If I didn't make a move, I knew Ron would lie there and not flex a muscle all night long. Placing my hand on his, I pulled it up to the fingertips on clitoris level and murmured something like, "There, now rub softly around and around."

Ron rubbed a few seconds and I started feeling warm. I sighed once, then he stopped.

"Don't quit now," I mumbled.

Ron pulled his hand away. "Who taught you that?"

"What?"

Ron sniffed his fingers, then reached over to the dash and put on his watch. "How do you know where I'm supposed to touch?"

"I know where it feels best."

"Did that steelworker touch you there?"

I pushed Ron and sat up straight, as close to my door as possible. "Of course he touched me there. I lived with him for three months."

Ron held the foam-wrapped steering wheel with both hands. His whole face drooped like a little boy's. "I never thought about you screwing him."

"What did you think I did with him? Besides, Mickey is a steel player, not a steelworker, there's a difference."

Ron's tongue pushed against his lower lip. "Not to me, there's not." His face turned from sulk to concern. "Was he a pervert, Lannie?"

I stared out the window at the bay. A silver moon was rising from Louisiana. I thought about Mickey's sly little smile whenever he wanted to try something new. "Yes, I guess most people would call him a pervert."

Teenage boys were a lot more naive before the common use of the pill and abortions and British rock and roll. I guess even "good" girls get laid in junior high now days. I'm sure little Marcie down the road saw pictures from *Joy of Sex* before she could even read—if she can read.

I go into that rap because of what Ron said next. He turned and picked up my hand and said, without irony or sarcasm, "You didn't like it, did you?"

Didn't like it? Didn't like making love under the steel, in truckstop men's rooms, in the van, tied down on a snooker table—I liked it so much I even amazed Mickey.

I looked into Ron's concerned blue eyes. "Sometimes he

hurt me, but mostly, I'd say I loved it and couldn't get enough. Why do you ask?"

Ron's big jaw sunk in his chest. He stared down at the plastic footprint he used as an accelerator pedal and mumbled, "I can't stand the thought of some pervert doing nasty things to you, Lannie. You're a princess to me. Why didn't you leave?"

"I didn't want to."

Ron turned his head to look away out the driver's side window. Blond curls on the back of his head fell over the edge of the collar on his Ban-Lon shirt. I touched the longest curl and said, "You need a haircut."

Ron didn't answer. I felt a swelling of sympathy for him. Poor kid, all the boys at school must know about my fling. I imagined the embarrassment of being a virgin with a girlfriend who was a known sleaze.

"If you let me," I said, "I could show you some things that might make you feel real good."

Ron turned, his face alight with hope.

———

It took work—Ron came if I so much as looked at the right spot—but by Christmas, he'd lost his virginity and I was pregnant with Cassie and Connie.

———

When Daddy found out in March, he sold my Chevy.

On Sunday afternoon, a grand council met in our den to decide Ron and Lana Sue's future. The Pottses arrived dressed for church. Mom, in her yellow slacks suit and matching fluffy slippers, pushed refreshments. Dad wore his golf outfit, Haggar slacks, Arrow shirt, cleats. He twirled a putter throughout the meeting, using it sometimes as a gavel, sometimes as a pointer. I took it as a possible weapon.

They made me put on a dress, an innocent, teenybopper thing with the waist down around hip level and pleats in the skirt—the uptown cheerleader look.

Daddy sat, scowling from his recliner. First the putter turned horizontally clockwise, then vertically like a Ferris wheel. By watching his eyebrows, I could always gauge his irritation level. Right then, they were flat and spread past the sides of his eyes. Darkness showed over his glasses. This should have been Daddy's take-charge hour, his finest patriarchal moment, but no one seemed to care whether Daddy took charge or not.

Neela Potts fluttered across the room, touching paintings and raving on about Mom's suburban granola. Mom blew ten minutes explaining the recipe, which was nothing but Wheat Chex, Corn Chex, and salty peanuts. Mr. Potts and Ron discussed Houston's chances against UCLA in some upcoming tournament. Mr. Potts's fingers pulled at the cuffs of his brown suit. He looked uncomfortable. I think he resented being away from his print shop more than he resented my seduction of Ron.

The grown-ups had maneuvered seating arrangements so Ron was perched on a low stool as far from me as two people could possibly sit in our den—as if his closeness might make me even more pregnant. Or as if we'd each been sent to the corner. When I looked over at Ron, he smiled and nodded. The smile was cute and open. Marrying him might not be such a bad deal, I thought, even if it did mean giving up the country-western fantasy. Ron was such a kid, he was bound to make a good father.

When Daddy's eyebrows showed completely above his horn-rims, his mouth twitched a couple times and I thought he might swat Neela Potts if she didn't shut up about the snack stuff. Finally, he cleared his throat with a faraway thunder sound and bounced the putter head off the foot cushion. Everyone turned to hear what he'd decided we were going to do.

Daddy started the meeting by making a big deal out of accepting the blame. "I guess I wasn't always the father I should have been," he said, knowing we were all disagreeing in our minds, "but I got so caught up in providing a good home for my wife and children that sometimes I forgot to provide that which is just as important, my time."

Neela said, "See there," to Mr. Potts, who probably hadn't eaten a meal with Ron in six years.

Daddy twirled the putter and frowned at Neela, then he launched into a long, boring explanation about why he failed and how "Grandma's blood" would always be the family burden, how he hoped the next generation could avoid the taint. The whole spiel ended with "We cannot change the past, we can only learn from it."

In the silence after Daddy's speech, Mr. Potts looked at his watch. Mom asked if anyone wanted more Coca-Cola, and Ron held out his glass without a word. I think he was afraid of Daddy's putter. Personally, I wanted to throw up—and not just because I always wanted to throw up that month. Daddy didn't blame himself for my condition. He blamed me. And Mickey. In Daddy's mind, nothing had been wrong before I ran away with Mickey and nothing had been right since. My morals were shot forever.

———

It was decided by Daddy, and everyone else agreed, that the day after our graduation, Ron and I would announce we'd been secretly married since a basketball trip to Baton Rouge, Louisiana, back in December. In the meantime, we'd keep our mouths shut. Which was silly because Roxanne knew I was pregnant and if Roxanne knew it might as well be published in the *Bellaire High Three Penny Press*.

After graduation, the women would throw me a bridal

shower so no one would be suspicious, then Ron and I would pack a few bags and shuttle off to Europe for a summer-long honeymoon.

"People won't gossip if they don't see you carrying," Mom said.

Neela patted my knee and murmured, "Maybe you'll miscarry, dear." No wonder Mr. Potts couldn't be around her.

Right before the baby was due, Ron and I were to return to Houston, where we'd be set up in a nice, frugal apartment and Ron would start pre-med at Rice. I was to be allowed one night course a semester. Other than that, I would stay home and do whatever Mom and Neela Potts had been doing since they were my age. Dad offered to support us through the collegiate years, but Mr. Potts looked up from his watch long enough to insist he'd pay half. By constant labor, he'd turned the print shop into a money-maker. You wouldn't think it by comparing family lifestyles, but the Pottses probably had more cash on hand than the Goodwins.

Neither Ron nor I spoke during the negotiations. Ron sat on the stool, his knees at elbow level, watching with interest. Whenever anyone looked his way, Ron smiled and nodded. I guess he wanted to be agreeable. I went into my nauseous resignation attitude, sighing quietly every time I heard "make the best of a bad situation."

After our futures were decided, Mom offered cherry-chocolate cake, but Mr. Potts said they had to run, he was needed down at the plant. Mr. Potts called his print shop a plant.

Ron pecked me on the cheek and said he'd pick me up the next day at eight. We were skipping school to drive over to Baton Rouge for the real marriage. Mom would come with us.

After the Pottses filed out, Mom got all ruffled about the untouched cake. She said Mr. Potts wasn't a very pleasant man, strong words for my mama, but that Neela seemed to have her head on straight. Daddy ignored her. He sat staring at me and twirling the putter slowly with his thumb and two inside fingers. I tried staring back, but I never was Daddy's match in an eye-contact showdown. Soon I gave up and looked at the floor next to his feet.

After ten minutes or so, Daddy emitted a spine-wrenching, gut-sinking sigh that I can still feel today. Then he stood and walked into the study. I turned on *The Carol Burnett Show.*

———

I make this scene out like Mom and Dad and the Pottses came together old European clan style and decided the future of their children. It wasn't that way at all. The next fifteen years of existing on automatic can't be blamed on my parents. Too many neurotics of my generation—namely Loren Paul—go around blaming every damn ingrown toenail on the people who raised them. I don't buy that.

The day after Loren introduced himself and I walked him into the stop sign, I took Ron to a bowling alley snack bar where we wouldn't be bothered. None of that gang of social climbers we ran with would be caught dead in a bowling alley. Over Dr Peppers and Twizzlers, I laid out the one element of my sexual education Mickey had skipped—child prevention.

Ron took the news well. He said, "Okay, let's get married."

I was glad he said that. We held sticky hands while I explained what I figured Daddy's reaction would be.

Marriage with honor was automatic, of course. Daddy couldn't play golf with an unwed mother for a daughter. Mom would have to drop bridge club. The college part I was sure about because I knew Daddy would never let me settle for a man without a degree. His diploma snobbery wouldn't allow it. I was even pretty certain he would insist on—and pay for—med school.

"Or we can elope and go live somewhere else," I said to Ron.

"I don't want to live anywhere else. Marriage and college

sounds good to me. Wonder if he'd send me to Rice?" Ron's only basketball scholarship offers had come from North Texas State and Oral Roberts. His feelings were hurt because Houston didn't even call his coach.

I squeezed his palms. "If that's how you want it, that's how we'll do it."

"That's how I want it."

So before I drove the Chevy down to Daddy's office, made an appointment, and broke the news to him—in front of his nurse, by the way—I knew what the repercussions would involve. I'd made my choice. The only detail I hadn't counted on was the summer in Europe, but that was okay too.

———

The process came about basically the way Daddy planned, the only surprise being that I spawned twins. Then, one year into med school, Ron decided he didn't like death and sickness and he didn't want to be a doctor. As well as I knew Ron's every thought, he still blew my socks out the window when he came home and announced he'd chosen dentistry.

"Dentist," I shrieked quietly so as not to awaken the girls.

Ron gave me his defiant look. "What's the matter with being a dentist?"

"You'll smell like spit."

Daddy didn't buy the change of plans. He led Ron into the study and closed the door. An hour and a half later they reached a compromise. Ron would become an oral surgeon and I would be a good mother.

———

Let's face it, I don't thrive on being the object of dependency. Parasites make me nervous. There's no quicker way for a man to bring on the *Crack* than by turning all clutchy-needy on me.

Knowing that, and looking back, I'm amazed at how much I enjoyed motherhood. Cassie and Connie were my darlings. Still are.

In the hospital, I thought something awful was wrong with me. I couldn't make a connection between my life and these two sucking, crying, sleeping, shitting objects. I was afraid they would break if I touched them. I thought I was an emotional freak with no maternal instincts, a spider woman.

Then one afternoon when they were a couple of weeks old, Ron drove over to Rice to talk with his faculty adviser and, in something I took as a miracle, both girls fell asleep at the same time. Up until then, I was sure they were taking shifts at keeping me on my feet.

Two blessed hours of rest later, I grogged back to consciousness. Shuffling into the kitchen, I poured a cup of coffee, lit a cigarette, and walked into the girls' room to see why they weren't howling. I had on my blue terry-cloth bathrobe and no shoes. The smoke burned my eyes. I'd only taken up the habit the week before and hadn't quite mastered cigarette technique. Roxanne tried to coach me on blowing it out one corner of my mouth or up at the ceiling, but my exhalations tended to hiss a cloud that floated into my face and stuck.

The girls' window was open and fuzzy Houston light washed over the room, reflecting off the butterfly mobile Ron's mother had hung over the cradle. Cassie slept on her side with a fist bunched at her mouth. Wispy auburn hair lay against her cheek. Connie's eyes were open, maybe focused on the nearest plastic butterfly. I imagined they were anyway.

Connie's eyes showed a deep, intense green, the same green as on a pack of Doublemint gum. Her hair was white and short, more fuzz than hair. She didn't have Cassie's cheekbones and her forehead was wider. Her lips were thicker.

The longer I stood looking down at my babies, the more

I realized how different they were from each other. And how different they were from me. For the first time, I saw them as little people, not pets or dolls or even a piece of me that broke loose and escaped. I'd created them, but now I would never be able to think or feel or act for them again. The helpless little creatures were on their own against one hell of a rough world.

"Holy Christ," I said to Connie and the sleeping Cassie. "This is neat." And—*Bingo*—I learned to love.

———

Ron wasn't home much the first ten years. Premed, med, dental school, residency, the process for mounting the ladder of financial security took most of every day. He kissed his women good-bye in the mornings and hello at night. Other than that, the three of us grew up pretty much on our own.

I mean, I was only eighteen and, except for that one three months of glory, I'd never slept away from my parents' house. I'd never been alone more than a couple of hours in a row and I didn't know what to do with myself while Ron was out learning to perform root canals.

The girls became my buddies. For the first couple of years, our talks were mostly one-sided.

"Do you think I should smoke pot?" I asked, holding them both upright in the bath basin. "Roxanne says it's fun. She says all the Volkswagen microbuses on the freeways are full of drug fiends having orgies. I think about that whenever I pass one."

Cassie cooed and splashed water with her palms. Connie stuck a bar of soap in her mouth.

Soon, however, they learned to give advice and criticism— lots of criticism. Connie was only four years old the first time she told me my shoes didn't match my earrings.

The girls sure were different from each other. For maybe five years, Connie was crazy about me. As a baby she cried whenever I left her sight. Later, Connie crawled, then skipped from room to room in the apartment, following me as I sorted the clutter, babbling all the while about her dolls and pretend evening gowns, asking me questions I never had answers to. Her curiosity-about-body-parts stage lasted considerably longer than I thought it was supposed to.

Early in her fifth year, Connie suddenly latched onto her daddy. Whatever he said was truth and whatever I said was suspect. Maybe she thought their blondness and large jaws set them apart from Cassie and me, or maybe it was the female version of Oedipalism. Almost overnight I moved from being the rock at the center of her world to the status of hired help.

"Mama was bad to me today," she said to Ron once. "I think we should fire her."

She stopped confiding and came to believe I wasn't as smart as she was. By the time she hit thirteen, Connie was convinced she knew more about makeup and clothes than I did. She was probably right.

All that's normal in a girl, I guess. At her age I thought my mom was a naive ninny. It hurts, but motherhood always has been a bum rap. I guess it always will be.

Cassie was quieter. We never had any trouble with Cassie. I don't remember swatting her bottom or making her sit in her room. I must have sometimes, she wasn't a freak or anything, but I just can't recall any need for discipline.

Cassie mostly played by herself. She was polite and friendly, more a cooperative little guest than part of a family unit.

She looks like me, dark, thick hair that she kept long way after Connie and all her friends cut back to the short and sassy look. She has high cheekbones and a long neck, almost Indian features. I don't remember her hands ever moving without a reason. Connie's hands were always twitching—twisting hair, scratching at itches, drumming rhythms on the table. In all the years I lived with Cassie, I don't remember her ever scratching herself. Isn't that odd?

It seemed to take forever, but all the schooling finally started paying off for Ron. We moved from the apartment to a town house and from the town house to a split level. We joined a couple of clubs for rich white people. Ron bought a Buick and a Volvo station wagon. Since I left, he's moved into an even bigger house and drives an Audi. He bought Wanda a Cadillac.

I look on those last four years we were together as our lessons period. Why can't upper-middle Americans learn how to do anything without paying someone to teach them? We bought Connie lessons in swimming, tennis, and coming out— whatever that was. Cassie took horseback riding and guitar, a combination I should have been suspicious of right from the start. Ron peer-pressured me into golf, cooking, and bridge, of all things. I should have left Houston after the first session when an old toucheefeelee guy in a woolen bow tie explained how to count points. Mickey would laugh himself into the hospital if I ever told him I took bridge lessons.

Between lessons and driving girls to or from lessons, I drank coffee, beer, or Bloody Marys, depending on the time of day, with Roxanne. The years never much mellowed cousin Roxy. She'd married a crooked state senator and dyed her hair twelve times. Cowboys still called my house and left obscure messages for her like *Amarillo Sunday night* or *Next time I'll use more rope*. Whenever I passed the messages on to Rox, she would laugh that vamp laugh of hers and look pleased.

———

We met at the Space Center Mall right after New Year's for lunch and drinks. Roxanne wore a leather vest with big silver buttons and nothing underneath, a calf-length rayon crepe skirt—royal blue—and cowgirl boots. When she swept through the door, a roomful of expense account bankers and brokerage consultant types choked on their carrot curls. Leading the hostess, Roxanne found us an octagon-shaped table next to three of the squirreliest-looking bankers in the place. The balding three-piece-suit must have been the manager and the other two suck-ups were junior loan officers. When Roxanne laughed the first time, old baldy drained his martini glass and turned the same red as a Coca-Cola can. She has that effect on a lot of businessmen. That's why she still prefers cowboy butt.

Rox waved across the dining room to the bartender and *yoo-hooed*. "Tanqueray on ice with a Pearl back, Biff honey." She turned to me. "What you drinking, Lannie?"

"Double gin gimlet."

She shouted this as I sat almost alongside the red-domed bank manager. He moved his chair as far from Roxanne and me as he could. Rox twirled as she sat so the audience and I could appreciate the total style.

"You look like a San Antonio hooker," I said.

Rox threw back her hair, which was a blue-blond that week, and yodeled a laugh that would make a Roto-Rooter man squeamish. "Hail, honey, I'm what San Antonio hookers wish they could look like."

"How many threatened species died for those boots?"

She lifted her left foot up to tabletop level. "You like 'em? Claibourne bought 'em for me. Tops are coral snake and he claims the toes here to be foreskins off southern sea otters." She flew into another gale of laughter. "You think they'd git bigger if I squeezed 'em hard?"

"I always knew you'd end up sucking pointy-toed boots."

The next table was reflected in Roxanne's vest buttons. Those bankers looked entertained as all hell. One of the junior loan officers pulled his chair around for a better view.

Roxanne rubbed one pale blue fingernail along the ankle

stitching. "Claibourne bought 'em 'cause I caught him coming out a whorehouse down on Ladybird Avenue."

"What were you doing on Ladybird?"

"Wouldn't you like to know?" she winked. I had no idea what that meant.

With the arrival of alcohol, we cut the spiffy patter and got down to business. I ordered crab crepes, Roxanne had a chicken fried steak, hold the gravy. We both drank what we could. Roxanne topped her lunch off with a sticky, dark dessert called a Stairway to Heaven.

She studied the chocolate gob from several angles, debating between an attack by spoon or fork. Then, all set for the first bite, Roxanne seemed to lose concentration. "We bought a sterling silver saddle yesterday," she said. "Sucker must weigh in at two-fifty."

I blew cigarette smoke on her uneaten bite of Stairway to Heaven. "What does a person do with a sterling silver saddle?"

"I'm gonna ride on it in the rodeo parade, if I can find a stud it won't bow back. We'll be the hit of the show."

"Sometimes you two work at being eccentric," I said.

"Do not."

"Hasn't anyone ever told you faking weird is just as pretentious as faking rich?" I think I got her with that one.

"Who you calling pretentious, Miss Racquetball-court-in-the-basement, Miss Swimming-pool-with-Muzak-you-can-hear-underwater? How many Princess phones do those girls of yours need? They only got two ears and one mouth apiece."

"The swimming pool's not ours, it's Daddy's. And the girls only have one phone each."

"How about them buttons they push to stick their hairless-balled boyfriends on hold?"

Our bankers about fell off their billfolds from leaning my way, and I was near sick of it. "Roxanne, you're not being fair. There's no buttons and there's no boyfriends. Cassie and Connie are too young for boyfriends."

She snorted and finally crammed some chocolate goo into her mouth. Roxanne talked as she chewed. "My golden taco was split at their age. Yours would have been too if you weren't so scared of your daddy."

She washed the chocolate down with a shot of Tanqueray. "Eccentric my ass, eccentric's a damn sight better than what you got with the dentist. He pull any fun teeth lately?"

Many conversations with Roxanne wound up with me defending Ron. Come to think of it, many conversations with Ron wound up with me defending Roxanne. None of my loved ones ever could stand each other.

"Ron's not so boring," I said. "He just works hard."

"Radio bingo without a card is more fun than a night out with your husband. He could put the Coast Guard to sleep."

"I happen to like him."

"You like stopping at red lights. Tell me, did he discover your right tit yet?"

I'd made the mistake at a luncheon somewhat similar to this one of confessing to Roxanne that Ron had reverted back to the old high-school pattern of necking—all interest in the left breast and none in the right.

Roxanne thought that was a riot. She wanted to buy him a girlie magazine with all the right boobs cut out.

In the reflection of one of the buttons on Roxanne's vest, I noticed our neighboring-table eavesdroppers frozen over their T-bones, awaiting my answer. Something had to be done.

I said, "He hasn't touched me since the mastectomy." Counting one, two, I whirled—caught all three copping tit stares. "*What the hell are you looking at?*" I shouted.

An intense interest suddenly developed in home fries and cole slaw. Baldy raised his lap napkin to his lips and hid.

I put my head on the table and sobbed. Roxanne, bless her heart, jumped right in and ran with it. Standing, she advanced on Baldy.

"The first time my cousin has the courage to go in public since the operation and you insensitive jackbutts ogle her mangled breasts." "Mangled breasts" came out as a near scream. "You should be *ashamed*."

I faked a stifled cry.

One of them stammered. I couldn't see which one but I imagined it to be Baldy, as he looked like team leader. "We're sorry, ma'am. We didn't mean anything."

"Sorry don't pick cotton, buster."

Pick cotton? All buzz of conversation died around us. I could hear dishes rattling in the kitchen and a slight wheeze from the table in front of Roxanne.

"What are you waterheads going to do about it?" she demanded.

In the silence, I figured the lechers had been punished enough and it was about time to bounce up, singing, "Fooled you, assholes," but Roxanne held my head down with three of her fingers. Evidently, she had something else in mind.

"Would it be helpful if we paid for your lunch?"

Rox appealed to her audience. "Isn't this just like a Texas stud? Destroys an innocent woman and thinks he can make it all hunky-dory by throwing money at her."

The silence was ugly. Finally the first voice said, "What can we do?"

Roxanne tapped my head. "Trot off to the ladies' room, honey, and gather your shattered pride while I have a talk with these dildos."

I ran from the room. It's a good thing fighting laughter looks the same as fighting tears.

When I returned ten minutes later, the bankers were long

gone. Roxanne sat in front of two fresh drinks and three hundred dollars in twenties.

"Now we know the price of insulting a woman in Houston," she said. "Plus I made them promise to send their wives a dozen roses before supper. They better do it too."

I picked up a stack of twenties. "Didn't know I was worth that much."

"Hell, honey, you're worth way too much to live with a dentist."

"Somebody else said those exact same words to me this week."

Roxanne demanded to know who and even offered her half of the three hundred, but, although she pestered me through two more drinks, I kept my mouth shut.

—

The who was my old flame, Mickey Thunder. Ever since Patsy Cline died and I lost my virginity, picture postcards had taken to appearing in our mailbox. Once in six months or so, a card arrived from some exotic nightspot like Kamloops, Alberta, or Tin Cup, Mississippi. The pictures were mostly large mockups of local crops with a banner cutline running diagonally across the card declaring whatever town this was as the capital of something—RUSH SPRINGS, OKLAHOMA, WATERMELON CAPITAL OF THE WORLD. PARSONS, KANSAS, BUCKLE OF THE BIBLE BELT. On the backs of these cards, pithy little country-western sayings had been scrawled in Mickey's drunken handwriting: *Never take a rattlesnake by its tail or a woman by her word.* Or: *When high on LSD, one should not look in a mirror.* Or: *Fucking with a rubber is like taking a shower in a raincoat.*

Less often, maybe once in two years, the phone rang in the middle of the night, always on the hour at one, two, or three, whatever closing time happened to be in whatever state the band was playing that night. The calls began with ridiculous, raving nonsense and ended in a fairly serious come-on.

"Run away from the dentist and meet me at the Holiday Inn in Fairbanks."

"Is this a marriage proposal?"

"Fuck no, Lannie, I wanta see if you can still suck a golf ball through a garden hose."

Ron didn't mind the calls. Mickey was so far beyond belief to him he never dreamed I might hop a flight to Fairbanks and show Mickey what I could still do. Ron took Mickey as wacko comic relief from my distant past that embarrassed me no end. He would tease me at breakfast the next day.

"Can your steelworker still drink beer through a straw up his nose?" Which always disgusted Connie. She couldn't understand why I didn't hang up or call the police. Cassie seemed more interested. She would ask where the band was playing and if Lacy had any new albums coming out.

A couple of years after I left Thunder Road, Mickey hooked the band up as backup to a second-level Nashville star named Lacy Rasher. She never was any Patsy Cline, or even Sammi Smith, but every now and then, Lacy cut a catchy tune that managed to place a bullet on the country chart. Her biggest hits were "Raisin' Cain or Raisin' Children," and "Pocatello on My Mind." Pocatello was a hit mostly because Willie Nelson sang a verse and played a double guitar break with Mickey.

What Ron didn't know was I secretly bought all Lacy's albums and played them when no one was around. I'd sprawl across the sofa-love seat combination and listen real close to the steel leads, imagining how Mickey's face looked as he fingered this run or that riff, how he might chew his gum quicker on the last chorus. I pretended I was the one to his left, closing my eyes and putting words to his beautiful music.

It should have been me. Some might call this jealousy, even though I always denied the emotion, but I thought Lacy wasn't all that hot. Her low notes came out as big-breasted gravelly groans. Also, I spotted an affected I-Was-Country-When-Country-Wasn't-Cool attitude flaw in her song selection.

I don't know why Mickey stayed with her all those years. I would bet, however, that it had something to do with booze and pussy. Mickey's last call came the week before Roxanne and I kicked butt on the bankers at Space Center Mall.

———

"Give me four lines of 'Wine Over Matter.'"

"Huh." I glanced at Ron. He'd rolled over on his back at the first ring, but hadn't quite come conscious.

"Just the chorus, Lannie, Choosie does the verses."

"Who is this?"

From the other end, his voice rose in a flat tenor, "*My mind's lost all feelin', the wine keeps it reelin'.*"

"Mickey, it's four o'clock in the morning."

"Put your teeth in, I'm on the phone."

"I'm married to an oral surgeon, remember. My teeth are in."

The sound of a scuffle came over the line, followed by a *clonk* as if Mickey dropped the phone. "I was talking to someone here. A few people came up to the room after last call and stayed for breakfast. Pretend it's in harmony, Lana Sue."

"I'm not singing over the phone to you, Mickey. I'm going to hang up and fall back asleep and tomorrow this'll be a bad dream."

For a moment there was silence. Mickey was pouting. "You're so beautiful when you sing, Lana Sue. It's when you talk that you turn into a pain."

"Mickey, don't be unreasonable. You're drunk and I'm not. On top of which, my husband is asleep right here next to me.

What would he think if he woke up and I was crooning into the telephone."

"Leave him, Lana Sue. You're worth too much to live with a dentist." His voice rose. "Don't drink that. Felipe Bob pissed in it." Behind Mickey I heard the sound of glass breaking. Then Mickey's voice again. "You were snorting on the can and he couldn't wait." Then more glass broke.

"Where are you?" I asked.

"The motel room."

"I know that. What city is the motel room in?"

"Hold on. What's the name of this place? Look in the tank on the back of the toilet, honey. I bought you a present. Spain."

"There's a town named Spain?"

"A country. Lacy's on a world tour, opening for Charley Pride and Minnie Pearl. We learned 'Kawliga was a wooden Indian' in Spanish. You know Spanish for Indian?"

"Indio."

"Charley and Lacy are going over real good, but there's a language problem with some of Minnie's material. You belong to a country club yet, Lannie?"

"I resent that question."

"Do your car windows go down when you push a button?"

"We have air conditioning. I don't do windows."

"You get your hair done by a male fairy hairdresser?"

"I don't have to put up with this, Mickey. Just because you haven't changed in sixteen years doesn't mean I'm not allowed to grow up." Mickey's end was silent except for someone coughing her lungs out in the background.

"What's that?" I asked.

Mickey talked like he was holding his breath. "Moroccan sticky."

"Oh."

"Listen, I'm sorry I gave you a hard time. Things have been

tough lately and I thought hearing you sing might help me feel better." I wondered what could possibly happen in Mickey's life to make things tough.

"Please," he said.

Ron was asleep on his side, facing me. His mouth was open and one elbow drooped over his head, exposing a blond armpit. He looked like he would sleep through a hurricane.

I sang it as a lullaby:

> *"My mind's lost all feelin'*
> *The wine keeps it reelin'*
> *Helpin' my heart take the fall*
> *And I'm mad as a hatter*
> *It's wine over matter*
> *But it's better than nothin' at all.*

How's that?"

Mickey said, "We're playing the Houston rodeo next month."

I don't know what I expected. "Sounds great," maybe, or "You haven't lost a thing." At least "Thanks." No comment at all pissed me off.

"You've played Houston before."

"You oughta come out this time. We'll be at the Bowie Knife all week."

"My husband doesn't like country music. I doubt if he'd go."

"Fuck the dentist and drive yourself over, Lannie."

"Don't hold your breath."

Mickey's voice came louder again. "You got it on backwards," he said. "That way gets come in the guy's ear."

The phone went dead.

———

Hearing Mickey always brought on a certain wistfulness. I

don't really care for wistfulness. It smacks too close to regret and regret is an emotion I don't abide. After his call, I held the phone in my lap and watched Ron sleep until the off-the-hook helicopter noise sounded. Gently laying the phone in its cradle, I slid from the bed, shrugged on my blue robe, and wandered downstairs to the family room.

Security lights from the street filtered through the humidity and windows to cast an unreal orangish glow on Ron's tuner. I sat on the carpet cross-legged, moving the dial until Suzie Burkburnett and "Mama" came through the speakers, filling me with that old warm feeling. God, I love country music.

> *Expecting and alone—again*
> *Mama, please let me come home—again.*

My wistfulness wasn't so much for Mickey himself. Mickey was just an old lover, the first, admittedly, who taught me some fanciful positions, but whose memory had faded into fuzzy mythology. What I missed was the music, the singing.

Onstage with everyone watching, I'd felt like somebody. I could make sad people feel better and lonely people understand they weren't really alone.

What I did back then mattered. I couldn't convince myself that Houston mattered. I mean, dozens of people tell you that motherhood is the most important job on earth. And I bought the line the first ten years. I truly believed I was forming future grown-ups. Only now, with the girls impatiently charging into adolescence, my part in the formation process seemed over. I found myself shifted into a nothing-but-a-job stance—maid, cook, chauffeur and, on Saturday nights after the news, weather, and sports, whore. I'd become the woman I made fun of. A thought surfaced: *I goddamn wasn't born to be a stereotype.*

For the first time in years—at least since I saw the

*M\*A\*S\*H* where Colonel Blake got killed—tears welled up on the inside corners of my eyes. No one needed me anymore. I felt like eating a candy bar. Squeezing both eyes shut, I doubled my fists and said, "Shit."

"Mama," droned to an end, and, after a Midas Muffler commercial, Emmylou came on singing "Play Pretend." Her voice rose so pure and holy, like running water in the mountains. Eyes still closed, I leaned back on both hands and straightened my legs. I sang quietly, just above a whisper.

> *"Let's play pretend, that you still love me*
> *I'll act as though you will always be here*
> *The kids will believe that we are still happy*
> *If you play pretend, that you always will care."*

In some three-two bar, I think it was Okmulgee, Oklahoma, I remember a boy at the first table behind the dance floor. He looked fourteen or fifteen, I don't know how he got in the bar so young, but I was sixteen and too young myself so maybe no one cared. This boy had real short, dark hair and blue eyes that never left me the whole first set.

I sang a few Patsy songs, "Walkin' After Midnight," "I Fall to Pieces," "A Poor Man's Roses," and did some backups on Choosie's "My-Wife-Done-Left-and-I'm-Gonna-Get-Drunk" standards. With each song, this boy flashed deeper and deeper into what must have been one hell of a religious experience. His face glowed like lit neon, his eyes practically shot sparks at me, I swear he didn't breathe for forty-five minutes.

Who knows what really happened? Maybe someone slipped him some redneck version of LSD and the kid saw me as Mother Nature reborn with a microphone in her hand. I was somewhat embarrassed and somewhat flattered. I mean, the whole place was watching this kid watch me.

We finished the set with "Tennessee Waltz" and, as Choosie went into "Pause for the cause, don't forget your bartenders and waitresses," I looked over at the boy. Tears streamed like when a rubber washer on an old faucet busts loose. His hairless chin dribbled. The boy's blue eyes shimmered in a saved-at-the-revival, basking-in-the-Promised-Land look of lost focus.

Mickey came up beside me. "What the hell did you do to that one?"

"I don't know."

"You'd think he never saw a twat before."

"Maybe he likes the way I sing."

Mickey laughed and spit onstage. We went out to the van for Johnnie Walker Red and when we came back in, the boy had disappeared.

———

"What're you doing, Mama?" Cassie stood by the door in her white flannel nightgown and long hair. For just a moment, I thought I was looking at myself.

"I'm thinking about the old days."

"When you were in the band?"

"Yes."

Cassie came in and sat on the edge of the end table with both hands folded in her lap. "Do you miss being in the band?"

"It was a hard life." I reached over and switched off the radio.

"Do you ever wish you'd stayed on the road?"

"No." I got off the floor and Cassie and I went to the kitchen in search of ice cream.

———

Closer to two months than one later, Roxanne called on a Saturday morning. I was drinking coffee at the breakfast nook, trying to schedule my day. The problem lay in dry cleaning. Cassie's riding lesson ran from noon to two-thirty, with Connie's tennis class from two to three. That left me with time for my Cambodian cooking school at twelve-thirty, but only if I drove the south side loop like an amphetamine-crazed astronaut.

However, it didn't leave time to buy groceries and pick up Ron's lucky cardigan at the dry cleaners. Ron was supposed to play golf in the morning and I knew both our days would be shot if I didn't bring home his lucky sweater. It was a sky-blue button-up with a reindeer on the back. Ron wore it because he'd once lucked in an eagle with it on. Also, he thought the sweater looked nonpretentious. Ron spent a lot of time and money on not looking pretentious at the country club.

The phone rang and Roxanne started right in. "He's in town. What're you going to do, Lannie?"

"I think I'll skip cooking class and pick up the dry cleaning. Who's in town?"

"It's rodeo week and I drank T'n'Ts at the Bowie Knife last night. Who do you think is in town?"

"Mickey?"

"The old pill popper himself. He wants to see you. I think the boy still carries a lump for you, Lannie, after all these years."

"Hides it pretty well if he does. I didn't realize you even knew the Mick."

Roxanne laughed—a sound like cutting cardboard with a butter knife. "Hell, me and Mickey Thunder go way back. How you figure he knew your address and phone number ever' time you and the dentist moved?"

"I thought he looked in the phone book."

"Wrong, my little housewife. Me and Galen drove over in his pickup to two-step last night and during the break, old Mickey walked up, sat at our table—pissed Galen off no end—and asked all about you. Seemed real interested in what the years have done to your body."

"How dare you call me a housewife?"

Roxanne shrieked again. "Which one of us is nursing a hangover and swollen thighs and which one of us can't decide if she ought to skip cooking class to pick up the dry cleaning?"

"Fuck yourself, Roxanne."

———

Roxanne's housewife crack pissed me off so much I didn't pick up the dry cleaning or make Cambodian cooking school. Instead, I pulled into a Tex-Mex drive-in on Hanover Boulevard and ate three of the greasiest enchiladas in Houston. The carhop had a pimple on her neck as big as Ron's class ring.

On the way to the stables, I daydreamed about hot fudge and creamed marshmallows on graham crackers. My sugar binges often begin as dessert fantasies. The daydream should have sounded a *Look out, Lana Sue* alarm in my head, but I doubt if it did.

Cassie stood by the driveway in her riding boots and Western wear jacket. Her hair was pulled back in a pony tail so she looked like a fourteen-year-old Elizabeth Taylor in *National Velvet.*

"A man was looking for you," Cassie said.

"What man?"

"There he is."

Mickey Thunder stepped from behind a hand-painted blue-panel truck with Tennessee plates. "Hi, Lana Sue."

It's odd to go around expecting something every day for years and then all of a sudden it happens. I didn't feel anything. "Hi, Mick." I opened the door but didn't get out.

He held out his hands. "Aren't you going to give your old buddy a squeeze?"

"I don't know." We stared at each other a moment. The

years hadn't changed Mickey a bit. Same gray skin stretched over the same knobby skull. Same straight, combed-over-his-ears hair. If Mickey had gained any weight, I couldn't see where. He was still the boy who all that lifetime ago had asked me if I was a cocktease.

"Your cousin told me you'd be here."

"Sweet of her to do that." I looked at Cassie. She stood by the front bumper, watching with no expression on her face—as if Mickey and I were on a television set.

I motioned in her direction. "This is my daughter, Cassie. Cassie, this is Michael Rossitelli."

"Call me Mickey."

"Mom's told me about you."

Mickey's eyes stayed on mine. "Don't believe anything she said."

I sat with both hands on the wheel, considering a way to deal with events. There didn't seem to be any middle ground between ignoring him and hustling him into the nearest motel. I wasn't sure which I wanted, but Cassie standing next to the car appeared to pre-answer the question.

Mickey came up a step and rested one hand on top of my door. "Lacy's got throat cancer."

"I'm sorry to hear that."

"Too many cigarettes, I guess. Tonight's her last gig. Monday, the doctors take her voice box out."

"Poor woman." I wasn't thinking poor woman. I was thinking, What in hell does this have to do with me?

"She'll be okay. A senator over in Louisiana's been after her to marry him for years. Now's his chance."

"It's still awful."

Mickey nodded a couple of times. He put his other hand on my door and stared down at me. "We need us a singer, Lana Sue."

My heart did a four-inch drop. The unfaced dilemma of my married life was about to be faced. "So?"

There it was. I looked at Cassie, trying to guess what she thought of the situation. "I'm too old for Nashville."

"We're not going back to Nashville. Choosie and me're gonna stick with Western honky-tonks from now on. No more rhinestones and record contracts bullshit, Lana Sue. It'll be just like it was when you were with us before."

I thought about before, the six bodies in a bed and the diet of soft drinks and candy bars. That might have been fine for a high-school junior, but I was a grown-up now. I'd become accustomed to clean bathrooms and sleep every night.

"You didn't need a girl singer before me. Why not go all the way back to the old days?"

Mickey shook his head. "Choosie's about whiskied his voice to death, and none of the new Bobs can sing for shit. You know how I am with a microphone. Besides, all our material goes with a girl singer. I kind of got used to it after you."

I didn't say anything for a while. The only ambition I'd ever had was to sing country music. But the idea of running out on Ron and the girls was ridiculous. I'd never for a moment thought of leaving Ron. Who'd fix his after-work Cape Cods? Not to mention what Daddy'd do if I took off with Mickey again. And it probably wouldn't last any longer this time than it had in 1963. Did I want to give up everything we'd worked to build for another three-month fling at the grubby life?

"No," I said.

"Lana Sue."

"No. Get in the car, Cassie."

"You want to grow old eating lunch at the country club and picking new drapes for the den? This is your chance not to die bored."

"Get in the car, Cassie." I stared into Mickey's eyes. His irises had picked up some gray flecks over the years. "Having a home and family and some money doesn't make a person bored."

"Does you."

"Let loose of my door. Cassie, are you getting in the car or not?" She shrugged and moved around to the passenger side.

"At least come hear us tonight. You owe yourself to see what you're giving up."

"I'm giving up lice, hunger, alcoholism, and sex with a child seducer."

"Who said anything about sex. I'm offering you a job."

"Bullshit."

Our eyes locked in a battle of furies. I was pissed. The bastard didn't want me. He wanted to save the band the trouble of finding a new singer. There'd be sex all right. I knew Mickey well enough to count on us sleeping together as a fringe benefit, but to Mickey, I was an interchangeable clit. He'd sleep with whatever female singer the band hired.

"I'm going home to fix Ron's supper."

Mickey released my door. "I'll leave your name with the guy up front. They'll let you in without a cover."

"I can pay the damn cover charge."

———

The part about fixing Ron's supper was a lie. He ate dinner that night at the Holiday Inn with three other doctors who wanted him to invest in a Biscuitville franchise in Beaumont. They told him it was a colored gold mine. After dinner, Ron called to say he was watching a basketball game in the lounge and I shouldn't wait up.

"Did you pick up my sweater?"

"Sorry. I'll drive over as soon as I feed the girls."

"You know I need my sweater."

"I'll have it tonight."

A little after eight, I knocked on the girls' doors to tell them I was going after the dry cleaning and I might stop by Roxanne's for a visit. Connie ignored me, an attitude she'd adopted for almost a week since I told her she couldn't sail on a boat with a college kid. As soon as I said no and we went through the "all the other girls get to" routine, Connie ran to Ron, who gave me half-assed backup.

"I don't see why you shouldn't but your mom said no and she's the boss."

At Cassie's door, I hesitated a moment before knocking. She'd know what I was really up to, and I'd know she knew. What if Cassie called me a liar to my face? I sure as hell couldn't deny it.

Cassie lay sprawled across her bed, watching a portable TV and reading a Judy Blume book during the commercials. She had on a black T-shirt that said BUY A HORSE across the back in red letters.

On the television, a woman with two heads and four arms spoke to an effeminate robot. "What's this?" I asked.

"New show called *Quark*. It's not very good." The robot scooted across the room, bumped into a doorframe, and fell on its side, beeping. The laugh track thought this was hilarious.

"I'm going out for a while. To pick up Dad's sweater and see Roxanne. Can I bring you anything?"

Cassie looked up at me and smiled. "No, thanks, tell Roxie I said hey."

"Sure."

As I left the room, Cassie spoke again. "Mom. You're going to be okay."

I turned back. Cassie's eyes were on the woman with two heads, not watching me. "Thanks," I said.

"No sweat."

— —

I paid the cover on the notion that it wouldn't do to let anyone know I'd been there in case I changed my mind and fled. Might as well have used my connections, though, because Choosie spotted me before my eyes even adjusted to the bar light. He came scrambling over, hugging and leering, carrying on in the been-too-long vein.

"My God, Lannie, you're beautiful as ever." He stuck a finger in my ribs. "See you've filled out some. You was too skinny before."

"Didn't you have teeth the last time we met?"

Choosie grinned, showing off two banks of brown, liver-spotted gums. "Yep. I sing better without 'em. Gives me resonance." Choosie had lost more than his teeth. If Mickey hadn't aged a day in sixteen years, Choosie'd grown old for the both of them. By my figuring, he couldn't have been much over forty, but sagging, bleached-out skin and a gray to balding head made him look sixty. His posture was more in the eighty range.

"You must have processed a lot of Dr Pepper and Jack Black since I left the band, Choosie. You look pickled."

He laughed and launched into a "same old Lana Sue" routine. I think he was under orders to be lovable so I'd rejoin the band. In the old days, a crack like that would have been answered with spit down my jeans leg.

"Not a big crowd," I said, checking out the general mill of cowboys and beauty-operator types grouped around two pool tables and a Space Invaders game.

"Early yet," Choosie said. "Rodeo ain't done for an hour. They'll be crammed in the rafters by midnight."

He led me by the hand up front to a round table surrounded by band members and two or three Houston snuff queens. An enormous woman with chins to her chest and boobs to her belt buckle scowled as if I'd been committing unnatural acts with her boyfriend.

I leaned to Choosie. "You always liked 'em big, but this is bizarre."

He grinned, showing gums again. "You should see her naked."

Mickey stood and pulled a chair over for me. "Real glad you made it, Lana Sue. I was afraid we lost out. What you drinking?" He had on a white T-shirt with a picture of Patsy on the front.

"I'll take a rusty nail."

A cocktail waitress who'd appeared at my elbow laughed at me. "Honey, we sell whiskey, scotch, or gin, on the rocks, with water, or Coca-Cola. Or beer. We don't serve pansy drinks."

"You got Jim Beam?"

"You bet."

"Pour me some in a glass."

I sat between Mickey and Choosie's fat queen. Lacy Rasher slumped on Mickey's other side with her head down on her folded arms.

"Is she drunk or crying?" I asked Mickey.

"Which would you be in her situation?"

He introduced me around to the band members, none of whose names fit the Bob game very well. "Warren Bob, Charlie Bob, and Felipe Bob, meet Lana Sue. She might be our singer next week."

At that, Lacy's head came up and she stared through unfocused eyes and stringy hair. "Already replaced me, you bastard."

Mickey put his hands over hers. "Life's gotta go on for the band, Lacy. You know that."

"Bastard." She leaned across Mickey and brought her face six inches from mine. Her breath was awful, her eyes frightening. Lacy studied me for thirty seconds. I didn't know how to come on. Normally, I would have said, "You push and I'll shove, bitch," but the woman had cancer. I could hardly blame her for hating me.

Finally she twisted to look up at Mickey. "She's a dog. An old woman. What you replacing me with an old woman for?"

"There's no call to take your problem out on Lana Sue."

Lacy shook her head wildly. "I don't have no problem. You got the problem." She hiccuped. "You guys'll fall apart without me. I can do fine without you."

Lacy fell back in her chair. "Whole damn band'll starve six weeks after I'm dead."

"You aren't gonna die."

She shook her head again. Her long hair swung like ropes. "Might as well. Gimme another drink."

Mickey held her glass under the table and poured a couple inches of Yukon Jack from a bottle. She sucked it down like a baby on a nipple. No one at the table except me would look at her. The guys mostly stared into their drinks, embarrassed. The women faked oblivion. Or maybe they weren't faking. Hell, I don't know.

When my Beam came, Mickey paid the waitress. So many names and stupid sayings were carved on the table that I had trouble finding a flat place to set my glass. The tables nearest the stage began to fill as people filtered down from the long bar. I had no trouble separating the construction workers turned Saturday night cowboy from the authentic rodeo circuit followers. The rodeo cowboys showed more confidence in their cowboyism. They didn't look at each other. Most limped and the inseams of their Levi's didn't rub. No one in the place looked like he actually worked with cows.

I felt shy around Mickey all of a sudden and he seemed to feel the same way about me. I don't know what we expected, the years not to matter or something along those lines, I guess.

But things had changed. I was playing at being real folks now. My cowgirl shirt came from Neiman-Marcus. I bought my jeans prefaded.

"Can Lacy still sing?" I asked.

Mickey raised a Lone Star to his thin lips. "Sure, why not?"

"How can she perform in her condition?"

"Voice box don't come out till Monday. She'll do fine tonight."

"She's too drunk to walk."

Mickey glanced at Lacy next to him. Her head was back and tears dribbed down her cheekbones, leaving little trails of mascara. "She don't have to walk to sing. Lacy's a pro. She's not gonna screw up her last gig."

Lacy mumbled something I didn't hear as her head fell to one side. She didn't look anything like the beautiful, peppy woman in tight pants and the sequined top who stood next to Mickey on her last album cover.

"'Bout time," Felipe Bob said. Nobody moved.

Mickey finished off his beer and reached over for a swig off Lacy's Yukon. "You coming to Lubbock?"

"What's in Lubbock?"

"Next job. We open Monday in a county-line club out in the boonies somewhere. Won't be much fun without you."

"That's a nice thing to say."

Mickey's skull face turned to me. "You coming?"

"No."

His long fingers tightened on Lacy's glass. She moaned once and burped like she was fixing to dry-heave. "Why come here tonight?" Mickey asked.

"I was curious. All those years I've remembered our time together in a certain way, and I wondered if that way was real or I'd built up a romantic sham."

"So which is it?"

My eyes circled the table from Lacy to the big woman on my left. "Seems kind of desperate to me."

One of Lacy's eyes opened. She muttered, "You can't take my place in his pants either."

Mickey touched one of her hands. "Time to work, hon. Go find the can and make yourself pretty."

Choosie's friend helped Lacy out of her chair and led her off to the bathroom. As Lacy stumbled away from the table, the fat queen looked back at me and snarled. I stuck out my tongue.

Mickey play-poked me in the shoulder. "Coulda been great," he said. "We could of blazed a country-western trail they'd sing about for a hundred years.

I blinked a couple of times. "I know, Mickey. But I'd rather be happy and secure than famous and wasted."

"Your choice." He stood up. I'd forgotten how much taller Mickey was than Ron. "Mount up, boys. Let's take her out with class."

The guys straggled onstage, picking up guitars and drumsticks, flipping on amps. They'd changed the order since my days. Mickey and Choosie still held down the sides, but Lacy's vocal mike was in the center between the bass and lead guitars. Mickey looked right at home behind his steel, stuffing his mouth with gum. He'd mounted a circular whiskey-glass holder off the tuning end of the board. Other than that, he was doing things exactly as he'd done them that New Year's Eve so long ago. I could have walked onstage and been sixteen again.

I thought about how it would feel to be sixteen again—to stand up there and sing through the smoke and barroom odors of sweat and beer. I thought about my girls. They didn't really need me anymore. Lord knows, Ron could get by fine without me, but if I jumped ship and abandoned Cassie and Connie now, wouldn't that be just cause for long-term mother hatred?

I'd been through way too much trouble the last fourteen years to grow old hated by my own children.

Connie was on the edge already. I hoped she might outgrow the resentment someday, but leaving her daddy would pretty much seal off that idea. What would Cassie think? I never knew what Cassie was going to think about anything.

Choosie's girlfriend flopped back into her chair.

"How's she doing?" someone asked.

"She'll be fine."

The band broke into a fast four-beat rhythm as Choosie stepped up to his microphone. "I'd like to welcome you-all here to the Bowie Knife Saloon and thank you for coming out. I know we're all gonna have an ass-kicking, gut-ripping good time tonight."

A couple of construction-worker cowboys whooped. I saw Lacy moving through the crowd. Her hair had been brushed and her makeup fixed. She appeared to be bouncing off the balls of her feet.

Choosie continued as the music wound behind him. "Right now, I'd like you all to put your hands together and give a big Houston welcome to Nashville recording artist Lacy Rasher!"

Lacy hopped onstage, grabbed the microphone with her right hand, and pulled it off the mike stand. "*Let's party.*"

More cowboys, real and drugstore, hollered back as Lacy kicked into "Setting the Woods on Fire."

She was beautiful. Energetic, alive, her eyes gleamed with excitement. She grinned at Mickey, clowned with Choosie on his breaks, directed the drummer by dancing. Leaning out from the stage, she winked at a star-struck kid at the next table over from us.

Lacy was a true professional. I played at being a singer—dreamed, pretended. I knew just how I would handle the adoration, how I would keep my down-home simple roots and not lose touch with the little people, what I would say when I accepted the Female Country Singer of the Year Award. But Lacy knew the job.

The fat girl nudged me with the mouth of a Lone Star. "Let's see you do that, cunt."

I drained my Beam and left.

———

The drive home found me enmeshed in one of those soul-searching self-examinations that I hate so much. Poets, artists, and Loren types love to hang around and wonder at themselves. Once a week Loren and I drive to town for breakfast and he'll order something like French toast. Then the rest of the morning while I'm buying groceries and returning library books, he clams up inside himself and explores the motivation behind choosing French toast instead of eggs.

"Mom always served eggs for breakfast. Could this be a reaction against her influence?"

I'll answer, "Zip your fly and decide what you want for dinner tomorrow," which brings on a whole new round of choice appraisals. The weeks before Loren staggered into the mountains in search of his pal, God, I could hardly get him dressed in the morning.

"Do you think people will realize my white socks symbolize a purity of spirit, or should I wear black? The black ones are clean."

"Jesus Christ, Loren, nobody cares."

The night I drove across Houston after leaving Mickey at the Bowie Knife, I found myself facing all kinds of disgusting truths, such as—was I capable of sacrificing my own potential for the good of my family? Or was this entire personal growth crisis nothing but an excuse for getting hold of Mickey's dick again?

The future loomed as a fork in the freeway with terrible as the exit and boring as the straightaway. I could do something remarkably stupid and immature—run away to the honky-tonks— or I could resign myself to a predictable existence—stay home. Both choices turned my stomach.

What was this predictable existence anyway? Four or five years of fighting with the girls, then the heartbreak of losing them. God knows how many years of being Ron's support system—unappreciated, unfulfilled, the whole feminist group therapy rap. Maybe I'd numb myself eventually. I could ease into more frequent drunks, go off on more sugar binges. The pain fucks might increase to semiannual, then seasonal. Maybe someday I'd get so bored I'd have an affair with a young hell-raiser. I could follow in Roxanne's footsteps.

Tawdry…trite…depressing…a fucking mess of a future. How had I got myself into a neglected housewife syndrome? Why hadn't I faced it before?

This story isn't even close to original. I think Grandma Moses wrote the first autobiographical novel of a woman screaming for her identity in an unhearing family. Finally she breaks loose, "*I must find myself*," and shocks the shit out of Hubby and the thoughtless children. The kids moan in terror, "*If only we'd given her room to grow.*" The husband cries, "*I should have bought her that kiln,*" and the wife goes off to a series of bad love affairs with raunchy yet vibrant men and finally finds happiness with a rock who cares.

Or doesn't find happiness. The plot changed about 1979.

———

Somewhere in here I ran a red light on Buzz Aldrin Drive and almost died when a black Cadillac with pimp windows barreled through and missed my front end. Scared the pee out of myself. A crash would have solved the immediate quandary, but I enjoyed being alive. Either one of my bad choices beat catatonic or dead.

Time to pay attention, I thought, turning on the radio and rolling down the windows. The night air was cool and smelled like bad milk. Running away might at least get me to a place where mold didn't grow on the bedroom walls.

That sounded nice for a second until I remembered there were no bedrooms where Mickey traveled. Only motel rooms and Howard Johnson food. I wondered if Ron and the girls would let me come home between gigs. Maybe there was no such thing as between gigs. Maybe the band never left the road. Did Mickey travel with everything he owned, or was there an apartment somewhere? Maybe even a house? Maybe even a wife?

I was contemplating leaving my family for this man and I didn't even know whether or not he was married. Sorry damn state of affairs if you asked me.

———

Ron's car sat parked in the driveway when I pulled up to the house. That wasn't a good sign. He might ask questions. Roxanne could have called while I was supposedly with her and blown my cover, although, at the moment, I didn't particularly care if my cover was blown. Many years of accounting for my whereabouts was beginning to chafe my so-called free spirit.

To hell with him. If Ron gave me any sass, I decided to turn snitty. No man—not even Daddy—has ever out self-righteoused Lana Sue Potts.

All three were in the den when I came through from the kitchen. At the sight of me, Connie turned off the TV and flounced from the room. I pretended not to notice.

"So, do we own a Biscuitville?"

Ron stood at his portable Sears Roebuck bar, mixing himself a vodka and cranberry juice. His big jaw jutted in that stubborn look that came over him whenever the team he bet on lost a ball game. "Maybe. Where have you been?"

"Out." I moved over and kissed Cassie on the cheek. She glanced up from her book and smiled, then looked back down.

Ron held his drink under the automatic ice dispenser until a couple of cubes plopped out and splashed cranberry on his hand. "Hope you didn't go anywhere public dressed like that."

I looked down at my Neiman-Marcus cowgirl shirt and designer blue jeans. At the Bowie Knife, I'd felt overdressed, and now I was being called slobby. "What's the matter with the way I'm dressed?"

"You look like a shitkicker."

Stomach muscles tightened, my scalp itched. Something was on the edge of happening and I was powerless to slow it down—even if I wanted to. "Maybe I am a shitkicker. Want to try me?"

Cassie's head came back up, her eyes studying my face. She knew Ron and I were courting disaster. I knew it also. Only Ron seemed lost in left field, oblivious to the possibilities.

"I didn't mean anything negative," he said. "I just wouldn't want you running into any of your friends dressed in your cowgirl costume."

It would be easy here to claim that I walked through the door and Ron came on nasty with no instigation. I could, with some success, blame his timing for our outcome, but that would be the easy way out. I know earlier I said leaving a man is ninety percent timing. However, in the case of Ron, timing doesn't answer all the riddles. What I think is, subconsciously, unconsciously, whatever the shrinks call it these days, I made my choice back on Buzz Aldrin Drive in one of those value-system-crystallization-in-the-face-of-death numbers. The Cadillac missed me, I cheated death, saw the way of the future, and went home looking for an excuse to do what I wanted.

Who knows if I would have pulled things off without Ron's help? I have no idea what the outcome would have been if he hadn't insulted me, but would-have-beens don't mean shit because he did.

"You get my sweater?" he asked.

"Nope."

"Why not?"

"I forgot. Mind if I fix a drink?" Ron stared at me while I poured an inch of Jim Beam into a brandy snifter.

"You forgot my golf sweater?"

"Guess you'll have to wear another one."

"How could you forget it?"

I looked him in the eye. "It wasn't important to me."

Ron watched while I slugged down my Beam. Then he spit out the only real insult he'd leveled at me since junior high. "You aren't worth much these days, are you?"

I said, "*Crack.*"

"What's that supposed to mean?"

"Means I'm driving to Lubbock."

———

Three and a half, going on four, years later I was living in Nashville when Ron called. It must have been early fall because I remember leaves in our backyard. Sycamore, oak, and a few elms ran down the hill to a little ditch creek with a fence and a cemetery on the other side. I remember standing on the back screened porch, chain smoking and watching the leaves most of the afternoon. They were pretty. I liked the way the flatness of the reds and yellows gave the yard a balanced, artsy look.

After a couple of scotches, the scene struck me as beautifully ironic in an American dream sort of way—that all these thousands of slick scammers and cynical pragmatists had chosen such a beautiful setting to work their cash flow magic.

Ace and I had been married over two years. He'd called earlier that afternoon to say he would be working late at the studio. I didn't believe him, but what depressed me was that I didn't care whether I believed him or not. At some point since our marriage, I'd adopted the Nashville attitude that the sex organs are nothing but business tools like the telephone and the Visa card, and I could hardly expect Ace to penalize his career for my security.

After I left Mickey in Utah things turned out about the way he predicted—which pisses me off. I can't stand Mickey thinking he knows everything about everything. Loren's the same way. I always seem to wind up with smartasses.

Ace wooed me away from Mickey and took me off to Nashville, where we fooled around a few months and came out with an album. The album zoomed to number sixty-four on the Billboard Country 100 and stayed there for two weeks, stuck between George Jones on the backside and Jerry Reed on the front. I did a couple guest shots on *Pop! Goes the Country* and the *Hank Thompson Ranch Show*, then my album sank into the Kmart cut-rate bin and no one called anymore.

Somewhere in there, for stability or legitimacy or something— hell, I'll never figure out why I pulled this one—I married Ace Roe. This was after he'd started that epileptic-fit-when-I-didn't-feel-like-sucking-him-off-business. Maybe Daddy's disease got me, or Grandma's blood. Maybe I just screwed up. Anyway, I was right back where I started—married, ignored, and frustrated.

I increased my scotch drinking and took four hot baths a day. I gained fifteen pounds hanging around the Kroger's bakery. Worst of all, I initiated a number of pain fucks with studio steel players. Nothing to compare with Ace's scorecard, but plenty enough to trash out my self-regard.

Along about the time Ron called, the idea was dawning that I'd messed up my life. The experiment of living the future for myself had lost its charm.

—

I answered on the second ring.

"Fucking yourself and me up is one thing, but you've gone too far this time."

"Hi, Ron, how's my babies?"

"Your voice sounds different, have you been drinking?"

"Of course I've been drinking. Did you call for a reason or simply to tell me I've fucked up our lives?"

I listened to his breathing a moment, then Ron said, "Your friend kidnapped Cassie."

Pictures of baby rapers and white slave traders flashed through my mind. "What do you mean, kidnapped?"

"Lana Sue, you are poison, you know that? And your lover Mickey is poison also. I can't believe what the two of you do to people."

"Back up. Mickey kidnapped my daughter? Is that what you're saying?"

"You know damn well that's what I'm saying. I'd bet everything I own you were in on it." He was crying.

I thought a minute. I hadn't talked to Cassie since her birthday in August. Back then she'd sounded fine. She was excited about enrolling at SMU. She told me she'd learned some new songs on her guitar.

"Ron, did Mickey really kidnap her or did Cassie run away?"

"What's the difference? My insides crawl when I think about that slime with my baby girl. And she dropped out of school. Your daddy's going to have your hide for this one, Lana Sue."

I shouted at the phone. "I didn't do anything!"

"You left."

I reached for the scotch bottle, but changed my mind. "Details, Ron. How long's she been gone?"

Audibly, Ron pulled himself together. "I got a letter today postmarked Denver, Colorado. Says she dropped out of school last week and joined the band. She says the school will refund part of her tuition and dorm fees back to me." Ron's voice was bitter. "She says she has to find herself."

How often had I used *finding myself* as an excuse to hurt people who loved me? "I wonder if Cassie's doing this to get back at me for leaving her?"

"More likely Mickey's doing it to get back at you for leaving him." That thought caused some grief. Mickey could be a mean fucker if he got his ass up, and ravaging my daughter would be just his idea of perfect revenge.

"Did she say anything to Connie before she left?"

"Hell, I don't know. Connie's so disgusted she pretends neither one of you exists. I can't get her to talk about anything."

I looked through the window at the softening late afternoon sky and the dying leaves. Outside was so pretty and inside was such a disappointment. I considered the people I had loved so far in my life. One daughter hates me, the other is ruining herself by following in my footsteps, my first husband blames me for every problem anyone has, my one true friend and lover is screwing my baby daughter to spite me, my present husband is sticking it to every would-be singer in Nashville— all of this caused by my good intentions. Shit, all of a sudden life was ugly.

"Are they still in Denver?" I asked.

"How the hell should I know? You traveled that circuit, you tell me."

"If they're in Denver, they'll be playing at the Powder Keg. It's not bad compared to some of Mickey's dives."

"I'm glad our daughter's being gang-banged in a clean bar."

"Ron, there's no call for that. I'll fly out tonight and get her. You'll have your daughter back by tomorrow afternoon."

Ron made a growl-laugh angry sound. "Don't fuck up again, Lana Sue."

———

The Powder Keg in Denver is the junction where the country in country-western connects with the western. The dancers make the difference. From the Powder Keg to northern California, you mainly see western swing dancing. The couples twirl and dip like jitterbuggers with spot-welded hips. East of Denver, it's all two-step—a never-ending, never-varying circle of shufflers with their hands placed in wrestling holds. For me, most two-step has all the spontaneity of a McDonald's hamburger, but that may just be another anti-East Coast prejudice I picked up from Mickey.

The place is definitely big. It used to be a National Guard armory or something. The walls are made from large stones mortared together like in a rock fireplace. A long bar stretches across the back and doglegs down the east side to a dance floor about half the size of a basketball court. Strains of "San Antonio Rose" drifted from the stage as I came through the door and made a beeline for the back bar. I could hear Choosie's voice crackling on the high notes.

Cassie stood dead center in Lacy's old position. They had her dressed up real nice—a calf-length skirt that showed off her tan boots and a white ruffled blouse with a jacket that matched the skirt. Her hair hung down on both sides of her shoulders, giving Cassie this pure-ranch-girl-come-to-Sunday-school look. She held her Martin kind of high and straight parallel to the stage. I was surprised how good the band sounded with an extra rhythm guitar. The mix was deeper, fuller, her chording set Choosie's fiddle free to soar in and out of the melody line.

I ordered a double scotch with a shot of Drambuie on the side. The plan was to hang back, mix myself rusty nails, and listen awhile—work on my position in the upcoming confrontation. The counterkidnapping would not be easy. My best bet was to act ungodly angry at somebody, but who? I could hardly come on self-righteously outraged at Cassie because I'd committed the same crime myself. Twice. At least she had the sense to wait until after her eighteenth birthday. I was still statutory when Mickey ripped up my hymen. Daddy could have made things ugly if he hadn't been too embarrassed to haul me into court.

It struck me that if anyone involved was behaving like a shit, it had to be my old pal Mickey Thunder. Hiring and sleeping with my own daughter was a dirty trick, reeking of ulterior, vengeful motives. I knew what a pervert Mickey could be in bed and he knew I knew. That was what rankled. He was using and abusing my baby daughter just to goose my imagination and screw me up—the asshole.

"San Antonio Rose" ended and after a few seconds of guitar tuning, Cassie began the first line of "Echo of an Old Man's Last Ride."

*I'm gonna ride me a moonbeam, someday, gonna take it to places and scenes faraway.*

Her voice startled me. When had it gotten so mature?

*Gonna rope me a comet and shoot me a star
Gonna ride me a moonbeam someday.*

Cassie's voice was a little deeper than mine, not so strong on the high notes, but her midrange rang out true and perfect, damn remarkable for a girl her age.

More than her beautiful voice, I was amazed by Cassie's face as she sang. Her face was alert, flushed with excitement. Her eyes bubbled with life-force.

She had always been such a calm little girl. Even at three

or four years old, Cassie's self-control frightened me. All her childhood, she gave the impression of peacefully waiting for something. Never unhappy, yet never happy, she didn't seem involved in her life. Now she was transformed. Whatever she'd been waiting for had come.

Joy practically exploded from Cassie's face. Not only was she involved in the moment, she was also damn good. I couldn't believe that was my daughter on the stage, my little girl. She was five times better than I'd been at her age and twice as good as I was now. How had Mickey known? Or had he known?

At the end of the first verse, Cassie looked over at Mickey and smiled. He smiled back and nodded.

*Now the next morning they found him, sitting under a tree*
*With his saddle and his rope by his side*
*His Colt .45 in his big gnarled hand*
*Was the echo of an old man's last ride.*

So much for dragging Cassie back to Texas. She was complete, fulfilled, her face when she smiled at Mickey glowed with smitten softness. She had, at least for the moment, pulled off what I'd been scrambling after for nearly twenty years— meaningful happiness. The pleasant life. I had no right, in fact, no desire, to threaten that.

Neither Ron nor Daddy would ever understand. For them, sucking Mickey's crank and performing in smoky honky-tonks was a terrible fate no matter how much joy it brought. I'd taken my shot at that route and failed, but I sure couldn't hold it against my daughter for wanting her own chance.

As the song ended, the crowd applauded and whistled. Cassie blushed and smiled and looked eighteen again. She said, "Thank you," into the microphone. I knew just how she felt.

Mickey leaned toward her, saying something. Cassie covered

the mike with one hand and said something back to him. She turned to the drummer, then back to the audience.

"This next song is an old classic the boys had a hit with years ago, but I just learned it yesterday, so ya'll will have to bear with me." A few people called encouragement. Cassie smiled and shook her hair back. "I'd like to dedicate this song to my dear old mama, wherever she may be and whoever she may be with. It's called 'Raising Cain or Raising Babies.'"

If I could prove that Mickey saw me back at the bar and put her up to that one, I'd shoot the bastard. *Wherever she may be and whoever she may be with.* Jesus. The words are even worse than the title.

I turned to the bar in disgust. Cassie could outsing her mother and look more beautiful and sleep with my old boyfriend, but she didn't have to be so damn honest about the whole thing.

"You look dejected," the guy sitting next to me said.

I hadn't noticed him before. He was skinny and wore glasses. His clothes looked slept in.

"I am dejected. That's my daughter singing that song."

He squinted at the stage. "You should be proud of her."

"She ran away from home. The tall sucker on the pedal steel is my old boyfriend and her new one. You ever hear anything so sick?"

"My son disappeared and my wife killed herself."

I turned from my drink and stared at him. The guy looked vaguely familiar, like someone I'd known long ago. I liked his curly hair. "That's awful. I'm so sorry, I must sound terrible complaining about my daughter."

He watched me in the mirror behind the bar. "I finished a book about them today. I don't know what to do next."

I felt almost embarrassed. My pain over Ace and Cassie and Mickey had me so worked up I'd forgotten that I still had them on some level or another. "Raising Cain or Raising Babies" might be an insult, but Cassie's voice was beautiful and Cassie was beautiful. I was proud of her.

"Listen," I said to the guy, "you want to go somewhere quieter and have a drink?"

# 15

Light filled the room and I woke up alone—which, I admit, is something of a novelty. Loren claims I've never spent a night alone since my first marriage twenty-one years ago. He made a big deal out of it on our honeymoon. The charge isn't true. I've slept alone plenty times. Plenty might be stretching it, but often enough not to be afraid to.

Knowing Loren, I know that he must suspect fear of sleeping by myself was why I left the day before his Vision Quest began. I call crock on the idea. If that was the problem, I would have stayed home and found a warm body to heat the bed. Why drive three hundred miles in search of a crotch?

Did I scamper off to bed with the nearest cowboy while Loren roamed the countryside, chatting with the ghosts of Scott Fitzgerald and Flannery O'Connor? Of course not. I can sleep alone if I choose to. I simply don't normally choose to.

While we're on the subject, let's discuss these cross-country death and truth jaunts. For many women, the Fitzgerald trip to Maryland would have been just cause for a *Crack*. No one could have blamed me for walking away, but I didn't. I hung in there, all the way to the Vision Quest.

We'd only been married three months and I was still flying around in ecstasy. I was nuts about the guy. Loren was the first man who thought I knew how to take care of myself. He trusted me to make decisions. If I was depressed he didn't blame my period. We had our cabin in the aspen grove with the creek and my own room. We fucked and ate great meals and walked in the woods, alone or together. Loren and I had the three goals of every country song—money, time, and love.

Then one afternoon, he came crashing in the back door while I was domestically going through his jeans pockets before dumping them in the wash.

Loren said, "Scott Fitzgerald wants to tell me the end of *The Last Tycoon.*"

I'm not illiterate. I know who Scott Fitzgerald is and before we were married, Loren told me about the writers' graves weirdness, but I was standing in the utility shed with my hands full of fuzzy candy and chewed-up straws. How was I supposed to make the connection that this guy Loren had to talk to was dead and buried in Maryland?

I threw him the keys. "Take the Toyota. It's gassed up."

"Thanks."

He was gone nine days. When he came home, I was so mad I didn't say a word about abandoning me in the wilderness.

"So how does *The Last Tycoon* end?"

"Scott wouldn't tell me, he changed his mind."

That was the first sign I'd married an idiot. And do you think I got credit for sleeping alone those nine nights? Hell, no. Loren pretends he trusts me, but I know in his mind I was up on the mountain humping backpackers the whole time he was gone.

———

Sometime in the night Thorne left the couch, so even though I didn't go to sleep by myself, I woke up that way, which should count for at least half credit. More important than being alone, I woke up fully dressed in Janey Axel's spacious shirt and green army pants. The woman must have been built like a lumberjack.

I stretched and blinked and worked on focusing on the log ceiling. Ten hours of sober sleep had done wonders for my stressed-out attitude. No nausea, no headache. After a cup of coffee and a good toothbrushing I might feel human again.

The room was large and airy and decked out like a hunting lodge lobby—dead animal heads on the walls, a glass-fronted gun rack by the bay window, chairs and couches with bent sapling arms and legs and red upholstery grouped around a bear rug and a stone fireplace.

Through the window, a Wyoming blue sky stretched off north above the Red Desert. Loren was up there, the other side of the horizon. I wondered what he would eat for breakfast. Would he fix it himself or had he found a new caretaker— probably little Marcie VanHorn from down the road. Loren has a thing for young girls. His books are full of thirty-year-old men fulfilling wet dreams with seventeen-year-old cheerleaders in tight sweaters and short skirts. I'd wring his neck if I caught him fulfilling anything with the little tramp.

Of course, if everything had moved according to plan, Loren was up in the mountains, fasting and waiting for some detached voice to tell him where Buggie ended up. Buggie. I shook my head to clear the early morning half-sleep mind associations. Now wasn't the time to think about Buggie or Loren. Coffee came first.

———

Maria sat on the kitchen floor, polishing drawer handles. The handles were made from tips of deer antlers. I've never polished a drawer handle in my life, but then mine were always wooden knobs or metal swinging things and it didn't seem important.

Only on a Wyoming ranch, or maybe a Montana bar, would drawer handles be made from an animal part.

My voice was a croak. "Coffee."

"On the counter." Maria held antler polish in one hand and a chamois rag in the other. Chewing gum, she concentrated on the smooth tip of the bottom drawer.

A full Mr. Coffee sat next to a Litton microwave that sat next to an Ashley wood stove that sat next to a Westinghouse gas range. The lineup shot to hell forever any theories of judging real folks from imposters by what they cooked on. The Mr. Coffee was spotless, shiny as a showroom jewel. All the other ovens and stoves, even the walls were equally blot free. I began to think I'd been wrong in liking Maria.

I found a cup and poured coffee. "Any idea the time?"

She glanced at a digital clock on the microwave next to me. "Seven-thirty."

"What an awful time to be awake." I sipped coffee while considering whether to stand and be uncomfortable or sit and risk a smudge.

"There's waffles in the oven and serviceberry syrup. I fried some bacon, but I got busy on the recipe files and it burnt up. I could make some more." She started to rise.

"No, thanks anyway, Maria, but I'll stick with coffee for now, maybe try some waffles later. Is something wrong with your mouth?"

When Maria looked right at me, her pupils appeared to have been hardened into tiny rat pucks and sizzled in a frying pan. This wasn't the same serenity-personified woman I'd met yesterday. This woman was a wreck and I suddenly realized why.

"Do you hear a train?" Maria asked.

"Holy smoke, Maria, you've been dancing in the snowflakes."

She looked down at her hands and gritted her teeth. "I found the Baggie in your jeans when I went to wash out the blood. I tried a little, then a little more. Forgive me, Mrs. Paul, I shouldn't have, but E.T. used to give me lines sometimes and I felt itchy, I guess. Then the cabinets looked dirty and when I hauled ashes from the wood stove I saw all this grease." She clutched her hands together. "It was fun at first."

I'm sorry, but I laughed—laughed so hard I spilled coffee on the shining floor. Maria'd buzzed her brains out and cleaned and snorted all night. On the one hand, her predicament was hilarious. I'd been in the position before. On the other hand, I felt so sorry for her because I'd been in the position before. It happened a couple of times while I was with Mickey and the band. Mickey was an alcohol and pills fanatic who generally regarded coke as a nasal form of herpes. But every now and then some bar owner or a roadie for a bigger band would offer up a pile, in seduction hopes, I suppose, and I'd come zipping back to the motel room about five in the morning, wide awake and ready to bust balls. Only Mickey and the boys would all be passed out like the drunks they were. I'd wind up reading heavy truths into the stock reports on all-night TV or making lists of the presents Ron and I bought the twins for Christmas and birthdays from the time they were two till twelve. It was awful. Some people enjoy the stuff. Many people must love it from what I read, but personally, I'd rather snort barbwire.

The memory made my throat tighten and my eyes ache. "I better get rid of that stuff."

Maria sniffed. "Please."

"Where is it?"

"I didn't know what to do so I hid the bag in the toaster oven."

"Why would someone with a toaster and three ovens need a toaster oven?"

Maria shrugged. "Janey bought it."

I set the Baggie on the kitchen table. We pulled up chairs

and drank more coffee, discussing the situation. I explained how I came to own an ounce of cocaine, leaving out the part where Billy G called me a woman. Maria told me about when E.T. used to give her snorts. He was after her body, but she never gave in because she was afraid of Janey, and after a while E.T. stopped hitting on her. This led to a general rap on Janey's character, which led to Maria's father and her boyfriend, Petey, and the treatment of Spanish-Americans in the oil fields. I like to never got her to shut up.

"What can we do now?" I asked.

"Nothing, the oil fields are as bad as ever. Janey's as bad as ever. If it wasn't for Thorne I'd move to Nevada and work in a trailer."

I couldn't picture Maria as a tiny hooker. Her posture was too good. "No, Maria, the bag. What can we do now with the bag?"

"You give it to the cowboys out in the bunkhouse. They're all a bunch of addicts anyway."

"Do you want some more?"

Maria shuddered. "God, I hope not. Maybe you could sell it. Cocaine is worth a lot of money."

"I don't know anything about selling drugs. Beside, that's kind of unethical, I think."

"E.T. loves to sell drugs. I heard him in the game room an hour or so ago."

"E.T.'s in the game room now?"

"He had the Grateful Dead turned up full volume."

"Doesn't anyone around here ever sleep?"

Maria spoke through clenched jaws. "You should have seen Darlene about four o'clock this morning. She was out by the barn doing something odd with a prairie dog."

I drained off the bottom of my coffee cup. "Whole Axel family's odd if you asked me."

E.T.'s game room resembled any one of fifty basement bars
I've seen in university towns. Obviously built for another
purpose—wine cellar, fallout shelter, maybe a canned goods
storeroom—these bars feature eight-foot ceilings, concrete walls,
and pillars or dull-silver conduits rising from the dance floor.
The fixtures hang about head level so direct light never quite
reaches the corners, an effect which causes nose and cheekbone
shadows straight from *Frankenstein Mauls Dracula's Daughter.*

I suppose it's a flaw in my age group that I thought "game
room" meant a pool table that can be converted to Ping-Pong,
a refrigerator perhaps, and a card table for Risk or a never-
completed jigsaw puzzle. Instead, at the base of the steps I found
two long rows of blinking video games leading to a back wall piled
high with more stereo equipment than a Muscle Shoals recording
studio. Between the rows of Donkey Kong, Indoor Soccer,
Radiation Ray, and Centipede lay a forty-foot boardwalk stacked
with albums, cassettes, reel-to-reel tapes, and trash. Lots of trash,
the kind of wrappers, bottles, bongs, peels, and used prophyls that
a country band leaves the maid after a month-long gig in one
hotel. I'd stumbled into the den of a renaissance derelict.

"Listen to this," a voice said.

"Turn On Your Love Light" by the Grateful Dead boomed
from the speaker bank, the sound bouncing from wall to wall
like the Ping-Pong ball I'd been expecting.

"Turn it down," I shouted.

The noise level dropped maybe twenty decibels. "What's
the matter, don't like music?"

"The bass is killing the mix. Sounds like Lesh is on Dueling
Cannons."

E.T. appeared from an alcove I hadn't noticed between
Frogger and Real Sports Football. "You know the Dead?"

He wore horn-rimmed glasses, which I hadn't expected. I

don't know what I did expect. Thorne was large and, judging by her clothes, so was Janey. Darlene was fat and ugly. I guess I expected a big, ugly drug fiend. Put Woody Allen's head on Richard Benjamin's body and you'll have a rough picture of E.T. Axel. He wore cut-off Levi's and a yellow, sleeveless I LOST MY VIRGINITY AT THE '77 PROM T-shirt. He blinked at least four times between his question and my answer.

"Of course I know the Dead. Why don't you go by Eddie or Ed? E.T. sounds silly."

E.T.'s posture was everything opposite Maria's. His forehead and hips led off with the shoulders hunched into a question mark position. "I had the name first. And, anyway, how'd you like to get stuck with a name like Ed? You're Dad's new woman, aren't you?"

"I'm nobody's woman, buster."

E.T. turned to one of the video machines. "I didn't mean to offend. Everyone says you're here to replace Mother."

"I guess I am, at least for a couple days."

E.T. slid his glasses at me, then back at the screen. "You're a hell of a lot nicer-looking than Janey. Mind if I call you Mama?"

"God, yes, I mind." I walked up and watched as E.T. pushed a button with his left hand and worked a lever with the right. I realized where E.T. got his posture. His spine was molded to the shape of a video game.

A burning building was pictured on the left side of the screen. A fireman threw a baby out the fourth-floor window to two other firemen on ground level with a net. When the baby hit the net, it bounced three floors back up and a little ways out from the building. At E.T.'s direction, the firemen scooted right and bounced the baby again. Meanwhile, however, the guy on the burning fourth floor heaved another baby out the window.

"That's gross," I said.

"It's fun. Not everyone can juggle babies."

The first baby reached ground floor on the right side of the screen where two stretcher-bearers caught the last bounce and shoved her, or him—the babies were asexual—into a waiting ambulance.

"What happens if you lose one?" I asked.

"Watch." E.T. moved the firemen out from under a falling baby. A high-pitched scream lasted a half-second, ending suddenly with a *pop* and a sound like a hammer going through a ripe cantaloupe. A moment later, a white cross and two blue flowers appeared down-screen from the firemen.

"My God, that's sick."

"The more you save, the faster they come at you. It's a lesson about life."

The word *life* used in the context of "Grand Scheme" made me think about Loren, which led to Buggie and babies again. I don't usually wake up obsessive or morbid, but then I usually wake up at home.

"This game's in bad taste."

"That's the idea, Mama. You got any Grateful Dead tapes?"

I ignored the question as irrelevant. "Do you sell dope?"

My question made him miss a baby. *Aighgh Pop.* "You asking as my new mom or as a naked chick Dad picked up in the bar?"

"Someone gave me an ounce of cocaine and I don't know what to do with it." *Aighgh. Pop. Aighgh. Splat.* The last baby landed on a fireman's head, knocking them both into crosses and flowers and ending the game.

"Cocaine?"

I showed E.T. the bag. He blinked fast as a strobe light in a disco dive. "Could I see that, Mama?"

"The name's Lana Sue."

"Come in here." By the wrist, E.T. pulled me into the

alcove between Frogger and Real Sports Football. It was more a wall safe furnished with two stools and a table covered by drug paraphernalia than the usual idea of an alcove. Stacks of reel-to-reel tapes sat on shelves around the walls. Tapes on one wall were locked into place by wrought-iron bars.

I nodded at the walls. "What're these?"

"Grateful Dead."

I picked one reel off a stack—RED ROCKS AMPITHEATER, DENVER, COLORADO, AUGUST 10, 1978 in blue ink on white adhesive tape.

"These're all concerts?"

E.T. pulled up a stool and hunched over an Ohaus triple beam scale. "Ten thousand hours. Largest collection of Grateful Dead music in the world, though there's a doctor in Berkeley might disagree with that."

"How did you get them?"

E.T. placed the bag on the scale. "Twenty-eight point one, it's a little short."

"I thought there were twenty-eight grams in an ounce."

"Twenty-eight point three-four-nine-five, to be more or less exact. Baggie weighs a gram, though."

I walked to the scale. He was right—28.1. "Maria was in it all night."

E.T.'s laugh came out as a cackle. "Maria's something else, claims she hates the stuff, but that girl can suck down a gram faster than coyotes on a rabbit."

Which reminded me. "Your dad called someone coyote ugly last night. What's coyote ugly?"

E.T. dipped a small silver spoon into the bag. He held it toward the light a minute, then bent over the spoon and made a noise like bad pipes in a cheap apartment. "Was he talking about Darlene?"

Since I didn't know the extent of the insult, I lied. "No."

E.T.'s spoon took another dip. "I'll bet he was talking about Darlene. Dad treats her worse than he treats me." The sight of cocaine outside the bag made my sinuses throb.

E.T. snorted up his other nostril, sniffed a couple of times, and looked pleased with himself. "Coyote ugly's when a guy wakes up holding a woman who's so repulsive he chews off his own arm rather than risk waking her. Want some?"

That seemed like an awful thing to say about your own daughter, but then my daughters are both beautiful and talented so I can't picture what it would be like to create a slug. Maybe Thorne's disappointment turned him bitter. I gestured at the barred shelf. "What are those tapes there?"

"Old ones from before Pigpen died. Dead haven't been the same without him. I've got a tape of the first acid test back in sixty-three. You know, Kesey, Merry Pranksters, the old hippie nostalgia. You can barely hear the sound. Guy recorded it on an RCA ghetto blaster with one of those microphones big as your thumb. Probably worth a hundred thousand bucks."

"You deal to make money for Grateful Dead tapes?"

"You got it. Here, pack your nose."

I didn't want to snort. Lord knows, I didn't want to snort, but thirty seconds later my head hummed like an air conditioner leaking Freon down my throat. Beneath the Dead tape, the room took on a low thump—a heartbeat.

I said, "Oh, hell."

"Good, huh?"

"The speakers are buzzing."

"Now the other side." He held another spoonful up to my face. The heartbeat doubled.

"Lana Sue what?" E.T. asked.

"Huh? My throat is closing."

"You said your name is Lana Sue. What's your last name?"

Pretend you're swimming in Chloraseptic. "Paul. My husband is Loren Paul." I sat down heavily. "He's a writer. Maybe you read *Yeast Infection*."

E.T. stared at me. His blinking was continuous, but it had gone half speed. Gave him eyes like a big turtle. "Did anyone ever notice you look a little like Lana Sue Potts? She was the singer for Thunder Road a few years back."

I was never recognized by a fan before. It felt neat. "I am Lana Sue Potts. Or I was. I've had two other names since then, but I kept Potts as my stage name, last time I was onstage."

"You're Lana Sue Potts?" I nodded. He blinked. "You were great. I saw you in Gunnison, Colorado, four, maybe five years ago. Holy cow, mama, you've changed."

E.T. leaped from his stool and ran out of the room. What's he mean, I've changed? And where's this Mama crap coming from? I stared at the Dead tapes on the wall, then back at the bag of cocaine crystals on the table. I missed Loren. He was up on the mountain searching for Truth and I was in a basement dungeon sticking foul shit up my nose. Made me wonder which one of us was really crazy.

The Dead tape stopped and after a blessed moment of silence, I came on—my album. I couldn't believe someone bought it. *There's not enough tequila in Texas, for me to go home with you.* I sounded pretty good.

E.T. rushed back into the vault. "Here." He shoved the album jacket at me. I looked down at myself standing in front of a lavender Rolls-Royce, wearing a blue, fringed vest that didn't connect between my breasts, ungodly tight white leather pants, and a blue cowboy hat. Ace chose the outfit himself. The album title ran across the top, cutting off part of my hat—*They Call Me Lana Sue.*

"I never did have any cleavage."

E.T. stood right in front of me. "This stuff isn't as good as what you did with Thunder Road. Why didn't those guys back you up?"

"We had a falling-out."

"Sounds like you've had your share of falling-outs."

How the hell would he know? The second cut was "Thrift Store Love." Ace had dubbed in all these violins and three black girls singing the last word of each line after me.

*When she boots you out the door.*　　Door.
*Don't come crawlin' here no more.*　　More.

Any of those three backup singers had a better voice than mine. Everyone knew I got the solo album because I slept with Ace. Hell, for all I know, they got the backup jobs the same way.

"I'll give you a thousand dollars for the coke," E.T. said.

"What?"

"The coke and a kiss."

"My ears are whining."

"A French kiss."

"That's the stupidest deal I ever heard."

E.T. reached into a drawer I hadn't seen under the table and pulled out a stack of hundred-dollar bills. He counted out ten, then stuffed the rest back under the table. "Darlene says you didn't have a dime when Dad brought you home. I bet you could use a thousand bucks."

"Who told Darlene?" "Thrift Store" ended and I kicked into a slick commercial version of "It's My Party and I'll Cry If I Want To."

E.T. stood too close to me and blinked. "You got the coke free. You can give away the French kiss, Mama."

"But why?"

"It'll be fun to think I crammed my tongue in Dad's new woman's mouth."

"You're all sick around here."

"Thousand bucks for the coke and a kiss."

I thought about the consequences. "You'll have to stop calling me Mama." He nodded and leaned closer. I could smell cocaine fumes on his breath.

Can selling a French kiss be considered prostitution? Daddy wouldn't approve, but at thirty-eight, I couldn't base decisions on what Daddy thought. Not after my life. But to French-kiss a blinker in thick glasses, a sleeveless T-shirt, and cutoffs—*ish*. This could be sinking to an all-new low, even for me.

A few moments later I'm standing there with my eyes wide open, E.T. clamped to my face, a thousand dollars and an ounce of cocaine on the table; my mind is pinging like a Kroger cash register; over this I'm singing, *It's my party and I'll cry if I want to, cry if I want to, cry if I want to, you would cry too if it happened to you*—when Maria's head comes through the door.

We stared open-eyed at each other a few seconds, then Maria said, "You better come upstairs, Mrs. Paul. There's a problem."

I broke free of the tongue probe. Made a sound like pulling a sneaker out of deep mud. "The problem is upstairs?"

"Please come."

I pocketed my thousand and followed Maria back through the flashing video games.

———

Remarkably enough, the problem upstairs was even stranger than the one in the basement. Maybe the weirdness quotient grows exponentially according to how many Axels are in a room.

With Maria in the lead and E.T. blinking along behind, we trooped up the steps and into the front living room and this fully developed scene: Billy G sunk in one of the red leather chairs, his head down in his arms; Darlene backed against a guncase, doing a high-pitched monologue that I couldn't follow except to tell I was the subject and the word *slut* came up every few seconds; Thorne, about halfway up the wide staircase, standing in a Napoleon pose with his arm swaddled in bandages, this perfectly appropriate Cary Grant smoking jacket, and blue-checkered boxer shorts. His hair stuck out sideways and pillow marks creased his cheek.

Darlene seemed to be threatening on behalf of Janey. "Mama's gonna kick butt when she comes back to get me. Daddy's butt, that naked prostitute's butt, your butt," meaning Billy G, I suppose. Her eyebrows rode low over her eyes and buckled as she shouted. Both hands fluttered like mating grouse. "Gonna kick every butt I tell her to kick. Then me'n Mama'll go back to Paris and leave this…this." Darlene lost words.

With his good arm, Thorne waved to me. "I just woke up."

"So I see."

"What's going on here?"

"Damned if I know." Maybe it was more sleeping pills than charm, but Thorne's face was so lovably confused, aloof, and taking charge all at the same time, I had this tremendous urge to shoot through the chaos and hug him.

Thorne ran his hands through his hair. "Maria, will you bring some coffee?"

Darlene spotted me and the tirade focused a little. She pointed one stubby finger. "Bitch."

I pointed back. "Gross slob."

Billy G came out of the chair and across the floor. His eyes snapped with a rose color—more an alcohol-induced bloodshot than any heartbroken teary redness. He held his peacock feather hat with both hands. "I just want to know why."

"Why what?"

"Why you're doing this to me. Do you hate all men? Do you hate yourself or are you just a screwed-up cunt?"

Somehow I ignored the cunt crack. "You're the one who said, 'I get hung up on no one and no one gets hung upon me.'"

He turned to E.T. "We made love all night. I must have come seven times." E.T. smiled and nodded.

I continued reminding him of his own line. "'Fast, meaningless good time,' you said. 'A basic quickie.'"

When Darlene screamed *slut* once more I began to understand Thorne's attitude toward his daughter.

Billy G advanced another step. "I pity you," he said.

"And we didn't make love. We rutted. You could have been replaced by a stiff dick nailed to a tree."

He didn't take that one well. When it came to vicious arguments, the kid was in over his head and he knew it. Billy G swung to Thorne.

"I respected you."

Thorne came down a couple steps. His face had an interested yet not really concerned, look about the gray eyes.

Billy G beseeched, "How can you steal another man's woman?"

"I'm nobody's woman, cowboy."

"*Slut.*"

Billy G held the knob thing at the bottom of the banister with one hand and his hat with the other. "Did you know that three nights ago she slept with her husband and two nights ago, me, and last night, you? Do you realize the kind of woman you're stealing?"

Thorne sent me a fuzzy look and said, "Doesn't sound like she's your woman, then, does it?"

"I'm nobody's woman."

"*Slut.*"

I remembered where I'd seen that look of Thorne's before. Years ago, when the twins were two, maybe three, years old, we used to leave them with Mom and Dad and go out country clubbing or lounge hopping with Ron's pre-med buddies. About two in the morning we'd swing by my parents' and wrap the sleeping girls in their blankets and carry them out to the car, and somewhere between Daddy's house and the car or between the car and bed, Connie would come to just for a moment and mumble, "I'm not sleepy, let me down," or something along those lines. I'd look into her beautiful eyes and love her. The expression in those eyes was the same as the one on Thorne's face the morning after his botched suicide.

Darlene put her fist on her hip and sashayed over to me. "I've slept with every cowboy in the bunkhouse."

I said, "You aren't just weird like the others, are you, Darlene?"

Her puckered lower lip and the bags under both eyes hung the color of bruised bananas. "Roy Rogers here and I did it last night. I made him spurt eight times."

Darlene's speech brought Thorne down another step and Billy G's hands up to his chest. "I never touched her."

Darlene twirled on him. "You said I was better than Daddy's whore."

Billy G appealed to Thorne. "I swear to God, sir."

"I know."

Maria appeared and handed Thorne a mug of coffee. He blew over the steaming surface and sipped. Billy G fell back into his original chair. Darlene continued her promenade.

In the charged silence, E.T. slid his arms around my shoulder. "Just now, Lana Sue and I were French-kissing in the basement."

Billy G groaned, Darlene slapped her forehead like an idiot. "Mama's gonna die." I gave E.T. a move-it-or-lose-it stare and the hand fell from my shoulder.

Billy G's head came up for one last supplication to Thorne. "Please give her back. I tried not to like her. I really tried, but I can't help it. You don't have any use for her, give her back."

Thorne looked amused. "Hell, I don't own her. We ain't even screwed yet. You want her so bad, take her."

Billy's face brightened with hope as he swung back to me, but I changed that real quick. "Lay one finger on me, sucker, and I'll snap your spine."

His jaw trembled and he twisted the hat around in his hands. I think, for about three seconds, Billy G was sizing up the odds of his spine surviving an all-out assault—the John Wayne approach of throwing me over his shoulder and marching me off to the bunkhouse. However, reason prevailed and his eyes dropped away. "You win, Lana Sue. I'm leaving. This state's too small for the both of us."

"I'll stay out of your way if you'll stay out of mine."

"Nope. Because of you I have to leave the home I love and go on the road." Out of pure spite, he added, "Maybe I'll go back to Chicago."

Before I thought up a catty-enough comeback, Darlene latched herself onto his arm. "Oh, darling, take me with you."

Billy G panicked. Jumping about five feet back and to his left, he gave off a little moan.

Darlene followed after him. "I've got money. We could go to California. Or France, my mother's in France. You won't ever have to ride a horse again."

The coward ran—out the door and across the lawn. My itch had caused another man to alter his life. Not that I felt remorse. I figure if these jokers can't maintain themselves after me, it's their own damn fault. This case was a bit more absurd than the others and took twenty-four hours instead of several years. Other than that, Billy G was nothing more than typical.

Darlene sat in his chair and glared at me. She muttered under her breath, "Slut."

"Gross slob."

E.T. trotted back down to the Dead. Thorne drank from

his mug. He looked across at me and smiled. "Can't have you chasing off all the help."

"Sorry."

"That's okay. Wait'll I get dressed and eat some biscuits, we'll ride around the ranch, show you some land."

"On horses?"

"Sure. Maria, how about some biscuits, and see if you can find something that'll fit her better. Looks like she's wearing a pup tent."

"Yes, Mr. Axel."

Thorne started up the staircase. He stopped and turned to me again. "Which Billy was that anyway?"

———

My horse encounter was put off until afternoon because, while Thorne was eating his biscuits, the phone rang. Then another phone rang, then when Thorne set down the first phone, it rang again. The head wrangler came in to talk about fetlocks. You can't just abandon an ongoing dynasty for a three-day drunk and suicide attempt. Sooner or later, fetlock problems have a way of catching up.

Maria and I sat around the kitchen, grinding our molars, while Thorne took care of bankers, oil foremen, and guys from two different kinds of stock markets. Finally Thorne looked up from one of the phones and shrugged an apologetic smile. "This may take awhile."

"No rush. Maria and I will be in her room, looking through clothes."

Maria's first-floor, back-of-the-house room was just what you'd expect. Small, neat as a curio shop, yellow enamel walls with a framed velvet painting of Jesus hanging over the bed. Photos of her father and boyfriend stood on the bureau. A neat stack of laundry sat at the base of the made-up bed. Next to a Silhouette Romance on the nightstand lay a small mirror reflecting a white powdery residue.

Maria lifted a pair of jeans off the laundry stack. "There wasn't much blood on these. They're still wearable anyway, if you don't mind a few stains."

"Does it look like I had an accident?"

She shook out the jeans and we inspected the few dark blotches. One Idaho-shaped smear could conceivably be misinterpreted as careless spotting, but only by the kind of person who looks for that sort of thing.

"They'll do." I was on the edge of the bed and slipped off my sandals and Janey's green army pants. "I can't stand this mountaineer uniform any longer. Does Janey still dress like this?"

"Not in thirty years. The shirt you used on Thorne's arm is beyond hope."

I slid into my comfortable old Lee Wranglers. "That shirt was an old thing I wear to do housework around the cabin."

"You do housework?"

"Sure. Do I look like a trust fund baby?" E.T.'s roll of bills crammed in my front pocket gave the jeans a lumpy look.

"I think you're accustomed to giving orders."

"It's a talent I pick up quickly."

Maria shuffled through the bottom drawer of the bureau. She pulled out a blue and gold football jersey—ROCK SPRINGS across the back shoulders. Number 38. "This was Petey's. He gave it to me when Janey ran him off the ranch."

The jersey fit real well, maybe a little tight in the chest. Petey wasn't a very big fullback. "Why did Janey run him off the ranch?"

Maria sat next to me on the bed. She picked up the Silhouette Romance and turned it over in her hands. "Janey thought we were in love."

"What's it to her?"

"My mother fell in love with a cowboy from the bunkhouse and I happened. Janey didn't want a repeat." I saw *passion* and *exotic nineteenth-century New Zealand* on the back cover of the book. Also something about daring privateers. "So you've lived on the ranch all your life?"

Maria stared at the nightstand. "Oh, no. Janey threw my father out as soon as I was old enough to travel. We lived in Cheyenne until Mama died and Janey offered me a job. My father still lives in Cheyenne. He lays tile."

Maria licked her right index finger and rubbed it over the mirror. Then she touched her finger to her upper gum. "My father doesn't want me working here, but I dropped out of high school and came over. Janey's frightened to death I will get pregnant and she'll have to make her own bed for a few weeks."

Maria handed me the mirror so I could massage my gums also. "The more I hear about Janey the less I like her." My mouth dropped into a dental memory. "I sure am glad I sold the coke. It'd be awful to do more."

"Yes, I am thankful to you for taking it away."

The mirror was wiped clean as Maria's kitchen. Not even a speck of white dust remained. I said, "That E.T. is a character. He's like a doped-up mole down there surrounded by Grateful Dead tapes. It's creepy."

"E.T. is not so bad. Everyone expects him to grow up like Thorne, which must be difficult. He told me he is afraid of cowboys."

"Must be tough being the son of a legend."

Maria nodded. She took the mirror, looked at herself a moment, then set it back on the nightstand, next to the book.

"I hope you didn't think I was really kissing E.T. when you came down there," I said.

"Of course you weren't."

"I mean, I was, but it was part of the deal. I had to." I ran the tip of my tongue between my upper teeth and lips. "Don't you just hate the way cocaine makes you feel?"

She looked at me. "Of course."

Maria and I held about ten seconds of eye contact before I spoke. "Let's find E.T."

———

His tunnel was dark as a cave. I blind-groped along the wall down each side of the stairwell. "Where's the light switch, Maria?"

"It's hidden. E.T. is afraid of rip-offs and Thorne. He hides everything."

I peered into the black. "Could he be in the little room full of Dead tapes?"

Maria was a step above, which made her the same height as me. Her voice came from next to my ear. "I do not know. Sometimes after a big score he holes up down here for several days. There's a flashlight in the kitchen."

I stood on the bottom step while Maria went back up in search of light. Because of my earlier snorts, the black hole of E.T.'s basement wasn't totally black. A yellow transparent curtain rippled before my eyes, and red dandelion bursts appeared to bounce from top to bottom. The room buzzed like a neon bar sign. My saliva glands craved vitamin C.

A couple minutes of womb sensations later the light bobbed down the steps, shining on the walls and my jeans.

"I changed the batteries," Maria said.

"Let me carry it." We stumbled into the basement, following the beam over trash and video games. The alcove was locked tight, but the little bugger had left a note and a Baggie tacked on the door.

*Mama—One frenchie wasn't enough huh? Got to have more of E.T.'s electric tongue. I ran into Rock Springs, but if you slip a hundred dollars under the door, you can have this as a substitute. Or you can have it free for another kiss. One from you and one from Maria.*

*Your new son, E.T.*

At my elbow Maria muttered what I took to be a Spanish curse.

"How much you figure is there?" I asked.

"Not a hundred dollars' worth. Hardly enough for one of us."

I tapped the Baggie with my index finger. The crystals sparkled in the flashlight light. "What should we do?"

"I wouldn't pay a hundred dollars."

"You'd rather kiss him?"

Maria repeated the Spanish curse.

"That's what I thought." I folded up a hundred-dollar bill and slid it under E.T.'s door. We found a flat-topped video game and snorted by flashlight. Maria was right, there wasn't enough.

———

Any person who lives in Wyoming, especially in a cabin at the base of a mountain, is expected to be crazy about horses. It's a responsibility. Anything less is interpreted as letting down the Western mystique. So this is something of a betrayal to admit, but I'm just not a horse lover. My first thought when Thorne said we'd tour the ranch on horseback was to ask if all the trucks were broken.

I'm not afraid of horses, exactly. It's just that they're awkward and sweaty and unpredictable. Like men. Except men are easier to handle.

Another way horses are like men is that the ones you see in the movies and magazines are sleek and beautiful, whereas in real life they're generally shaped wrong and look funny around the nose. And they're stupid—horses, not men, necessarily. A horse's intelligence rates somewhere between the turkey and the armadillo. Which is actually a blessing, since most horses loathe humans and would kill if they only knew how. You don't run into many *My Friend Flicka* mares in love with a master who climbs on her back and yanks at an iron peg stuck sideways in her mouth, all the while chanting, "Atta girl, go get 'em baby."

Back in high school, Roxanne was always dragging me off my towel at the country club pool to follow her down to the stables so we could pet the horses and flirt with the help. She still loves the whole horsemanship game; spends thousands of dollars on outfits and saddles; speaks in pithy little Texasisms like, "That stallion's hotter'n the tail pipe on a chopped-down Harley." She's the only female rider I know who wears spurs.

I think Roxanne's deep interest in corrals and horses is based on the same thing as all her other deep interests. She just naturally gravitates to any hobby involving spread legs.

When Loren and I first moved into the cabin, our nearest neighbors, Lee VanHorn and his daughter, Marcie, took us on a three-day pack trip in the Teton Wilderness. My horse's name was Alex Trebeck. He was a pink-white edging to jaundice color with blood-filled eyes. He hated me.

Marcie was fourteen back then. She rode with a set of Walkman plugs in her ears and her head down, reading Loren's *Yeast Infection*. For all the nature Marcie absorbed those three days, she could have stayed in her room.

At night around the campfire, she asked Loren questions about his sensitivity and the creative process.

"A mind like yours must be an awful responsibility, Mr. Paul."

Loren squinted his eyes to affect a pained poet look. "It's the burden of my life."

"I'd love to write novels someday. My mind is full of great ideas for plots, all I need is help getting them on paper."

I hit the fire coals with my wienie stick, showering sparks into the night. Burden, my ass. Loren eats up that writer's sensitivity myth. Keeping him from taking this tender esthete act seriously is a full-time job. That's why, whenever he's around, I say he's "typing a book" rather than "writing a novel." Otherwise Loren'll start thinking he's Eugene O'Neill and the regular rules of life don't apply in his case. The last thing he needed back then was a fourteen-year-old disciple.

Marcie's young face turned to me in the firelight. "You must feel so honored to live with such a gifted husband. I mean, to know that while you're cooking dinner, he's in the study creating works of literature."

I waved the glowing end of my stick dangerously close to Loren's smudged glasses. "Yes, Marcie, it gives my life meaning to know I'm washing the socks of a genius."

Neither Marcie nor Loren caught the sarcasm.

About then, Marcie's father came into camp and said Alex Trebeck had broken his hobble and run into the forest and I better go catch him. We chased that mangy animal up canyons and across creeks for two hours while Marcie and Loren sat on stumps, sipping cocoa and admiring each other.

Later, at home, Loren said, "That Marcie VanHorn sure is mature for her age. Her perceptions are right on target."

"Lay one finger on her and I'll sew your penis shut."

———

The foreman led a semishort pinto from the barn. "Name's Suzy Q," he said. "Treat her firm or she'll graze." The foreman was real small and real old, I'd say early seventies. A handlebar mustache flowed off the sides of his mouth like twin ermine tails.

I stood with both hands in my pockets. "Is she gentle? I haven't ridden a whole lot, you know. I mean, some, on bridle paths in Houston and a pack trip up by Jackson, but I haven't ridden all that much. I think I need a gentle one."

The foreman spit. "She's broke." His mustache tips were greased to antler points. I imagined you could turn his head by holding them like real handlebars. Of course I'd have to wear gloves to try it.

Working with his good arm, Thorne buckled and cinched leather things on a giant brown horse named Laredo. He kneed the hell out of the horse's belly before pulling the final belt tight. He grinned at me. "You afraid of horses?"

"Of course not."

"Get on, then."

Thorne mounted and waited while I held Suzy Q by the horn, put my left foot into the stirrup, and stood there, bouncing up and down on my right leg.

"Thought you'd been on a pack trip," Thorne said.

"I was. Three days. It was awful."

"Didn't you have to get on and off your horse that three days?"

Suzy Q's legs moved away from me. I followed her around in a circle. "Someone always gave me a boost," I said.

Thorne watched as I followed Suzy Q's butt around another 360. "You allergic to horses?"

"Why do you ask?"

"You keep sniffing like you've got a runny nose."

Finally Thorne nodded to the foreman, who stepped over and clasped his hands together under my right foot. Together we pushed me into the saddle. "Keep her head up," he said.

The foreman's name was Gritz or Grits. I think it was Gritz as in a legitimate last name, but he was old enough to have been the original cook on *Rawhide* and cowboys back in the early twentieth century had the same names as their horses—lots of Texas and Pecos Johns. Now they're all Butch or Snuffy. I actually met a steer wrestler in a bar outside

Meeteetse who'd said his name was Billy Joe Bobby Jack. "You call me BJBJ."

I sat on Suzy Q, holding the reins with both hands, wishing Roxanne was here to tell me how to start her. I knew it took some kick action, but I didn't want to kick too hard for fear of pissing Suzy Q off. "Gedup" had no effect.

Gritz went over by Laredo and squinted off south toward some gray ledges on the horizon. "Got time to look at something, boss?" he asked.

"If it's that mare's fetlocks, no."

"It's something else. Out behind the barn."

Thorne shifted in the saddle toward me. "Ever see a barn like this?"

I went with the safe answer. "Nope."

"Janey and I built her before we built the house. She'll hold forty thousand tons of hay. You could fly a plane through the front and back loading doors without touching a thing. I did it once."

I thought of Loren. He'd like anyone who called a barn she. "I hear it's got two flush toilets."

Thorne squinted at me as if I was being sarcastic. "Those're Janey's."

Gritz still stared at the horizon. "Wish you'd come have a look."

"Better be important." Thorne swung his horse and started off. Without me making a move, Suzy Q followed.

---

Behind the barn we found four or five cowboys standing in an arc around a crucified prairie dog. Its front legs were held on to the crossbar by thick rubber bands. Its back legs dangled free in front of the tail.

I said, "That's sick."

Thorne stared for thirty seconds or so. Then he sighed real deep. "Darlene?"

Gritz shrugged.

"How'd she kill it?" Thorne asked.

"Nobody's gone close enough to tell."

Thorne glanced at the cowboys. "You afraid to get near it?" Cowboys don't like being called afraid. One of them stepped forward and knelt in front of the cross. "Head looks bashed in."

Thorne sat looking at the dead prairie dog for another thirty seconds. His eyes were worn out like they'd been yesterday at the hospital. He blinked a couple of times. "Throw it out," he said. Then he wheeled Laredo and trotted south. Suzy Q followed.

———

We rode up an old washed-out Jeep track. I wanted to ride alongside Thorne and discuss the situation, but Suzy Q was born to follow. She stuck her nose about eight inches behind Laredo's rump and stayed there. I kicked and tugged and pulled, finally got her over into the other rut, but the stupid horse wouldn't pass Laredo's tail.

I ended up talking to Thorne's back. "You think some-thing's wrong with Darlene?" I shouted.

He glanced back at me, but didn't answer. We swung down into a gully and I had to lurch way back to keep from falling off. Then I fell forward and hung on to her neck as we climbed the other side. Roxanne would have been tickled.

Up on the flats again, I kept on as if Thorne had asked for my opinion. "I mean, a lot of kids don't like their parents. My daughter can't stand me. My husband is embarrassed by his mom. Lord knows what I think of mine. But that's all normal resentment. Darlene's not normal."

Thorne's back moved up and down above the saddle. He had good posture for a cowboy—or maybe the prairie dog and my prattling made him tense.

"Even E.T.'s normal, more or less," I said, "in a sick kind of way, but I think Darlene's sick like a disease, like cancer or something, where E.T. and my daughter are sick more like mumps."

Thorne twisted in the saddle. "You been talking to E.T.?"

"I saw him this morning." Thorne seemed to have forgotten E.T.'s crack about French-kissing in the basement.

He slowed Laredo to a walk. I urged Suzy Q up the rut, but she still would have none of it.

"Those two and their mother are all I did this for," Thorne said. He paused to take in "this," which was desert as far as we could see, spotted here and there by a few cows and a fence line. A windmill turned over by the eastern horizon. "And not one of them gives a shit."

He reined Laredo to a halt. Suzy Q stopped behind them. "I almost killed myself yesterday, but I didn't. I'm glad I didn't." He thought that one over a moment. "So, today, problems don't matter. Today I ride my horse on my land and spend time with you. Today is mine."

Thorne glanced back at me to see how I was taking the speech. I smiled, so he continued. "I haven't done anything for me in years. Today I do."

"What're you going to do?"

"I don't know. I'll think about it."

A couple of miles later, Thorne led off through some willows down a gully and out into a low flat area with a pond and an old collapsed homesteader cabin. We tied the horses to a rotten trough and peeked through broken glass windows at a couple of moth-eaten mattresses and an ancient barrel stove. An empty Delaware Punch bottle sat on a shelf beside some black tins.

"How long ago'd these people leave?" I asked.

"Thirties, I figure." Thorne pointed out a pile of Colt .45 cans in one corner. "My hands use it ever' now and then during a blizzard. Janey and I almost stayed here one night when my truck threw a rod. A rattler came under the door and she made us leave."

"I wouldn't sleep with a snake."

Thorne grunted. "Was raining like hell outside. Spent the night in the cab of the truck."

At the pond, Suzy Q finally consented to stand beside Laredo. After the horses drank, Thorne hobbled their legs so they could shuffle around the clearing searching for grass. Thorne pulled a shower-curtain-looking blanket out of his saddlebag and spread it in the shade of three six-foot sagebrush.

"Let's see what Maria sent for lunch," he said.

"This is a picnic?"

Thorne smiled. "Can't ride a horse without workin' or eatin', and I ain't workin' today."

He pulled out a pair of small rib eyes and a half-dozen eggs, a homemade loaf of bread, two potatoes, a grocery store basket of strawberries, a can of Crisco, and a skillet. And a pint of Ten High.

"That Maria's wonderful," Thorne said.

"You should throw Janey out and marry her."

He took a slug of Ten High and eyed me over the bottle. "I got you."

I'd been on these picnic-down-at-the-tank deals before in Texas and on the road with the Mick, so I knew that however innocent the afternoon begins, there'll always come a "Gee, it's hot, let's skinny-dip" suggestion, and once a man has your clothes off, he starts taking things for granted. Sooner or later it leads to a shoreline free-for-all. About the best you can hope for is the guy lets you get back to the blanket.

I thought about the situation as we gathered dead sagebrush for the fire. This time wouldn't be just morphine-in-a-dick like I'd wanted from Billy G. Making it with Thorne would matter in some way. Everyone at the ranch took it for granted I was there as a romance and sex object. Thorne acted as if the issue had already been decided. So did I.

But Loren was only three days back. I was married to Loren. Even though pain fucks weren't really cheating, this would be. I hadn't committed adultery on Loren before, wasn't real sure I wanted to.

"How do you like your steak?" Thorne asked.

"Medium rare."

"Eggs?"

"Over easy."

I expected the next question to be "sex?" and was all set to say, "Let's wait awhile." However, Thorne seemed more interested in his meat.

I watched his fingers as he worked around the fire. He used mostly his right hand as the crook of his left arm was still bandaged. Even one-handed, though, each movement showed control. I'd never been around a man who knew exactly what he was doing before. It was unnerving. If I did say, "wait awhile," I wasn't going to mean a real long while.

We ate the steaks, drank some more Ten High, watched a small herd of antelope come down the ravine. Thorne rolled over on his back and propped his bad hand on my knee. "Sure is peaceful," he said. "Can't remember last time I felt peaceful."

I looked at the water, which was still as glass. "My daughter Cassie'd like it here. She loves horses and real ranch stuff. I've been around cowboys in bars for years, but I've never seen them much at their work. It's interesting."

Thorne snored.

So much for skinny-dipping after lunch. I sat on the blanket next to him, tossing pebbles into the pond and watching the ripples. The countryside was so quiet, not even a grasshopper to break the drone of Thorne's breathing and my pebbles as they plopped into the pond. I traced his face with my index finger while he slept. The corners of his eyes had deep lines. I made up little stories about how he got the scar, imagining something dangerous and fun, a grizzly maybe or a border-town whore.

An old cow came across the rise and drank from the other side of the pond. You'd never see one cow out by itself in Texas. When I was little, before Dessie turned gay or I discovered sugar sadness, back when Mom laughed, Daddy used to take us on drives outside Houston in our watermelon-green Dodge wagon. We'd see cattle standing in the shade of oil pumps, and black people sitting on crates in front of section road gas stations. Wyoming doesn't have section roads or black people, at least not up in Jackson Hole. There's more one-eyed bears in Teton County than there are black people.

Every drive we'd find a wind-beaten cafe and stop for apple pie heated with cheddar cheese on top. I must have been five or six then, because by the time I was eight Daddy'd traded the Dodge for an Oldsmobile. Then he bought a new house and took up golf and raising saffron. Funny how you date times by the car that goes with them.

Thorne's eyelids flew open. He lay still a moment, searching the sky. Then he sat up. "What happened?"

"You took a nap."

He looked from the pond to the ravine to Laredo and Suzy Q grazing on weeds. "A nap."

"You were so peaceful I didn't have the heart to wake you up."

Thorne blinked a couple times. He ran his hand through his hair. "I never slept in the daytime before."

I handed him the pint of Ten High.

Thorne held the bottle to his mouth, but didn't drink. "My dad didn't believe in naps. He said when the sun's up, you work, when it's down, you sleep."

"When did you eat?"

"On the edges." He drank from the bottle. "And noon. Straightup twelve, Mama had dinner on the table. They called lunch dinner when I was a boy."

"I know that. I'm not as young as you think."

Thorne seemed to be adjusting to his recent nap. He leaned back on his right arm and took another swig. His eyes traveled over my body. "You sure look good, Lana Sue."

I've never been smooth at taking straight-on compliments. I prefer slightly smartass repartee where I can get in a few flirty licks amidst the wordplay. Simple sincerity is kind of embarrassing. What I did this time was mumble something along the lines of "thanks" and reach for the bottle.

Thorne didn't notice my embarrassment. He was still amazed at his own decadence. "Sleeping in the afternoon," he went on, "how about that?"

"How about it?"

"I thought I'd come to an age where I'd never do anything I hadn't already done over and over."

I took a good swig. The Ten High cleaned up the rough edges left by E.T.'s coke, relaxed my tight forehead. "Hell, we're on a roll. What else have you never done before that you always wanted to do?"

"Let me think."

"I could shampoo your hair, or give you a pedicure. Have you ever been fed grapes while lying on your back? I can sing. When was the last time someone sang you a lullaby?"

"Sixty years ago, at least."

Sixty? I hadn't realized Thorne was quite that old. A sixty-year-old man might be a first even for me.

A shine came into Thorne's right eye. He licked his bottom lip. "I thought of something."

"Uh-oh. I can tell what you thought by the gleam in your eyes."

"You thought of it too?"

"Naked swimming foreplay, am I right? Then man-on-top-gets-a-sunburn?"

Thorne laughed. "Hell, no. I've played that game plenty of times." He took the bottle back. "I want you and me to make love on a galloping horse."

"Horse." My voice squeaked. "I don't like horses. They can't stand me. Whatever makes you want to get laid on a horse?"

"I saw it in a movie once. Looked exciting."

"Wars are exciting, but I'd rather not be in one."

Thorne's look was defensive and slightly hurt. "We don't have to. You just asked what I always wanted to do and I told you."

"Wait a minute, let me think." I reached for the bottle, but he hadn't had his turn yet, so I waited while Thorne drank, then handed it to me.

I took a big burning slug of Ten High. Thorne's proposition shouldn't have come as such a surprise. Every cowboy wants to bring his horse in on a three-way hump. They're like bikers with Harleys and golf pros on the eighteenth green. Just a couple weeks ago Loren had suggested we borrow a horse from the VanHorns and make it on the run. And Loren's not even a cowboy. He's just a regular pervert.

It was a matter of self-worth and pride. Both as a singer and a wife-girlfriend, I've always considered my calling to be fulfiller of fantasies. I mean, I'm desirable, dammit. Men dream of someday meeting a woman like me and I find a lot of pleasure in making dreams come true. I'd never said no to a kinky position yet, and with Mickey Thunder as my first teacher, that's a pretty dramatic claim. But *on a horse—a running-over-the-prairie horse?* Jesus. I hate horses.

By then, Laredo and Suzy Q had hopped almost around the pond to where the lonesome cow stood, chewing and blinking. Thorne would want to commit this act on Laredo, of course. Suzy Q lacked the pizzaz. Laredo was tall and brown with mean eyes. I wondered if the woman in Thorne's movie faced forward or back. Either way would be insecure and I can't stand insecurity, especially when I'm fucking.

Thorne straightened his legs on the blanket, then crossed his right ankle over the left boot heel. He didn't say a word or even glance my way, but his eyes had that tired, vulnerable look again. By not trying to push me into guilt sex, he was making me feel guiltier than ever. My whole idea had been to hang around for a few days, giving him a pleasure jolt he could look back on in his old age. I couldn't very well deny his first wish.

I threw down more Ten High. "Bareback or in the saddle?"

Thorne grinned. "Bareback."

———

When she was eleven or twelve, Connie used to buy *Seventeen* magazine every month. I remember a column in it called "My Most Embarrassing Moment," in which girls would confess true-life social blunders like thinking a big date was on Saturday when it was really on Friday, or taking the school bus two hundred miles to a band concert and finding nothing but a salami sandwich in your piccolo case. Most of the I-coulda-died situations didn't strike me as all that awful. Nothing comparable to a heavy flow on white slacks or telling Mama you're getting another divorce. Loren says the most embarrassing thing that can happen to a man is for his wife to commit suicide.

Horrible thought. Anyway, if *Seventeen* ever asks my opinion, I'll claim mounting a horse naked as my most embarrassing moment. People who give human characteristics to animals are total idiots in my book, but, I swear, Laredo laughed his ass off.

Thorne mounted first. He sat way up there, brown as old Tony Lamas on his face and wrists, a kind of blank newsprint color everywhere else. His belly sagged some and there was extra flesh on his lower back. He held his right hand across to the left side. "Hop up."

Without stirrups, "hop" wasn't the proper word. Finally— after a scene from a bad Polish joke—I sat astride Laredo's upper spine, facing Thorne and hanging on for dear life.

"Don't squeeze so tight," he said.

"I can't help it."

"That's not a saddle horn."

He nudged Laredo and stared off at a slow walk. "Put your hands on my hips," Thorne said.

"I can't let go."

"You've got to let go or you'll never get it in."

"Let's just ride a minute, try some foreplay. I think I'm pretty dry down there."

Thorne kicked Laredo into a trot which caused a sensation like riding a giant bowling ball down steps. *Bang, bang. Bang.*

"This won't be smooth unless we go faster," he said.

"Stop."

Thorne pulled Laredo to a halt. He tried to pry my fingers loose, without much luck.

"Your hair looks pretty in the wind," Thorne said.

"Is it over? Did you get off?"

Laredo stood on top of a little knoll thing with me facing east and Thorne west. I know that horse was amused.

Thorne gave up on my fingers. "Tell you what, let's stick it in at a dead stop, then go from there."

"Stick what in?"

"Put both hands on my legs and raise yourself up. Then lower yourself on to me."

"Like this?"

"You've got to let go first."

I heard a *thunk* and Laredo reared up on his hind legs, slamming me into Thorne. We hung there for what seemed hours as Laredo kicked in the Heigh-ho, Silver position. When he came down, I banged back on his neck, then I flew—over the ears and past his evil eyes. I felt a momentary altitude gain before my hip and lower back smashed into a rock and my head came down hard. Laredo's back hooves flashed by inches before my eyes.

A rock whizzed through the air over my head and I turned to see Darlene at the base of the knoll.

*"I'm pregnant,"* she screamed and let fly another rock. This one caught Laredo in the neck, causing another six seconds of bucking bronco. Thorne stayed with him, though I don't know how. I'm not sure if he'd seen Darlene yet.

*"Can't you hear me?"* she yelled. *"I'm going to have a baby."*

I said, "No, you're not."

She heaved a rock at me, missed by eight feet. Then she whirled and ran.

———

Thorne leaned forward, soothing Laredo, whose nostrils flared and blew. The horse stood stiff-legged, shivering. I think he was braced for another rock.

"You okay?" Thorne asked.

"I don't know."

"Any bones broke?"

I lay back on the dirt to check my body parts. My toes moved so I figured my spine wasn't snapped. My hip hurt like hell. With my fingers, I touched the beginnings of a goose egg on the back of my head. "No, I don't think anything's permanently broken."

"You're all right, then." Thorne guided Laredo over to where I lay. He held his right hand out. "Hop up."

I didn't move. "Thorne, you've got to talk to Darlene."

"I know it."

"She's sick. All these bizarre claims are cries for attention. You can't ignore her anymore."

Thorne took his hand back and sat up. "You a child psychologist?"

"No, but I raised two girls."

"One hates you and the other lives with your old boyfriend."

I was surprised he remembered that. "Yeah, but they're happy—enough anyway. They don't do bizarre things like Darlene."

"Either one ever catch you fucking on a horse?"

"Good point."

"Hop up."

"I'd rather die."

————

A hundred yards away we found tire tracks leading back to the pond and Suzy Q and nothing else. No blanket and picnic leavings, no saddles, no clothes, worst of all, no shoes.

Thorne said, "Damn her."

I shuffled past Laredo and into the pond. About knee deep, I turned around and sat down, spreading my feet straight. The cool mud soothed my aching butt—some. My feet stung. I wanted to cry, but my head hurt too much.

Thorne was off Laredo, checking his lower legs. "Think all the bucking bruised a hoof," he said. "We'll have to ride double on Suzy Q going back."

I leaned back until my head lump was in the water. "You'll ride Suzy Q. I'm going to stay here and die."

Thorne walked to the water's edge. "No use being dramatic, Lana Sue. Come on." He held out his right hand again.

I sat up. The water trailed off my hair and down my back. "Thorne, I'm serious. You'll never get me on a horse again."

"Walk, then." He turned away.

"My feet are shreds already. I can't walk."

Thorne came back to the water. His penis had shrunk to the size of a broiled Vienna sausage. "Lana Sue, you're not being tough. The first rule of getting bucked off is you gotta climb right back on."

"You want tough, bring Janey back."

"I don't want Janey. I want you."

"And speaking of tough, who tried to hack his arm off yesterday? Was that tough?"

I hurt him on that one. Thorne's whole face sank. He gave up and turned old.

"I'm sorry," I said. "I'm just real upset and in a lot of pain. I had no right to say that."

"Yes, you did."

"No, I didn't."

Thorne went around the pond to untie Suzy Q's hobble. I leaned back with my bump in the water, studying the sky, then sat up and watched him get the horses ready for the ride to the ranch house. Thorne wouldn't look at me. In fact, he looked everywhere else but at me. After checking bits and belts, he stood between the horses with both sets of reins in his good hand, then he mounted Suzy Q. He held her reins in his left hand and led Laredo with his right. The three of them came over to where I sat in the pond.

Thorne's eyes focused up on the horizon behind me and to my right. "I'll send someone in a truck with some clothes."

I said the only thing I knew that would save the old guy. At the moment, I felt so low, maybe I even meant it. Hell, I never know when I mean it. I said, "I love you, Thorne."

He didn't move for a long time. I guess he was considering saying, "I love you too," but the cowboy finally got the best of him and he just blinked a couple of times and led off toward the ravine. As the horses reached the edge of the clearing, I called out, "Thorne."

He stopped with his back to me.

"When you send someone with the clothes, don't send E.T. He thinks I'm naked most of the time anyway."

Thorne looked back and smiled.

———

Thorne was right, of course. Men are almost always right when they tell me things about myself—not that it does either of us any good. It's just that "tough" had never been one of my goals. Roxanne is tough. My sister, Dessie, is tough. They'd both have bounced up off the rocks and jumped back on Laredo. Roxanne would be flying across the prairie, right now, head back, laughing, soaring into the orgasm of a lifetime. Dessie would have gone after Darlene and either seduced her or beat the living crap out of her. I was the only one who would squat on her ass in the mud at the edge of a stagnant tank in the middle of the goddamn desert and feel sorry for herself.

But I had excuses. People are supposed to be upset three days after their marriage breaks up. I missed my cabin and my creek and my cats. Darlene and E.T. weren't my problems. I admire versatility, but making it on horseback just isn't me. Maybe I wasn't as exciting and open as I'd hoped. Maybe I was getting too old to strike out into the unknown whenever the known turned dull.

I missed Loren. In fact I missed everyone I'd ever

loved—Cassie, Connie, Mickey, Ron, even stupid old Ace. Buggie, whom I loved secondhand and had never even met. Mama. Daddy. How could I have gotten so entangled with so many lives and wound up naked and alone? What a screw. Belly deep in mud, aching all over, the tears finally came.

———

Maria found me there a couple of hours later. She was so short, I could barely see the top of her head as the truck bounced over the wagon track from the homesteader cabin. I was real glad to see her. Two hours is about my mope limit, and, as the sun began its slide toward Utah, my depression was rapidly changing to cold boredom.

She parked by our picnic sagebrush. Where the day before Maria had been calmly efficient about providing me a wardrobe, today she was mostly amused.

"Fate will have you wear Janey's pants," Maria laughed—more of a smirk than a laugh. Her smile showed gleaming teeth and part of her top gum.

I tried to stand, but my hip stiffened into a spot weld. "You bring towels?"

"Of course." Maria walked down to the water's edge. "Do you always lose your clothes?"'

I pulled my feet under me and raised myself out of the muddy water. My hip creaked. It was bruised the same dead banana color as Darlene's lips. We finally had something in common.

"I never lost more than a sock in a dryer until I met your boss."

"My father says if you lose your shirt more than once, you'll get a reputation."

"I've got a reputation, thank you."

Maria wrapped me in a couple of towels. Then she slid under my arm and helped me stagger toward the truck. I was more stiff than in any pain, except for my feet.

"Did you bring shoes?" I asked.

She reached into the truck bed for a pair of bright yellow hightop sneakers with skull-and-crossbone patches on the sides.

"These're E.T.'s," I said.

"No one else has close to your size foot."

"Then he knows about the latest escapade."

"Everyone knows. Darlene went out in the daytime and Thorne rode into the barn naked. It caused talk."

Maria lowered the gate so I could sit down to dry off and pull on Janey's lumberjack suit. My feet were a mess.

"I'm sorry I lost your boyfriend's jersey."

"I'll get it back from Darlene."

"Could you get back my nine hundred dollars?"

"E. T.'s money was in your pocket?"

"All except the hundred you and I snorted."

"I doubt if you will see it again. Darlene's not too good with money."

"Couldn't be worse than me."

---

Nine or ten cowboys lounged around the front of the barn when Maria and I pulled up to the house. They pretended not to look at me while I pretended not to look at them. I don't know what they were hoping to see—tits or blood, I suppose. Nothing they hadn't seen before. Cowboys used to be one of the last groups of American males with breast obsessions, but now that every ranch in the West has a satellite dish, I imagine the era of going apeshit over an exposed nipple has vanished into history.

Maria led me, limping, up the stairs and into a guest room. The room was cheerful. A vase of lupines and Indian paintbrush sat on a nightstand next to a queen-size bed.

"You will be wanting another bath?" Maria asked.

"Maria, you're a godsend."

"This one has no temperature control or whirlpool. Would you prefer using the tub in the master bedroom?"

"I prefer to hide here."

Maria disappeared into the bathroom, so I sat on the edge of the bed and waited. The coverlet was an off-white fiberfill comforter with a ruffled thing around the sides. I couldn't help wonder who had chosen it. No one in the family was into ruffled sides. My mom would have loved it.

The sound of running water came from the bathroom. Maria reappeared in the doorway. "There's aspirin in the medicine cabinet and Grand Marnier under the sink. Do you think you'll be needing anything else?"

"Who decorated this room, Maria?"

She looked around at the pictures and paintings on the walls. "Darlene threw almost everything she owned out of her room three years ago. I saved the dresser, that chest, some of the pictures. Janey sticks old stuff in here sometimes. I guess no one decorated it."

"Whose coverlet was this?"

Maria studied the bedspread. "Darlene's when she was young, I think."

I felt the ruffles with my hand. "Was Darlene ever normal?"

"Not the five years since I've been here."

As the tub filled, I wandered around, touching little empty jewelry boxes and poking into closets. A nice cedar chest sat at the end of the bed, but it was locked. I lifted one end for a weight check; the box was too light to hold much. I still wished I could find the key. On the left side of the dressing table mirror there was a Remington print of an Indian lying in the snow, spying on a covered wagon train. The frame was nice, teak or something.

On the right side there was a photograph of the Axel family

in front of a large boat. E.T. and Darlene stood in front, holding a giant fish between them. E.T. had its head, Darlene its tail. I figured it was an ocean fish because of the wide fin. Thorne was behind Darlene with a hand on her shoulder, and Janey—I suppose it was Janey—hovered over the fish.

I lifted the photo off the wall. Judging from E.T. and Darlene, it looked like a scene from maybe ten years ago. E.T. was just as skinny as now, and had the same "What, me worry?" look in his eyes. His sweatshirt was aqua blue with a Miami Dolphins logo on it in white.

Darlene was the one I stared at the most. In the picture, she looked two or three years younger than E.T., although she doesn't anymore. She wasn't smiling—that would be asking too much—but she didn't seem terribly angry either. Like any twelve- or thirteen-year-old on vacation with her parents, Darlene appeared embarrassed and bored. Her facial color was pale, but nothing abnormal. It was considerably darker than the fish's belly. You couldn't say that nowadays.

Thorne stood smiling and patient, possibly even proud, although whether it was pride in family or pride in being able to supply the fishing trip, I couldn't tell. I wondered who took the picture. I imagined a guide.

Janey was almost as tall as Thorne, only huskier. I wouldn't call it fat—husky. Imagine Telly Savalas in a dark wig. That's unkind. Janey just looked like a ranchwoman who'd been expected to do a man's work all her life. Wyoming prides itself on being the first state of sexual equality. They have a saying: "Wyoming—where men are men and women are too." Janey seemed to have gotten herself caught in the saying.

Before my bath, I washed down three aspirins with a Dixie cupful of Grand Marnier. Afterwards, I turned off the light and lay down on Darlene's old coverlet and fell asleep in Janey's clothes and E.T.'s sneakers.

—

People might wonder why I came out of the bath and completely redressed down to the skull-and-crossbones sneakers before I slid onto the coverlet for some rest. The truth is, all this losing clothes stuff was making me paranoid. I know it had only happened twice, and the day before I hadn't actually lost my clothes—I only destroyed an old shirt and stained a pair of Wranglers—but the whole thing had me spooked. It was not outside the realm of possibility that Darlene might smash through the door with a double-headed ax and come after me, and that's not the kind of scene I care to handle nude.

Several times in my life, I've had periods of not knowing the realm of possibility. I used to like it. With Mickey I never knew what the hell might happen. That first couple of weeks in Nashville I thought my potential for stardom had no limits. Fat chance.

However, the last few years I have observed in the world that your general ratio is eight bad surprises for each good one. Eight people get run over by trucks for every one who finds true love from an unexpected source. Therefore, I've decided uncontrollable news is bad and should be avoided. And if you sense the unavoidable coming, meet it with your shoes on.

This is a pretty lengthy justification for dressing after a bath, but one of Loren's prime symptoms of a man fucking up is that he wakes up with his shoes on, and I wanted to explain that this wasn't a case of fucking up. It was a case of being careful.

Turns out I was right, too, because about the time I dropped off, someone scratched at the door.

Another one of Loren's sayings is: Beware of people who scratch your door. God knows where he comes up with this stuff, but he's always right. A book of Loren's pithy axioms could get a person through most situations in life.

The scratch brought me wide awake. I lay there, wondering if it was someone at the door or rats in the walls. It came again, then the door cracked open an inch, E.T. slipped through, and the door shut again.

"Hsst."

"Turn on the light, E.T."

By the time my eyes adjusted, he was sitting next to me on the side of the bed. "Hi, Mama. You like my sneakers?"

I pulled myself up and sat with my back against the headboard. "They're fine. Thanks for the loan."

"I heard you had another adventure." He was dressed the same as that morning, only with a sleeveless, very faded jeans jacket over his T-shirt. When he leaned forward, I could see an embroidered Grateful Dead album cover on his back. Behind his horn-rims, his blinking had taken on a gentle up-and-down sagging motion, like waves washing onto a Gulf Coast beach.

"Have you seen Darlene? I need to talk to her about nine hundred dollars."

"Darlene has your money?"

"I want it back."

"Then you can't pay for any more toot with money?"

"I came down, E.T. I don't want more toot."

He pulled the coke from his jacket pocket and snorted right in front of me. The bag was considerably lighter than it had been at seven-thirty that morning, which meant E.T. either sold a lot or did a lot or both. He plugged one nostril with an index finger and sniffed. A speck of white powder perched on the end of his nose.

"Once Darlene gets hold of money, it's gone. I never have figured out what she does with it since she never leaves the house. Until today. I think it's a good sign that she went outside in the daylight, don't you?"

"She went outside to break my neck."

"She's got to start somewhere." He held out a heaping coke spoon of the powder. "Want some fun?"

"What's it cost?"

He grinned, showing teeth. "We'll work something out."

The only reason I even wavered is because it's hard to turn down something that a lot people are desperate to have. I didn't want the crap. Effects from this morning's buzz were all gone except a vague pain in my spine, and that was nothing compared to the real pain in my hip. Had E.T. been offering some kind of prescription painkiller, I might have gone with temptation, but the sight of cocaine crystals just made me nauseous.

"I can turn your brain to happy gas." E.T. said.

"I don't want gas for a brain. What I'd really like is to rest awhile."

E.T. was shocked. "No toot?"

"Sleep."

He grinned. "How about my shoes?"

I looked down at the yellow sneakers. "They're awfully wide. You must be quite a swimmer."

"You want to buy my Dead tennies?"

"No, I don't want to buy your Dead tennies."

He reached for my feet. "Then give them back."

I swatted his hands away. "When you get my sandals from Darlene, I'll return your tennis shoes."

"I want them now."

"You can't have them now."

E.T. sat back and did another snort. At this rate he was sure to have a heart attack by midnight and it would be my fault. I could just see Thorne's face when I told him I killed his kid.

E.T. seemed to be hyperventilating. He wheezed, "You're stealing my sneakers."

"How can I buy them? You know Darlene took my

money. You don't accept Visa, do you? There's a Visa card in the Toyota."

E.T. pouted. "That's my only pair of yellow sneakers."

"I'd like to help, but you're not touching these shoes."

I knew damn well what was coming. The boy was unrealistic. He gave me that dumb grin again. "Maybe we could work something out."

"You want to trade dirty old tennis shoes for sexual favors?"

He shrugged. "They aren't so dirty."

"Leave or I break your glasses."

"Mama—"

"I'll dump your coke out the window."

"That's going too far."

I stared into his dull, blinking eyes. "You know I can do it, E.T. I am no longer putting up with colorful behavior."

"We could do a toot and laugh about the day. I'll give you a free snort."

"Out."

After he left, I got up to turn off the light and look at the Red Desert stretching away in the moonlight. Shadows moved behind the curtains in the bunkhouse windows. A couple of horses trotted around the perimeter of a corral. A soundless jet crossed the sky like an east-moving star. I've never had the temperament for standing in dark rooms, staring moodily out at the view, but this time it was kind of nice.

I remembered when I was nine or ten years old and Daddy made us turn off Jack Benny to go stand in the backyard and look at the first Sputnik. We craned our necks while he pointed and pointed and Mom kept saying, "They all look the same to me," until I finally figured out which star was moving through the others. There must have been thousands of satellites cross the night sky since then, but I haven't seen any except the first.

My peaceful time-out lasted maybe eight seconds before the

doorknob rattled and the hinges squeaked. I blew up. "*No toot,
no sex for sneakers. No nothing. Now leave me alone.*"

"Sneakers for sex?" It was Thorne's voice.

"I thought you were someone else."

"If it's one of my children, I don't want to hear about it."

That was fine by me because I didn't want to talk about it.
We stood in the soft darkness for a few moments, watching
each other. I wondered what the repercussions of saying, "I
love you," would be. Would he run away or latch on? Or
neither. Maybe he wouldn't expect anything or be afraid of
anything. That was doubtful—men who can accept love are
rarer than hare-lipped cover girls.

"I thought you might be hungry," Thorne said. He held out
a white pizza box.

"What time is it?"

"Nine, maybe nine-thirty. Why?"

"Don't turn on the light. I've had all the glare I can handle
for one day."

His dark form moved across the room and set the box on
the bed. "I was driving around and got hungry. Thought you
might like some pizza."

I crossed to the bathroom and reached in to flip on the light-
switch. With the door open a few inches, it gave the bedroom
a relaxed, easy glow.

"You bought a pizza?"

"Hamburger and onion."

"How'd you find a pizza parlor in the desert?"

Thorne kind of chuckled. "There's a Shakey's in town—
Rock Springs. After I left you I drove around all afternoon and
ended up there."

"That's forty miles."

"More like two hundred the way I went." He took a bite.
"It's still warm. I came the direct way back."

Pizza smelled good. It wasn't hot, but it wasn't cold yet either. "You've taken off your bandages," I said.

"Got in the way of driving."

"Let me see." The cut ran sideways, drawn together by long, black stitches. "Does it hurt anymore?"

"Some."

We ate the pizza in silence, both of us staring at the closed window. Afterwards, Thorne set the box with some crusts on the floor and we held hands awhile. I started to talk about Jackson Hole and my cabin, but that kind of petered out when it led to Loren.

Thorne told me about a pet pig he'd raised as a boy. He'd named it Teddy after Teddy Roosevelt. It was one of those "only thing I ever really loved" stories, the kind that ends with the pet winning a blue ribbon at the county fair and finding itself auctioned off to the slaughterhouse. The moral being: You only kill the ones you love. It was a sad story to hear coming from a sixty-something-year-old man. Thorne still grieved.

Afterwards, he leaned forward and almost kissed me, but didn't. "So, you want to get married?" Thorne asked.

"No."

He seemed to accept my answer. He didn't push it anyway. Much later he leaned me back on the bed and we made love. I don't think Thorne had been with many women other than Janey.

There's something touching about being with a man who's somewhat clumsy in bed. It's as if he's going on desire and emotion rather than technical experience. Makes me feel more appreciated, less like a judge at a gymnastics meet. It's not something I'd want to do every day, of course, but the lack of fire is made up for by how good I feel about myself afterwards. It's like the glow I used to feel on Christmas morning with

Connie and Cassie. Or that dizziness after I donate to a Red Cross blood drive.

Later, Thorne slept with his head between my breasts. I lay there awhile, staring at the ceiling, thinking, and wishing for a cigarette.

———

I awoke to confusion—shouts outside, doors slamming, orange light on the window, feet running in the hall. Gritz's mustache appeared above the bed.

"Barn's on fire, boss." He didn't say it with any more urgency than "Time for breakfast" or "Rain coming." By the time I realized what he meant, Gritz was gone and Thorne was pulling on his jeans. I ran to the window. Flames licked from the hayloft. Slivers of fire crept up the eaves. Men ran in and out the loading doors, saving machinery, tools, and tack. A guy pulled on Laredo's reins as the horse fought to go back in.

"Holy Christ," I said, but Thorne was already out the door.

I threw on Janey's clothes and E.T.'s sneakers. As I ran down the hall, I have to admit my first thought was how glad I was that the fire wasn't in the house. I flashed a vivid picture of myself running naked from the burning building into E.T.'s waiting arms. Even the mental picture was horrifying.

The front yard wasn't nearly as chaotic as I'd expected. There was a lot of noise and rushing, but everyone seemed to be doing his job. Five or six cowboys were hauling out the last of what could be saved. Another five or six worked with hoses down by the windmill. The hoses were obviously worthless. The barn's entire roof was burning. The fire made a sound like rushing air. I could hear the loft breaking up, falling into the main floor.

Thorne and Gritz stood about halfway between the house and the barn. I don't think either one was aware of my presence.

"Get those men out of there," Thorne shouted. "Anything inside now is gone."

Gritz shielded his face with a raised arm. "Laredo was the only horse in the stalls and we saved him. This'll cook the chickens."

"How much hay?"

"Not much—fifteen, twenty ton. I sure hate to lose that saddle."

"I hate to lose that barn."

I don't know which one screamed. I heard a sound and turned to see E.T. dragging Darlene through the loading-bay doors. He had her around the middle, half dragging, half carrying, while she thrashed her arms and legs, a child in a temper tantrum. They were almost out when she bent over and bit one of his hands. He jerked. She broke free. She ran a couple of steps back into the fire, fell, and he caught her again. By then, Thorne and another cowboy were there to help.

They dragged her away from the fire, Darlene screaming and crying the whole way. Her face was black from the smoke or soot. Her shirt tore off, leaving her in a bra white as the exposed skin.

All the cocaine added to the adrenaline fear-rush must have blown E.T.'s circuits because he floated along behind the scene looking practically calm. Serene maybe, like a shock therapy patient. He drifted over and said, "Hey," seemingly oblivious to the fire at his back and Darlene's hysterics.

"You okay?" I asked him.

"My Dead tapes are safe."

Darlene calmed down enough to blame Thorne for the fire. "This is your fault, you started this."

Thorne held both her wrists. He looked into Darlene's fierce eyes. "Your mother and I built that barn before you were born. Why would I burn it?"

"Because you hate yourself."

An explosion blew a wall of hot air out the front of the barn, knocking two cowboys off their feet. I saw Billy G get up still clutching the hose. I hadn't destroyed his life after all.

"What was that?" Thorne shouted over the roar.

"Fifteen gallons of gasoline," E.T. said. We all turned on him. "She bought thirty gallons, but left fifteen in a tank by the back door."

"Where'd she get the money to buy that much gas?" Thorne asked.

Darlene jumped at me and shrieked. Then she whirled back at Thorne. "Got you, got you," she laughed, "I bet you don't bring whores home while Mama's away now, Daddy dear."

Thorne slapped her. She fell into the dirt and stared up at him, her black face reflecting the firelight. E.T. screamed, *"You son of a bitch,"* and jumped on Thorne's back. Thorne spun around, clawing at E.T. until he worked him up on one shoulder. Then he lifted E.T. and threw him across the yard and onto Darlene. Out of breath, Thorne pointed at them. "You two are off the ranch. You're out of my life. It's suicide or throwing you out and I'm throwing you out."

Darlene pulled the hair out of her eyes. Tears ran clear, scar-like streaks through the black of her face. She pulled herself up on her hands and knees and hissed, "Mama knows everything you do."

Back in the crowd of onlookers, I thought of my daughters and Buggie, my parents, Loren's mother. You can't stop loving someone just because they're a disappointment. Loren needed me. I needed him.

I said, *"Crack."*

No one heard except Gritz. His mustache turned until he was looking at me from one eye. He said, "Good riddance."

"Didn't know you cared, Gritz."

He spit and moved away to help Billy G and the others with the hoses. In the flickering, flashing light of the burning barn, I turned and walked to the Toyota. E.T. never would recover his sneakers.

# Part Five

# *16*

ON THE FOURTH DAY, IT RAINED. NOT AN EXCITING SUMMER thunder-head rain like the storms that used to rip across the city in Houston. This rain was more in the line of a cold mountain drizzle. I woke up completely out of the spiritual enlightenment mood. Maybe it was the dream about Buggie and Ann, or maybe I missed Lana Sue. Maybe I was just hungry. Whatever the cause, all my religious fervor pissed out across the wet ground.

What I really wanted was a hot bath, two giant towels, a steak and eggs breakfast, and to hold Lana Sue for an hour or so. Then I wanted to make love—oral first, then vaginal—and drink three cups of coffee with real cream. Nothing even vaguely connected to a day of Fig Newtons, drizzle, and climbing a mountain.

I hung the daypack in a low Doug fir and draped my wet sleeping bag around the branches. It was fiberfill instead of goose down, so I figured to be somewhat warm the next night, even if I had to sleep damp.

The bag formed a sort of canopy over one spot of almost dry earth. My legs had to stay out in the rain, but I made the rest of myself as comfortable as possible, considering. Five or six Fig Newtons later, I flipped open the Spell-Write notebook and wrote, *I now understand why most world religions sprung from the desert climate.* I chewed another Newton and watched rain drip off a big whitebark across the ledge. The mist was so fine that the tree seemed to be gathering moisture from the air and manufacturing raindrops.

The whitebark made me think of God, which made me think of Buggie. Where was my son? Even if I could narrow it down to dead or alive, that would be something. Not knowing anything was a pain in the butt which, as time passed, was taking all the kick out of my new life with Lana Sue.

Here I was with a perfect wife, big bucks, a cabin in the woods within the sound of running water, all the time I needed to write or love or do whatever I felt like doing—my life's goals accomplished and it wasn't worth stale crap because my brain was stuck in one agonizing rut. *Where the fuck was my kid?*

I skipped three lines and wrote, *Ignorance of an answer is worse than the worst of all possible answers.*

I mean, I knew where Ann was. Or at least I knew where Ann's body was. She'd brought a husband's worst nightmare to reality. My wife killed herself. Try facing that fact one day at a time.

However, over the last four years, I'd been forced to pay the bills, brush my teeth, tie my shoes, change the oil in the car. I'd taken hundreds of walks in the woods. I'd earned Lana Sue's understanding. Somehow I'd worked out a way of dealing with Ann's death—I'd come to a sort of quiet, sad acceptance. But there was no way of accepting Buggie's fate, no way to deal with it and let go.

So, I worked out my cockamamie theory that God could be finagled into coughing up a few answers. Cheyennes did it. Jesus did it. Confucius, Max Brand. If all those people could weird themselves into visions of truth, so could I. And God owed me more than a simple dead or alive. If Buggie was dead, I wanted some real whereabouts information. No more hocus-pocus; religion is an extensive wine list, pick your vintage and pop the cork. I demanded truth.

Lana Sue let me run with the obsession until I started talking to Buggie and God instead of her. Now she was gone and the purpose of the search was suddenly fuzzy. The entire process had one final goal: freedom to live wholeheartedly with Lana Sue. But to reach that goal, I'd lost her. I was working backwards.

The thing to do was to run to the top of the mountain, get this religious catharsis jive over with, and go find my wife. My live wife. The wife who made me happy and life worth the mess.

I spoke to the dripping whitebark. "God better be there when I make the top of the hill because I'm not hanging around until He shows up."

The whitebark just dripped. I wasn't crazy enough yet to hear talking trees. Maybe at the top.

With that, I shrugged on my daypack, then pulled my sleeping bag around my head, shoulders, and back, and trotted off into the wet forest—must have looked like a jogging hunchback in a nylon shawl.

---

After Ann's suicide, I decided that any artificial mind diversion was a cheat and had to go, so I stopped drinking alcohol and watching television. Life suddenly got real. Each morning I woke up on the couch, terrified. I ate a bowl of Corn Chex and half a grapefruit. Then I sat at the kitchen table and worked on *Disappearance* for eight hours. What had been the facing of one loss became the avoidance of another.

After I finished my day's work, I fixed a box of Kraft Macaroni and Cheese and popped open a Dr Pepper. I sat on the couch to eat and didn't get back up until the next day. I could sleep for short periods on the couch in my clothes. Any attempt at the bed or undressing brought on vivid images of Ann in her coffin, then Ann rotting under the ground. I saw her face decompose. The hollows under her cheekbones went first, then the indentations on her temples. Her neck turned stringy. Her eyes opened. I woke up terrified.

This went on about three months. The landlady dropped by for the rent, which I couldn't pay. She knew the circumstances, however, and didn't have the heart to throw me into the street. Once she brought a casserole dish of mulligan stew, but I couldn't eat meat yet. I set the dish out the back door for the neighborhood dogs.

I remember doing a hundred push-ups one night. It took a couple of hours. Another time, Ann's boss from the day care came over. I pretended she was with the KGB and I was being questioned for thoughts against the state. I found a dead daddy longlegs and buried her in one of Ann's hanging plant pots. The plant had dried up the summer Buggie left, so I figured I'd get some use from the dirt.

The police called and made me drive downtown to see another dead little boy. It wasn't Buggie.

I came to hitchhiking in Nevada. The driver was an old lady wearing white gloves and a box hat with a net over her face. She asked why I wanted to see Max Brand's grave. She said she couldn't stand graveyards, hadn't been in one since Mr. Dodd died.

"Who's Mr. Dodd?" I asked.

"He was my husband."

I wandered the San Joaquin Valley for several days before a cub reporter on some newspaper told me Max Brand was really Frederick Faust, who was buried in Italy. After that, I wound up in jail in Hannibal, Missouri, on a drunk and disorderly charge. Mark Twain isn't buried in his hometown either.

I spent three days in jail—with some very strange people—before a deputy decided I couldn't still be drunk. A psychiatrist was called in and the final upshot was my brother, Patrick, flew up from Texas and took me back to Denver.

By then, Patrick had gone big in Alcoholics Anonymous. It was his life and religion. I think he spent as much time on AA as he used to on alcohol, but at least he got more done and he was easier to be around. He also had more money. Draining swamps for real estate had been lucrative since he sobered up. Patrick paid my back rent and a couple of months to spare. He took me to Kroger's and bought a shopping cart full of frozen dinners and organic vitamins.

As I drove him out to Stapleton International, Patrick told me to straighten up and join AA, even though I wasn't necessarily a drunk.

"AA is like having a real family," he said. "Haven't you ever wanted a real family?"

"You bet."

Patrick flew away, I went home and back to *Disappearance*.

———

In late June I hooked back up with the brick cleaning company. I enjoy cleaning bricks. It's outdoors, physical, yet not too heavy. The hammering is controlled, almost gentle. You can't just go crazy and start smashing mortar. Even then, I wasn't into smashing.

After cleaning bricks all day, I wrote in the evenings and on weekends. Nights, I drank beer and watched television. I found a midnight-to-dawn radio talk show that was hosted by a woman whose voice was soothing. Her name was Kathy, like my sister's. Only cranks and lonely people telephoned her, so I turned the sound off whenever a call came in, then I turned it back up in time to hear Kathy's voice again. Real late at night, right before sleep, I downed four measured ounces of Jim Beam and three aspirins—not a bad combination.

I'd had to start *Disappearance* all over after Ann used the manuscript to light the baby-bed fire. The book was probably better for it. The first three-fourths were about Buggie and the last part dealt with how we were treated and what it felt like after he left. I wrote a lot about guilt, anxiety, and loss.

One night it was too hot to sit in the duplex watching *Odd Couple* reruns, so I climbed into the Chevelle and circled Denver for a few hours. I drifted all over the city, cruising the franchise strips, watching people in the other cars. At a Big Boy on State Street I met a girl who claimed to be a prostitute. I'm not certain how it happened, or if I drove down there looking for a hooker or what. She certainly didn't try to entrap me. She hardly spoke a sentence.

"Twenty dollars," she said.

"Are you really a hooker?"

"Do I look like a Girl Scout?"

She looked like someone's teenage daughter was what she looked like. A baby-sitter maybe, the kind that drinks giant forty-ounce bottles of Coca-Cola and chews gum while she talks on your phone. She was dark, with pretty eyes and a tiny overbite. Long silver earrings dangled from both ears, but the right ear had a second fake diamond post up in the cartilage.

"What's your name?" I asked.

"Teresa, listen, I need a yes or a no here."

"How old are you?"

"You want my life history or you want to get laid?"

She was young and vulnerable and I was old and couldn't afford her. However, I hadn't been laid in just over three years. Abstinence that long changes a person's standards.

"I'll do it if you'll wash off some makeup," I said.

"That'll cost extra."

She took me to a hotel room straight out of a bad French movie about artists and heroin addicts. The place was almost too bare to be filthy. I'd have run away if the naked light bulb had been more than forty watts.

"Do you live here, Teresa?"

"You want straight, oral, or half and half?"

When we came to the actual act, I failed. As I fingered Teresa's little nipple, I remembered the last time I'd had sex, the day Buggie disappeared. That was the last time before she died that Ann and I talked as friends and lovers, the last time she trusted me.

"I'm sorry," I told Teresa.

"Happens all the time."

I paid her ten dollars an hour to lie next to me and hold me while I slept. The next morning, I awoke with an erection and finished the job.

Every couple of weeks the rest of the summer and early fall, I drove down to State Street and found Teresa. I looked at it as letting the air out of my tires before the pressure mounted and I blew a tube. She looked at it as business. Even though she hardly ever spoke more than five words, I suppose I would have eventually gotten involved in Teresa's personal life. I generally do when I sleep with a woman.

However, sometime in October she disappeared. I hung around eating pie in the Big Boy for three nights straight, but Teresa didn't show. No one answered when I knocked at her room. I tried asking the more obvious hookers on the street if they'd seen her. A couple knew who I was talking about, but no one seemed to know where she'd gone. The women offered to do the task for her, but my heart wasn't in it. I'd grown fond of Teresa. I didn't feel like trying another whore.

Eventually I wandered home and went back to letting the air out of my tires the old way, by hand.

—

I finished *Disappearance* on a Saturday afternoon in November. The last scene took place in the same graveyard that holds Peter Pym and Mary Louise Wolfe. A backhoe rests behind a canvas canopy. Seven or eight day-care teachers and moms watch as Ann is lowered into the ground. I stare off through the falling snow.

The scene was sad and emotional to write, but to tell the truth, after dwelling on one subject for over a year and then typing four hundred pages on that subject, I was burnt. Anyone who has ever lived day and night for a goal, then reached that goal, knows what I mean about the post-finish depression.

I skipped two lines and typed THE END. My fingers on the keyboard were a strange greenish-yellow color. The keyboard itself was dusty. A dirty thumbprint showed on the space bar. Why hadn't I seen those things before? I hit the line return a couple more times, then typed WHAT NEXT?

There were me and my ghosts and my manuscript—too many entities for one small duplex. Someone had to leave right away and I had a horrible feeling that if it wasn't me it would be the manuscript. Five more minutes alone in a room with that book and I would have burned it again. By the time I reached the Chevelle, air came in short gasps. I felt like a family fleeing poltergeists.

I drove all the way to Boulder and back before I could catch my breath enough to think in a straight line. There was a yearning of some kind. I wanted to be near someone I knew. I circled State, searching for Teresa, then I drove up to Denver University just in case some old English professor might be wandering through the parking lot. I got to thinking about Ann. She would have been proud that I finished a book. She always had more faith in my writing than I did. At least until Buggie disappeared.

I cruised the apartment complex where we lived when we met. A light was on in her place. A cardboard skeleton left over from Halloween hung in the window.

One year on my birthday, Ann found a baby-sitter and took me to a gigantic restaurant out by the Interstate named Los Gatos. That would be the place to stop and drink the yearning into nostalgia. Ann had been happy the night of my birthday. Maybe I'd feel close to her there, close to the real Ann that I met, not the dazed Ann that I lost.

I circled the off-ramps until I realized Los Gatos no longer existed. The big rock armory building had been transformed into a country-western nightclub. As a rule, I wasn't much interested in cowboy music. The words swung back and forth from self-pity to smug, and I don't much care for that pair of emotions. No one admires the crap he wallows in.

However, I wasn't familiar with any other nearby bars, and I'd developed a sudden craving to be around people. From the Chevelle, I watched the crowd of men in long-sleeve shirts and women in tight jeans with wide belts as they milled in and out of the horseshoe-shaped front door. They certainly qualified as people—not the sort of people I'd ever talked to, but, by then, I was pretty well out of people I'd ever talked to. Anyhow, whether they would speak to me or not, I could always kill the craving with Jim Beam.

———

I spotted Lana Sue Goodwin while she was paying the cover. She'd gained some weight and her hair was styled like a grownup—all swirls and differing lengths. Her eyes were tight, as if the skin had stretched. Much alcohol had been processed since high school, but this was definitely Lana Sue. How could I forget a woman whose name I'd carried on my butt for eighteen years?

She beelined for the back bar to an empty stool three or four down from where I nursed a Jim Beam on the rocks. In the mirror, I watched her order a double something, a single something, and an empty glass. She held the double glass the way people do who need what they're holding, not the offhand way of a woman at a cocktail party. Same with her cigarette. Something since graduation from Bellaire High had made Lana Sue nervous.

The cowboy on her other side asked her to dance, but she shook her head no without looking at him. When he got up to ask another woman, I slid down the bar and stole his stool. I don't think Lana Sue recognized me. She didn't even see me. As she mixed her drinks, then swirled the glass, Lana Sue appeared totally oblivious to her surroundings. For a moment, I thought nothing mattered to her except for what she was thinking about, then I realized her eyes weren't foggy at all, they were fixated on the band way down at the other end of the room.

It wasn't a bad band as far as cowboy music goes. I didn't know squat about country western, but the tune was kind of catchy and familiar. I caught myself tapping my sneaker along to the violin's melody.

They were an odd-looking group—a pretty girl in a Dale Evans outfit stood out front holding her acoustic guitar way high in front of her, several inches higher than most rock and rollers hold their guitars. Three guys in matching cowboy shirts played behind her and what looked like two old winos held down the sides of the stage. The winos had on clothes like I would wear to shoot pool.

The pretty girl sang a song I recognized called "Echo of an Old Man's Last Ride." It's about suicide. The words are interesting—outside your usual country-western theme.

Lana Sue turned sculpture behind the veil of wispy blue smoke curling up from her cigarette. Her hands didn't move.

She didn't blink. I watched closely, but saw no sign that she even breathed until after the last note of the song. Then, as the crowd cheered and applauded, Lana Sue exhaled a monumental sigh. Her eyes went all slick and she used both hands to bring her drink up for a sip.

I was staring at her face from about eight inches away, yet she never noticed me. She chewed the corner of her lower lip for a moment, then touched her tongue to the midpoint of the upper lip. As the girl singer gave a little speech introducing the next song, Lana Sue's face changed. First there was distress, pain. Then her face lit in a smile. Then she chugged down the rest of her drink.

I used the same line I'd tried so many years earlier when she walked me into the stop sign. "You look dejected."

She stared at me, still not remembering. "I am dejected. That's my daughter singing that song."

I looked at Lana Sue's daughter onstage. The resemblance was a hoot. Same dark, thick hair, same wide mouth and high cheekbones. Same long neck. "You should be proud of her," I said.

"She ran away from home. That tall sucker on the pedal steel is my old boyfriend and her new one. You ever hear anything so sick?"

What I did next was a cheap shot. I took all the pain and tragedy and realism of Ann and Buggie and turned it into a line. There's no defense except to say that I really wanted to talk to someone that night.

"My son disappeared and my wife killed herself."

Again her face changed. The lines beside her eyes softened, her forehead momentarily relaxed. "That's awful. I'm so sorry, I must sound terrible complaining about my daughter."

I looked away. "I finished a book about them today. I don't know what to do next." She sat staring at me while I watched her daughter sing. I didn't recognize the song. Lana Sue's daughter looked young, seventeen or eighteen years old at the most. I started counting the years since high school. How old would Buggie be now—eight and a half, going on nine. How much younger than Lana Sue's daughter?

"Listen," Lana Sue said, "you want to go somewhere quieter and have a drink?"

———

I have a confession to make about that tattoo. I thought a tattoo would make me look tough. At first I was going with a picture—a lightning bolt or a snake—but then I decided a woman's name would give me a tragic past that girls in Bellaire High would lather up over. For a week, I was torn between *Roberta* for Roberta Nesslebaum, the girl who sat in front of me in civics, or *Zelda* for Zelda Fitzgerald. Still not knowing which one to choose, I made an appointment and waited a couple of days for inspiration to strike, which it did in the form of a stop sign on Bissonnet Road. The truth is, I was on my way down to the tattoo parlor when I met Lana Sue. It wasn't love at first sight or precognition of the future. Lana Sue was a name more or less pulled out of a hat.

Not that I hadn't thought of her often over the years. In the shower, I'd soap down her name and wonder where she was and whether or not she remembered me. I used to make up stories about her. For years I had her as an exotic dancer in Las Vegas. Then I gave her a job studying chimpanzees in Zambia. Never in my wildest fantasies was Lana Sue ever a washed-up country singer or a mother.

———

Lana Sue took me on a jukebox tour of Denver. She said the wino pervert who stole her daughter was the foremost authority on jukeboxes in the Central and Rocky Mountain Time zones.

"The man's brain is a Wurlitzer filing cabinet," she said. "It's his one redeeming quality."

"He has good taste in women."

"Mickey runs on a take-what-he-can-get system. Cassie and I were dumb luck."

We zipped her Avis rental up Arapahoe to a tavern with the Fontella Bass version of "Rescue Me." Then down Sheridan to an all-night cafe owned by a guy claiming to be Gene Pitney's cousin. "Town Without Pity" played three times while we polished off fried chicken blue plates. Then back to the bars for more rusty nails and obscure 45s. A live recording of "Lovesick Blues" on Columbus. "Mack the Knife" at a gay bar on Speer. Lana Sue drove us way the hell up some canyon to a dirty dive that served nothing but Pabst Blue Ribbon and had a jukebox of trucker singles, all by men named Red. Check out this list: "Neon Playboy" by Red Steagal, "Nytro Express" by Red Simpson, "Truckin' Trees for Christmas" by Red Sovine, "Pin Ball Boogie" by Red Foley, and the last one, my favorite, Red Rubrecht singing "Hold On, Ma'am, You've Got Yourself a Honker."

After the Red inundation, she brought us back all the way from the Speedway to the Coliseum on nothing but Patsy Cline. Lana Sue claimed a spiritual connection to Patsy—said they'd both suffered on their knees before the Nashville cocksuckers. I had trouble picturing the metaphor.

About the fourth version of "I've Got the Memories But She's Got You," I realized we were both blasted out of our gourds and the situation was shaping up as a definite score. Lana Sue had been singing along with the jukeboxes for forty-five minutes. Between songs and bars, we held hands and she told me about her lousy husbands and darling daughters. She said if

I'd find an all-night Eckerd's she would buy a golf ball and a garden hose and show me a neat trick.

We wound up driving way off down Santa Fe almost to Castle Rock, where she pulled into a nice little motor court featuring a coffeepot in every room and paper cutouts you were supposed to cover the toilet seat with before you sat down. Lana Sue jumped on with an enthusiasm I'd only dreamed of, but I took forever in coming. I guess I was too drunk.

We stayed in the motor court for four days. On Sunday, I suggested we transfer over to my duplex, but Lana Sue said that pain fucks don't work in a private residence.

"Too much history in a home," she said.

"But I've got a refrigerator."

Several things Lana Sue said—like "pain fucks"—let me know she was using me as a form of grief therapy, that it wasn't my wisdom she was after. I don't mind being used if it'll get me fucked the way Lana Sue fucks. Jesus, she was an experience.

Monday we drove back to the bar to pick up my Chevelle and see if her daughter was around. The car was okay, but the band had moved on down the road. Lana Sue didn't seem too distressed. Other than that trip and a couple of lunch breaks at Arby's, we stayed in the room, mostly in the bed. It was my first shot at marathon sex. I loved it.

———

I also didn't think the sex was quite as impersonal as what Lana Sue had in mind. Sometime Tuesday afternoon I mentioned this fact.

"I think you're starting to like me."

Lana Sue gave me a light nip to the ear. "Honey, to me you're just another dick in the night."

"That wasn't my dick you were talking to at six-thirty this morning."

We were lying naked, side by side, with our heads at the foot end of the bed. A Domino's Delivers pizza box was on the floor and *Wheel of Fortune* played on the silent TV screen.

Lana Sue fed me the tip bite off a slice of Italian sausage pizza. "You figure out the puzzle yet?"

"Admit it, Lana Sue. I'm having a good effect on you." The puzzle was T _ _ _ _ _ _ _ _ _  _ _ _  T _ _ _ _  T _ _ .

"Of course you're having a good effect on me. We're setting a Colorado record for orgasms per entry."

I took another bite of her slice. "Tippecanoe and Tyler too."

"What?"

"Tippecanoe and Tyler too. That's the saying."

"What's it mean?"

"Something to do with politics."

On the show, a contestant got the C. He looked like the old janitor we had back in junior high.

"You were smoking three packs of Larks a day before you met me."

"So what. Look at this sauce on the sheets. The maid will think we're perverts."

"Today you smoked less than one."

"We've either been asleep or screwing all day. When would I have had time to smoke?"

"A true addict would have found the time."

"Bullshit, Loren. Are you certain it's Tippecanoe?"

The N came up. "And we're drinking Dr Peppers right now." I pointed to the evidence on the floor. "Three days ago it would have been scotch."

Lana Sue dropped a fat chunk of crust back in the box and rolled onto her side to face me. "What's the point here, Loren?"

I retrieved the crust. "You talked about your past and your problems for hours last night. You listened when I talked back." I rubbed her third eye with my thumb. "Your forehead is starting to relax for the first time in days. You should have seen your eyebrows that night in the Powder Keg."

"Sex relaxes me. It has nothing to do with you."

"I think it does. Fondness is hard to hide."

"Watch me."

"I caught you smiling when I came out of the shower this morning. You were glowing."

"I don't glow."

"Admit it, Lana Sue. You're beginning to fall in love."

Lana Sue rolled on over to face the ceiling. Her breasts rose once and fell. I've always liked Lana Sue's breasts. They aren't very large, but they don't sag a bit. They look energetic.

"Do you realize the implications of what you're saying?" Lana Sue asked. "If what you claim is true—it's not, but if it was—I'd have to get dressed and leave right now."

The stupid janitor got both P's but still couldn't solve the puzzle. "Why?" I asked.

"Why? I'm a married woman. I don't have affairs."

"You've never done this before?"

"I've done *this* plenty times. *This* is a crotch form of morphine. What you're proposing is heightened sensitivity, which is the last thing I want."

"I can make your life better."

"Don't confuse me, Loren. When I get confused I go home."

———

One thing I admire about Lana Sue, she doesn't use the door as a power play device. She has never once threatened to leave me that she didn't actually wind up leaving. Sometime that night, Lana Sue must have finally realized a growing fondness for me. Nothing was admitted aloud, but I know she felt something strong because the next day she had me tail her to the airport where we put ourselves through an emotion-packed good-bye scene and Lana Sue flew off to Nashville. I moped around the loading lounge awhile, worked out a reasonable that's-that attitude, then drove home to my duplex and Buggie's manuscript.

———

I don't know if Lana Sue would have returned to Denver on her own impetus or not. She had this falling-in-love-and-splitting-up-is-all-timing theory that I don't, as a rule, buy. My opinion is she would have created the timing and come back anyway. Hell, we were in love. Love is great compared to lonely nights and scotch.

However, this is all conjecture, because, lucky for me, Ace took care of the timing. When Lana Sue arrived home that afternoon, she found Ace in the Jacuzzi performing unnatural acts with the Sugarez Sisters, Carly and Monetta, a singing duo from Ox Point, Wisconsin.

Lana Sue made death threats. She towered over the Jacuzzi like the Statue of Liberty, threatening to bean Ace with a fully charged electric Dust Buster until Carly Sugarez lost stool control and fouled the water. I understand a mass of glassware was broken, phonograph albums fell like rain, counteraccusations were hurled, doors slammed, lawyers phoned—Lana Sue was back in my arms by midnight.

## *17*

UP HIGH, NEAR WHERE MINER CREEK RIDGE MEETS THE Sleeping Indian's belly, there was a clearing maybe two miles long and a quarter mile wide. I wandered waist-deep through an amazing array of flowers—larkspur, paintbrush, cinquefoil, balsamroot, more color and variety than a Rose Bowl parade. If it hadn't been for the misty rain, the pollen would have killed me. The flowers were such a treat that, for a moment, I forgot all about Buggie and Lana Sue. I didn't think of myself for over an hour.

At the top of the clearing, the tree line came from both sides to form a point. Thirty yards or so downhill from the point, a snowmobile sat facing south, its treads astraddle on an old pock-marked aspen trunk. I approached with suspicion. One doesn't expect to come upon machines in the wilderness, at least not this far back. My first thought was of booby traps. I know that is a paranoid first thought, but after the flaming chokecherry bush and those shots the day before, I was in the mood to take incongruities personally.

My second thought ran to the possibility of a dead snow-mobiler. My car was parked ten miles down the hill, but in winter no one plowed the road for another ten miles back toward town, which meant if this guy had been alone when he wrecked or broke down, he was probably rotting somewhere in the vicinity.

I touched the red leather seat. A piece of chrome on the blue metal-flake body read POLARIS TXL. The choke had been left clear out and the key was still in the ignition. I opened the gas cap and sniffed. The rider hadn't abandoned her from lack of fuel. Leaving my daypack in the flowers, I shrugged off my sleeping bag poncho and hopped on the snowmobile. There's a futuristic Woody Allen movie where he finds a two-hundred-year-old Volkswagen that starts right up. Woody says, "Those Nazis really knew how to build cars." No such luck with the snowmobile. The ignition didn't even click. I pumped the gas a couple times, squeezed the brake bar, pushed in and out on the choke. Nothing much else to play with—definitely a dead toy.

I leaned forward with my hands on the handlebars, *vrooming* in the back of my throat. The scene needed a most-plausible-explanation story as to what happened at the time and why no one had returned to haul the snowmobile away to a garage. How would you move a snowmobile off a mountain in the summertime anyway? Even though the machine straddled a log, it looked more left behind than wrecked. My guess was a midwinter breakdown, abandonment, then as the snow melted, it gradually eased down onto the log.

The speedometer splintered. A moment later, I heard the shot. I looked left, down the hill, at a man standing in plain sight, aiming at me like I was a fear-frozen antelope. Dirt spit next to my leg. I rolled off the far side of the snowmobile. There was silence, then my daypack jumped a foot and another shot boomed up the hill.

Facedown in the wet dirt, I waited without a move. I'd starved and come into the mountains in hopes of a hallucination. Expectations swung from Thunder Gods to sermonizing hawks, but wishful thinking made me wonder if this might be the moment. Another shot into the log and I rejected that idea. Like Buggie's disappearance, this trouble was too real.

Sliding to the front of the snowmobile, I peeked out between the log and the front runner blade. Whoever it was wasn't about to content himself with one flurry and a fadeout like he had yesterday. Rifle held under his armpit, the man advanced slowly toward me, picking his way through the field of flowers.

"Asshole," I whispered, "what did I ever do to you?"

The man still wore gray khakis and the red wool shirt. His limp seemed more pronounced than before. At one point, he held his left hand up as an umbrella for his eyes while he squinted at me through the rain. I repeated myself. "Asshole."

Obviously, staying put was out of the question. That left a mad dash up the hill into the trees or a ground-hugging slither using the flowers for cover. The thirty yards between me and the edge of the forest was carpeted by knee-high goldenrod, but I couldn't tell if the cover was thick enough to hide in or not. Looking up through the flowers, I could see him easily. Could he see me looking down? The rifle didn't appear to have a telescopic sight, but the man was almost close enough for that not to matter. However, he'd missed so far, which meant he was either a poor shot or he was only trying to scare the living shit out of me after all.

I forced myself to breathe slowly, stopping for a short break between each inhale and exhale. It wouldn't do to hyperventilate and pass out. I'd hate to get killed in my sleep.

Desperate plan time—I had to make the woods and then hide. Make the woods came first. A triple-blade Boy Scout knife lay in my daypack not fifteen feet to the right. If I could reach it, I'd have some chance at climbing another tree, then slitting the bastard's throat as he walked by.

Another check showed the man had stopped moving

forward. His face was toward me, I suppose waiting for the break he knew had to come. If anything, the rain lightened a little, giving him a clearer view. Hugging dirt and praying like a Cheyenne—Oh, Mother Earth, I am a part of you. Oh, Mother Earth, I am a part of you. Don't let this asshole kill me, Mother Earth—the crawl seemed to go on forever. Mud slid up my nose. My eyes itched like hell. I figured even if he couldn't see me through the weeds, the blossoms above shook like dozens of little waving hands pointed straight down at my butt. I always did hate goldenrod.

Just as I reached the daypack, he put a bullet into the snow-mobile's gas tank. Jesus, what an explosion. I fetal-positioned as, first, tremendous heat scorched past, then snowmobile parts rained a metal hailstorm. Then I was up and running.

———

I tore through the trees, whipped by wet willows, scratched and pulled by wild roses. Almost broke my ankles in a couple of clumsy falls, lost the daypack somewhere near the crest. Running like a maniac wasn't much use either. The soft ground yielded a set of tracks so visible that any idiot could read them—even a city-hired hit-man idiot. I might as well have put up road signs.

And I'll tell you what I was thinking as brambles tore my arms and rocks chopped at my feet. The pain in my lungs was remarkable, but even so, all I could think charging down the back side of that ridge was this: *Holy Christ, I'd like to get laid right now.* Brushes with death always bring out my horniness. By the time I hit the creek, I had such a hard-on I was running in a stoop.

However, I hadn't read seventy-five Max Brand novels for nothing. I jumped in the freezing creek—which took quick care of the hard-on—and floundered up the stream, away from my telltale footprints. "Let's see that sucker track the Jimmy Stewart of Jackson Hole," I muttered between wet tumbles. Soon the creek narrowed into nothing more than a streamlet draining a series of pink summertime snowbanks. I found an outcropping of rocks to skip across, leaving not a single track. The outcropping led to a pile of broken slabs left by an ancient slide off the top of the Sleeping Indian. After poking around a few minutes, I discovered a huge cracked boulder over a one-man crawl space. The killer couldn't follow in there if he wanted to. I turned around, shrugged my body into the crack, and went back to imagining Lana Sue's body.

No matter what anyone thinks about Lana Sue, I've never heard a word of criticism about her body. The thing I like best about it is the color. It's a dark, rich color, kind of like a polished teak coffee table. Sometimes I turn off all the lights in the cabin except the television and lie next to her on our bed, just watching the colors of her body. It's a perfect body for being on top.

In the dark hole there, I got to comparing Lana Sue's body with Ann's. Ann was much lighter, freckles sprinkled her neck and arms. Her butt was bigger than Lana Sue's, but her breasts were about the same size, only they hung different. It was difficult to imagine Ann's body without imagining her dead.

At sixteen, Marcie VanHorn had bigger knockers than Lana Sue or Ann. I'd never seen her entire body, but Marcie didn't leave much to picture. Lately she'd taken to wearing a nylon tube around the top and cutoffs so tight she had to carry her car keys and change in a little pouch she hung around her neck. Marcie was into long dangly earrings and painted toenails. Lord knows what I saw in her other than willing adoration.

From Marcie, I went on to my usual fantasy women—movie

starlets. I pretended Debra Winger was in the crack with me giving me head. Then I pretended I was licking clit on Mary Steenburgen. The girl who played Bailey on *WKRP in Cincinnati* climbed on even though I couldn't remember her real name. I combined all three fantasies into one doozy of an orgiastic daydream.

This'll show Lana Sue, I thought. I may not break marital vows technically like she does, but I can have a hell of a time pretending.

———

Lana Sue and I have been together for two and a half years and I still haven't managed to cop a stance on this adultery thing of hers. I suppose that's because she has yet to cross the line, that I know of. There were unconfirmed suspicions after the Scott Fitzgerald trip to Maryland, but nothing was ever disclosed.

However, sooner or later, Lana Sue's desire for side action will have to be faced. She's told me too often about fooling around on past husbands and, although I'm an idealist, even I'm not dope enough to think a spouse will change habits simply because she happens to marry me.

Lana Sue draws a moral distinction between adultery and what she committed while living with Ron and Ace. She claims her extramarital humping is medication, no more ethically objectionable than terpin hydrate and codeine cough syrup. She expects me to understand that if I cause her pain, or confusion, or even boredom, she'll go out and score a couple of orgasms off a stranger, then come home to me, and everything will once again be dandy. She forgets I'm the prime example of painkiller gone romance, which, for me, blows her rationalization right out the window.

And do you think Band-Aid sex is a two-way street, that I can scratch itches for the purpose of giving our marriage strength? In country-western terms—fat fucking chance. One screw-around would give Lana Sue excuse enough to become the female Hitler of my life. I'd have to shoot her to get her off my face.

Which I knew might happen when or if Lana Sue ever returned from her present huff. I'd made a mistake just before coming up the mountain, what turned out to be a mistake in vain, and if the limper with the golf tan didn't kill me, Lana Sue would.

———

Early the first morning of my Quest, I was upset about Lana Sue being gone and probably with someone else, so, after shopping at Safeway, I packed my mountain provisions and drove down to Marcie VanHorn's. Since she's only sixteen and lives with her father, I took along an old bundt pan we'd borrowed last February when Lana Sue baked me an angel food cake with white icing for John Steinbeck's eighty-third birthday.

Marcie answered my knock wearing a white gauzy cotton top and Levi's cutoffs cut off right at the crotch. She had a Diet Dr Pepper in her right hand. I could hear MTV blaring in the living room behind her.

She kissed me on the cheek. "Say, hey, good-lookin', haven't seen you in a couple weeks. Want some Cheetos?"

"I'm on a fast."

"A what? Come on in. Dad's gone to church."

Lee VanHorn is Catholic and owns Russian steam bath franchises strung all over the West. I've always taken for granted he's in organized crime because my only experience with steam rooms is from TV and movies. No one but gangsters ever takes a steam bath on television.

Lee is one reason I never followed up on Marcie's invitation to sleep together. I always imagined I'd go to sleep with her and wake up with a horse head. The other reason is that Lana Sue threatened to sew my dick shut if she ever caught us.

Marcie led me into the living room. On the television, a guy with long curly hair and no sleeves in his shirt was killing his father and mother. The action was accompanied by a song extolling bitterness and anger.

I said, "Music videos are the root of all evil."

Marcie plopped down in an easy chair and reached for the Cheetos. "This one's gnarly. Wait till you see the end."

"Gnarly," I said. I stood in the center of the room, holding the bundt pan with both hands.

"Why are you on a fast?"

"Do you realize kids of the fifties coped with the A-bomb? Then the sixties brought easy sex and mind-warping drugs. But it wasn't until that stuff started"—I pointed at the guy with the curly hair who was in the process of destroying his parents' house—"that the rate of teenage suicide doubled."

Marcie glanced from me to the screen. Some other sleeveless guys milled around the wrecked house, dragging chains. "Doesn't make me want to commit suicide. Makes me want to eat."

We watched until the song ended and another bleak outlook on life began. "Mind if I turn it down?" I asked.

Marcie nodded with a flip of blond hair. "This bunch sucks eggs anyway."

In the quiet, I said, "I brought your pan back."

"You didn't have to. Dad's always in church on Sunday morning. Have a seat. How's the great Wyoming novel coming along?"

"I'm having trouble with inspiration."

"I can relate, buddy. I have this photography project going, been working at it all summer, but I just can't seem to get inspired." Marcie leaned her head back and dropped a Cheeto into her mouth. Her bare feet hung over the side of the easy chair. She looked ready for the taking.

I sank into a cane chair with some kind of leather strips for a seat—probably elk gut.

"I had an inspiration last night."

Marcie reached down for her Diet Dr Pepper. "Why go on a fast, you're too skinny now?"

No time for spiritual apologies, I dived into the purpose of the visit. "I was wondering if you'd enjoy having sex with me this morning."

She looked across at me and grinned. "Why, Mr. Paul."

Marcie was the only girl I'd ever flirted with, at least consciously. I wasn't sure if *Why Mr. Paul* was humorous indignation or well-intentioned acceptance. I set the bundt pan on the floor and continued.

"Before—you know, that pack trip summer before last, you asked me to help with your virginity—"

"Believe me, I solved the problem."

"I figured as much. Anyway, you were only fourteen then and Lana Sue and I were newly married; Lana Sue can be quite a forceful personality, you know."

"You were afraid she'd break your legs."

"Anyway, I turned you down at the time, but now, what with this fast and all, I've reconsidered."

Marcie swung both legs to the floor. "Reconsidered?"

"Yes, I'd be willing to make love to you now. If you still want to."

Marcie crossed the room and sat on the arm of the cane chair and leaned over and kissed me lightly, maybe like a daughter, maybe like a playful coquette, I wasn't sure. Tentatively, I lifted one hand to touch her back.

"Loren, you're so sweet," she said. "When I grow up, I'd be honored to go to bed with you." She love-tapped my nose with hers. "You know you're my favorite novelist in the whole world, but I'm just a kid now."

"What?"

"I can't fuck grown-ups. It would confuse my identity."

I pressed on her back. "You were a kid at fourteen."

She stood up and moved over by the television. "I was too young to know I was young then. Your artistic temperament in *Yeast Infection* blew me so away, I'd of done anything for you back then."

"How about doing something now?"

"I respect you so much for not taking advantage of my vulnerability."

What kind of woman says gnarly one minute and vulnerability the next? Bruce Springsteen broke into a sweat on the television screen.

I saw my morning-comfort screw slipping away in the wind. "I think of you as a grown-up, Marcie."

"You don't even think of yourself as grown up."

"Then we're even. You can pretend I'm in high school."

Marcie turned and pushed a button, blacking out Bruce Springsteen's face. "There is one thing I'd like from you, honey-bunny."

Honey-bunny? Debauchment botched, it was back to the flirty old mentor act. "Sure, sugar, how can I please you?"

"I'd like to see your penis."

I picked the bundt pan back up and set it on my knees. There's a difference between seducing a teenager and flashing one. Flashing seemed tawdry, especially three days before I was scheduled to meet God.

Marcie turned on the enticing charm. She ruffled my hair and tweaked both ears. "Come on, Loren, do it for art."

"That's my line."

"I just want a little peek. Please."

I never refuse a woman who says please. I'd have probably made it with her back on the pack trip had she only begged. Ten seconds later, Marcie was ogling my lap.

Her mouth twitched. I couldn't tell if she was appreciative or suppressing a giggle. "Perfect," Marcie said.

"That's what I've always thought."

"Come here." Marcie grabbed my hand and dragged me from the living room into the kitchen, I held up my pants with my other hand.

"Are we going to make it now?"

"Not today. Today we make art." The kitchen table was covered with black velvet. Next to the refrigerator, a Nikon sat atop a tripod.

I tucked back in—fast. "Oh no, Marcie, honey. I'm no pervert."

"Loren." She faced me with both hands on her hips. "Where's your youth? Nobody'll know it's you." She lifted the black velvet to show a silver-dollar-sized hole. "You stand behind there and hold the cloth as a backdrop. Nothing shows but the dick."

"Marcie, this is kinky."

"Seducing me wasn't kinky?"

Nothing left to say—I dropped my pants. Before Marcie snapped the photo, she pulled a Rock Cornish game hen out of the refrigerator and set it next to my penis.

"What's that for?"

"Makes the shot artsy. A prick by itself is just another dirty picture."

"But why that?"

"It'll develop to look like a chicken. The perspective'll make your thing seem huge."

"Oh, yeah."

"Right now it won't, though." Marcie reached down and squeezed once. "That's better."

"Try again. It'll grow more."

"We don't want it sticking up like a carrot. It's supposed to hover next to the hen—like a phallic UFO."

"One more squeeze. I'll make it hover."

Marcie laughed. "Oh, Loren, you're such a card."

She dashed from the room, leaving me standing alone with the false chicken. I looked down the front side of the velvet at my lonesome dick. I've felt detached from myself often in life, but this time the feeling was eerie. I had a terrible premonition of Lee walking in to get a beer. What would I say? "Hi, Lee, how was church?"

"Got it," Marcie said, coming back in the kitchen.

"Got what?"

She shook baby powder on my penis and the Rock Cornish game hen. She rubbed it into the hen, but not me.

"Don't want any shine," she said.

"That makes sense."

Marcie moved some lamps around. Then she stood behind the tripod and focused. "Out-a-sight," she said. "This'll be gnarly."

I said, "Gnarly."

———

I let Debra Winger, Mary Steenburgen, and Bailey from WKRP have their way with me for a good while. Jessica Lange stood outside the crack, watching with desire, but I cut the fantasy off on her. I was wet and hungry and someone was trying to kill me. This was no time to break in a fourth woman.

In fact, I had some trouble relaxing with the other three. Sooner than I really wanted to, I crawled from the crack to survey the situation. I stood, relieving myself in the direction of the Sleeping Indian's nose. Because of the killer, I could no longer daydream my way across the mountains—which is how a Vision Quest is supposed to work. No one can see spirits when every rock might camouflage a sniper. The temptation was to call off the meet and go home.

However, I'd gone to a lot of trouble so far and Buggie's whereabouts was still unresolved. If I gave up now, I'd still be the same old partial husband to Lana Sue, still giving myself shit instead of letting go and accepting life. I squinted at the lightest spot in the clouds. By rough estimate, I figured the time as five o'clock with at least four hours before sunset, another hour after that until total darkness. The run to the top of the mountain would take two hours tops. That gave me three hours to find out what happens to a person after he dies and clear out. I could drop down a ravine on the other side of the mountain, shiver in safety all night, then walk into Jackson in the morning. Marcie or Lee would pick me up and drive me home, where I'd load my Ruger Magnum and come back after the Chevelle and anyone else who happened to be in the vicinity.

Of course, none of it came true. Fifty yards into the forest, I found the magic setting I'd been searching for. Low-lying cloverlike carpet with no underbrush; ancient, flat stones matted by green and orange lichen; the bark on the trees dripped with life—not plant life or even animal life. The bark hummed like running water. No birds, no squirrels. Other than the low hum of the trees, all was silent as if the air itself muffled and absorbed any sound that might dare enter. A place for Gypsies to chant in lost languages and Druids to sacrifice ripe virgins with long, long hair.

Across the clearing, an elk skull grew from the fork of a limber pine. At first I thought he was a bizarrely twisted branch. I approached at an angle, walking twenty degrees or so to his left. The horns had eight points on each side. He had three groups of teeth in his upper jaw, two back toward the cheeks, and one set of six that stuck out the front in an intense overbite. A long, thin cavity showed where his nose had once been. His forehead was flat as an egg pan.

The skull would have been intriguing yet dead had I not looked into the eye sockets. This is impossible to describe without sounding like Greta the Cosmic Cow—which is a wimpy way to sound—but the scene reeked of metaphysical boogiehood and to describe it, I must offend some otherwise nice people. Like Lana Sue. Lana Sue would gag at this, but the damn eye sockets were empty holes and something else at the same time. Call it alcohol withdrawal, Impossible Shit, or God Himself, I don't know. All I know is some *thing* was aware that I stood there looking at it.

I decided to go for broke, believe what I wished to be true, and asked the question.

"What happens after we die?" I asked. The elk had no bottom jaw, but if a dead object can communicate, I don't see why it would need a working mouth.

"Where is my son Buggie?" I asked. The trees hummed. Far above, an eagle shrieked the exact sound, only thirty times louder, made by the lungs of a gasping asthmatic.

"One more chance, elk, where's Buggie?"

A voice boomed, "You killed him, bucko."

My heart twisted. I swung around to face the black hole barrel of a rifle.

The man came a step closer. "What is this place?"

"I didn't kill Buggie."

"You come here to perform religious ceremonies?"

"I just found it today, but, yeah, I guess so."

"You guess so."

"I didn't kill Buggie."

We dropped into some form of defiant eye contact. His were silver-gray like his rain-matted hair. He had a politician look-square jaw and slightly bloated nose. I wondered why he hadn't worn the golf hat indicated by the tan line.

I said, "Tell me what's going on,"

"I shall shoot you until my bullet supply is exhausted, then I shall abandon your body to the carrion eaters."

I glanced at the rifle. It was a Winchester—a Magnum of some kind. "What kind of bullets?" I asked.

"What?"

"What kind of bullets will you exhaust on me?"

"One sixty-five twenty grains—what's it to you?"

"I just wondered." I glanced to the elk for help, but if this was God, he didn't appear to be a God who gets involved. In fact, it was beginning to look more skull and less deity by the minute.

I thought of something. "Is Buggie dead?"

"How should I know? Ask your friend there." The man swung the barrel to the elk, then back at me.

"You said I killed Buggie. You wouldn't think that if you didn't know he was dead."

"Stand aside, over there. Keep your hands visible." He limped to the elk and grabbed one horn. I winced. The man tried to shake the elk. "Tree's grown around it," he said. "Must have been embedded for years."

"Is Buggie dead?"

The man bent to inspect the fuse point where elk and tree had grown together. "He must be. Annie would never have allowed you to drive her to suicide if the boy was still alive."

"You knew Ann?"

He scowled and jerked the rifle back at my chest. He almost pulled the trigger right then—the struggle for control was visible.

"Ann didn't know whether or not Buggie was alive," I said.

"You believe that?"

"She'd have told me if she did."

"Death was her way of telling. You wouldn't listen to any other way."

"Ann killed herself to get my attention?"

"You got it, bucko."

I stood with my hands visible, watching the man inspect my elk head. He ran his hand down the right antler to the button at the skull. Then he brushed some pine needles from the nasal cavity. I took him for a maniac, which meant I was safe for the moment, he would be in no hurry to kill me. Maniacs always explain themselves before they blow your brains out. They want you to agree that killing you is the proper course of action.

However, the timing confused me. The guy's appearance was awfully convenient to the theme of the Vision Quest. It'd been six years since Buggie left and almost four since Ann's death. Why did this character show up on the one day I'd planned for explanations?

"Why today?" I asked.

He paused to eye me again. "I've observed you for the last four weeks. My vacation ends tomorrow."

"You're killing me today so you can get back to work?"

The man nodded.

Even my assassins are tacky. "What kind of job do you have to get back to?"

"I own a Dodge dealership."

"I'm being stalked by a vengeance-crazed car salesman?"

"You have no idea who I am?"

"Not exactly."

"I was Annie's family, the only person who loved her. And she loved me. And you don't even know my name. She was a stranger to you, wasn't she?"

"She never mentioned talking to an old guy."

One-handed, he dug out his wallet and handed me a card.

I was embarrassed for him. "Listen, mister, killers don't pass out business cards."

"Just read the damn thing."

WALT SMITH DODGE/OLDSMOBILE in twenty-four-point type above the logos of both companies. Then underneath, it read HIGHWAY 101 AND GLENWOOD, COOS BAY, OREGON. I couldn't recall a Walt Smith from Oregon. Ann was so long ago and in a completely different life and frame of mind, but I'd remember anyone as close as this guy claimed. The name Smith was familiar.

"Holy shit, you really are family."

He smiled, showing capped teeth. "Ann is my daughter."

I couldn't believe it. "She told me about you. You're nuts."

He swung the rifle in my direction, but I was too blown to take the threat seriously. "Didn't you once shoot at some guy on the freeway?"

"I'm going to shoot at you now."

For the first time, I spotted the resemblance to Ann and Buggie, especially Buggie. It was in the brow and forehead area, and the stubborn look of his eyes. "Why the grudge, Mr. Smith? We both loved her and she's gone. You and I should be empathetic companions."

He jerked the bolt action back, then forward. "You abandoned Annie when Fred disappeared. You killed her."

He'd said what I sometimes late at night suspected. However, at the time, it seemed the opposite. From the moment we lost Buggie, Ann had fallen into a closed-off trance, almost a spell. I tried to talk, tried to touch her. I cried at the same times she did. I was there for Ann, at least through that first summer while we searched. But then we returned to Denver and I started Buggie's book. She started barbiturates.

I said, "You abandoned her when her mom died."

Smith pulled the trigger. Dirt belched up next to my right foot.

"This is too Western for me, Walt. What say we cool it?"

Another shot bit tree bark behind my head. I froze, hoping not to piss him off any more. My mind, however, raced. He'd worked the bolt before the first shot, which meant, like most hunters, he didn't walk around with a shell in the chamber. My Ruger down in the cabin had a three-shot magazine. I wondered what the odds were of all Magnum rifles being the same.

Walt shouted, "My little girl loved me, you hear that? I mattered, not you. When Fred died, you ignored her and she turned to her daddy."

"So where was her daddy the afternoon she killed herself?"

He fired again.

Lana Sue stepped from behind a tree. "Stop frightening my husband."

———

Holy Christ, was I glad to see Lana Sue. She had on a rainproof poncho and this floppy hat we'd bought in Venice. She carried my daypack in one hand with the sleeping bag bunched under her arm. Her eyes were beautiful.

"Aim that thing somewhere else," she said. "I've had it with men and guns."

Walt lowered the rifle so it pointed into the ground a couple of feet in front of me. With his left hand, he pumped three more shells into the magazine. "Who are you?"

In hopes of a hug, I took a step toward Lana Sue, but neither she nor Walt encouraged the gesture. "This is my new wife, Lana Sue. Lana Sue, this is Buggie's grandfather."

"You must be kidding."

"He says I killed Buggie and caused Ann's suicide and now he's on his vacation to kill me."

"Jesus, Loren, I leave you alone for four days…"

I shrugged. "Anything interesting happen to you while you were gone?"

She stared at me a moment, then dropped my pack on the ground and turned to look at the elk. "And who's this?"

"I thought maybe it was God, but I was wrong."

She studied the elk without comment, then slid out of her own daypack and bag. "You hungry?"

"Starved."

"We could both use a drink."

Alcohol sounded awfully good right then. "How did you know where to look for me?"

Lana Sue pulled a fifth of Jim Beam from her pack and tossed it to me. "Marcie. I figured you'd trundle on down there soon as I topped the rise."

"I returned her bundt pan."

As she leaned over her pack, Lana Sue eyed me under the brim of the French floppy hat. "You hit on her."

Was this wifely intuition or had Marcie ratted? Marcie was a sport, she wouldn't rat. "I deny it," I said. "Marcie's only sixteen."

"So?"

The Beam went down like liquid battery acid. I loved it. "Why did you come looking for me?"

Lana Sue tore the seal off her own bottle of scotch. That's one of the things I admire about her. Even in the backcountry, she'll haul one bottle of my drink and one of hers.

"Lana Sue," I asked, "why are you here?"

She poured scotch into a Dixie cup. "I missed you."

Men with rifles hate to be ignored. Walt Smith thumbed another shell into the chamber and fired up at the pine tops. "You two don't seem to understand what's happening here. I am going to kill Loren now, so let's cut the chatter."

Lana Sue drained her Dixie cup. "What about me?"

"I don't know. You're a problem."

Lana Sue offered him the scotch bottle. Without lowering the rifle or taking his eyes off me, Walt took a long swallow. From the way he drank, I could tell the last couple days of pure living had been just as hard on him as it had on me. I poured more Beam down my throat into a stomach that had had nothing but Fig Newtons for four days.

He drank again. "I don't believe in killing anyone who doesn't deserve to die."

"Good attitude," Lana Sue said.

"And you don't—so far as I know yet. Did you ever abandon anyone?"

Lana Sue reached for the bottle to refill her cup.

Walt continued, "I don't suppose you'd promise not to tell anyone I shot him?"

"I'd promise anything to stay alive."

"Lana Sue," I said. She smiled at me.

"But you wouldn't keep your promise."

"Suppose not."

"This is a fix. I've never had to execute anyone from selfish motives before."

More items spilled from Lana Sue's daypack—a bundle in white butcher paper, a box of Noodle-Roni, a pack skillet, a Glad Bag with what appeared to be real coffee. Lana Sue talked as she sorted. "I'm not the one to help you. I don't want me or my husband shot because I love us both and don't think either one of us deserves to die."

Mr. Smith pointed at me with the gun barrel. "He does."

"You have a name?" Lana Sue asked.

"Walt Smith."

"Okay, Walt Smith. What say we eat something and have a few drinks, you can explain to me why Loren should be shot. Maybe when you're through, I will promise not to tell."

I said, "Lana Sue."

——

I was put in charge of the fire. Lana Sue had supper detail while old Walt retired with the scotch bottle to the far side of the clearing where he rested on a rock and kept an eye on me; Lana Sue was allowed occasional Dixie cup refills.

"You look tired," she said on one of her trips to his rock.

"I am tired. Chasing that fool has played havoc with my body clock. Can't wait to finish him off and go home."

The butcher bundle was a pound of hamburger. Lana Sue's daypack also held salt, pepper, and dried onion flakes. "Hand me my pack," I said. "There's paper I can use to start the fire."

Lana Sue brought the pack to where I squatted placing rocks into a fire circle. "If you're looking for the knife, he shot it."

"Shot it?"

"I checked when I found the pack. The blades are bent to hell—won't open."

Lana Sue was right. The bullet had passed through my notebook and lodged in the Boy Scout knife. I wadded some back pages for the pit.

"I also read that stuff," Lana Sue said.

"These are my private thoughts."

"You nearly broke up our marriage for *being happy is nicer?*"

"Was a revelation to me."

"Loren."

"I never thought in those terms before."

"Any cow knows being happy is nicer."

"I'm not a cow."

Later, while I sat cross-legged, feeding the fire, Lana Sue showed me the soft side of herself that not everyone is allowed to see. As she knelt beside me and broke hamburger into the frying pan, she touched my hand. "I'm sorry I took off when you needed me, Loren."

"I'm sorry I went spiritual and didn't pay attention to you."

Her hand squeezed once, then let go. "It's my own fault. I knew you were a ding when we married. In fact, that deep crap was one of the things I loved most about you—never understood your thought process, or wanted to for that matter, but I loved you for it. I just didn't think you'd ding out on me."

I watched her hand moving over the skillet, stirring the burger. She held the spoon like a pencil with her index finger pointed into the pan. "I fixed the vacuum cleaner."

She stopped. "Come on, Loren, I apologized and meant it. You don't have to lie to me."

"I fixed it. The belt was on backwards and was rubbing that center doohickey that spins. I even cleaned up the mess afterwards."

"Amazing."

"You underestimated me again. You always underestimate me and every now and then I don't deserve it."

She leaned the skillet to drain the grease. It made a sputter sound on the wet grass. Walt sat up. "What's going on over there?"

"Supper," Lana Sue called. She balanced the skillet back over the rocks and continued talking to me. "It's just that you act like such a stupid genius sometimes, like a college professor or a poet, all cerebral and no brain."

"I can wash dishes and I can clean bricks. Don't call me a poet."

Lana Sue poured water from my canteen into the skillet. Then she added the Noodle-Roni. "I'm sorry," she said. "You're in the right this time."

"Did that ever happen before?"

"Not that I can recall."

I scouted around the clearing for more sticks. There wasn't much deadfall in sight of Ann's father, but whenever I drifted behind the trees, he made throat-clearing sounds and thumbed his bolt. I think the alcohol affected him more than it affected me or Lana Sue. The person at the barrel end of a gun hardly ever gets as drunk as the guy on the trigger—even if he drinks a lot, which I did.

Up close, the elk's gray eye sockets didn't seem nearly as knowing as they had from across the clearing. Maybe Lana Sue and Walt Smith affected it. Mystic beings don't normally reveal themselves to more than one person at a time. I rubbed that flat forehead, then spread my hand so my thumb went in the right eye hole and my middle finger in the left. His head had a petrified calcium feel to it, like chalk in a pool hall. The tree had grown a full half inch around the base of one antler, which meant the skull hadn't moved in a long, long time. If this was an aware-of-itself entity, I imagined whoever was in there must have been bored stiff before we came along.

Back at the campfire, Lana Sue lowered her voice. "You think this is best dealt with blasted?"

"The only way." I threw on a whole stack of wood, hoping Walt was the kind who mesmerizes on flames.

Lana Sue sipped her drink. "What's the odds this murder thing is for real?"

"Hell, I don't know. He's had plenty of chances and hasn't killed me yet."

"I didn't like the part about never having had to execute from selfish motives before."

That word *before* had been ominous. "Let's not play it as a bluff and wind up dead fools."

Lana Sue blew across a spoonful of the skillet mess. "There's no plates and only one spoon. We'll have to share." She tasted and made a face. "Wish we had some basil."

"You'd think he couldn't kill someone he's shared a spoon with."

———

The mist lifted as we ate supper so I stretched my damp sleeping bag out next to the fire and sat on the foot end. Lana Sue took off her floppy hat, letting her dark hair tumble across her shoulders. As she leaned over the fire, she cupped her hair back with her left hand the way a girl will when she drinks at a low water fountain. I caught Walt staring at the back of her head, but I don't blame him. Lana Sue is beautiful.

He ate considerably more of the burger-Roni mix than either one of us did—another sign that killers are less nervous than victims. I saw no evidence that he carried a pack or a sleeping bag, or anything, for that matter, other than his ever-present Winchester. I wondered if he'd slept on the ground for four nights.

"How long you been up here?" I asked.

He looked at me through the heat waves over the fire. "I lost you on Sunday."

"He was with Miss Pimply Seducer." Lana Sue wasn't about to drop that subject, even in the face of death.

"Be that as it may," Walt continued, "I found your car that afternoon and remained next to it, hoping to execute you there, until yesterday, when I grew fearful you might not return before I was due in Oregon."

"I never heard of an assassin on a deadline," I said.

"Our midsummer clearance sale starts this weekend."

"Where'd you sleep last night?"

"I didn't."

I took a deep pull on the Beam. We were all sucking down whiskey at an alarming rate. Walt and Lana Sue appeared to be in a scotch competition, which meant they'd soon run dry and make a transfer to my bottle. I figured to process my rightful ounces before the time came for sharing.

Walt cleared his throat. "This must be disappointing slop for a last meal."

"Look at the sunset," Lana Sue said. Dutifully, I turned to admire the pink fluff in the west. The sun dropped between the mountains and the cloud layer, sending out orange-gold fingers the color of Miller beer in a dark bar.

"Real nice," I said.

Walt looked at me instead of the sky. "Annie wrote me a letter."

"I've never seen so much pink in a sunset," Lana Sue said.

I leaned way back, making a pillow out of my daypack. "It's the altitude. Down below, the pollution gives it a purple glint."

"Three weeks before you made her kill herself, she sent me a letter."

Lana Sue's temper flashed. "Are you going to appreciate the sunset or not?"

"Don't interrupt me."

"Don't threaten me."

They stared at each other with all kinds of unspoken communication. I jumped in to ease the tensions. "She's upset because you called supper slop." That didn't defuse either of them, so I went on. "Ann and you didn't communicate the whole six years I was with her. Why at the end?"

"Because you betrayed her."

"Did you write back?"

Walt jerked and stood up. Even though the Winchester rested in the crook of his arm, it was aimed through the fire, directly at my crotch. Gave me a sudden need to pee.

"She wrote that your carnality caused the loss of her child."

"Ann never used the word carnality in her life."

"She said Fred heard you screwing her and ran away and something got him."

Lana Sue said, "My cooking isn't slop."

"Then after you'd robbed her of her child, you decided to cash in on the grief. You were writing a book that would sell her private hell to the reading public."

"Did you write back?" I asked again.

He took a step toward me. "Fred was gone, you were as good as gone. All Annie had left was his memory and you stole that."

The last pink in the west turned ruby as the sun flattened on both the bottom and top. His accusation about Buggie stuck. I drove him away. Making love had never been the same since. Just when I'm supposed to let go and live the moment, I always wonder who my dick is killing this time. But this idea that I caused Ann's suicide was one step too far. I wrote the book to purge grief and guilt, not steal her memories or make money.

"I deny it," I said.

"Annie claimed that if you finished the book she would never hold her son again and she would die. She said she burned it once but you didn't care."

Lana Sue asked, "What did you do when you got the letter?"

Walt exhaled deeply through his nose and turned sideways so he appeared to be talking to the elk. "Nothing."

Lana Sue held her Dixie cup with both hands. "Your daughter was in trouble and you did nothing?"

Walt glanced at Lana Sue, then at the fire. I figured if he drew deeply enough into his own thoughts, I could pull a stick from the coals and throw it in his face. He spoke quietly. "When Lisa passed away, I almost went with her."

"Lisa was Ann's mother?" Lana Sue's voice was kind.

He nodded. "Then Ann ran off with that greasy foreigner she called a guru. She got away and I had to stay and raise her brothers and sister."

I lifted a stick from the fire. The hot end glowed a deeper red than the sunset. Walt kept talking more to himself than us.

"Then Annie moved in with some hippie, then she gave birth to an illegitimate son—all without a word to me."

"So you didn't answer when she needed you," Lana Sue said.

Walt came back to alertness. "It's not my fault she died. He's the one. He was living with her. I couldn't know."

I blew on the tip of my stick. The glow went neon, then darkened. "Who abandoned who out there on the coast?"

"You shut up."

"Ann told me you blanked her out after your wife died."

"I told you to shut up."

"She left with the fat Maha-whatever because you wouldn't speak to her."

He cocked the rifle. I turned to Lana Sue. "Walt here mails a bulletin out every Christmas with a list of where the kids are, who's married, who has kids. After Buggie was born, he dropped Ann's name from the lineup. She said he made her feel dead."

"You bastard. I will kill you."

"Buggie was the bastard. That's why you never acknowledged his existence."

"I swear, I'll beat you to death with my bare hands."

"You're too old."

Lana Sue's turn to defuse. She moved quickly around the fire to stand between Walt and me. "Maybe you feel guilty," she said to him.

"Don't play psychiatrist with me."

"And you transferred your guilt to anger at Loren. You blame him so you won't blame yourself."

"He abandoned my baby."

"So did her mom, her dad, and her child."

"Hand me the fucking bottle."

"Everybody killed her, Walt. Not you alone and not Loren either."

"I'm still going to shoot the asshole."

———

We all observed a moment of liquid silence. Lana Sue carried the supper leftovers into the darkness and scraped the mess into a chiseler hole. Walt went hypnotic on the elk. Or maybe he was scotch-stunned. If I'd thought he was totally oblivious, I'd have plowed his scalp with a rock, but he blinked now and then and sighs escaped. The rifle stayed in the ready position.

I poked the reddest coals into a square pile, then tossed on my largest chunk of kindling. As I watched his sharp face in the near darkness and firelight, I imagined Walt's brain slithering with distorted remembrances—like one of those experiments where they dump two hundred mice in a cage built for twenty.

Some turn to insane hyperactivity, others go catatonic. Cannibalism and rape erupt. Birth defects by the dozen.

"It's okay," I said.

"After I kill him, we can rest," Walt said to the elk.

"I have to pee now."

———

Someone should write an ode to blind-drunk urination. First, you have to stand up, which is an unnecessary challenge. Then, find a place, find your fly, miss your leg, get it back in. The most debasing moments in a man's life often come while he's pissing drunk.

I thought these things as I leaned on a tree trunk and listened to the whiz. I thought about Ann's barbiturates. At least, stoned on reds, you don't have to excuse yourself every ten minutes. I've lost some crucial bar pickups because of you-don't-buy-beer-you-only-rent-it.

I also thought about obsession. Walt Smith was obsessed by the memory of his daughter. I was obsessed with finding Buggie. I'd always believed obsession was the only way to accomplish anything or really feel anything in life, but, using the two of us as examples, it seemed obsession causes an outlook twisted to the point of stupid. Lana Sue wasn't obsessed by anything and she was the only sane one of the bunch.

"You going to stand there with your pecker out all night?" Walt asked.

"Maybe."

"It's my turn."

I tucked in. "This is a big forest, Mr. Smith. No need to take turns."

He punched my ribs hard with the rifle barrel. "Your contempt is suicidal."

"What contempt? I respect your position here. I just don't care to die."

"You should have considered that five years ago when you abandoned my Annie."

"I should have known this would happen?"

"Right, bucko."

The bucko shit was getting old. Back at the fire, Lana Sue gave me the hug I'd been waiting for. "I'm glad I found you in one piece," she said.

Her hair on my face smelled nice, like the rain. I wondered something. "Other than Marcie telling you I was on the mountain, how did you manage to find me?"

"She's statutory, Loren. And her daddy owns guns."

"I mean, there's a lot of land up here."

"Only one trail from the parking lot up the ridge, though, and there was this smoke at the top end of the meadow."

"That was a snowmobile."

"Can't tell by looking at it now." She pulled out of the hug, but kept hold of my hands. "Then I saw your daypack up by the woods. After that, I just wandered uphill until I heard the first shot."

"Pretty good timing."

Lana Sue smiled. "You're my husband. I could track you anywhere." Then she kissed me—a solid wife and lover kiss, none of this lovable fuck-up stuff. "I missed you a lot," she said.

"I'm glad you came back."

I felt her hands on my shoulder blades. "It's an odd world out there, Loren."

"Odder than here?"

She glanced behind me at the drunk car salesman who planned to shoot us. "Be a toss-up right now." I was standing close to the fire so the backs of my legs got too much heat, but I didn't want to let go of my hold on Lana Sue. It seemed a long time since I'd touched a human being.

"Here's the plan," I said. "We drink him unconscious, then we walk out of here."

"Nine miles across pitch-black wilderness drunk on our butts?"

"Okay. We drink him unconscious, then break the rifle in half. What's he doing over there?"

Lana Sue released the hug and moved so the fire wasn't between her and Walt Smith. I jumped away from the heat. "Still communing with nature, I think."

"I hope I can commune that long when I'm his age." I turned to look at Walt. That brought my front to the fire and cooled my calves.

"Drinking him under is our best bet, Loren, only I want you to pretend to pass out first."

"Shouldn't be hard. Why?"

"He'll relax more when you're not a threat. Besides, he's not likely to shoot you while you're asleep."

"Murder's all right, but only if the victim is awake?"

"It's the cowboy code. He's waiting for you to come at him or try an escape or something. He's on his way back now. Drink a lot and pass out. Only leave enough for us." *Drink a lot and pass out.* I could handle that.

I sank onto the sleeping bag next to the Beam bottle. A sliver moon with Venus off the bottom tip rose through the trees behind the old elk skull. An owl swooped across the clearing and away, but I was the only one who saw it. I wondered what kind of owl it was and if that mattered and whether it would matter more if I was immortal. Dying tonight seemed somehow probable yet impossible at the same time—like death always seems, I suppose. I would miss Lana Sue singing country songs on the toilet early mornings while I sleepy-fussed around the kitchen making coffee. And the taste of cold water. And the opening theme music to *M*A*S*H* reruns. That song is comforting, it gives continuity to life, even though the title is "Suicide Is Painless."

Walt approached, tucking the wool shirt in with one hand. His two-day beard gave him a cleaned-up-wino look— nothing like a car salesman. I asked myself the old Nixon question. "Would you buy a used car from this man?" Depended on the deal.

Right now he was staring at Lana Sue. "How come a good looker like yourself ended up with trash for a husband?" He swung the barrel my way.

"Lucky, I guess."

Walt leaned off to one side and drank from the bottle. "Look at him over there, nodding like a heroin addict. He's a simpleton."

Lana Sue studied me a moment, considering the observation. I smiled at her. "Loren's my honey," she said. "My sticking point."

Walt made an ugly snort sound. "Makes me want to puke."

"So don't look at him."

His stare returned to Lana Sue, only this time it was more a leer. "Maybe we could work out a deal."

"No."

"You don't even know the terms."

"I know the terms."

"You'd rather I shoot the asshole?" Sounded like a reasonable question to me.

The firelight gave Lana Sue's cheekbones a shadowy, Cheyenne mystery woman look. "Four days ago a man said he'd commit suicide if I didn't sleep with him. Then three days ago a kid offered to sell me his shoes for sex. I said no to them and I'm saying no to you."

"So you'd rather see your husband die than be nice to me?"

"My cunt doesn't prevent murder or suicide. Or bare feet."

I raised my head off my hands. "Did the guy kill himself?"

"Nope."

"Did you sleep with him anyway?"

"I told you what I said, Loren."

"I know what you said—what did you do?"

This got me a particularly nasty stare—so nasty in fact that I didn't buy the bit. She'd been up to something. Lana Sue took the bottle back from Walt. "You have a stroke recently?" she asked him. The smoke made them shift around the fire, away from where I slouched.

"Three years ago in February. Does it show?" The heat over the fire gave them an unsubstantial, watery look. Kind of artsy.

"You limp like my uncle Bart. He fainted into a sand trap a few years back. Couldn't speak for a month, but they physical-therapied him so well you can hardly tell now—except he can't whistle anymore and he carries his left leg some when he's tired. Like you."

Walt passed from the watery far side of the fire to the more solid left. The rifle still pointed between my eyes. "It was mild, nothing really. I was back on the lot by summer."

I twisted the top off my Beam bottle and took a good slug. Lana Sue smiled and lip-synced *pass out* at me. Then she continued, "So, Walt, was it around the stroke that you developed these avenging angel urges toward Ann?"

"Hand me the scotch." Walt eyed Lana Sue as he drank. With the bottle almost empty, we were headed toward a *vomit à trois*.

"I resent the insinuation," he said.

"What insinuation?"

"You imply that my mental capacities were lessened by my sickness, that my defense of Ann is a disease-caused blip on my personality."

"I wouldn't have said blip."

"You better not. I should have killed him at the funeral itself."

I raised my head. "You should have come to the funeral itself."

"I was there."

"Horseshit, you didn't even know she was dead."

"Don't curse at me, bucko."

"One more bucko and you eat that rifle." This was the Jimmy Stewart side of me rising to the occasion. Walt's mouth twitched a couple times and made a chewing motion. For a moment, he appeared on the edge of calling my bluff. What would Jimmy Stewart do then?

Walt stared into the fire. "Her doctor phoned the day it happened. He said you were too much a mess to think of me."

"Ann and her family were enemies. I saw no call to notify anyone."

Walt turned to Lana Sue. "I was at the cemetery. It snowed and some of the women who worked with Annie had been Christmas shopping before the service."

Lana Sue touched his shoulder. "It must have been very hard."

"After the prayers, he sat in the car and took notes. Can you believe the monstrosity? My baby is dead and he's recording impressions."

"I'd of gone insane that week if I stopped work on the Buggie book."

He raised the rifle butt to his shoulder and took aim at my chest. "Your wife was dead. She deserved a little insanity."

Lana Sue tried to step between Walt and me, but he moved away from the fire, keeping me in range.

"Don't kill him," Lana Sue said.

"Look at him, he's taking notes right now."

She glanced back at me. "I wouldn't doubt it, Walt. But he's all I've got. Don't kill him."

I wasn't taking notes. I was wishing I could be sober enough to think about the things Lana Sue was saying. I'd never understood what she saw in me—always figured I needed her more than she needed me. But now it seemed pretty strong both ways.

Walt stepped past Lana Sue and stood five feet away with the rifle on me. "You're incapable of love. Ann told me about your mother and brothers. That bastard was the only thing you ever cared about, and when he was gone, you killed my baby."

"I care about Lana Sue."

"Annie was your wife."

"I cared about her too—at the time. Hell, I married her."

Walt lowered the rifle and stared at me. He blinked twice, then swallowed. "What color were Annie's eyes?"

"What?"

"For reasons I'll never understand, this woman loves your worthless hide." He nodded his head toward Lana Sue. "For her, if you cared about Annie enough to recall the color of her eyes, I'll only shoot out your kneecaps. I will not take your miserable life."

"Be tough to survive blown kneecaps this far from the road."

"The two of you will manage."

I thought about Ann the first day we were together when

we took the picnic basket to the cemetery and Buggie climbed the grave markers even before he could walk. Her hair had been so clean that day. The sky had been so blue—it seemed to match her eyes. "Blue. They were a light blue."

Walt grew very calm. "Annie's eyes were hazel. The Ann in your book had blue eyes."

"Are you sure?"

"You lose, bucko."

Lana Sue hit the rifle as he fired. With the second shot, a hole appeared in the sleeping bag next to my hand. Another shot and the Jim Beam bottle exploded.

Lana Sue screamed, "I'll do it!"

Walt stopped. "Do what?"

"I'll fuck you for his life."

Walt and Lana Sue stared in each other's eyes for a few intense seconds. He took a step toward her. "Right now. In the dirt. With him watching."

Lana Sue nodded.

"Why?"

"I don't want Loren dead."

He turned to me. "And you'll let her, won't you?"

I looked at Lana Sue. Her hair blocked out most of her face, but I could see her right eye, staring at the ground, waiting. I thought about Buggie and the day he disappeared. He'd caught a trout that morning. Ann and I made love for the last time. With effort, I pulled my legs under my drunk body and made it to my feet. I faced Walt across the fire.

"No."

He pretended not to understand. "What's that?"

"You'll have to shoot me first."

"Your choice." The rifle came up, dead center on my chest. He squeezed the trigger and we all heard the empty click. I drunk-rushed.

Walt two-hand-swung the barrel into my left ear and I went down onto his feet. Grabbing both legs, I lifted him clear off the ground. He cracked me again and we both fell. On my back now, I kicked his face, but he made it to his knees and drew the rifle back, this time holding the barrel, swinging the stock. On his left, I saw Lana Sue move in with a rock held over her head in both hands. Then Walt's club came toward me, the night strobed once and darkened.

———

Nineteen seventy-eight or -nine, must have been -eight because Buggie wasn't quite four, I sat at the kitchen table working on a scene near the end of the second Western. Ann gave Buggie a big chunk of Colby cheese and a slice of whole wheat bread and sent him into the backyard to play. She stood at the sink window in blue sweats, her Bronco jersey, and no shoes, humming as she Woolited Buggie's no-longer-needed snowsuit.

The scene was an important one. Someone—a woman—had locked my sheriff in his own jail and he had to break free in time to save another woman from violent death. I was torn between picking the lock and dynamiting the back wall. Dynamite seemed more dramatic, but there were logistical problems.

Suddenly Ann squealed, *"Holy shit,"* and ran out the back door. When I reached the patio, she was dragging Buggie away from the body of an owl.

Buggie said, "Bird sick."

More than sick, the owl was dead. It lay on its side on the concrete, its head and shoulders spotted by yellow bite-size pieces of cheese, the bread slice balanced across the exposed wing.

Ann tried to turn Buggie's face from the sight, but he would have none of it. "I feeded him. Make him better."

I couldn't blame Buggie for wanting to see the owl. Even though the cheese made it a little bizarre, he was still huge and beautiful. His face was a white heart curved back like an inside-out bivalve set around two black pits for eyes. Nothing back in my Texas pet cemetery came close to this owl.

I knelt over the body. "Wonder what kind he is?"

"What difference does it make?" Ann said.

Buggie twisted in her arms. "Feed him. Make it fly."

I touched the wing feathers. "Afraid he's a goner, Bug. Let me get the bird book, we'll see what we've got here."

It was a barn owl, a young male as best as I could make out. I showed Ann and Buggie the markings. "See this cinnamon streak down here. The book says this makes him look ghostly at night."

Ann didn't care. "Get rid of it."

"I'm not real sure how to go about that."

"Throw it in the Mini-Mart Dumpster."

Buggie gave her his hurt look. "Feed the bird. Now."

"You can't throw a predatory bird in a Dumpster. This is a noble creature. I don't think it's even legal that he died in our backyard."

Ann picked Buggie up and carried him toward the back door. "Just get rid of it, Loren. Gives me the creeps."

"We could have him mounted."

"No."

Burial didn't feel right. I considered hauling him into the mountains and leaving him on the ground for the mice and ants—a completion of the nutritional wheel of life sort of thing—but he was so beautiful, rotting would have been sad.

So I cremated him.

I sloshed a quarter inch of kerosene into the bowl of our outside barbecue grill. Then I gently picked the owl up and placed him in. He filled almost the entire bowl. Out of respect for Buggie, I left the cheese on his face. Standing way back, I threw lit matches at him. The first couple went out in midair, but finally he *whooshed* and burst into a fireball.

The feathers gave off a burnt fingernail smell. His legs curled. Through the flames, I could see the cheese melt into his eyes. I mumbled a vague spirit-to-spirit prayer with no idea what it meant.

What brought on this memory, besides the owl itself, was that vaporous waviness in the heat above the fire. At one point, I looked up from the burning owl, and through the heat waves, I saw Ann and Buggie pressed against the back window. Ann's face filled the top left of the frame with her dark blond hair hanging down above Buggie's eyes, forehead, and two chubby palms. The effect was as if they floated a few inches below the surface of a clear, gently rippling pool. They looked far away, detached, dead.

I sprayed the owl good with lighter fluid and went inside.

———

High mountain light and the odor of smoke filled the clearing. I rolled over, coughed, then sat up and blinked at the blue, cloudless sky. Sometime in the night, someone had covered me with the sleeping bag. Gathering it around my shoulders like a shawl, I staggered to my feet shakily, looking at Lana Sue as she fussed around the campfire.

Her hair was down and she was wearing a bone-colored sweater and blue jeans. I could smell the coffee boiling. She kept her face turned away, not looking at me.

"I'm sorry," I said.

When Lana Sue swung my way, I saw the glisten of tears. "You better be."

"I am."

She was up and in my arms. "This is the last time, Loren, you hear me? I'm never going to save a man again—not even you."

I sunk my hand into the hair on the back of her neck. "My head feels cracked."

When Lana Sue pulled back to look in my eyes, a hint of smile crossed her face. She touched my blood-matted ear. "You were more drunk than hurt."

"Right now I feel more hurt."

"Should have seen the knot on Walt's skull. I thought I'd killed the poor schlock."

"Poor schlock?"

"I kept imagining what I'd tell the police when I got to town."

I pulled the sleeping bag over both her shoulders. We leaned together, touching foreheads. I asked the question. "Would you have done it?"

"Fucked him?" Lana Sue's body gave a little shudder in my arms. She looked up at me. "I guess I couldn't let him kill you."

"Thanks."

Her eyes turned fierce. "But I guarantee you'd never have seen me again."

"That's fair."

Lana Sue ducked under the sleeping bag and walked to the fire pit. "It's been a hard five days, Loren. Splitting up isn't as much fun as it used to be."

"Can I have some coffee?"

She folded a bandanna several times, then drew the blackened pot from the fire. I walked over and stood behind her while she sprinkled in salt to settle the grounds. "When did he leave?"

"Dawn. Couple of hours ago. I hope he makes it down all right." She poured coffee into my Sierra cup.

"Bad shape, huh?"

"Old Walt is no longer a threat." She motioned toward the elk skull. "His gun's over there." She'd done an amazing job of breaking up the rifle—must have been fifteen separate pieces in a pile. "I threw all his bullets in the creek."

We drank coffee in silence, looking first into the fire, then out at the beautiful day. Sunshine glittered off the cliffs in a way it never glitters below nine thousand feet. The flowers and pines gave off a fresh scrubbed odor that mixed perfectly with the coffee. Even the elk skull seemed to have formed a smile, or maybe a more balanced leer.

Lana Sue caught me looking at the top of the Sleeping Indian. "So you still think God or some talking rock is up there waiting to tell you about Buggie?"

"I don't know."

"If you're going up, I'm going with you."

The coffee was the best I ever tasted. "I'm not going up."

When Lana Sue took the cup, she held the back of my hand a moment. "Can you live with me in the present while the past is still unresolved?"

From this side, the peak didn't look like a sleeping Indian at all. It looked like a mountain. Maybe all I had to do was scramble up the ridge for an hour to find out if Buggie was alive or dead, and, either way, where he had gone. But it didn't matter so much. The thing I'd really wanted to ask was whether death brings on another stage or total eternal blankness, and whichever way the answer came down would have no effect on how I planned to live. I'd still get up in the morning and pull on my pants and drink a cup of coffee with cream. I would go on loving Lana Sue and writing dumb little books in hopes of making someone else's life more pleasant. I would watch the sun and the weather, the cycle of plants and animals. I would do all I could to enjoy the everyday. Oncoming death couldn't change squat about ongoing life.

"This catharsis crap is a bitch."

"Like shitting bricks. You having one now?"

"I suppose so."

"You're realizing being happy is nicer, right?"

"Something like that."

Lana Sue kissed me. I could taste coffee in her mouth. "I think you're ready for country music, Loren."

"Let's go hear some."

———

We walked back through the long meadow with the blown-up snowmobile. In the sunshine, the flowers were even more beautiful than the day before, although the rain had freed a hurricane of pollen. Lana Sue told me about her daughter.

"The band's playing in Cody week after next, Loren. It's only a hundred fifty miles and the drive through Yellowstone would be pretty."

"So let's go."

"I think you'll like Mickey Thunder. You two are a lot alike in strange ways."

I walked on the trail behind Lana Sue, admiring her ass among the flowers. Curiosity overcame tact and I took a chance on spoiling the mood. "You make it with many men while you were gone?"

Lana Sue stopped a second, then kept on. "One or two, depends on how you count."

"How do you count?"

"One didn't matter and the other wasn't any good."

"Was the one that didn't matter as good as me?"

"Course not. You're technically good and emotional at the same time. That's a rare combination." Lana Sue picked a columbine and tucked it behind her ear. "Loren, when I drove to the VanHorns' to find out where you were, Lee sent me in to talk to Marcie in her darkroom."

"Marcie told me she's into photography."

Lana Sue glanced back at me. "I saw some pictures coming out of the dryer."

"What about this one who wasn't any good? Does that mean he mattered?"

"There was a dick that looked just like yours, only it was enormous, big as a chicken."

I tripped over a stone in the trail—almost fell into Lana Sue's back. "Couldn't have been mine. I'm just barely above average."

She swung around and eyed me. "I could spot your tool anywhere."

It was one of those scenes that demand eye contact. Otherwise the woman knows you're lying in your teeth. "I'm not enormous, remember?"

Lana Sue smiled. "When I figure out how you two did it, I'll murder you both."

"What about this guy who wasn't good, but mattered. I'm not certain I like that."

Lana Sue laughed aloud and I loved her for it. "You know what I've decided, Loren. You and I deserve each other."

"I'll take that as a compliment. Let's go home."

# EPILOGUE

*"TESTING, TESTING. IS THIS THING ON? LOREN, THE DIAL'S NOT moving. I can't tell if the machine's recording."*

*"It's on."*

*"How the hell do you get this to come on?"*

*"It's on already."*

*"Are you sure? I don't think so."*

*"Look at the red light."*

*"That means it's on?"*

*"That means it's on."*

*"I'm going to play it back and see. I don't think it's on."*

———

*"You satisfied now?"*

*"The sun is about to set, Loren. Shouldn't you be out on the fence?"*

*"I thought I might miss it once. Just stick around and see how you wrap things up."*

*"Outside, Loren. I need privacy."*

*"You gonna tell about humping more cowboys?"*

*"Out."*

———

Since Loren got three chapters to my two, he's letting me do the epilogue—prologue—whichever comes at the end. Only, one more day in front of a typewriter and I'll scream, so I made him buy me this Japanese machine with the first advance from his publisher. Nice of them to pay him before we finish the book.

Anyhow, I'm much more comfortable with a microphone in my hand. We'll hire some high-school girl from Future Business Leaders of America to transcribe the thing. I imagine Loren will make a pass at her and I'll catch him and, in all likelihood, we'll be off on another book.

Loose ends: I got Loren off the Sleeping Indian without any more gunfire. We spent the next day and a half in bed, asleep mostly, but occasionally rousing ourselves for simultaneous food and sex. At first Loren hauled his rifle along whenever he went outside. And he made dozens of long-distance phone calls to his mother, both brothers, practically everyone he knew in high school. Told them all he truly loved them and he was through with cosmic assholehood.

Along the same lines, I wrote letters of reconciliation—make that apology—to Ron, my dad, and Connie. It seems such a waste to be disliked by someone you love. Dad wrote back, through Mom, that there was nothing to reconcile, that everything was model between us and always had been. Ron didn't answer. Connie sent me a chain letter for women only. The letter said to mail a dollar to the top name, put my name on the bottom, and spread it on to ten friends I trust.

The one I didn't write was Cassie because there seemed to be no reason to reconcile or apologize. Wrong again.

Two days ago, I was repotting an impatiens when Loren showed up from town with the groceries and mail. I'd just reread the last of my book pages that morning, so I was thinking about Thorne Axel. He'd had enough knowledge to figure out an address or phone number, but—so far, anyway—I haven't heard a word about how that deal came down. Been tempted a time or two to call Maria, just to see if everyone on the ranch is still alive, but I guess I won't. I made my choice and the direction I didn't take is none of my damn business.

Loren came banging through the back door and plopped two brown bags on the table next to my dirt-covered newspaper. "What's wrong with the bush?"

"Root bound." I touched the lip on one sack. "You bought dog food again, didn't you."

Loren looked across my hand. "I forgot."

"I forgot" didn't mean he forgot to buy dog food. It meant he forgot both our dogs died last month. Within three days, Rocky's liver, then Josie's heart gave out.

"I was thinking about something else." Loren stared out the window a moment, adjusting. He always forgets the dogs are dead and, when I remind him, it's like the grief starts over at the beginning. I went back to my impatiens.

"There's a letter from Cassie," he said. "She's getting married."

Cassie writing a letter was more a shock than Cassie getting married. I always figured she'd marry someday, but a letter... "Who to?"

Loren pulled himself from the window, adjustments made, the dead dead, the living live. "Who do you think?"

Dirt hit the floor. "Not Mickey?"

"We're invited to the wedding." Loren flipped the letter across the table. Then he opened the refrigerator and peered in.

I said, "I'll kill the prick."

Loren spoke to the vegetable bin. "I thought you and Mickey are best pals."

"I won't have that washed-up drunkard married to my baby."

"He'll be your son-in-law." Loren pulled a limp squash from the refrigerator. "Did we ever eat one of these?"

"That bum will poke anything with a hole. How could Cassie marry a man like that?"

Loren threw the squash into the trash bucket. "She's expecting."

I lunged for the sugar, but Loren beat me to it. He turned quickly, opened the liquor cabinet door, and traded the sugar bowl for the scotch bottle. "The letter's not so bad. I think she'll be happy."

"Happy?"

It was addressed to both of us—

*Dear Mom and Loren*
*The band is playing West Las Vegas during the tractor pull next month so while we're there Mick and I are going to wed. Ya'll should come. We could sing duets like up at Cody the end of last summer. They were pretty tart harmonies I thought. Roxanne's coming and maybe Connie but I don't know. I'm knockered. It's cool fun except when I get sick. Mick says you'll make a hunky-dory Grandma.*

*Love ya Mama*
*Cassie*

I put the letter facedown in potting soil and closed my eyes.

"Do you think *tart* is youth jargon or something country western?" Loren asked.

"I never heard it before."

"I'll ask Marcie next time I see her."

"She told Roxanne before she told me."

"And Connie." Loren poured scotch into a coffee cup and handed it to me. "I was comfortable," I said.

Loren nodded.

"I figured I did it myself, so I couldn't very well give her crap for sleeping with him."

"That's true."

The scotch burned some going down. "But to marry the bum."

Loren measured himself a shot of Beam. I went on, talking to myself. "Mickey used to claim he was Peter Pan. He lured young girls to Never-Never land and played with them until they decided to grow up. Then they left."

"Was the fiddle player Captain Hook or Tinker Bell?"

I gave Loren my nastiest stare, but he missed it. "Now that bad-breathed child molester wants to marry my daughter. They won't last six months."

"You can't stop it."

"I can sure as hell try."

"Keep your mouth shut. If it doesn't last six months, you'll be here for her. Nobody runs to a mama who can say 'I told you so,' or she'll stay with him long after she should leave just to prove you wrong."

"Maybe." I looked across at Loren. He looked cute with his curly hair and smudged glasses. "You sure are smart for a man who doesn't even know if he's wearing underwear."

His hand traveled down to belt level, checking. "Did he really relate to that Peter Pan thing?"

"Pete was the role model."

"Ever notice that in the end, Mary Martin comes back twenty years later and kidnaps Wendy's daughter?"

I couldn't decide between nicotine, alcohol, sugar, or a sex marathon. Finally settled for all four, pretty much in that order.

———

*"You missed a great sunset. The moon came up full just as the sun fell behind Rendezvous Mountain. It was a winner."*

"*Tell me about it.*"

"*What's with the sniffles, Lannie?*"

"*Hell, I don't know. I've been way too emotional lately. You know I started crying during a damn phone company commercial yesterday. It was stupid—some guy called his fat mama to say he loved her and I fell for it.*"

"*Jeez, you're getting like me.*"

"*Suppose I could do worse.*"

"*So why are you crying now?*"

"*Loren, I'll be forty years old in only sixteen months.*"

"*Fourteen.*"

"*And you know what I want to do?*"

"*Grow younger.*"

"*I want to borrow a horse from the VanHorns and make love at a full gallop.*"

"*Tonight?*"

"*The moon's full.*"

"*Can we borrow two sets of spurs?*"

"*So, where's the off on this machine?*"

"*Is the book finished?*"

"*As it'll ever be.*"

"*Here.*"

CLICK

# About the Author

Rebecca Stern

REVIEWERS HAVE VARIOUSLY compared Tim Sandlin to Jack Kerouac, Tom Robbins, Larry McMurtry, Joseph Heller, John Irving, Kurt Vonnegut, Carl Hiaasen, and a few other writers you've probably heard of. He has published nine novels and a book of columns. He wrote eleven screenplays for hire, two of which have been made into movies. He used to write reviews for the *New York Times Book Review* but was fired for excessive praise. He lives with his family in Jackson, Wyoming, where he is director of the Jackson Hole Writers Conference. His Sandlinistas follow him at www.timsandlin.com.

# Tim Sandlin's Complete GroVont Series

## Is Now Available from Sourcebooks Landmark

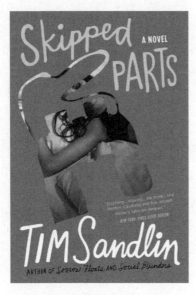 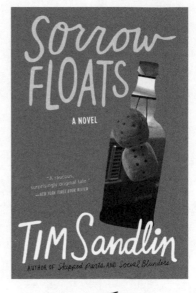

**Skipped Parts**

978-1-4022-4171-0
$14.99 U.S. / $17.99 CAN / £7.99 UK

**Sorrow Floats**

978-1-4022-4173-4
$14.99 U.S. / $17.99 CAN / £7.99 UK

Welcome to the ribald, rollicking, and sometimes peculiar world of Tim Sandlin's GroVont, Wyoming, where family is always paramount, no matter how strange.

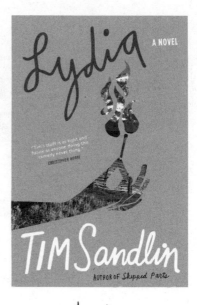

Social Blunders

978-1-4022-4175-8

$14.99 U.S. / $17.99 CAN / £7.99 UK

Lydia

978-1-4022-4181-9

$24.99 U.S. / £16.99 UK

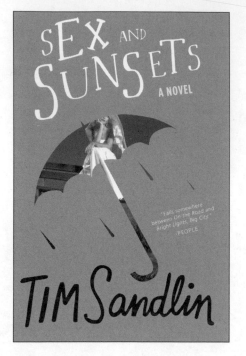

"Falls somewhere between *On the Road* and *Bright Lights, Big City*"
—PEOPLE

## Sex and Sunsets

At twenty-nine, Kelly Palomino's a little off-kilter but settled into his career of professional dishwasher. His big, blonde, ex-hippie wife has left him for good.

So it's with no particular purpose that Kelly positions himself on his porch across the street from an Episcopal church in Jackson, Wyoming, to witness a singular sight: a dark-haired bride in full regalia punting a football over the rectory before turning resolutely to walk down the aisle.

It's love at first sight for Kelly, and he'll do absolutely anything and everything to get his girl...

978-1-4022-4179-6 | $14.99 U.S. / £9.99 UK